Praise for *PRETENDING*:

'*Pretending* is the thoughtful, intelligent, urgent novel we need in a post Me Too age. It is both unsettling and hopeful, enlightening and entertaining. Holly Bourne examines the darkest of subjects while retaining incisive wit, absorbing narrative and a totally loveable lead'
Dolly Alderton

'MAGNIFICENT. The whole sorry mess of gender and sexual politics wrapped up in a compelling story told by an ADORABLE heroine. I feel educated and empowered from reading it. Brutally honest and righteously angry but still HUGELY enjoyable and engaging. I BOW DOWN!'
Marian Keyes

'So relatable, powerful and thought-provoking . . . This is a vivid, contemporary exploration of the darkest side of relationships, anger and powerlessness, but it's filled with joy too'
Daisy Buchanan

'Searingly honest, intense, and insightful, this is a profoundly moving novel'
Louise O'Neill

'Every page brings another eye-wateringly relatable moment and I couldn't put it down. I was constantly laughing, crying, and nodding aggressively at every page'
Lucy Vine

'An extraordinary book . . . It's feminist and angry and compassionate and hopeful'
Julie Cohen

'Such unbelievably dark themes . . . yet *Pretending* still has a joy and a lightness of touch that makes it easy to breeze through'
Caroline O'Donoghue

'Smart

Praise for *HOW DO YOU LIKE ME NOW?*:

PRETENDING

Holly Bourne is a bestselling author. Alongside her writing, Holly is passionate about gender equality and is an advocate for reducing the stigma of mental health problems. She is also an ambassador for Women's Aid, working with the charity to spread awareness of abusive relationships.

Pretending is her second adult novel.

Also by Holly Bourne

How Do You Like Me Now?

PRETENDING

HOLLY BOURNE

HODDER

First published in Great Britain in 2020 by Hodder & Stoughton
An Hachette UK company

This paperback edition published in 2021

1

Copyright © Holly Bourne 2020

The right of Holly Bourne to be identified as the
Author of the Work has been asserted by her in accordance
with the Copyright, Designs and Patents Act 1988.

A CIP catalogue record for this title is
available from the British Library

Paperback ISBN 978 1 473 66817 1
eBook ISBN 978 1 473 66815 7

Typeset in Plantin Light by Palimpsest Book Production Limited,
Falkirk, Stirlingshire

Printed and bound in Great Britain by Clays Ltd, Elcograf S.p.A.

Hodder & Stoughton policy is to use papers that are
natural, renewable and recyclable products and made from
wood grown in sustainable forests. The logging and manufacturing
processes are expected to conform to the environmental
regulations of the country of origin.

Hodder & Stoughton Ltd
Carmelite House
50 Victoria Embankment
London EC4Y 0DZ

www.hodder.co.uk

To Good Eggs

I hate men.

There, I've said it. I know you're not supposed to say it. We all pretend we don't hate them; we all tell ourselves we don't hate them. But I'm calling it. I'm standing here on this soapbox, and I'm saying it.

I. Hate. Men.

I mean, think about it. They're just *awful*. I hate how selfish they are. How they take up so much space, assuming it's always theirs to take. How they spread out their legs on public transport, like their balls need regular airing to stop them developing damp. I hate how they basically scent-mark anywhere they enter to make it work for them. Putting on the music *they* want to listen to the moment they arrive at any house party, and always taking the nicest chair. How they touch your stuff instead of just looking; even tweak the furniture arrangement to make it most comfortable for them. All without asking first – *never* asking first.

I hate how they think their interests are more important than yours – even though twice a week all most of them do is watch a bunch of strangers kick a circle around a piece of lawn and sulk if the circle doesn't go in the right place. And how bored they look if you ever try to introduce them to a film, a band, or even a freaking YouTube clip, before you've even pressed play.

I hate their *endless* arrogance. I hate how they interrupt you and then apologise for it but carry on talking anyway. How they ask you a question but then check your answer afterwards. I hate how they can never do one piece of house-work without telling you about it. I hate how they literally cannot handle being driven in a car by a woman, even if they're terrible drivers themselves. I hate how they all think they're fucking incredible at grilling meat on barbe-cues. The sun comes out and man must light fire and not let woman anywhere near the meat. Dumping blackened bits of chicken onto our plates along with the whiff of a burp from their beer breath, acting all caveman, like we're supposed to find it *cute* that we may now get salmonella and that we're going to have to do all the washing-up.

I hate how I'm quite scared of them. I hate the collective noise of them when they're in a big group. The tribal *wahey*-ing, like they all swap their IQs for extra testosterone when they swarm together. How, if you're sitting alone on an empty train, they always come and deliberately sit next to you en masse, and talk extra loudly about macho nonsense, apparently to impress you. I hate the way they look at you when you walk past – automatically judging your screwability the moment they see you. Telling you to smile if you dare look anything other than delighted about living with stuff like this constantly fucking happening to you.

I hate how hard they are to love. How many of them actually, truly, think the way to your heart is sending you a selfie of them tugging themselves, hairy ball-sack very much still in shot. I hate how they have sex. How they shove their fingers into you, thinking it's going to achieve anything.

Jabbing their unwashed hands into your dry vagina, prodding about like they're checking for prostate cancer, then wondering why you now have BV and you still haven't come. Have *none* of them read a sex manual? Seriously? None of them? And I hate how they hate you a little just after they've finished. How even the nice ones lie there with cold eyes, pretending to cuddle, but clearly desperate to get as far away from you as possible.

I hate how it's never equal. How they expect you to do all the emotional labour and then get upset when you're the more stressed out one. I hate how they never understand you, no matter how hard they try, although, let's be honest here, they never actually try that hard. And I hate how you're always exhausting yourself trying to explain even the most basic of your rational emotional responses to their bored face.

I hate how every single last one of them has issues with their father.

And do you know what I hate most of all?

That despite this, despite all this disdain, I still *fancy* men. And I still want them to fancy me, to want me, to *love* me. I hate myself for how much I want them. Why do I still fancy men so much? What's wrong with me? Why are they all so broken? Am I broken for still wanting to be with one, even after everything? I should be alone. That's the only healthy way to be. BUT I DON'T WANT TO BE ALONE. I hate men, that's the problem. GOD I HATE THEM SO MUCH – they're so entitled and broken and lazy and wrong and . . . and . . .

Hang on . . .

My phone.

HE MESSAGED BACK!!!
WITH A KISS ON THE END!
Never mind.
Forget I said anything. It's all good.

'I think I'm going to fall in love with him,' I tell Katy, as we stand by the dilapidated kettle, waiting for it to gurgle into a lacklustre boil.

'Maybe a little bit soon for that, don't you think?'

'I know. But I also, like, *know*, you know?'

Katy closes her eyes for a little longer than necessary, which is fair enough. I can hear what I sound like with my very own ears. I am not this person. I am not this woman. Although I am, I am. 'You're getting carried away again, aren't you?' She's washing out our mugs using the tiniest amount of Fairy Liquid, which has the note 'please use sparingly' on it, like the charity we work for can be saved from financial annihilation by more efficient washing-up.

'It's been five dates! *Five*! Do you have any idea what a milestone that is? I googled it, and it really, really is.'

'Didn't we talk about googling relationship stuff, April?'

'I can't help it. We work in an office with unrestricted Internet access and I'm not Gandhi. And even he, I am sure, would google "what to expect after five dates" if he was in my position.'

She laughs loudly enough that heads jerk up around the office. I *shh* her as I pour the coffee out of the cafetière into three mugs. She splashes in the milk equally and I giggle with her, but I can't help but feel a twinge of hurt at her

5

amusement. Katy's been married for four years, to a man who completely and utterly adores her. She's all smug and I-wouldn't-be-like-that and chilled, which is so easy to be when you've been married for four years, to a man who completely and utterly adores you. I would be just as chill if I was married to a man like Jimmy. Bored as fuck, but chill.

We clatter back to our desks, through an office fizzing with Friday energy. The end of the week is tauntingly in sight. Shoulders relax as people tap at their keyboards, meetings are laced with jokes, and the radio's been cranked on. No one is working quite as hard as they should be and their Monday-selves will hate their now-selves for being so lax. But that is then and this is now and I have a sixth date and a whole weekend and the hope of the beginning.

I attack my phone the second I'm sitting down. The sweet agonising apprehension of waiting for a red blob containing a message alert – my future mood totally dependent on it. For a millisecond, as I wait for my screen to unlock, I imagine it all disintegrating. Maybe I'm overhyping the connection, maybe he won't have replied, maybe I'm delusional and mental and he's figured this out and will now ghost me without explanation. I'll have to start over again. Pick myself up and out of the dust again. Try to find the faith again. A dark chasm yawns open in my stomach . . . but wait!

There's a message!

He's replied!

I've been rewarded for leaving my phone at my desk while I made coffee. I successfully tricked the Love Gods with my trip to the kitchen to make a hot drink. They thought I was ambivalent about Simon's reply and therefore sent it to me, but the joke is on them because I didn't even want this coffee. I just needed a reason to be away from my phone.

'Your phone buzzed,' Matt tells me unnecessarily as I stare at it in my hand. He's peering at me over his monitor, his eyes kind through the thick black rims of his glasses. 'Is it Simon?'

I nod. 'I think so. Can't open it to tell yet though, can I?'

'Why not? Of course you can.'

Katy plops his drink down in front of him and he nods a thank you. 'Google probably told her not to,' she says, taking her seat next to him. She pulls her keyboard towards her and starts clacking earnestly.

'It's not just that,' I protest. I open my top drawer and put my phone in there so I can't see it. It nestles in on top of some used-up notepads and promotional postcards we give out at student unions. 'I just don't want him to think I've spent my whole day checking my phone to see if he's messaged.'

'Even though you have . . .' Matt puts forward.

'Yes, but I've done other interesting things and had other interesting thoughts too.'

'Like . . . ?'

'Well, we just had that meeting.'

'Which you brought your phone to . . . and spent the whole time looking at your lap.'

I shake my head and take a slurp of my unwanted tricking-the-Love-Gods coffee. 'OK, OK, so I'm a pathetic mess and Simon's going to find out how crazy I am and dump me and then I'll die alone in my flat, and my cat will eat my face because cats have no loyalty.'

'You don't have a cat,' Katy reminds me, still typing.

Matt points at me. 'Write all that out to him and send it back.'

'What? Say "please don't dump me when you find out I'm crazy. You're the one chance I have to not have a cat eat my decomposing face"?'

He points harder. 'Yeah. Go for it. Stress-test it. See what happens. If he's the guy, he'll get it.'

Katy and I shake our heads at one another. Katy has been with Jimmy so long she's completely out of the game, but even she knows that's wrong.

'You know that's not how it works.'

Here's the thing: I really don't understand why love has been so hard for me. I am pretty. I am smart. I have a goodish job. I have friends. I have hobbies. I am funny. I am self-actualized. I dress well. I don't have particularly high standards. I am not expecting to be rescued. I am realistic about what relationships are like. I know they take work. I know nobody is perfect, let alone myself. I know I have to 'put myself out there' and I have been doing that. I am a good conversationalist. I am happy on my own. I am.

But, like, I still want a relationship.

I *really* want a relationship.

Not because I think it will complete me or solve all my problems. Not because I want a big wedding and to look pretty in an expensive dress. Not even, really, because I want to have children because, if I had to, I could survive not having them.

I want a relationship because it's a really normal and natural thing to want. And yet, it's not been happening for me. It's so exhaustingly hard. I don't understand why it's so hard . . .

But maybe it won't be hard any more. Not with Simon.

God, I really, *really* like Simon.

I attempt to lose myself in my work. My important work in my important job in my independent life. I try to be better than this. Less needy than this. Less obsessed than this. It's my shift answering the inbox this afternoon and that's always a traumatic ball-ache, so I need to be efficient and get through my emails and be all the things I know I'm capable of being. I type up the notes from the meeting about safeguarding procedure. I plan next month's buddy timetable and send it out to the volunteers. I go to another meeting about budget cuts, how to make it work on much less than we have and how we will probably get even less next year but we are positive that actually it will be OK. I'm hyper-aware of my phone in my top drawer, however. The unread message thumps through the oak like it's the still-beating heart of a murdered body I've tried to bury, like the Poe story. I stare into nothingness for many a moment to obsess about the contents of the message. He won't be cancelling tonight, will he? He seemed really up for it last night. He explicitly used the words 'looking forward to seeing you'. He put a kiss on the end. But what if he's changed his mind? What if his ex rang him randomly last night and told him she still loves him and they've been up all night rampantly shagging and he's only just remembered he's got a date tonight?

'*Whoops, I should probably let her know,*' I imagine Simon saying, laughing with carefree abandon as she wraps her arms around his neck. Her name is Gretel, I've decided. For some reason, whenever I fantasise about perfect women who behave perfectly in relationships, I always call them Gretel. Gretel kisses his face and says, *'Well you can't go now, can you? Not when we are about to elope to Gretna Green,'* and— OH MY GOD, WHAT IS WRONG WITH ME? Why is this weird image of him and his ex in my head? I don't know him, it's only been five dates, and why am I doing this to myself? I have to open the message. He's going to be cancelling. I know it, I know it. I should get over the disappointment now, rip off the plaster, give the wound oxygen to heal and . . .

The drawer is open. Phone retrieved, alongside a scattering of postcards that rain onto the grey carpet like shrapnel. I jab my finger on the scanner to unlock it, already wondering if my housemate Megan will be free tonight to commiserate-drink with me. I open the message.

Simon: Hey, are you having a nice Friday? Shall we meet at 7pm in Gordon's Wine Bar? X

The usual knee-jerk of emotions scurry in. Euphoria! He messaged! He likes me! I like him! I've not imagined the attraction! Human beings can meet and like each other and make it into a thing and I can be one of those humans! I can do relationships! I can totally do them! There's nothing wrong with me after all! Yes! Oh I like him so much! Gordon's! What an idea! I love that place! I hate it normally but it's so perfect now! Yes! Oh, he really is perfect! I think I'm going to fall in love with him and it will always be perfect! Silly me! Whoopsie! Silly, silly me for doubting this.

Hang on . . .

I just full-on *hallucinated* him having amazing make-up-sex with his ex-girlfriend. I even christened her 'Gretel'.

That's not normal, is it?

Bloody hell, that is *so* un-normal.

What is wrong with me?

HE CAN NEVER FIND OUT HOW UN-NORMAL I AM!

Matt glances over and sees my shaking hands clutching my phone. He takes his headphones off and gestures towards it. 'All OK? You look like he's sent you a death threat?'

I look up, flustered. 'He wants to go to Gordon's Wine Bar.'

'Woah, even worse than a death threat.' He ducks just before I jokingly thwack the top of his head. 'It's good that he wants to see you again though, isn't it?'

'I guess.'

'Are you going to reply?' He talks slowly, like a teacher would say to a child, 'that's a lovely painting, are you going to add a sun to the sky?'

'I mean, that's the obvious thing to do, isn't it?'

'Tends to be the pattern. They message. You message. So on and so forth.' He goes to put his headphones back on, before pausing, holding them out either side of his ears.

'Oh God, what is it?' I ask. 'You're not about to give me some brilliant dating advice, are you? Like "if it's right there's nothing you can do to fuck it up, and if it's wrong there's nothing you can do to make it work" – because I did not have you down as the inspirational quote kind of guy.'

'No, actually, I was going to talk to you about your shift.'

My heart stiffens. Vision smears. I know where this is going.

'I had a look at the inbox and there's a heavy one in there. I'm your buddy so I just thought I'd give you a heads-up and—'

I cut him off. 'I know what you're trying to say, but I'm OK.'

'You sure?'

I smile through it, though I can recognise all the familiar triggers *zing-zinging* throughout my nervous system, setting everything off again. Turning all the switches on across my body. I'm in the dark dark dark of the worst that life can be. The white wallpaper dissolves behind my eyelids. The embossed pattern swirling. I'm here in the room and things have got out of hand and I'm not sure how because it all happened so very quickly you see, but the wallpaper and . . . *No.* I'm not there. I'm here, in an office. On a Friday. I'm totally safe.

'I'm sure,' I tell him.

He must believe me because he puts his headphones back on. Matt can't handle the office's choice in radio station. Essentially, if a song isn't written by some sad bloke tormented by low self-worth and memories of all the exes who got away, Matt doesn't want to listen to it.

I return my phone to the top drawer without even thinking about it, Simon's message temporarily forgotten. I plug in my own pair of noise-cancelling headphones. I know it's Friday, and it's fine that everyone wants to listen to Magic FM, but I can't read about sexual violence to Wham!. I put on *Piano and Rain*, log in to the charity's inbox, and wait to see what horrible thing a man has done to a woman today.

It's bad, my shift. I mean, it's always bad, but I'm almost gasping as I read through this message in the charity's inbox:

Message received: 15:34

Was it rape? He is my boyfriend. I don't understand. Did he mean it?

Matt's checking on me more than he's letting on. I sense every one of his head twitches, feel his eyes dart towards my face.

I stand up suddenly. 'My round for tea. Anyone?' I announce in an overly-chirpy voice.

He pulls his headphones around his neck. 'No tea for me. You OK? Honestly April, I'm happy to do this shift if you'd rather not.'

'I'm *fine*!' I collect my mug and make a thumbs-up/thumbs-down motion to Katy to see if she wants in. She shakes her head. I act like the day hasn't shifted entirely, like my life doesn't feel like a shaken snow globe. 'Tea coming right up,' I mutter to myself.

I stand in the grotty kitchen, gulping down the tea without tasting it. I'm in the office. I am safe in the office. I am in the present moment. God, this office is a shithole. When I was little, I imagined an office with men in dry-cleaned suits

and silken ties and women in power heels with perfect mani-
cures. People would shoot up floors in a sleek, glass lift and
have meetings overlooking the London skyline. That is not
what a charity office looks like, especially a charity office in
a never-ending financial crisis. Since the cuts, we've had to
relocate again. We're now uncomfortably snuggled above a
high-street estate agent. Twenty of us share a unisex loo where
everyone can hear everything and there's no window to let
the smell out. There are no freshly cut flowers at reception
or state of the art touchscreen thingamajigs – just an office
rota for who's answering the phones this week and some old
lumpy computers we got cheap from an office sale. Oh, and
too many desperate young people needing help and not
enough of us to help them effectively.

I make myself go back to my chair, then I reach into my
clogged handbag and rummage for my lavender oil. I dab it
onto my wrists and inhale deeply to further ground myself in.

'Honestly,' Matt interrupts again. 'April, I can take over.'

I look up and smile at his concerned face. Matthew is one
of the few things about this job that doesn't totally destroy
my faith in men. 'You are lovely,' I tell him, because he is.

'Ice cream afterwards?'

'More than lovely.' I take another deep sniff of my scented
pulse points and read through the email message again. I start
taking notes, making sure I've caught everything, all the frag-
ments of her story and her pain. Then I minimise the window
and double-click on my 'template answers' folder, pulling up
the Word document entitled 'Raped By My Boyfriend'.
Because being raped by your boyfriend is so commonplace
the charity has a template answer for it. I tweak the template

that contains all the important phrases about it not being her fault, and there being no right or wrong way of dealing with this, and ask her if there's someone she trusts whom she can talk to. I signpost her towards specialist organisations that can help her further. I offer hope that, in time, she will be able to make sense of this and not let it define her, or her life. I slurp from my cup and check my reply for typos. Then I put the cup down, have one final read-through, and press send. My breathing's not quite right. It stays lodged in my diaphragm like a lump of wet clay. My computer beeps sharply to inform me my reply's been received. I picture it arriving in this face-less girl's inbox – wherever she is in the country. I imagine her refreshing her screen, waiting for this reply, and now it is here. I hope it helps. I picture her feeling soothed by it, less alone. Her crying, but a good sort of crying, a cry that leads you to the start of a hard, but right, path.

I'm helping I'm helping I'm helping, I say over and over to myself, and let the thought seep in, spread out, and calm me down again.

Matt again. Looking over my monitor. 'Just read through your answer,' he says. 'You got the tone spot on.'

I sigh and hang my head back, staring up at a loose ceiling-tile. 'Cheers buddy.'

'Just say when, re the ice cream. The rest of the inbox is pretty standard. You've got a 23-year-old virgin to look forward to, and someone who wants to know if you can get pregnant from a toilet seat.'

I smile up at him. 'I can't talk about my job on my date tonight, can I?' I ask. Simon is back in my thoughts now that I've pushed through the trigger. Hope blossoms through my bloodstream. 'Not sure if sperm on toilet seats is appropriate date-conversation fodder, is it?'

'Google it,' Matt smiles back.

I start to type.

'Oh God,' he says. 'You're actually googling it, aren't you?'

Here are the ways that I think Simon is different and why I might therefore fall in love with him: he always messages back. He seems pleased to see me. His parents aren't divorced. He has not declared I am the love of his life yet, which is appropriate, yet he seems to like me the more he sees me, which is also appropriate. He has a steady job and isn't a failed musician or a failed novelist or a failed actor and only doing the steady job because he failed and is bitter and weird and depressed because of it. He volunteered for the homeless shelter that one time, which is where I met him, so he is not dead inside. He has a sister, which we all know helps things along. He is attractive, but not in a way that means he gets hit on all the time and is therefore too big-headed and likely to cheat. He makes me laugh, and I make him laugh. He is a really good kisser. When I stalked his ex-girlfriend online, she was roughly equally as pretty as I am, if not slightly uglier and, from what I can make out by the date-stamps of the photos, they've been broken up for one year and two months which is a good amount of time for him to emotionally recover. He seems really into me . . . so far.

I spot him before he spots me, so I get to enjoy that giddy thrill of watching a man wait for you. Oh Simon, I really do want to fall in love with you if I can possibly help it. He looks handsome in his work stuff – the sleeves of his blue shirt rolled up to show off his tanned arms. He's already ordered a bottle of red – remembering I prefer red from last time. He's managed to score us a tiny barrel table and two stools outside. He's on his phone, scrolling with his thumb, oblivious to the loud weekend braying of everyone drinking around him. Then, sensing me, he glances up. His eyes crinkle as he smiles, which, according to the relationship expert Roald Dahl, means the smile is really genuine. I wave bashfully and smile back, also a Roald Dahl one. This is it, you know. This could really be it. A man doesn't smile like that unless this could be something. I walk over, highly aware of myself, wishing I hadn't had that second glass of wine at after-work drinks. I hadn't meant to, but London's been boasting a most unusual heatwave, and, determined not to waste a moment of it, we'd carted some wine to Regent's Park around the corner. I wanted to soothe the lingering aftertaste of my shift. Plus, after googling it, I had the dawning realisation that maybe Simon would want to have sex tonight and promptly freaked the hell out. Wine has now diminished the fear that it won't work or *it* will happen again. I just feel floaty and convinced it will all be fine, even though I've not used my vaginal trainers in ages.

We don't quite know how to greet one another yet. The last time I saw him, we were pinned against some wall by the Tube station, kissing so hard it's a miracle we weren't arrested. I'm sure that's in both of our minds now, yet we're back to formal courtship.

'Hello you.' He kisses me on the cheek, while I sort of turn it into a hug.

'You smell great,' I find myself saying tipsily, as we pull apart. 'We'd have totally genetically healthy children.'

I die inside for exactly two seconds until he snorts with laughter and my stomach relaxes again. He laughs widely, showing off at least three fillings which is still sexy to me because I'm off my tits on oxytocin.

He leans in and sniffs my neck. 'Mmm, you smell like you came from a diverse gene pool.'

'Our children won't even need to get vaccinated.'

Then we're kissing in a way I'm normally against people doing in public, mimicking the finale of our last date. Wiping away the polite greeting. The wine's temporarily abandoned, the surrounding *rah-rah*ing crowds of Friday drinkers fade into a Vaseline smear, and I'm tasting Simon's mouth and really feeling quite certain this must be love.

I break off. 'Please don't sniff my butt like a dog though,' I say.

He showcases his sexy oxytocin fillings again. 'But that's my best move.'

We settle into our bottle of red and the euphoric fizzing of connecting with another person you really fancy.

It's all been worth it, I decide, as he picks up the bottle and drains the last of it into my glass. All of the heartache and the break-ups and the terrible dates, and the ringing various female friends, saying I'm exhausted and can't do this any more, and the constant worrying of 'will this ever happen to me', and the crying until I choked, and that year after Ryan where all I did in my empty hours was google ways to kill myself that wouldn't damage my mum too much when she found my body . . . it's all been worth it because of now. Simon. This. The way we are slotting in together.

'I'm not like the other guys who work in finance,' he's saying, sloshing his wine around his glass so it's licking the rim but never quite splashing. 'They're all just in it for the money but I'm not. I'm an ombudsman; I'm just there to make sure they behave. You say you work in finance and everyone just assumes you're a banker wanker, but someone's got to keep them in line.'

I nod my head heavily, looking like I'm trying to under-stand some of the number nitty-gritty he's now explaining to me when, really, I'm having the very terrible thought that he works in finance, and this means he earns good money, even if he's not a banker, and that's quite useful you know, because I work for a charity so I'm always broke. Maybe he has enough savings to buy a house? Then I can live in it? And then, if we get married, it will sort of be my house too? I mean, I like Simon for Simon – not for his money. But the money is useful. Hang on, what the hell is he talking about now? I blink away our three-bed Victorian conversion in Greenwich. 'What was that?' I ask.

He reaches over the barrel table to take my fingers again.

'I was just asking about your job. You're always quite quiet about it.'

'Well, yes, that's because I'm an advisor for a sex and relationships charity. I can't really talk about it on dates. It's all very uncouth.'

He squeezes my hand harder. 'We're on our sixth date, April, I think things can get a bit *uncouth*.'

Then he does that thing men do with their eyes, when they're making it super clear they really want to have sex with you. *Oh God, here it comes. It will be OK, it will be OK. If he's The One, it will be OK.*

'So, your job?' he prompts, leaning back and returning his eyes to normal. 'Tell me about it.'

'What do you want to know?'

'Well, do you like it there?'

'I love it there.' I brandish my wine glass with excitable abandon and let the joy of my job cancel out my unfurling anxiety. 'I mean we're constantly running out of money; we couldn't even afford a Christmas party last year. But the work is rewarding and my colleagues are great. My job is split,' I explain. 'I spend half my time on organisational stuff – sorting out our volunteers, our safeguarding policies etc. Basically I'm in charge of recruiting volunteers, training them, keeping them, and ensuring they know what the hell they're supposed to be doing. Then I spend the other half of my time doing shifts on our front-line services.'

'And they are?' He looks only half interested now, but maybe I've just imagined him glancing at his phone?

'Well, I work on our online service. People send in their questions about sex and relationships and we write back.'

'Sex questions? You must get some fruity stuff.'

I laugh and finish my glass, feeling the warmth of it dribble through me. It is date six and I'm starting to feel comfortable with Simon. Nothing to do with all the wine, I'm sure. 'Nothing shocks me any more,' I tell Simon, my potential future husband.

'Is that so?'

'Oh yeah. You can't be a prude with this job. I mean, on my first day there, I had to chair a meeting about our anal sex policy.'

He almost spits out his wine. 'And what *is* your anal sex policy?'

'Do you mean mine, or my place of work's?'

He swallows hard, and I'm pleased with myself for that line. I laugh again and enjoy his squirming. 'Told you I'm unshockable. In my defence, you started this conversation. Though my colleague, Matt, told me not to bring up work for a while longer.'

His head tilts. A smirk tugs across his face. 'Oh, so you've been talking to your colleagues about me?' He puts his glass down so he can reach over and take my hand again.

I nod shyly, unable to even describe how amazing his skin feels against my skin. 'Why? Have you told your colleagues about *me*?'

It's his turn to nod. 'I may've mentioned I've been on a few dates.'

This is it. I *told you* this was it! If he's *telling* people about me, that must mean he's falling too. My muscles untwist themselves, heaving sighs as they relax into giddy abandon. I try to drink in the moment around me and commit it to memory, so I can recap it accurately for our grandchildren. The sweaty sun in the sky, the smell of the nearby Thames in my nostrils, my exact outfit, his exact outfit, the precise location of our barrel table, the noises of the groups around us. It's all so wonderful that I make a fatal mistake.

I believe.

And therefore I start to relax.

'I always wonder what it must be like to just have regular relationships with work colleagues rather than really intense ones,' I ponder, brushing the rim of my wine glass against my bottom lip. 'When you work for a charity like We Are Here, in order to be professional, you have to immediately have highly-personal and unprofessional conversations.'

'What do you mean?' Simon asks, tipping his head back a bit too far to get to the wine in his glass. It's not the most attractive look but it doesn't matter because he's potentially my future husband and therefore everything he does is adorable.

'Well, if you work with upset people telling you upsetting things, like we do, it's unhealthy to have an I'm-at-work bravado, you know? We've got to feel healthy in ourselves to handle the users appropriately. You can't take on a shift on a helpline if you're in a bad way. That's irresponsible. You may accidentally let it seep into your responses. So, my colleagues and I are, like, super close. We always have a buddy to debrief to after each shift, and we have to talk about our emotions all the time. I know basically every terrible thing that's ever happened to them, and vice-versa. That way we can all know our triggers, and look out for one another during shifts.'

Simon's face screws up. 'Triggers?' he asks.

I nod. I really do love talking about my job. Our little charity. It's been such a source of good in my life since Ryan. 'Yes, subjects that upset you – usually because of something that's happened in your past. At work, if you're triggered by a particular topic, you may be too upset and therefore need to let a colleague take over.' I smile fondly, thinking of Matt and Katy and all the others in our little microcosm of support. 'So, we are all *very* close. Like, I know my buddy cannot handle anything to do with alcoholism because his dad was an alcoholic. And, my manager isn't so good on the STI type questions, because she's phobic of germs, and one of our volunteers, bless her, isn't so good on anything to do with drugs.' I look up at Simon, still grinning, expecting him to be grinning too. So, it's a shock when his face isn't the face I imagine. Instead, he's leaning back, looking slightly bored. I see him punch his thumb onto his phone to check for notifications and my stomach twists.

'Whoa, all a bit heavy, isn't it?' he says, nose wrinkled.

I can taste the change of vibe in the air. I detect his discomfort and feel instantly self-conscious and stupid.

'Do you want to go somewhere else?' Simon very deliberately changes the subject, arms crossed in front of him. 'Or,' he says, raising one sly eyebrow and changing the vibe further, 'we could just grab a drink at mine?'

I'm still emotional when he drops the sex hint, trying to locate how and when I messed up. I make myself smile, while I do the basic-level psychology needed to figure out what's going on. 'I guess we could head back to yours?'

I'm stressed that I've upset him, feeling like I'm wobbling backwards on the edge of a ledge, arms flailing to keep balance.

But sex . . . sex always grounds you with them again. I now want to have sex with him, not because I'm horny, but to make things OK. Offer myself as an apology for being myself.

He stands quickly and puts his arm around my back as I scramble up. A crowd of drunken suit-wearers push past, claiming our table before I've even disentangled my handbag from my stool. I'm still mentally processing as we're spat out onto the pavement next to Embankment, where a *Big Issue* seller mumbles a desperate plea for sales. I'm trying to get back into the good feeling. Have I just imagined our connection vanishing? Probably. Especially as . . .

There's no time for further thinking. Simon has pulled me into him, moaning as our lips meet. We make out in front of the *Big Issue* vendor for twenty solid minutes, London blurring to nothingness. I forget how much kissing renders me incapable. I lose all sense of fear as biology takes over, flooding me with the druggy high of chemistry. Simon breaks off, takes my hand and drags me to the Tube station, all eyebrows raised and the-sex-is-going-to-happen-soon. I instruct myself to feel excited rather than tense.

There's four minutes until the next Circle line train so we kiss again, breaking apart only to debate whether to change at Tower Hill.

'It'll save us two minutes,' I say.

'What's two minutes?' Simon replies, pulling me back into him.

The Tube hisses its arrival. We stagger onto the half-empty carriage. Under the glaring lights, we silently agree to shelve the PDAs, and sit opposite one another. The kiss escapism lasts a whole Tube stop before my anxiety shows up. I stare over at Simon and start oh-so-predictably freaking out about everything that's happened and is about to happen. He's pulled out his phone, scrolling through with a glazed expression. Why isn't he staring over at me adoringly, like I am him? That's the first twinge of angst. Then, just as we're clattering past Monument: Why did he go all weird when I brought up my job? Was I too much? I'm always too much. Why haven't I been practising with my trainers? Will it work? Will I be able to?

Don't say anything, I instruct myself. Don't bring it up. Enjoy this. Have the sex. Get the closeness back. You know how to have sex. You've done it before. Fall in love. This man clearly likes you. Look! He's just looked up from BBC Sport and winked! A wink! What a lovely, romantic wink . . . oh, he's gone back to looking at his phone now, but that's OK. You can't expect him to gaze at you adoringly the whole Tube journey. That's asking too much. You're asking too much, just like always.

But my mouth is open and the words are already out:

'Simon? Is everything OK?'

He glances up from his screen and wrinkles his nose for the second time that evening. 'Yes, why?'

Stop talking, stop talking, stop talking, stop talking.

'I didn't mean to go on about my job . . .'

'Don't worry about it. It was just a bit too much for a Friday, wasn't it? Look! This is us!' He reaches out to entwine fingers again and I step out onto the platform, feeling a little bit like I've been punched in the face, but also like it's my fault and I'm the one who needs to make it better.

'I cannot wait to get you back to mine,' Simon whispers into my neck before kissing it.

I make a non-committal sexy-sounding noise and try to gear myself up. What did he mean by 'a bit too much'? I'd hardly said anything. Why are those two words *always* used about me?

We steer through the Friday night energy, dodging clumps of scantily dressed revellers, and the swaying drunks looking for the meaning of life in their Ginsters pasties. Simon kisses me as we wait at the bus stop. Each kiss soothes the angst and pulls me back into the moment. As we get on the bus I try to tell myself I'm being silly and reading too much into things, like I'm always told I do. I try to get myself into the mood for sex, mentally checking I've got myself ready for it. I'm wearing nice matching underwear. I shaved in the shower this morning. I've got condoms in my bag, and a toothbrush. I hope there are no specks of loo roll stuck around my vagina. Maybe I can use the bathroom before-hand, just to check?

The loud *ding* of the stop button being hit. Simon's standing up.

'This is us.'

I clamber up, trying not to fall as the bus lurches into the stop. He gets off first and holds out his hand. 'M'lady,' he says, kissing the top of my own hand.

'Sire,' I reply, though I'm having an inexplicable moment of finding Simon totally repulsive. *You're a cheesy twat*, I think. *Fuck you for being weird about my job.*

Then it passes, as promptly as it arrived. I laugh and do a little curtsey.

Simon's pulling me towards his flat, muttering sweet-anythings like the director's commentary on a film called

Everything A Woman Secretly Wants to Hear. 'You're so beautiful, and sexy. I really, really fancy you. You're amazing.'

The words dissolve in, like honey in hot milk, and erase away all the doubts putting their hands up. I feel potent with power, high on how much he wants me. If he can just keep up this level of adoration for every minute of our lives together, that will compensate, surely, for the fact he can't handle one minute of me talking about my job being hard, or the fact he *is* a bit cheesy actually, and . . . oh. We've just got into his flat and, looking around, it's an atrocious mess. It's filthy. There's crap everywhere. It's like him and his housemate are feral. *Eww. Eww eww.*

'Sorry. The cleaner's not coming until Sunday morning.' Simon lifts my arms up above my head to remove my top before I'm ready to remove it. I mean, we're still in the cluttered entrance. He's not even pretended we are going to drink coffee.

I could've done with a bit more reassuring small talk beforehand but now my top is off and Simon's behaving how all men behave when they get a whiff of laid. His eyes have that angry urgency to them, and now he's plunging his tongue into my mouth. It's gone all primal. I feel like . . . bait? *Oh God, brain, stop thinking!* I try to focus on kissing him back and losing myself in instinct and feeling good and sexy and doing all the right things, but, yes, I do have one eye open, to take in his flat and try to figure out what that means about his character. It's hard to deduce much through the mess. It's typical men-living-with-other-men stuff – two lazy boys and an easy-to-assemble pine table from IKEA littered with wilting *Evening Standard*s. I twist him around so I can get a view of the kitchen. I'm unimpressed with the stack of washing-up and crumb-laden surface. I mean, he's 33 and he can't wipe a counter top?

'Let's go to my bedroom.' Simon's erection strains against his suit trousers, his shirt half-unbuttoned.

'OK.'

We crash around, attached by the lips. He carries on undoing his shirt so I put my hands up the back of it and sort of scratch him so I can feel like I'm contributing. His grunting noises amplify their urgency and we smash through the door and arrive in his room. There's a Welsh flag hanging on the curtain rail, which surprises me because he doesn't sound Welsh. *Is* he Welsh? Do you need to know if someone is Welsh or not before they put their penis inside you? *Oh God – shut up brain! Enjoy the sex. What is wrong with me?*

We fall backwards onto his unmade bed with a *doof* and a giggle. The intimacy of his laugh turns me on a bit. It feels real and right again and I'm back in the game. My brain clears enough for me to tug off his shirt and chuck it to the floor like an actual vixen – well, not an actual vixen, they don't have opposable thumbs. *Shut up brain, shut up brain.* Simon gently guides my pelvis up to try and take off my skinny jeans. He does marvellously, until they get stuck on my shins. I lean down to help him.

'No,' he smacks my arms away and yanks.

Shocked, I say, 'I was just trying to help.'

'Well don't.'

He struggles to get them off a while longer, muttering, 'What the fuck *are* these things?' Then, once he's finally yanked them off my feet, he beams at me, all cocky and voila! Like he didn't just smack me. Like I was supposed to find being told off sexy.

I'm not sure what to do so I lean up and kiss him, craving tenderness for counterbalance. But he wraps my hair around his fist, pulling me towards him roughly, using his other hand to try and unclip my bra. I know this one has a tricky clasp and he'll struggle but I've learnt that he won't appreciate any pointers. So I run through all the things I like about him to try and get myself back into it, pretending it's not taken over a minute now for him to get the hang of it: Simon always replies to my messages within an appropriate level of time. He makes me laugh. He is not like other people who work in finance. I remember how hard we giggled on our first date because the waiter was so incompetent and kept ignoring us. I remember how, on our second date, he turned up holding a bunch of tulips because I'd told him they were my favourite. I remember the lovely message he sent me last week, when I had to rain check because I got struck by the office lurgy, telling me to get well soon. *Nobody is perfect*, I think to myself, as he rummages himself out of his boxers and silently instructs me to slide out of my knickers. *I'm so lucky I've met him*, I think to myself, as I wait propped on my elbows while he faffs around with the condom. *This could really be the start of something*, I think to myself, as he leans me back. I take three, subtle, deep breaths just as he's about to enter me, stressing that it won't work that it will hurt that it will be awful and my life is ruined . . . but . . . oh thank *God* he's made it in and we're having sex. I sigh in relief, my entire body relaxing. Simon mistakes the sigh for satisfaction and lets out a matching one. He pulls my face towards him to stare into my eyes.

That's nice actually. I like that. It's tender and real and safe for two whole minutes of missionary. But then his eyes leave mine, his face closes off, and he gets rougher, thrusts more forcefully, like it doesn't matter if I'm there at all. Why do they always do this? Why? I need him to look at me. I need him to see me. I need to feel like this is something. But the porn urge has overridden him and I feel like nothing once more and I'm losing it, spiralling away from this room and him and into the darkness, holding on by my fingernails.

But it's about to get worse. He pulls out and, without asking, without checking, without kissing me or showing me any tenderness at all, he starts arranging me into the doggy position. It's so cold and unfeeling and no, *no*! Where has he gone? Why is he acting like I'm not here? My anxiety builds and builds, my stomach curdling as he yanks my hair. The nice man I thought I could fall in love with is gone and I panic . . .

I can't.

I freeze. Primitively suspended in the moment. Fear soaking through me.

He doesn't notice, or maybe he's pretending not to notice. Either way, he's getting ready to start again, despite me stiffening up, but *no* . . .

No no *no*.

Not this way.

Please not this way.

The white wallpaper.

No. But *oh God*.

This will be so much easier, *so* much easier if I just go along with it.

But I can't.

I can't.

'I'm sorry,' I squeal. I roll myself over so I'm no longer bent over the bed. I fight the urge to kick him away and run out of the room.

'What the hell?'

I glance up to see panic bleed across his face. His mouth hanging open, lips slightly curled.

Shit. I've ruined it, I've ruined it, I've ruined it. I'm terrified and want to run away but I also can't handle his face now that I've ruined it.

'I . . . don't understand. What's going on?'

'Can we just not . . . in that position?' My voice is more squeak than voice. 'Not tonight.' I desperately grasp at an excuse. 'I want to see your face.'

'Oh,' Simon says, standing there naked. 'Oh,' he repeats.

'OK, cool.' I say and unravel myself and make myself lean up to kiss him, to try and get it back. I reckon I could drag myself back into the moment if he could just be a bit more tender. We can recover, this is fine, he's still a good kisser . . . or is he? He's hardly kissing me back. I can taste the hesitation. And, when I glance down, I can see the deflating impact of my behaviour.

Shit. Shit shit shit shit.

I shouldn't have said anything.

What's wrong with me?

Why did I do this?

Anxiety pulses through me, panic starts hitting the button. I break off, even though I know talking about it will make it worse. 'Is everything OK?'

Simon's eyes are wide; Simon is not OK. 'Yep.' He winces as he says it. Then . . . 'I mean, well, actually . . .' He sits down on the edge of the bed, away from me, signalling the end of the sex and, I'm quite certain, the end of us. My throat closes up in self-loathing. I long for an alternate reality where I just let us continue. Where I am the sort of woman who loves a porn-style pummelling by someone she's sleeping with for only the first time. 'I'm just . . . well, you've made me feel bad. I wasn't doing anything wrong . . .' he trails off, hangs his head.

'I know you weren't! Sorry! I'm so sorry. I just . . .' I don't want to tell him about it, but I also don't know how to explain it without telling him about it. I will try and make it breezy. I can do that, surely. 'It's just . . . umm . . . I had a bad experience a long time ago and so I need a bit more time sometimes . . .' His eyes widen, panic well and truly flowing through him now. My heart's bending over on itself, but I'm still determined to save this. 'Look, it's nothing, I was really enjoying it. Hey? Hey . . .' I fling myself at him, wrap my naked legs around his waist and kiss him even more desperately. I rub my hands down his back, scratching his skin, trying to be all alluring like the women in the movies.

He ignores me though, and just stares at the wall. 'I . . . I don't think I can have sex now,' he announces, before standing suddenly, shedding me like a coat he's dropped to the ground and striding to the en suite. I watch him take a piss. I watch him as I gather my clothes to myself, my heart close to snapping. I expect him to sit down and say maybe we can talk about it. Although I'm disorientated, I reckon I can power through this, make light of it, laugh our way back to sex. He doesn't talk about it though. He turns off the light and strides back towards the bed, like I'd said nothing, like we're a stale couple who have been married a million years. And with that, Simon, the man who I thought may be the love of my life, is a stranger again. All the connection just got pissed down the toilet.

He smiles awkwardly. 'It's late, and I've had one hell of a week at work. Shall we just go to sleep?'

I nod, shoving my dress back over my head to shield my naked body. He leans over and kisses me on the forehead. 'You all right?' he asks, making it clear the only acceptable answer is yes.

'Yes.'

Satisfied he's a nice man because he bothered asking, he clambers under his slightly-smelly duvet and rolls onto his side. 'Night,' he says with his back to me.

'Umm, night.'

There's one toss, one groan, and one turn, while I blink up at the ceiling next to this stranger. Then Simon does the impossible.

He sleeps.

I'm not even under the duvet by the time his breathing falls into a steady hiss and his body goes heavy. I take a deep breath and calmly bend to pick my knickers off the floor. I shrug my dress to my nose and smell the cigarette smoke and sweat from the day. Then I lie back next to this man in the dark and actually contemplate the possibility of being able to fall asleep too. I would like to. To be able to check out of reality right now, to pretend whatever the fuck just happened didn't just happen. I could wake tomorrow, refreshed and

35

bright-eyed and bushy-tailed, and somehow laugh it off and say it's nothing before seducing him into having good sex and getting us back on track again.

Maybe some girls would find that possible?

Although, I bet those girls wouldn't have behaved like a complete frigid nutter in the first place . . . Girls like *Gretel*.

That's the thought that sets off the crying. A few tears seep down my cheek, sinking into Simon's dirty pillowcase. I sniff and wipe my face, staring at the blackness of the ceiling. Simon stirs and I sniff louder as I play out a fantasy in my head. The fantasy that he will wake up to see I'm upset, and it will create an outpouring of love from him. He'll sit up, turn the light on and say '*Hey, hey, what's going on?*' and I'll say '*I'm sorry I made it weird.*' He'll tuck my hair back and say '*I'm sorry I made it weird too.*' We'll laugh about how awkward it was. Then he'll tuck my hair back again, because, let's face it, you can never have too much of that, and he'll say, '*I'm really sorry, April, I didn't mean to freak out. I'm so glad you confided in me about what happened, and, now I've had some time to digest it, it's nothing. I really, really, like you, and I'm so excited that we met.*' That's all the talking we will need. We'll collapse into one another and kissing will turn into mind-blowing sex – the sort that will totally erase the painful misfire we just shared.

This fantasy calms me for a moment. I turn over and watch Simon's contented face, bathed in the artificial orange from the streetlight outside, the rise and fall of his breath. My fantasy triggers a deep stirring of love for him. This perfect man in my imagination.

A minute, it lasts. Before the truth builds itself around me.

The truth that I've ruined it with this man, and he has ruined it with me. What sort of person is capable of falling asleep when the woman whose body you were just inside of is clearly very upset? In one final attempt to wake him and see if he can be the man I want and need him to be, I snuffle. To no avail. He stays solidly unconscious. And that's when my anger at him flips into anger at myself in my predictable trauma response. The shame and self-blame bombard themselves through my body, filling me with loathing.

I've fucked it up, I've fucked it up, I've fucked it up.

Like I always fuck it up, like I always fuck it up, like I always fuck it up.

Because I'm too fucked up, too fucked up, too fucked up.

The tears gain momentum. My chest starts heaving with the effort of controlling the sobs. The saltwater soaks my hair, drips off the edges of my face. Eventually, the sobs are too huge to contain. I tiptoe politely to Simon's en suite so I can get on with the serious business of totally falling apart. At first, I try clinging to the toilet to cry, but he's left skid marks all over the rim and just the sight makes me gag. I put the loo seat down and huddle on the bath mat.

He didn't even clean the skid marks off the loo before I came round. That is how little you mean to men who mean things to you. You're not worth the effort of scraping shit off a toilet for.

I end up foetal, forehead on the floor, my lungs heaving as I free-fall into despair. At some point, I hear Simon's flat-mate let himself in. I bite my lip and whimper silently as I listen to his getting-ready-for-bed noises. I hear him make something in their kitchen, the sound of the TV coming on low, some late-night comedy show with canned laughter, the scrape of food being eaten off a plate. I imagine how Simon will tell this faceless man what happened. I picture his shock. The words he will use. 'A bit too damaged, unfortunately'. 'Better off without that.' 'Oh well, plenty more fish in the sea.' The sound of a light being switched off. The kitchen extractor fan runs itself to a stop. The flat falls quiet again.

I'm aware of how very alone I feel.

All my loneliest moments in life involve a man asleep when he knows it's likely I'm crying.

I have only two options: a) to be the weirdo who disappeared in the night, or b) to be the weirdo who is still there in the morning. I pick b), as a stupid part of me is still determined to make this work somehow. I cannot handle the humiliation of being so very wrong about him. We may very well wake up sober, and be able to talk about it. I surely didn't imagine the closeness between us? We don't even have to go into it, I don't even particularly *want* to go into it, but just talking, like we were so good at earlier this evening, could get us on the right path again.

At around 3 a.m. I crawl back into Simon's bed and attempt to lose consciousness. I play back my favourite memories of what we've shared so far. Our first date, our first kiss, his smell, his . . .

I wake with a start.

My head throbs from too much wine and too much crying. My mouth festers with dryness. Simon is awake, sitting upright in bed. I swear he grimaces when he realises I've stirred. Any hope I harboured dies with the grimace. My gut kicks into the familiar feeling of impending break-up – the slurry in my stomach, the wobble of my top lip, the resigned inevitability of it.

'Morning,' I say.

'Morning.'

'Did you sleep OK?'

'Yes, you?'

I nod my lie and notice him not leaning down to kiss me.

'Do you want breakfast?' he asks. 'There's this place around the corner. They do good avo on toast. You like that, don't you?'

He wants to end this over breakfast so he feels less like a bad guy. I cannot do this. I cannot have someone say kind things to me again over sourdough when they are also telling me they never want to see me again. No amount of avo on toast can take the sting out of rejection.

'It's OK.' I put my hand up. 'You don't have to.'

'It will be nice.'

I shake my head. 'Simon, can we just talk about what

39

happened last night already? You don't have to buy my breakfast.'

Even in my anguish, there's a part of me that enjoys watching a man's inner turmoil when it becomes obvious he's going to have to talk about his emotions. Simon's eyes widen, like he's a vegetarian that's accidentally bitten into a meat pasty. I leave him in the silence he needs and brace myself for impact.

'I didn't mean to upset you,' he says, finally, without making eye contact. 'I'm still not sure what happened.'

'Well, you didn't ask me what happened, did you?' I point out. 'You didn't talk to me about it at all. You just went to sleep.'

He takes the hit, hesitates, and then recovers. 'Yes, sorry about that. I was just shocked, and you see, I'm so stressed with work. I could've handled it better, I admit.'

I wait for the 'but'. I arrange my face into battle mode.

'But . . .'

Here it comes.

'The thing is, I'm not really looking for anything serious at the moment. And—'

I cut him off. 'Don't lie.'

'What?'

'You are. Just not with me. At least own it, Simon.'

He runs his hand through his hair, and that's the moment I notice his receding hairline. The widening space above his forehead. He's got a year or two, max, before those two patches merge and then he'll have to start shaving it off. 'I don't understand why you're being like this.'

'I just think we're both old enough for the truth.' I sigh and shake my head.

'We're not exactly old . . .'

'We're in our thirties.'

'That's not *old*.' He looks genuinely offended that I've suggested such a notion. I shake my head again and wish there was a betting website where I could put my life savings on the odds that he's referred to himself as *Peter Pan,* proudly, in the last year.

'Look, anyway, let's just get on with it.' It's rather incredible that I'm not crying. In fact, I sound quite chill and disconnected and sassy and all the things I'm sure would've kept this relationship going if I'd been able to summon them last night instead of being triggered. Simon seems equally as thrown at my character transformation. Doubt settles in just above his eyebrows. He's going to follow through though because he's still not making eye contact.

'I really like you,' he starts. It's how this always starts. 'You're pretty and you're smart and you're funny and you're kind.' I nod. All of those things are true. They don't seem to make me lovable though – too unchill and broken for that. I wait again for the second 'but'. The 'but' that's been the butt of all my misery my entire adult life. 'But, to tell you the truth, I've not been feeling it . . .' he trails off.

I close my eyes. I count to three. I take deep breaths. I let the rejection, once again, soak through me.

He can't handle the pain he's caused me. Simon thinks he is a nice guy. Maybe he even is, to women who aren't me. He's started scrambling around for modifiers to make himself feel better. 'You're great, you're so great. Last night was just . . . well . . . Again, I'm sorry. I don't know what's going on with me.'

I manage to look up at him. 'For fuck's sake, stop lying.'

He jerks back, his demeanour switching into defensive-mode right away. 'I'm not!'

'You are, and it's boring. Just tell the truth. *God.*'

'Look, stop making me into a villain! As I said, I've not been totally feeling it, but I thought there was enough there to see where it went. And, well, last night . . . I'm just not sure I'm the right guy to take on something like that, April, OK? I'm not evil for wanting a normal sex life rather than . . .'

The word 'normal' hits harder than a bullet. It explodes on impact. He doesn't finish his sentence. He's made it clear: I'm the problem, not him. He crosses his arms. He can't physically look at me. Bottom lip stuck out. All 'look what you made me do'.

I stand. I can't, I just can't any more. I will cry I will cry I will cry, but I won't give Simon the satisfaction of seeing that. 'Goodbye Simon,' I say, putting my sandals on with as much dignity as it's possible to muster.

'We can still get breakfast,' he tells the floorboards hollowly.

As I stuff my belongings back into my handbag. I can practically hear him whinging to his mate.

She was acting like I was such a jerk, but I was the one offering to take her out to breakfast! I was the one trying to be mature about the whole thing! Nightmare! She's just taking whatever happened out on me which is so unfair. I'm not a bad guy. I was just being honest.

Or even worse, he won't mention me at all. I'm not significant enough.

I bend over, my heart feels like it's going to tumble out of my mouth. I'm thirsty, and hurting, humiliated, and done.

He doesn't follow me to the door. He just sits with his face in his hands, concocting a way, I'm sure, to make himself the victim in all this.

'Have a great life!' I shout over my shoulder as I leave, wincing as I say it, because it sounds like a line in a really crap movie. I wait for the lift, playing out one last desperate fantasy. Imagining him chasing me out, catching the lift before the doors close, telling me it's all a big mistake, that he will do anything to have me back. I want him to want me, even though, if I give myself time, I know that I don't want him. Not really. Not the real him I wasn't given the time to get to know.

The doors slide open. I step inside. They slide shut, without any chases and dramatic revelations. I pull out my phone, seeing if there's a message from Simon, telling me to wait.

Instead I have five messages from Megan:

Megan: You've not come home. IS TONIGHT THE NIGHT?

Megan: What's sex like? I've forgotten.

Megan: I've eaten your leftover lasagne. Sorry, but not really. If you didn't want me to, you should've come home tonight and stopped me. You know what I'm like.

Megan: Yes, I'm totally victim blaming you right now.

Megan: I've eaten your Gü pudding too . . .

Even she isn't able to make me smile. I blink and blink and blink. The lift doors *ding* open and I'm spat out onto the dirty, littered streets of London on a Saturday morning. I lean against the wall of Simon's new-build beside a couple of pigeons pecking at a patch of splattered vomit, and watch

43

the buses lurch past, joggers jog, and cyclists cycle, and wait a moment or two before I reply. These are my last moments of showing the outside world I'm capable of having a relationship. Right now, only Simon and I know we've disintegrated. My friends and colleagues still believe that April might have the ability to meet a nice man and get past date five. Their doubts about me are fading. They're thinking 'how nice'. As soon as I message Megan to reveal the ending, that veneer will collapse. The narrative will revert back to April trope. I'm going to have to go through the painful and humiliating process of telling everyone I told about Simon that, no, actually, it didn't work out. I'll have to endure the re-explaining of what happened, the 'well he doesn't deserve you anyway' lies when, secretly, they're thinking, 'hmm, I do wonder if there's something not quite right about that one' before they get on with their own business and their own lives and their own relationships that they seem to find so, *so* much easier than I do.

April: On my way home. It's over. Before it even began. Not good.

No one asks if I'm all right as I weep silently along the District line, staring out at the blackness. Two tourists, armed with cameras and stinking of sun cream, notice the tears and discuss my predicament in a hushed language I don't understand. But they decide to do nothing.

The moment I get signal, my phone vibrates with replies.

Megan: Fuck
Megan: I'm so sorry hon.

Megan: I'm here. I've just run out to get replacement Gü.
Multiple Gü.
Megan: You WILL get through this.

I shakily reply 'I love u xxx' and focus on trying to ravel myself back in again. It is just a man. One man. I can handle this. I've been here before. Many, many times. I focus on my ribcage expanding and contracting, on my breath coming in and out, even if it is in short, sharp bursts of sadness. The carriage judders to a halt at South Kensington and I'm the first to get out when the doors slam open. I cannot handle the crowds of dawdling tourists, not today. I jump off and run to the steps, elbowing a stressed mother pushing a buggy towards the Natural History Museum exit. She shouts after me, and I find myself muttering 'fuck off' as I run past. I don't even feel guilty. All I can think is that she deserves it, with her three children and her life all together, getting in my way when I'm falling apart and will probably never be able to have what she has – no matter how hard I try. I dodge down the side roads, to the little mews where Megan's flat hides. I scrabble with my key, the tears really streaming now, and, when I'm through the door, Megan is there. Arms wide open, a chocolate Gü in each hand, looking just as upset as I feel. I fling myself into her and cry myself dry.

Here are the red flags I ignored about Simon because I was so desperate for him to be the end of dating hell: yes, he did always message back but he never called me. Every time we arranged to see each other, I had to fit in around his diary, not the other way around. His parents are still together, but he mentioned during our third date, after three martinis, that 'I really don't think they love each other, or ever have', which is bound to impact his view on healthy relationships. He rarely asked me any questions about myself and looked bored at the answers. He once referred to his ex as 'a bit crazy'. He sneered when I mentioned my friend Chrissy and her battle with depression, saying it's 'a bad habit'. He admitted he only volunteered at the shelter that one time to meet women and thought it was funny.

The main red flag? He said he was looking for a 'partner in crime' which everyone knows is shorthand for 'a woman who isn't real'.

'I still don't understand it,' I tell Megan, lying on the sofa, exhausted and blotchy.

'There's nothing to understand. He's just a dick.' She's curled her feet up under her and the gold from the sun hits her black hair, turning it grey.

'Is he, though?'

'Yes.'

'He's not done anything wrong.'

'He's a man, of course he's done something wrong.'

'No, it's me. There's something wrong with me.' My voice breaks and Megan leans over and gently strokes my leg and whispers the sorts of lies one has to whisper to someone in my state.

'There, there. He isn't worth it. You can do so much better.'

I lurch up. 'I don't *want* to do better, that's the point! I'm prepared to settle! I'm thirty fucking three. I'm not expecting fucking . . . fucking . . . *Gaston* to turn up at my door.'

Her whole face quivers with laughter.

'Stop it!'

'Who *ever* wanted to date *Gaston*?'

'You know what I mean. I'm so confused,' I say, huddling my legs up, my voice flat. 'I thought it was going so well. I'm mental. I'm actually mental. There must be something seriously wrong with me.'

'No,' Megan replies firmly, continuing a steady pat of my leg. 'There's something seriously wrong with *men*. Men don't deserve women. How many times do I have to tell you?'

I pick up one of Megan's scatter cushions and bury my face in it. 'If only I'd just been more chilled out.'

'You mean, if only you'd had sex you didn't feel comfortable having, you'd have "won" a relationship?'

'Yes,' I mutter into the Laura Ashley.

'And you really want to be with someone who doesn't respect your sexual boundaries?'

'But isn't it fair enough to want sex in the doggy position? No wonder he freaked out. That's pretty vanilla! I'm too weird and difficult and no man will ever want me because I'm a mental, high-maintenance FREAK!' More tears arrive.

Megan reaches over. 'Not into the Laura Ashley,' she says gently, which makes me laugh-cry. 'Look, the right guy, well, not even the right guy, but a guy with any decency could've handled you not wanting to get hardcore doggy-styled the first time you slept with them. That's quite extreme for a first time. You're not a freak! I mean, if anything, it was just bad manners.'

'And I *can* have sex from behind,' I say. 'I can even enjoy it. I just need to feel safe first. Not have it happen right away.'

'Exactly. That's totally healthy considering what happened. Simon is just an insensitive, selfish, dick. If he really wanted a true relationship, which means liking someone for who they are, he wouldn't have just freaked out and used it as an excuse. I mean I can't believe you told him about . . . you know, and he just *blanked* it.'

'I don't blame him. I wish *I* could just blank it.' I wipe under my eyes, and use the back of my hand to clear up the snot. 'I keep torturing myself with this imaginary woman called Gretel,' I say, more tears falling. 'She's based on this girl I worked with years ago, just after I graduated. I only knew her a few months, but every man in the office was *obsessed* with her. She was really confident and sexy and sure of herself. She had this cool fringe and managed to get Glastonbury tickets every year because she "knew someone".' I shake my head. 'All the men in our office fell in love with her, and she kind of got off on the power she had . . . Now, whenever I'm feeling insecure, I always compare myself to this weird made-up version of her and feel crap. Gretel has sex from behind and loves it. She's brilliant at sex. Nothing fazes Gretel. She's easygoing and laughs all the time, and spends her life going on adventures. No man who dates her ever gets over her. She's never needy or insecure or jealous and therefore she's rewarded by the pick of all the men in the universe.'

Megan crosses her arms. 'She sounds like a right dick.'

'Oh my God, she was a total dick. All the women in the office hated her.'

'She's also NOT REAL,' Megan bellows, leaning into my hair. 'There is literally no woman out there who doesn't have insecurities about *something*. Gretel sounds like a sociopath, if you ask me. Both the real one and your imaginary one. All these men falling for her would've realised she was just as fucked up as the rest of us eventually.' She reaches out and puts a hand on my shoulder. 'There's nothing wrong with you, April,' she says quietly. 'Nothing. I mean, you're not perfect, no one is, but you can't torture yourself with this idea that other women are more chilled out, because they're not.

Also, who wants the pick of all the men in the universe? Men are terrible!'

I hug my knees to my chest. 'But so many women seem to be in happy relationships,' I protest.

'*Seem* to be.' Megan gestures out like a magician's assistant. 'There you have it. God knows what they're putting up with and shutting up with in order to make it "work" with the stupid fucking man they're stuck with.'

Megan is in the enviable position of having completely given up on romantic love, and, as a result, is probably one of the happiest, most content people I know. I mean, it helps that her parents are loaded, so she's inherited a two-bed flat in freaking *Kensington* but, as she says herself, 'what I inherited in money and property, I also inherited in a fucked-up family dynamic and major issues'. She reaches out and pulls my head out of my knees. 'Think of all the married women we know, then look at their husbands. Is there a single one of them, a single one that you don't think is a bit of a dick and wonder how she puts up with him?'

I pause as I run through all my 'happily married' friends' husbands. There's Joel, Steph's husband, a Chelsea season-ticket holder and has therefore never once spent a whole weekend with her, apart from their two-week honeymoon. Even then, she says he watched football on the hotel TV the whole time. Then there's Stu, Kim's husband, who corrects her on her grammar in front of people. Even Katy's husband, Jimmy, is someone she constantly complains about. 'He just doesn't do anything,' she'll moan. 'It takes so much effort sometimes to get him to just mend a bloody shelf without me asking a million times.'

'So, these are my choices?' I ask, spelling them out on my fingers: 'a) accept that all men are problematic cretins who don't deserve us, but try to find one to love anyway. Which is what I've been trying to do, but men don't seem to want to be with me because I'm not like Gretel, despite the huge personal compromises I'm making in trying to love their pathetic arses. Or b) give up, live my life without a man, continue using a vibrator and find a sperm donor if I get really desperate to have children?'

Megan points to herself proudly. 'And you will notice I've gone for option B. Look how happy I am. How *young* I look.' She jabs the uncreased skin around her eyes.

'I want there to be more options than these. I get more options for how to take my fucking coffee. I'm so depressed.'

Megan tilts her head. 'I know, hon. It hurts. And I'm sorry.'

'Is there . . . am I . . .' I can hardly make myself say it, the inkling in my stomach that makes me feel sick and useless and desperate. 'Am I just . . . unlovable?'

Megan pulls me into her so tight that I can smell her Chanel Coco Mademoiselle. Only Megan would still wear perfume on a lazy Saturday. 'Of course you're not unlovable! You're so lovable, *I* love you!'

'You have to say that because you're my friend.'

'No. Because it's true.'

'I'm too damaged for love. Ryan fucked me up beyond repair and men can sense that. They want someone perfect; they want a Gretel.'

'Everyone's damaged, hon,' she reassures. 'And men are the most damaged of all. It's nothing to do with you. You know it. Deep down, you know it. And, how many times do I need to tell you? Gretel ISN'T REAL.'

I hear her words and I know they are right but I still don't believe them. I remember the look on Simon's face when I revealed a tiny part of myself that wasn't easy-going. It's the face I've seen time and time again, over the years and the heartbreaks. So many different men, with different features, temperaments, eye colours and bone structure – yet all with the same drawing up of the eyebrows, the lowering of their chin, the face they pull when they realise you are too much and they're not sure they want you after all (though they'll still be willing to sleep with you and hide all of this until you catch on).

I can't do it any more.

I can't see that face on a man again. Especially as so many of those men weren't even all that. It's exhausting feeling so permanently powerless.

What does it say when a man you're willing to compromise on isn't willing to compromise on you?

'Are you OK?' Megan leans forward, her face the picture of concern and love and understanding. The sort of face it would be amazing to see on just one boyfriend, just one. If men could love women the way women love each other, everything would be terribly easier.

'I'm such a reluctant heterosexual,' I admit.

Megan squeezes my knee. 'I know, honey. Aren't we bloody all?'

Things I've tried, to make it work with men

Being truly authentic and open and myself

The result?

'I've never had to have *this* many *conversations* about my *feelings* before. It's all a bit too much.'

Backing off and playing it cool

The result?

'There's something missing, you know?'

Just allowing it to happen naturally: 'The right guy comes along when you're not looking for him'

The result?

I did not have sex for a year and a half.

Being 'less picky'

The result?

I ended up ruining my life for two years with Ryan and all the things he did to me.

Being 'more picky'

The result?

Literally no matches. At all. On any dating service. But then I was so traumatised after Ryan, I only liked about one in two hundred.

Going for someone older and more mature
The result?

'I like you, April. But I'm not sure I like you enough to introduce you to my children.'

Going for someone younger with less baggage
The result?

'You're not, like, one of those crazy 30-something women who are desperate for babies, are you? Oh my God, you *are*, aren't you!'

Being open and brave, and never losing hope: 'Just keep putting yourself out there'
The result?

Simon.

I lose the rest of my Saturday in a wretched spiral of loathing and self-doubt. I hate myself for how hard I'm taking this. I hate myself for how un-normal I seem to be. So it was six dates, so he didn't like me, so he's actually a dick, so he's not The One after all. So what? I know that's what I'm supposed to be thinking. I'm supposed to shimmy like Beyoncé and know my worth. I'm supposed to go out and get hammered and show him what he's missing, and, in doing so, not think about him once. Then Simon will subconsciously realise I've moved on and it will prompt him into realising what a huge catch I am and, unable to believe he's lost me, he'll turn up and make a heartfelt plea. But it will be too late. I'll tell him to go home. I will be too full of healthy levels of self-esteem for a shit like Simon. He will torture himself every day for the rest of his life about what he missed out on. I will never think about him ever again.

This is what would happen to Gretel.

I'm not Gretel though. I am April.

And instead April goes through every single message we sent, focusing particularly on any nice ones, to further prompt her heartache. April loses her whole day in a Google hole, reading psychology blogposts about different attachment styles, and occasionally stumbling with her laptop into Megan's room whenever she has a breakthrough.

'Simon is an avoidant attacher,' I announce, eyes wide with the revelation, like I've just started speaking in tongues. 'He told me his parents moved him around loads in the first two years of his life. Look! Look here! It's just his attachment style. If I can convince him to go to intense psychotherapy, in about two years we'll be perfect for each other.'

Megan doesn't look up from her *Times* Style supplement. 'I'm disconnecting the router.'

'I still get 4G.'

'I'm confiscating your phone.'

My mum rings for her weekend phone call to hammer home the existential crisis.

'How's it going with the new fella?' she asks, ripping open the wound and tipping some gangrene into it. I don't even have to reply. 'Oh dear. Already? Again? I wish you'd listen to me and stop doing this to yourself.' I lift my head upwards and focus very hard on the crack in my bedroom ceiling, the one that makes it look like its hatching. Mum sighs down the line. 'What happened this time?'

'I don't know.'

'I thought it was going well?'

'SO DID I!'

I shout so loud Megan runs into the room to check I'm OK, Sudocrem decorating her face in little splodges. I point to my phone and mouth 'my mum' and she nods in understanding and retreats.

'I didn't mean to upset you, darling, I was just asking.' She's all sniffy and snippy and acting like she's the victim. Oh yes, this is how phone calls with Mum go. It's like paint by numbers, but you replace the numbers with emotions like 'guilt' and 'exasperation' and 'shame'.

'I know, I know. I'm just upset.'

'So he dumped you?'

'Well, we weren't technically going out.'

'Did you sleep with him?'

'Mum!'

'You did, didn't you? How many times do I need to tell you?'

I close my eyes and try to take yogic breaths. 'Mum, please.'

She isn't listening; she never listens. Instead she goes off into the same old nonsense I've heard since I was a teenager. How you can't trust any of them and I'm crazy for even trying. How, if I'm so determined to try, I shouldn't sleep with them too soon. How you should make them have to wait for it. How they will not commit to you if you're already giving them what they want. How you should only expect the worst anyway. I've never told her about what happened with Ryan, as I honestly can't handle her thinking maybe I deserved it for being such a naive wench. Since Dad left when I was 3, I don't think she's even spoken to a man other than Jeremy (Jezzer) the postman. She fills the void with Bridge Club and Book Club and Church Club – swimming in pools with all the other divorced, embittered women who can never recover from the hurt of being left thirty years ago.

'I'm sorry April,' she says eventually, after telling me, in detail, about how you cannot trust any man: I just need to take one look at my father. 'I know you had high hopes for this one.'

'I did. I feel so stupid now.'

'Don't *you* feel stupid. *He's* the stupid one to let you go. You're a lovely girl. You have so much love to give.'

'Pity nobody wants it.'

'I want it. Megan wants it. All your friends at work want it.'

She's always quite nice, Mum, once she's puked up all her lemons.

'Yeah yeah, I know I know.' I roll my eyes. 'I still feel stupid. You know? For thinking he could be different, he could be the one?'

'Everyone always thinks they're the one at the time,' Mum says. 'Otherwise why would we bother? You have to think they're different in order to put yourself through it. It's only when you're out of it that you realise how insane you were to think that.'

Megan returns with a cup of tea. She hands me the mug and leans her face into my phone. 'Hi Susan!' she calls. 'How's it going?'

'Oh, it's Megan!' Mum sounds excited. 'Put her on.'

Even in my sadness, I'm able to smile as Megan takes the phone to give us a break from each other. 'Hi Susan, how's Bridge? You're such a shark! Yes, yes, I'm doing well. Job fine. My new manager is a trash bag, but that's what you expect in PR. Oh, we're just going to watch TV tonight. Don't worry. I'm taking good care of her. What's that? Oh, yeah, we'll probably just re-watch *Dawson's Creek* as usual. If things get really wild, we'll crack out season one of *The O.C.* Yes that Sandy man really is quite something, isn't he? Those eyebrows!' Megan laughs and I hear Mum's laughter crackle out tinnily from my phone.

There is love, I remind myself. There is always love to be found. Not the love I really, really, want, but, for today, on this terrible today, I have all the love I need.

That's the sort of thought Gretel would have, I realise.

That night, I lie in bed and, for the first time, I let myself really feel all the pain that men have put me through. I've tried so hard not to think about it for so very long but it's all catching up with me. I can feel my heart closing as I stare up into the darkness that's never that dark. After all this time, it's finally giving up. I've determinedly clamped it open, every morning of every day since I first decided to try and love a man. Despite all the knock-backs and reasons not to and shattering disappointments, I've always picked it up off the floor where it's been discarded, blown off the dust, admired the new scar, put it gently back into my ribcage, and prised it open again. I know that the opposite of love is fear. That it only works if you believe.

I don't think I believe any more. In fact, I think I'm beyond not believing. I think I'm finally, finally, allowing myself to feel pissed off.

So I'm lying here, in my 33-year-old body that isn't getting any younger, and I'm thinking of all the horrible things men have done to me and this wide open heart of mine.

There was Tommy, in sixth form, who told everyone I just 'lay there like a brick' the day after he took my virginity. Then there was Tommy again, who cheated on me with Jenny Cartwright and everyone in the whole school knew it but me. There was his laugh when I confronted him. 'I thought you knew?' he'd said, like it was all my fault.

Then there was my overcorrection boyfriend at university, who couldn't be more sweetness and anti-toxic-masculinity and wrote me poems and pushed them under my halls door, but also needed to be loved in a way that no one could ever offer, bled into me, making my life his life and my friends his friends and always said 'I don't mind' whenever I asked anything. When I left him after graduation, he couldn't handle his 'investment not maturing' and swapped the love letters for long emails about what a total prick I was as a person.

There was the date that went for a piss at the pub and never came back.

There was the guy who told me he wouldn't go down on me because I tasted like chow mein.

Then there was Ryan . . . whom I met aged 25, when I was insecure and scared by how long I'd been alone for and who was the most perfect boyfriend for six months, and made me believe I was going to save his life – but then couldn't handle it, or me, when I couldn't. Then two years of arguments, always concluding that it was all my fault, of anxiety pulsing through my stomach, wondering what Ryan I would get that day – the rare, amazing Ryan, or the man who told me I spoke too much and laughed too high-pitched and cooked all my food wrong and who never wanted to touch me. Until those two times where he raped me coldly and clinically – and it took me years to call it that because I was so confused and filled with self-disgust that I felt I'd just let it happen.

Then there was the fallout of Ryan after he moved on to some poor 24-year-old, whom, I know from the low moments when I spy on him, he still calls Hashtag Soulmate on his insta. How I tried to have a one-night stand, like you're supposed to do when you're 27 and heartbroken, but how I couldn't have sex and screamed in piercing agony, pushing him off me.

Then there was the hospital appointment, my legs in stirrups, and the year of using numbing gel and vaginal trainers to try and fix what he'd done to my body and being too scared to leave the house, let alone consider dating.

Then there was John, two years afterwards, whom I told about Ryan and who then used it against me. Telling me it was clearly 'too soon' for me to have a relationship if I ever dared behave imperfectly, before dumping me.

Then there's been all the micro-aggressions of dating hell since. The ghosting, the guy who is happy to date you for two months, and, then, only when pressed, admits he 'sort of has a girlfriend'. The slight winces new dates make when you say something that doesn't match their idea of what a woman should be. The last-minute cancellations, the hours of my life waiting for a man who is late, checking my phone, and pretending I don't mind when he finally turns up. So much rejection, gaslighting, entitlement, pushiness, scorn, manipulation, power play, compulsive lying, on and on it has gone. And, every time, no matter what men do to me, I have taken some time out to recover and then hurtled back into the ring, determined to try again. You can't lose the faith otherwise you lose the opportunity to spend your life with someone. *You've got to keep trying*, I told myself. *This time will be different*, I told myself. *You can't love without fear*, I told myself. *There must be someone*, I told myself. *They can't all be broken*, I told myself. *Other people have managed it*, I told myself.

I can't tell myself lies any more.

I'm lying in bed. I stare at the ceiling. I can't see the cracks but I know they are there. And I'm finally hardening. Not because of Simon. (I admit that, yes, maybe I am overreacting to Simon. Simon is just a man. Yet another not-good-enough man.) I'm hardening because I've realised something.

I actually, physically, mentally, spiritually, can't do this to myself any more. I can't put myself through it. It's not worth it. Because what is the prize? A man? A man who will never quite give you what you need, and never quite do enough around the house, and never quite comfort you in the way you need comforting, or fuck you in the way you need to be fucked, who will never quite deserve you but yet believes *he* deserves the medal for staying with you, a man who will always prioritise sport, who will smell and shit and burp and fart and lie and cheat and be lazy and get complacent, even if he wasn't to begin with, who will inwardly roll his eyes over time, who will let you take the strain if you're stupid enough to have children with him.

That's not a prize.

It's how to ruin your life.

'I let go of this,' I say out loud, to my shitty cracked ceiling. My heart is closed for business. And not in a when-I-meet-the-right-guy-I'll-take-it-back way. I'm honestly done.

I'm not just done. I'm angry.

So. Fucking. Angry.

I mean, aren't *you*?

I hate men.

I hate how annoyed they get when you dare show any negative emotion – usually triggered by them. Acting like you've let the side down with all your pathetic emotions and ruined the fun. How they secretly think you shouldn't be upset because *they* wouldn't be. The judgement that lingers like putrid BO whenever you confess an anxiety or sadness.

I hate how they don't believe you. That if you're ever stupid enough to tell them about something another man has done, how they look for the holes in your traumas and widen the hole until you doubt it really happened – sometimes without even saying a word, just by pulling a face they don't even realise they're pulling. How sometimes they just ignore what you've said. Block it out because it ruins *their* day that you dared to get yourself violated by one of those nutcases who definitely isn't them or anyone they know and now you wanna talk about it, goddammit?

I hate how sometimes when they tickle you in a play fight, they hold you down to show off their superior strength and you squeal like it's funny but also the threat is there.

I hate men because the threat is always, *always* there.

I hate men because they're so lacking in *exhaustion* from not constantly feeling in danger. They walk with this general easiness, like they've earned it, rather than taking a moment to examine their luck that they're not terrified of violent rape whenever they leave their house.

I hate men because they only ever want you for the idea of you – all the good, sexy bits and not the messy, traumatised bits. Bits that are traumatised BECAUSE OF MEN.

I hate men because they've made me hate myself. I hate men because I could've been someone so much better, and greater, and cooler, and comfortable if it wasn't for them. I hate men for not loving me when they're the ones who made me unlovable. I hate men for making me hate myself for wanting one to love me. I hate men for the amount of time and energy they take from my life in the quest for it.

I hate.

I hate.

I hate them.

I don't want them to love me any more.

I want them to feel as powerless as I've always felt.

I want them to pay.

I go out the next morning and get to the shops just as they open. The air con of the book store is so welcome that I want to pitch a tent and live in there. Though, after the pitying look the bookseller gives me ringing up my purchases, I'd be too embarrassed to stay.

'Where have you been?' Megan asks when I return home, sweating. 'You seem happier.' She's sitting in a nest she's made on the sofa – her favourite thing to do. She drags all the covers off all the beds and arranges them around her like a spiral of puffy candyfloss while watching *Dawson's Creek* and doing impressions of Joey Potter's wayward mouth expressions.

'I am happier, thank you.' I dump my heavy shopping bag down on the table, lean into a back stretch, and wince as I smell my already-smelly armpit. 'Isn't it a bit hot for the nest?'

'I need the nest,' she says. 'My manager just told me I have to arrange the freaking launch event for our new jewellery line in only six weeks' time. Because, you know, emailing your employees with giant projects on a Sunday morning is *totally normal*.'

'Hon, that's amazing.'

'It's terrifying and stressful, is what it is.'

'So you thought the best way to tackle this challenge was to wrap yourself in *my* duvet and watch an episode of *Dawson* for the eight trillionth time?' I perch on the edge of the sofa.

'I've given myself this sacred Sunday to pretend it's not happening, then I'll have the nervous breakdown tomorrow.' She looks up at me from her array of blankets and taps a space next to her. 'Joey's about to slouch her way through a horrific rendition of "On My Own", care to join?'

I do. I've seen the Beauty Pageant episode countless times before, but I flop down next to her, though not under the blankets. We wince our way through her cover of Eponine, Megan pausing it at random intervals to yell 'ERGH DAWSON IS THE WORST!'

When it finishes, she's up right away, digging through my shopping bag.

'Megan! No!'

'What did you get? You never buy books! Oh my God, April,' she digs one out and holds it like it's contaminated. 'What the hell? Is this a joke?'

I grab the book off her. 'No.'

Her mouth drops open, and she digs into my Waterstones bag to unearth worse books with even worse titles. I try to stop her but I can't. Megan gets them all out, turning each one over and reading under her breath and then staring up at me. 'Is this what Simon has done to you? I didn't realise it was this bad.'

'No! It's fine. It's nothing. I'm fine, honestly.'

'Yeah, you're clearly totally sane. All these books are signs of such high self-esteem.' She jabs at them with her finger. On the floor lie six books with the following titles:

Why Men Love Horrible Women
How to Win Him
Calling in Your Soulmate

The Laws of Love
Make All Men Want You
How Not to Scare Off Your Soulmate

All of them have various grand claims on their covers. Things like 'Find the love of your life within 30 days', or 'Use the law of attraction to pull in lasting love'. Even Oprah has endorsed one.

'I'm just trying something out,' I tell Megan. 'I'm doing some research.'

'For what?' She picks up *Calling in Your Soulmate* and holds it upside down, like it's a dead mouse. 'Are you method acting in a play called *The Importance of Being Basic*?'

'Ha. Something like that.'

'Honestly, what's going on?'

Do I tell her?

Because I know what I'm planning is mental. And mental in a way that's so mental that even your best friend isn't going to pretend it's OK.

'Nothing's going on. I'm just interested, that's all. In all this stuff you're told about how to meet guys. I thought it might help the relationship advisor part of my job.'

'So it's nothing to do with getting dumped yesterday?'

'No!' It's to do with getting dumped consistently throughout my entire life. 'And it's just for work.'

'I don't believe you and neither would the most gullible person in the whole of gullible land.'

I shrug and pluck the offending book out of her hand. 'Please, just leave it?'

She must see the pleading in my face. 'OK then,' she

relents. 'As unhealthy coping strategies go, reading is better than doing smack. That stuff is all bullshit though, you know that, right?'

I nod my lie. 'Total bullshit.'

She looks up at me with wide, kohl-lined eyes. 'Are you OK though? Seriously? You'd tell me if you weren't, wouldn't you?'

'I really am all right, I promise.' And it's the truth. I reach down and begin to pick up my shopping. 'In fact, despite these books looking like evidence to the contrary, I actually feel the best I've felt in a very long time.'

As the sun steadily bakes the city hotter and stinkier, I stay indoors, flipping through the pages of the books that will help me. The hours smudge into one another, lost in a haze of sweating my way through the earnest pages, stopping here and there either to make notes, or to get ice cubes out of the freezer and squeeze them under my armpits.

'Great idea,' Megan says, spotting me in the kitchen and coming over to copy me. She gasps as the ice hits her. 'You sure you don't want to come back into the nest?'

'I'm fine. I'm just chilling in my room.'

All of the advice in the books, I find, I kind of knew already. What with all the panic pre-date googling I've done over the years. Plus my 33 years living life as a woman. Since the moment I plopped out of my mother's womb, I've absorbed through osmosis how a woman should behave if she wants a man to put up with her. From the passive princesses winning princes in fairy tales to the magazines I read as a teenager, telling me what hairstyles boys liked, what their body language meant, if our star signs were compatible, and how to talk to them at parties, to every film I've ever watched, where the girl has to chill out and get over herself and give up what she really wants in order to win his heart. I mean, if *Grease* taught me anything, it's that you need to get the ratio of Madonna:Whore perfectly right before you're allowed to float off into the clouds with some jerk who tried to date-rape you in a car park. The books all confirm my suspicion: in order to be loved by a heterosexual man, you must not need or want to be loved by a heterosexual man.

As I turn the page of each one, I feel more and more alive. It's like I've finally taken the red pill and woken up in some pod that reveals just how ludicrous it all is. If these books are to be believed, all men are the same and none of them want a woman who is real in any way. It makes my past dating nightmares become so much clearer. No wonder I've been so 'unlucky' – I've been too honest, too myself, not seeing it as a game to win.

It gets dark but the heat doesn't relent. Megan puts the last of the ice under her armpits around eleven o'clock and calls 'goodnight' before heading for her room. The city around me is hushed – the neighbours quiet and sleeping or getting ready for the week ahead. Even with my windows wide open to try to keep cool, it is tranquil. I feel like the only person awake, which is ridiculous because it's London and if I got up and put some clothes on I could probably find some open club nearby, snort coke and jump into an adult ball pit or something.

I put my last book down and try to prepare myself for the unattainable idea of a good night's sleep. A fantasy comes into my head, clear as a drawing scratched in sharp pencil. I'm sitting across from a faceless man, at some nice little place somewhere. There are candles on the table. I can sense his nervousness. There's sweat on his forehead. His hands tremble on his knife and fork as he cuts into an artichoke.

'Are you OK?' I ask, serene and peaceful and radiating a glow that you just cannot bottle. 'You're being weird.'

He laughs, all *bahaha*. 'Am I? Sorry, there's just . . . just . . . something I want to say.'

'What's that?' I look over at this man, struggling to eat his artichoke, and make it as easy for him as I can. 'You can tell me,' I say. 'Whatever it is, you know you can tell me.'

The man sighs and puts his fork down, and reaches over to clasp my hand. 'I know I can. Sorry. I don't know why I'm so nervous. The truth is . . .' he looks up into my eyes, so wide and open and vulnerable, 'I . . . I . . . I love you, Gretel.' He gets it out. He squeezes my hand tighter. His voice is thick with emotion, eyes wet, vulnerability bleeding out all over the table.

'Oh,' I say.

'Look, you don't have to say it back. It may be too soon for you.'

I reach out and take his other hand. 'It's not that, it's just . . .'

'What?' he asks desperately. 'What? What is it?'

I look over at this man, who stands for every man who has ever broken me. Who has ever told me I'm not this enough or that enough. Who has made me feel defective for wanting to love them, for wanting anything from men at all in exchange for my body and my thoughtfulness and my energy and time. He's taking the hit for them all. Like

Jesus – the Jesus of Tinder. I let go of his hand and I tilt my head. I say his name.

He's on the edge of his chair, his artichoke forgotten. He's waiting for the 'I love you' back, for his life to finally begin with this unicorn of a woman he's found.

'Yes?'

'My name is not fucking Gretel.'

Then I stand up, and I leave him with his confused broken heart and his unfinished artichoke and I never see him again. How powerful I feel, for once.

I don't see any reason not to start right now. So I sit up in bed, the sheet sticking to my stomach with sweat. I lean over and pick the phone up from the floor where it's charging, squinting as my eyes are hit with its white light. I turn the brightness down and re-download the dating app I deleted after my third date with Simon. But this time I set up a different email address for it, and, when asked for my details, I type out a different name.

• Gretel's Guide To Getting Your Guy

Feeling lost in love? Trapped in a powerless cycle of endless dates? Desperate to finally have a man drop the big L?

Hi, my name's Gretel, and I'm here to help you finally cross the finish line. All you have to do is pretend to be someone else . . . Me.

You see, I'm just your regular everyday Manic Pixie Dream Girl Next Door Slut With No Problems. i.e. Exactly what all men want.

I'm a high-worth woman who is independent but still really needs a man Only when he's in the mood to feel needed that is. When he's not in the mood to feel needed, don't worry, I'm off backpacking somewhere and whoops-a-daisy he misses me now. Who would've thought? I have such a strong character, but don't worry, it's not too strong. It includes things like having a dirty laugh, and standing up for refugees. Don't panic, I don't stand up for anything that makes him feel personally uncomfortable because he's slightly guilty of being problematic in that way. I won't go all 'strong' on him about sexual violence, or the pay gap. Nah, I'll stick to Malaria, or homelessness, or something.

I'm excited to wake up every morning. I have such a fabulous life, filled with exciting but non-threatening things, and he feels so lucky to be part of it. My resting face is serene. I glow. Everything about me just glows.

I don't really nag, because I don't get upset by the stupid stuff. He never has to worry about upsetting me because I'm never insecure. However, every so often, I will lightly whimper on him, just so he can feel manly when he snuggles me into his arms. He's so good at comforting me about the mild thing I'm upset about that doesn't freak him out or make him feel helpless. I won't have PTSD from a rape or an eating disorder or anything – I would never get raped, that's totally not my thing. And I won't have any serious mental health problems that require patience. I don't even get PMS because I'm on hormonal contraception so he also never has to use a condom. What a win.

I'm feminine, of course. Not in an obvious, insecure way. We've established already that I'm not insecure. How *repulsive*, for a woman to be insecure. Not me! Where were we? Oh yes, I'm feminine. Don't worry, I never take too long to get ready. I'm naturally beautiful. I don't realise it, of course, that would be egotistical, but I'm also confident in how I look. I'm feminine in an effortless way. I'll randomly shove on some flowery dress and I'll reek of womanliness so much that the flowers may just float off my dress and follow me around like Pocafuckinghontas.

I've got an edge to me though. I can totally be one of the guys. In fact, he loves to bring me out and watch how well I fit in with them and how they all look at me and wish I was their girlfriend. I make the perfect crude joke. I have an interest in whatever boring-as-bollocks sport he's into. Not because I'm pretending to – I *actually* find it interesting.

Pretending

I'm one of those people who will wake him up one morning and say, 'let's go on an adventure' with a glint in my eye, and both our passports in my hand.

I'm not a pushover, that's important to note. I won't let him walk all over me. I completely and utterly know my worth, and, if he doesn't show me the respect I deserve, I will let him know it. Somehow I manage to do this in a magical mystical way that never feels like 'nagging'.

My cool job means I have money, so I don't need him in that way. But, I don't have a silly, intimidating amount of money. Maybe just the same as him, ideally a tiny bit less.

I always smell good.

I dance like I'm lost in the music.

I'm not fussy about where I sleep.

I have a brilliant appetite but I'm never fat.

I like to have sex however he likes to have it.

I reach orgasm through penetration alone.

No man can believe his actual luck when he meets me.

Oh, by the way, I'm not fucking real.

The morning rolls around, as it always does. I wake sticky and dehydrated, mangled in my sheet. I take a cool shower but am sweaty again by the time I've dressed.

Megan's face down on the kitchen table, thumping her head into the wood.

'Looking forward to work?' I ask her.

A groan is her reply.

'You're always fine once you're there.'

'No I'm not. I can't believe I wasted all yesterday watching *Dawson's Creek.*' Her hair spills all over her head so her entire face is completely obscured. 'How are you anyway?' her hair asks me.

I smile and find I actually mean it. I take out the porridge oats and start the laborious process of cooking them into the most boring, unsatisfying breakfast food ever, no matter how much agave syrup I shove on top. 'Dead inside,' I reply. 'But in a good way. A useful way. I feel like I'm at the start of something good. Less dramatic.'

Megan sits up, flicking her hair back like a mermaid exiting the water. She analyses me stirring my healthy sludge. 'Oh my God, you mean it,' she says. 'Have you given up on men? Even despite all those terrible books you bought?'

I nod and stir. It feels good when I nod. Like I've just lost twenty stone of bullshit. 'Yup. I *told* you they were for research.

You have no faith in me. But, yes, it's over. It's all over. I feel amazing!'

Megan's out of the chair, pulling me in for a hug. 'Aww, hon. Welcome to the Happiness Club!'

'You've literally just been banging your head against a table.'

'That is true. But job stress is so much easier to handle now that I don't have stupid man-stress to deal with. Look how far I've come with my career since I've stopped dating.'

I nod again; it is not to be argued with. There has been a very definite shift between pre-fuck-it Megan, and post-fuck-it Megan. I scooped her off the floor so many times at university and then all through our early twenties. She made my reaction to heartbreak look like I was competing in the stiff upper lip Olympics. I've seen her screaming outside an ex's house at least twice, sobbing and demanding to be let in. Rumours that she was mental ran amok amongst her posh boarding-school friendship circles, and she was deliberately not invited to at least two fancy-pants weddings a few years ago. After every man-gone-wrong, I've picked the pieces off the ground and handed them back to her, and when she's screamed and said she didn't want them, I've picked them up again and eventually forced her to piece herself together.

Then we've been through Zen periods, where she's realised that 'Mikey From The Jubilee Line' or 'Connor's Little Brother' probably, on reflection, wasn't the love of her life. During these phases she's gone to the gym every day, meditated, and started nudging her way up the corporate pole of jewellery PR. Until she's met 'Joe' from 'this thing' and 'it's just sex, I don't want a relationship anyway' and, suddenly, she's screaming at Joe's window and work have pulled her in for a disciplinary.

But, three years ago, when she decided to just stop, she picked up the pieces herself without prompting. She started going in to work early, leaving late. Then she applied for this new position at a jewellery company that was much more her style – all graphic, plastic-but-high-end novelty necklaces worn by quirky celebrities and millionaires who live in East London – and she walked it. It's incredibly stressful and I've seen her bang her head on the table like this multiple mornings, but I've not seen her cry since that day. She has consistently remained 'Megan'.

I tip my porridge into a bowl and join her at our table, chucking some blueberries on top in a futile attempt to improve the thing. 'I don't think I can handle work today,' I admit, dipping my spoon in unenthusiastically. 'Everyone is going to ask how Friday went, and I'll have to tell the whole damn thing all over again.'

'So, don't tell them.'

'You know I don't have that capacity. I literally can't keep anything in. I even told my dental hygienist about him.'

'Why?' she asks.

My spoon full of porridge stops on the journey to my mouth. 'What do you mean?'

'I mean, why do you tell everyone everything?'

'I don't know. I just do.'

Megan gets up and stretches her arms over her head, leaning left into it and making a small straining sound. 'I just wonder what you get out of it,' she says, 'compared to what they get out of it. All these helpful advice givers.' She bends down and touches her toes. 'I just worry sometimes that you come out of it confused, and they come out of it feeling much better about themselves.'

The porridge sticks in my throat. I take a sip of tea and force myself to swallow. 'It's a bit early for Megan psychotherapy, isn't it?'

She pats my head, then picks up an oversized plastic rainbow-necklace from the side and shoves it unceremoniously over her head. 'Probably. I'm just using you as a distraction from how much shit I have to get through at work. I dunno though. Be careful today, April. At work, I mean. Don't fall into that trap of being the untogether one whom people care about deeply, but whom they also use to feel more in control of their own lives. Even if they don't mean it, don't let them put that on you.'

Then, with a collecting of handbag, a muttering of 'why do back-to-back meetings fucking exist in this fucking world?' and a kiss blown in my direction, Megan is out of the door. Leaving me with my half-eaten breakfast and too many thoughts to be having at this time of the morning.

The heatwave is hanging on and nobody in London can believe their luck. This morning BBC News threatened it could last the whole summer, but everyone's still seeing it as a treat rather than a warning. I walk through the red-brick streets towards the Tube station, dodging a collection of teenage schoolgirls giggling in navy uniform, and smelling of sun-lotion mixed with vanilla perfume.

The Tube is too full to get onto. The doors clunk open to reveal a comedy sketch of commuters stuffed into the carriage, like that clowns crammed into a car trick. Despite this, people are still determined to force their sweaty bodies into the impossible situation. I stand back and watch the spectacle, and, somehow, space is found for most of them. The doors slide shut and the Tube rattles off, leaving just me and a few other stragglers waiting.

Do people really use me to feel better about their own lives?

Am I really that person?

When the next train whirrs in, it's much emptier, and I feel smug at the tiny win against London. I even manage to get a seat, putting my blazer down so my bare skin doesn't touch the gross cushion. The stench of one man opposite is so putrid that he could be used as smelling salts. Sweat's already drenched his business shirt, and he's eating a cereal bar so aggressively that crumbs of desiccated oats are spraying from his mouth like a whale's blowhole. He finishes it with a *chomp* and dusts off his remaining mess like a rhino scent-marking a river with their own shit.

I hate you, I think, as I look at this man.

Once I get to Baker Street, I treat myself to a coffee, so I'll be slightly late and won't have to handle all the 'how did it go's?' I stand outside Pret and watch everyone scurry to work in a haze of self-important Tasmanian Devil tornadoes. Simon once said 'Pret coffee is shit', when it literally all tastes the same to me.

'Fuck you, Simon,' I say out loud, taking a hearty swig. 'It's just fucking coffee, you tosser.'

This anger is new, the bitterness fresh out of the box. I have been many things in my life – frantic, desperate, obsessive, silly, motivated – but never cynical. Never angry. But it's like I've only been pushing it down, letting it form pockets of hatred in my body like undetected tumours, and now they've all burst and the cancer of it is spreading rapidly.

I finish my perfectly-adequate coffee and check the time on my phone. It's 9.34. I toss my cup into the rubbish bin next to the homeless man, fibbing when I say I don't have any change, but feeling like I'm still a good person because at least I didn't ignore him. I walk up the street to our office, punch in the entry code and climb the dingy steps. I take a breath and stand outside the door for one moment, composing myself. Something I've never done before. I draw the curtain shut on my personality and push through into the keyboard clacks and furrowed brows of Monday morning.

'Hi April.' Mike, our CEO, nods as I walk past and slide

behind my desk, pushing aside all the unfinished crap I'd abandoned there Friday evening. Matt and Katy nod 'hello' too and I nod back. I never just nod back. Usually I bowl in, dramatically unveiling my latest drama in the swirl of my coat being taken off, and letting everyone in on the hilarious mess that is my life. Today, I just nod.

I switch on my computer, put my headphones on, and open up my emails. There's the usual quicksand to wade through, sent by the people who check their inboxes over the weekend, to prove to us all how much harder they work. I roll my eyes and bash out my responses. We're about to recruit a new batch of volunteer advisors, so I lose an hour to tweaking the wording of the advertisement.

At ten thirty, Katy waves her hand to distract me away. 'Coffee?' she mimes.

I shake my head, even though I'm desperate for more caffeine. She doesn't mean 'coffee', however. She means standing in the kitchen and debriefing our lives. My life, mainly, since I usually have the most drama to tell. I'm bashing too hard on my keyboard and clicking the mouse button like it disrespected my mother. I feel like there's a million tiny Bunsen burners in my veins, slowly bubbling my blood, and I'm not sure where this anger is coming from but it's really demanding to be felt.

I wait until Katy sits back down with her drink before I go up and get my own. I close my eyes as I wait for the kettle to boil, focusing on my stomach going in and out with each breath to see if that helps dislodge all the putrid rage.

'April, happy Monday,' Matt says, joining me with an empty mug.

I flicker my eyes open and smile with closed lips. 'Morning Matt.'

'Good weekend?' he asks. 'More importantly, good date?' The kettle clicks off and he pours the water into his cup even though I was here first and I was the one who put the kettle on.

I blink for a long time before opening my eyes again. 'I don't want to talk about it,' I say, taking the kettle from him.

Matt almost pauses in mid-air. I don't think he's ever heard me say that combination of words together. I don't offer further explanation either. I smile tersely again, tip some milk into my drink, hand him the bottle, and return to my seat. Apparently, no, you don't have to share your life's dramas. You don't have to play the part of 'poor little April why can't she make it work'. You can just make coffee and go back to your desk, without vomiting up your vulnerability as a way of making people like you.

Matt and Katy's side-looks make me angrier throughout the morning. In fact, everything makes me angrier. It's like I've only just discovered the emotion. I always thought anger was something to suppress and squash down and make peace with. I think I knew, somehow, that if I tapped into that particular reservoir, it would be the undoing of me. But it's now time to unleash it.

'You all right, buddy?' Matt's head pops up from above my computer monitor, before my shift starts at eleven. He is clearly taking the tactic of pretending I'm not being difficult today. 'I'm here if you need me.'

'I'm fine, cheers,' I tell the computer screen, still *click-click-clacking*, entering all the various passwords and security codes I need to get access to the inbox. I sense, rather than see, his head retreat back down again.

There are ten questions to get through this shift, which is quite a lot for midsummer. Swallowing my mouthful of coffee, I open the first question and read it under my breath.

Message received: 23:07

I've just moved to Birmingham for my job and I'm feeling really lonely. I'm too shy to go out and make friends and so just spend my time looking out of my flat window. I'm too proud to tell people how hard I'm finding it. How do I make friends?

I click into our shared folder and get out the 'I'm lonely' template, personalising it for this yet-another-victim of modern life. I fire it off, and open up the next one.

Message received: 01:23

am i pregnant? my period is late

This question is standard despite the fact it's impossible to tell if someone is pregnant, a) without a test, and b) through a computer screen. I open the relevant template telling them to go to the doctor, while emotionally supporting them, and hit send.

I fly through the next couple. Someone has chlamydia and is too scared to message his past partners. One is not sure if they are gay or not because they watch gay porn but don't want to have gay sex in real life.

It's question number six that gets me.

Message received: 11:32

I've never used a service like this before, and I'm worried I'm being silly. It's just my boyfriend did something weird the other night and it's really upset me but I'm probably just being stupid. We went out clubbing at the student union and he came back to mine. We were both completely wasted and all I wanted to do was pass out but he wanted to have sex. I said 'no' and pushed him off a few times because I just wanted to sleep but he kind of held me down with his body and we had sex. I was so drunk I couldn't really push him off and just kind of froze. Then we went to sleep. I'm really confused. Is this normal? I don't mean to make a fuss. I love him. He's my boyfriend . . .

I shake my head and throw my head back to the ceiling. 'For fuck's sake,' I mutter as my stomach liquefies.

'Are you OK, April?' Matt's head appears.

'Yup.'

'That one literally just came in, otherwise I would've given you a heads-up. I'm really sorry.'

My teeth are gritted and I smile through them, forcing myself to look at him. 'No need to be sorry, I told you I'm OK.'

Matt won't relent. 'Two shifts in a row though, that's not fair.'

'It's not like it's unusual.'

'Let's have a proper debrief in the park when you're done . . . I insist, come on. Any excuse for ice cream.' He's humouring me, which is both endearing and frustrating at the same time.

I nod, stand, and spend way too long doing a wee before returning to my desk to send my reply. I close off my anger, as it is not appropriate to let that seep into my response, and I push the pain down deep into the slosh of my tummy until it is absorbed into me. I pull out the template from the 'favourites' folder, I personalise it, I check it through, I hit send, I wish this would stop happening.

Why won't it stop happening?

'Ready?' I say, a bit later, once I've dealt with the last message on the list.

Matt takes off his headphones. 'Can I meet you there? I need to print some stuff off first.'

I nod, desperate to get out of the office. 'I'll see you on the bench.'

I don't say goodbye to Katy as I pick up my bag and leave. I'm still mad at her after what Megan said to me this morning. She looks a bit hurt as I swish on past, but she's stuck in a volunteering spreadsheet, trying to sort out all the shift changes due to people taking summer holidays. I rush down the stairs, my breath not quite filling my lungs each time, and run out into the chaotic London street, the heat smacking me like a sucker punch, making me sweat within seconds.

I want to scream.

Why is there nowhere in London to scream? Surely there must be some pop-up fucking primal screaming booth? I'm five minutes from Regent's Park and stumble towards it with too many emotions and nowhere for them to go. Heat drifts up from the pavement, cooking my skin, making my blood boil hotter. I can hear my phone going in my bag but I ignore it. I reach the park entrance and dart through the wrought-iron gates. It's quieter in here. My phone goes again. Again I ignore it. I do not know what to do with my rage. It's consuming me. Eating up my stomach like a hungry parasite.

I sink onto a bench dedicated to a lady called Gladys who always loved this place. I try and let the ducks quacking on the pond distract me from myself. They scuttle about, picking at nothing on the ground or dousing themselves in the sludgy black water.

Soon enough, Matt arrives with strawberry Cornettos. 'Be quick, they've almost melted.' He hands me mine and sits alongside me.

'Cheers.'

The only noise for a while is the sound of us rescuing drips off our melting cones with our tongues. The syrup in the sugar hits my blood and I feel it rejuvenating me, kicking me back into myselfness.

'What did you need to print off?' I ask, once we're done. I hold out my hand and take his sticky wrapper.

'It's cheesy, but I reckon it will cheer you up.'

'Not like you to be cheesy, Matt.'

His eyes laugh behind his glasses as I return from the neighbouring bin. He is a proper wotsit, it has to be said. He once showed me the Valentine's Day card he'd spent two weeks making for his boyfriend. It was a hand-sketch of all his favourite things. Though it would've been more romantic without the butt-plug.

He gets out a stack of papers from his pocket, unfolds them, and rustles them like a newsreader. 'I just thought, after another tough shift, you could do with some affirmation about why we do this.' He coughs as I sit down, and starts to read off the page:

'Dear Are You There, thank you so much for your reply. I was feeling really lost and scared, but now I feel less alone and like I know what to do next.' I resist the urge to roll my eyes at how . . . Disney this all is, because I don't want to hurt his feelings, and I let him move onto the next page. And that's the one that gets me.

'Thank you Are You There. Your service has helped me realise that I was, in fact, raped – which still feels weird to be typing. I rang Rape Crisis, as you suggested, and they've been brilliant and I have a counselling session set up for next month. I don't know what would've happened if I hadn't found your charity. I already feel a bit like me again.'

My throat tripwires. The edges of my heart melt a little. 'OK, OK, OK,' I say. 'I get the point, Oprah.'

'Are you sure? I've got loads more. I'm in the middle of compiling the user satisfaction survey to help fundraising with our bid for Comic Relief.'

'I get the gist, thank you. I really am fine.'

'She says, with the vein still bulging in her forehead.'

I laugh and scatter some of the ducks that had started edging towards our feet in the hope of cone crumbs. 'I honestly am fine.'

'I know you are. But it helps to be reminded of why we put up with the harder bits of this job.'

I reach over for his sheet and reread it under the glaring light of the sun. Getting feedback is quite rare in our job and we're trained to cope with this. Because we're an online service, you don't get to see or hear the impact you've had very often. Ninety per cent of the time you send off your advice and never hear anything ever again. It's a shame because the feedback is what gives me the high. I used to read and reread these comments when they came through, letting them pour balm over my wounds, but now they're losing their impact a bit. I get that Matt is just trying to help, but when I look down and see what this girl has written, I don't feel soothed that I'm helping so much, more angry that she had to go through this in the first place.

I hand it back to him. 'I do hate men,' I tell him.

'God, tell me about it.'

'Obviously you don't count.' I have to admit Matt does not fall into that bracket. Some men have levelled up. They're rarer than vaginal orgasms, and most of them are gay, but some of them are good.

He grins again. 'Remember what they said in training. If you worked for a charity that deals with victims of dog bites, you'd start to believe that all dogs bite. Whereas, the truth is, at least four dogs have walked past us since we sat at this bench, and not one of them has bitten us.'

'Yeah, yeah, whatever.'

'Don't forget, I can always take over your shift.' He lifts up his arms, stretching to reveal sweat marks under his shirt. 'Ready to go back?'

It really is filthy hot out here, but I want to stay out a little longer. I shake my head. 'I'm going to have five more minutes, if that's OK?'

He shrugs. 'Hey, I'm not your boss.' We high-five before

he lollops off, and I watch him till the sun eats his silhouette and I can't see him any more.

'I already feel a bit more like me again.'

My face cracks a smile. I'm helping. It's worth it because I'm helping. I sit with my eyes closed, letting myself get to the threshold of a bit too hot for a few minutes. All I can hear are the gentle quacks coming from the pond and the low but steady roar of traffic circling the park. Peace settles into my skin until I'm jolted by the vibration of my phone.

I look down to find a fish wiggling in my net. A match from the new profile I set up last night. The app's reminding me I only have a day to reply. I swiped yes for twenty men at random, just to set the ball rolling on whatever it is I'm planning. I'm still not entirely sure.

CoffeeIsTheAnswer: Hey – how's it going? It's soooooo sunny today!

I don't even open his profile before I fire a message back from my fake account.

PartnerInCrime: Why are you on a dating app on a Monday? Don't you have gainful employment?

I'm expecting a bit of a wait for the next message. I stretch my legs out and ready myself to return to the office. I do not expect my phone to go again. 'No actual way,' I mutter, retrieving it more out of disbelief than interest.

CoffeeIsTheAnswer: Lol. Don't worry. I'm a taxpaying normal citizen. Just on lieu time as I had to work yesterday. Enjoying the sunshine! Why are YOU on the app on a Monday?

PartnerInCrime: I'm just on a break from work, been eating a Cornetto in the park.

Straight back. We may as well be playing ping pong.

CoffeeIsTheAnswer: Lol. Seriously? Wish I could get away with that at work. What amazing job do you have? Nice to dating app meet you, btw. My name's Joshua.

I can't help but laugh at his formal tone. No one's ever introduced themselves to me on an app before. Well, unless sending a photo of their flaccid penis counts as a formal introduction, which, let me tell you, I can't imagine Mr Darcy doing back in the day. I look down at my phone and a strange feeling of calm settles upon me. I watch, almost detached, as my thumb thuds out a reply.

PartnerInCrime: *curtsies* Nice to meet you, Joshua. My name's Gretel.

• *The First Hurdle – Gretel's Guide to Dating App Etiquette*

It's probably worth pointing out that women like me, Gretel, don't need dating apps. I just tend to meet men naturally, you know? I have such a busy and interesting life that things just happen, sparks just ignite; it's crazy where this path called life can take you. So, I'm only really on here *ironically*, or because one of my many friends told me to, or because I'm one of those women who sometimes really craves hot sex with a random stranger, but not because I have any underlying self-esteem issues and use casual sex as validation.

But, if you're not a woman like me, and you do have to use them, you pathetic, desperate mess, then remember this is the *fun* bit. Dating apps are just a great way to meet as many men as possible, so you feel like there's an abundance of them, because, remember, the only way to not act like a needy freak is to feel like there's always an abundance of men. Even though most men you meet on dating apps make you want to puke, scream, run away and hide, and generally lose the will to live . . . well, at least there's an abundance of them, babe! Can't go getting all emotionally attached to the miracle few who aren't psychopaths.

When it comes to setting up your profile, think in terms of advertising. You want to sell the 'idea' of you rather than the reality. The less detail you have on there, the less reason you're giving that abundance of psychopaths to say no to you. I mean, they need a 'sense' of who you are, of course, but leave it at around five per cent and let them fill in the blanks themselves. I mean, if you're really lucky, you'll end up with someone who totally loves only about five per cent of you anyway. So showcase a little bit of you and make it interesting – we *all* like going to the cinema and having meals with friends! – but not so interesting to be off-putting. He can't adequately project if you give him too much information.

Maybe have a perky question on there or a quirky fact about yourself as a means of prompting conversation. Have you ever got a Blue Peter badge? Have you ever broken a world record? What's your favourite album right now? Do you worry constantly that you're going to die alone because online dating is so soul destroying and essentially treats human beings like fucking items you can go shopping for and you worry the only people left on here are the ones who are too fucked up but does that mean you're also too fucked up and maybe you're in denial about it? Hang on, not that last one. Don't *ever* put that last one in, whatever you do.

Josh: All right Grets? I've decided to call you Grets. Is that OK?
Gretel: Absolutely not.
Josh: Shit sorry.

Josh: I really am sorry.
Gretel: Chill. I've just been in back-to-back meetings all day.
Josh: Oh, thought I'd pissed you off ;)
Gretel: Takes more than that.

'Who you messaging?' Katy asks, the next Monday, pushing her keyboard away, signalling she wants a chat. 'Is it Simon?'

I smile kindly and realise the smile is authentic. To be fair to her, she has left it a whole week before asking what happened with him. The suspense must've been killing her.

'Simon is no more.' I shrug and actually mean the shrug.

'Oh, shit, I'm sorry. I shouldn't have . . .'

'Don't worry. I'm fine. This is someone new, Joshua.' I point to my phone.

Katy's eyebrows raise. The eyebrow raise says, 'Another one? Already?' But her voice just squeaks: 'Oh, exciting! How did you meet?'

'We've not met yet. We're just messaging.' I stand up. 'Coffee?'

She nods. 'Yep, great.'

I wave to Matt to get his attention. He's on shift and has his headphones on to drown out the office chatter. 'Coffee?' I mouth. He gives me a double thumbs-up.

Katy and I clatter over to the kettle and lean against the countertop as we wait for it to boil.

'Well, it's great that you're putting yourself out there again,' she says, in what I'm sure is a means-well way. 'My sister went on, like, two million dates before she met Darren. She said modern dating is all about throwing spaghetti at the wall and seeing what sticks.'

'I thought the saying was throwing shit?'

She laughs. 'Same thing?'

'Same thing.'

We go about spooning sugar granules into mugs.

'So, tell me about Joshua,' she prompts, pouring water into the cafetière.

'There's not much to tell. We've just been messaging.'

'You have a photo?'

I pull his profile onto the screen and show her.

'Oh, he looks nice! He has a kind face.' She commandeers my phone, taking it fully off me and flicking through the rest of his snaps. 'Oh, he's climbed Mount Kilimanjaro, that's cool.' I nod. I guess it is. 'Oh, he looks quite hot in this one.' I lean over and nod again, non-committal. I've hardly looked at photos of Josh. Past Me would've closely studied each one for any insights into his soulmate potential. Psychoanalysing every atom of every photo. Wondering what climbing Mount Kilimanjaro means about his childhood, and wondering if getting that out of his system means he'll now be ready to be a good father or something. Now, since my epiphany, I can see the photos with detachment. I look at the Mount Kilimanjaro pic and bet he cannot believe his fucking luck that he gets to put that on a dating profile. I imagine how great he feels every time a new match says, 'Mount Kilimanjaro? Wow, cool', and he can then talk about how amazing it was, and how important it is to push yourself. If I'm ever to love someone who has climbed Mount Kilimanjaro, I will love the person who does it and yet never, ever, tells anyone. Maybe they'll quietly tell me on their deathbed. 'Oh, yes, darling, something I forgot to mention. I climbed Mount Kilimanjaro once. Yeah, in the dead of night. Didn't want anyone to see me. No, never took any photos. It was cool, I guess, but it didn't change me as a person. I was just bored one day and happened to be in Kilimanjaro so I thought I may as well.'

That man, I would marry that man in an instant.

Though he wouldn't marry me because I'm not Gretel enough.

Katy pores over the rest of the collection Josh has put together to convince women he's worth a swipe. There's the 'him laughing in a group' one, and the 'him at a coffee making course to show he has interests' one and the 'him taken from an angle where his cheekbones look better than they are' one. She hands my phone back and says what she's said many times before: 'I've got a good feeling about this one.'

'Hmm.'

'No, I really have.'

I add milk to Matt's drink and hide a smile. There's this kind of determined optimism coupled-up people force upon single people about their chances of love. I used to cling to their words like they were wise oracles, believing them when they said, 'of course there's someone out there for you' and 'you are so lovable'. But now I'm thinking it's all bullshit. I mean, there's a lot of evidence to the contrary that suggests no, I am not lovable. Out of all the men I've been with, only one has actually said the words 'I love you' out loud, but then he also raped me and emotionally tormented me so I don't think that really counts. I mean, it's surely crossed Katy's mind that maybe there is something significantly wrong with me? That, maybe, actually, there *isn't* someone out there who can put up with all my countless personality failures? Whatever it is, Katy seems happy that I'm back sharing with her again and it's nice not to have the awkwardness of me freezing her out. It's nice to know I can still relate to her when I'm not just performing the 'poor vulnerable April' act.

I hand Matt his coffee and he mouths 'thank you', still engrossed in his shift. I clatter down in my chair, and think I should probably look through the inbox, to check he's going to be OK. Make sure there are no addicts in there. Two weeks ago we had someone write in about their alcoholic father and Matt went to the bathroom for a very long time. I enter all the security codes and pull up the list of questions that came through overnight. There's someone who wants to know if you can get pregnant from pre-cum. There's someone who thinks their penis isn't big enough. There is a boy who is really struggling with a break-up from his university girlfriend. So far, so non-triggering for either of us. Then I click on the next one and know right away, just from reading the first line:

Message received: 11:02

I'm probably making a big deal of nothing, I'm just a bit confused . . .

My mouthful of bitter coffee intensifies. It takes a moment to swallow. I click off the question and glance over at Matt, who is fixated on his screen, *tip-tapping* out a reply, nonplussed. I feel a huge swell of gratitude towards him, that he's the one taking this shift and not me. That he's the one who has to unpick the inevitable clusterfuck of a young girl's pain and confusion over his cup of not-very-good coffee. I try to distract myself from what Matt's dealing with by powering through my emails. I am emailed to be told my budget has formally now been cut by two thousand pounds and yet I'm still expected to do all the things I'm supposed to do with less money. I am emailed about another email to say to ignore what's been said in the previous email I haven't got to yet, and told that the real email will be coming in an upcoming email. I'm emailed about a meeting we're having to discuss how the charity can reduce the amount of email it sends.

When I get a moment, I log in to my personal inbox and sigh when I see the subject title.

From: ChrissyHartley123@gmail.com
To: AprilS1987@gmail.com
Subject: Hen Do

April!!! How are you?? OMG, it's so weird that you're not on Facebook and such any more. Makes me realise how much I rely on it to communicate. HOW ARE THINGS? I realise I have

NO IDEA because I also use social media to know everything that's going on with my friends' lives. TERRIBLE, isn't it? We should meet up properly soon and have a really long catch-up. I miss doing that. Sorry I've been rubbish. It's just been such a whirlwind planning the wedding. Especially as Control-Freak-Chrissy has, of course, insisted on doing it all herself. Oh God, I'm talking about myself in the third person . . . Not good.

ANYWAY, I had the hen do all set up as a group chat online, and then realised you can't see it. I know you said you're free that weekend, but I've not given you the deets. Here they are: Right, so we're going to Brighton. Nothing cheesy! I promise! We are too old for penis straws and butlers in the buff now, I reckon. 33 is not 27! We've got the top floor of a nice restaurant booked for the whole evening, so we can just stay there and get wankered. MAYBE, if we're really drunk, we'll end up in a club. But, to be honest, there's at least five of us either preggers or breastfeeding, so I reckon we'll just end up going back to the Airbnb and chatting with cups of tea. Then we'll go for brunch the next day, maybe pootle around the Lanes. Very chilled! It all comes to £150 which I hope is OK with you? Again, sorry. All of this is in the group and I totally forgot to loop you in. My bank deets are 44-52-87 and 90827536. I'll email again about trains down. SO EXCITED TO SEE YOU! I can't believe it's coming up so soon. WHAT IS HAPPENING? WHERE DID THE TIME GO?

So much love and hugs,

Chrissy xxxx

I swear when I see the amount at the bottom, frantically doing some maths in my head to add in the cost of train tickets and meals and 'of course we can't let Chrissy pay for anything on her hen do so let's all pitch in to cover it for her'.

Katy jolts me out of my thought-processing. 'So?' she asks, leaning around her computer, big smile on her face. 'When are you going to meet Mr Mount Kilimanjaro?'

I take another sip of coffee. 'I'm not sure if I *am* going to meet him. He's not asked me out yet.'

'Feminism remember!' she shrills. 'You can totally ask him out, you know?'

'I know I can,' I say. 'But I'm not sure I want to.' Plus, the books say you shouldn't. Everyone says you shouldn't. Men need to hunt and gather you. Plus, Gretel isn't sure yet. She's too busy getting her nose fucking pierced or something.

'Oh hon,' Katy sighs, her face sinking into sympathy I don't need or want right now. 'I'm sorry things didn't work out with Simon, but I think it's important to keep putting yourself out there, you know? You've got to keep the faith.'

'Who needs Jesus when you've got a man who climbed Mount Kilimanjaro?'

She laughs. 'You know what I mean. I really do have a good feeling about this one. Honestly, from the moment I saw his picture, I felt something. I get things like that sometimes.'

I glance back at my emails and a reminder jumps out to remind me I've got my clinical supervision this afternoon. 'Did you have a good feeling when you met Jimmy?' I ask, only half-interested in the answer.

'I did actually. I remember it so clearly. After our first date, I came home and wrote in my diary, "I know this sounds dramatic, but I think I've just met the man I'm going to marry".'

I smile and say 'aww'. And think: *literally every woman thinks that after a good first date.* If I'd actually married all the men I thought I was going to marry then I'd be like Henry VIII combined with a sex cult-leader and multiplied to the power of Katie Price. 'That's cute,' I say.

'I know.' I watch her soothe herself with the memory, its magic making her think fondly of her husband for a moment or two.

'Well, we'll see. He's not asked me out yet.'

'He will.'

'Well he might not.'

'He will. And like I said, I've got a feeling about him.'

'Don't tell me, you think maybe this one could be different?'

It's too hot to be asked such pressing questions.

'Have you considered, April, that it might be time to think about retiring from this particular role?'

My clinical supervisor for work is a psychologist called Carol. She's arranged neatly in her chair, pretending to be all wise and knowing, despite the fact it's about ten million degrees in this office and I can see sweat glistening on her top lip.

'Why would I want to do that?' I squiggle about in my plastic chair, wipe the sweat from the underside of my thigh and cross my legs.

'Well, some themes are starting to repeat quite often in this supervision. Most notably, how these shifts are altering your general view of men.'

I nod. It's true.

'You're coming up to two years working on the front line of this charity, that's right, isn't it?'

I nod again, knowing where she's going with this. Front-line workers tend to break around the two-year mark, especially in roles where you're helping victims of sexual violence. I was warned about this by Mike when I first took the extra work on. It's almost expected that you'll resign before you get too soured and angry.

'I don't want to stop,' I tell her. 'I know it triggers me occasionally and makes me angry, but I don't want to stop.'

'Why not?'

I don't answer. I dodge her gaze and look around the cluttered, sweaty mess of our office's meeting room. A brainstorm from an earlier meeting about new revenue streams droops helplessly from the wall, with the words, 'become a donkey sanctuary' scribbled across it as a joke.

'April?'

'I don't know.'

'We've discussed before that this may be linked to your own personal experience of rape?'

I wipe the sweat off my legs again and re-cross them. 'Well of course it's something to do with that.'

'You used to say that this role helped you work through what happened to you, but do you feel like maybe that's changing? That maybe you've hit your limit? There's nothing wrong with that, you know.'

Once more, I don't reply. My skin feels like it's erupted into cactus spikes.

'I have to do something,' I tell her. 'I have to feel I'm resisting somehow.'

'To make up for the fact you weren't able to resist when you were assaulted?'

Why didn't I tell him to stop? Why did I let him do that to me? If I 'let' him, then surely it wasn't rape? No no no. You know it was, you know it was.

I dig my fingernail into my thumb, take a breath, and look back up at my sweaty supervisor. 'Probably.'

'Are you OK, April?'

'Yes, I'm fine. Look . . .' I pick the skin around my nail bed. 'What's the psychological perspective on revenge?'

'Revenge?' she asks, writing the word down on her notepad, probably with a red flag symbol.

'I'm just asking hypothetically,' I say, in case she blabs to Mike even though these sessions are supposed to be private. 'Have there ever been any studies into whether revenge is *helpful*?'

'Embitterment is a common emotion for victims,' Carol says, dodging the question. 'It's not unusual to desire that someone who hurt us should hurt too.'

'What if it's not just one person you're mad at though?' I ask. 'What if it's a whole group of people?'

She makes another note then puts her pad down. 'April, we've spent many of your supervisions talking about how this job, combined with what happened to you, has given you a negative view of men. And, despite me trying very hard to work through this with you, it only appears to be getting worse.'

'That's not my fault, that's men's fault.'

'We've spoken many times about how every man is different, every human is different. A few bad apples do not reflect half the human population. You help a lot of alcoholics and drug addicts in your role, and yet you're not coming here telling me everyone is an addict.'

I resist the urge to roll my eyes. I resist the urge to do a lot of things that I really want to do: scream, swear, force her to read the emails I'm forced to read every day, and then yell 'Do you blame me? Do you get it now? Do you?! DO YOU?!' Get her to break. Cave in. Lean forward in her sweaty chair and whisper, 'Look, I'm a woman too, I get it. Yes, men are awful, fucking broken and awful, but I'm not allowed to say that because then I'll get struck off, but I promise you I'm secretly agreeing with you' . . .

'. . . As I've said, these feelings only seem to be getting stronger, and it doesn't seem to be having a good impact on your mental health. Your company understands these things often have a time limit. It's not like you'll get fired, you'll just step into something different. Something less in your face.'

I'm a bit panicked now. I don't want to stop my shifts. I'd only ever been a project manager before coming to We Are Here, lost and scared and not recovered from Ryan. But, after a year, and after organising the training of so many volunteers, I'd been asked if I was interested in training to do shifts too. It was the first thing that eased the pain a bit. That made me feel worthwhile, rather than a broken pile of pieces. 'Are you going to tell Mike on me?'

She smiles and shakes her head. 'You know these slots are confidential. I'm here for you, April, and only you. I'm saying this for your benefit. I can't force you to stop.'

'I just don't think it's fair, what you're saying. Making out that my reaction is wrong. I think hating men considering everything men do is a completely normal response. I shouldn't have to "work on myself",' I air quote, 'in order not to get upset when men routinely rape women.'

She reaches out her finger to punctuate my rant. 'But they aren't all the same.'

'Yes they are!'

Suddenly I'm standing and I'm yelling, with sweat dripping down the back of my legs. I'm also shaking and trying not to cry and my throat feels stitched shut and Carol is looking worried, trying to get me to sit my hot flesh back down on the sticky chair.

It takes a moment or two to pass, for me to gain control of whatever's just happened. I keep saying 'I'm fine, honestly I'm fine', which isn't very convincing.

'April,' she says, once I'm sitting down and my breathing is vaguely back to normal. 'Be kind to yourself. Maybe at least think about taking a break from your shift work.'

'I can't.'

'You can, and it doesn't have to mean anything. It's just a break.'

'I'll think about it,' I tell her, when I know I won't. But I play good employee and allow the supervision to return to normal. Carol and I go through some of my answers to the email questions I found tricky, and we tweak a template answer for the virginity questions that wasn't quite working.

What if revenge is good?

Do we ever allow ourselves to ask that question? What if turning the other cheek is not the answer? Because I'll tell you what. I've lived my whole life as a girl and I've turned so many goddamned cheeks I'm surprised I have any skin left on my face. And yet it's never once made me feel better. Not like how I feel when I think about Gretel.

'Do have a think about what I've said,' Carol says when the fifty minutes is up.

'I will.' I stand up to go back to the office. I can see Matt waiting through the glass wall, pulling that nervous, 'trying not to look like I'm about to go into therapy' face, as he sits on the chair outside. I push through the glass door and high-five him, like we're on a WWF tag team. 'You're up,' I say. 'Want some tissues?'

'You're hilarious,' he mutters, but he smiles as he steps in. I hear Carol say, 'Welcome Matt, take a seat', before the glass door closes again.

I walk around a bank of desks and arrive at my own, where Katy has left a slice of cake with a note: 'post supervision treat'. She's in a meeting, so I can't thank her. Instead I sit down to emails and more emails, just as my phone vibrates.

Josh: So Gretel, how about we do that thing where we actually meet in person and politely try to decide if we fancy one another?

It's such a smooth message that you could spread it on toast. Credit where credit is due.

I wait an entire day before I reply.

It's not even hard. I have back-to-back meetings the rest of the afternoon. I go out for drinks after work, and then meet Kerry, a friend from the charity I used to work for, and we sit through an hour of OKish theatre at Soho Theatre. We go for drinks afterwards and she complains about her husband being so busy and stressed since his promotion.

Megan's still up when I get in, mood-boarding the launch event she's just been chucked into doing, magazines cut up and discarded all over the flat, so I stay up and help her, and we finish a bottle of wine, and say we can't believe we are up this late on a school night, and shit, we're going to be hungover tomorrow. I fall into bed without taking my make-up off, and wake up way too thirsty at 3.30 a.m., down a pint of water and then manage to get back to sleep, kicking my covers off in the muggy heat. Then I press snooze three times instead of two, which throws off my morning routine, and I have to rush around, layering on the deodorant because this heat will not break, and run out the door to the Tube, the red brick of the posh flats blurring past me, thinking how atrocious it is to be running when it's this hot. I collapse onto a train and wipe the sweat off the bits of me it's appropriate to wipe in public. The carriage roars into the tunnel and is swallowed by darkness, and it's only then that I think of Joshua and of his invitation.

I read back the message. It still makes me smile.

Gretel hits the 'reply' button.

Gretel: Sure, why not?

Joshua suggests he and Gretel meet on Tuesday, but Gretel can't do Tuesday, even though she can. In fact, Gretel switches her drinks with her university friend, Vicky, to Tuesday so now she's not even lying about being busy, she is just actually busy, being so bloody great at living life. Gretel suggests Thursday instead, because it's important she show Joshua that she is interested in meeting him. She doesn't want to put him off just yet, but he also needs to know how busy and great she is. Joshua suggests they go out for cocktails at this place he knows. She says sure. Thursday it is. Cocktails it is. Can we make it six thirty instead of six because I have a thing? It's not real, she just needs him to know she's the sort of girl who has things.

• Test One – Gretel's Guide to First Dates

First dates are nerve-wracking, so it's totally natural to be nervous.
Just don't *show* your nerves, all right? That will put them off. Meet
somewhere fun to show off how fun you are because you really
want them to see you're fun. Dinner is a bit too formal. A cinema is
not right because you can't talk to one another, and you won't be
able to entrance him with all your eyelash fluttering and hiding the
more negative parts of your personality. Maybe a casual drink?
But somewhere interesting. You know what? It's sort of better if you
let him decide where you go. Remember, it's the first date, you have
to be *casual*.

Of course you should make an effort with your appearance, but don't
make it obvious you've made *too much* effort. Not too sexy, not too
prudish. Remember – channel Goldilocks. Stay in the middle of the
sexy spectrum. Stay in the middle of every spectrum. Be as bland
as you fucking can to trick him into wanting to spend more time with
you. With all that said, it's really important on a first date to keep the
bland chat interesting. The important thing about first-date
conversation is that it should be breezy but also create an emotional
connection. Dodge the dreaded 'small talk' and ask him deeper
questions like 'why?', and follow that with more 'whys?'. He will start
opening up and he'll associate the emotional connection with you. If

he asks you questions, it's your chance to show him how cool, and busy, and interesting, and kick-ass, yet sensitive you are. Mention how much you want to travel to Africa and that you're thinking of booking a ticket soon. All men want to be with a girl who wants to go to Africa. Don't mention exes. Ever. I mean, *duh*. Yes, you are both single in your thirties so that means, without a doubt, that somewhere along the line for both of you some shit has gone seriously, painfully, wrong, but now is not the time to acknowledge that elephant in the room! So, keep it light and pretend you want to go to Africa. If you really want to go to Africa, even better! Remember not to swear and steer away from contentious subjects like politics or art or your emotional responses to life's hardships. Keep it positive!

Oh, if you're going somewhere to eat, make sure you don't order salad. Men don't want to spend the rest of their lives with someone who orders fucking salad. Order whatever you like because you're strong and independent and don't care what anyone thinks, just don't order salad; even if you're in the mood for salad and that's genuinely what you feel like eating, don't eat it, OK?

When the bill comes, make sure you offer to split it because this is modern life. But, also, if he wants to pay it, then let him so he's not emasculated. You can pay on the next date – but we're getting ahead of ourselves. This is still only the first date here. You're not on the second yet, are you, you fucked-up mess reading advice about first dates?

If the date has gone well, and there's sexual chemistry and an emotional connection and you've not ruined all that by revealing any unattractive human traits, then the big question is, do you kiss? Clearly sex is a no-no, you slut. Kissing is OK though. Sort of. As long as you follow some simple tips, sorry, I meant rules: Let him kiss you. Do not kiss him first. Even if it's clear he wants to kiss you, don't lean in. Ideally don't kiss until dates two or three anyway. Let there be build-up. Oh, and afterwards, wait for *them* to contact *you*. Don't do it first, because: men. Anyway, you're too busy being awesome and high-value and not needing them very much to even be worrying about messaging him, right?

It only works if you know there are plenty of men out there that you can spark with and you never worry about dying alone. You can't go out dating with the fear that you may die alone. I mean, that's essentially the sole reason of dating – to meet someone so you don't die alone – but you're not allowed to think that. You have to accidentally find love on the date you're going on to try and find the love of your life. Otherwise you're just desperate and I can smell that from here – jeez.

I'm weirdly calm as I get ready in the cramped office bathroom. No matter how many first dates I've been on in my life (clue: a *lot*), they've never lost their nerve-wrackingness. I've never been able to overcome the sheer weirdness of sitting with a stranger, both of you trying to figure out if you're capable of falling in love with one another. The instant judgements you both make, telling the same stories that you know go down well, but clearly not too well otherwise you wouldn't still be going on dates. I'm not wearing my usual first-date outfit but instead what Gretel would wear to a first date.

He would want Gretel to look effortlessly amazing, which, of course, takes a shit load of effort. If Gretel was real, she'd just tumble into the date straight from work, her face glowing, and hair piled up – looking just as extraordinarily beautiful as she does when she wakes up next to you in the morning, probably with a blowjob or something. In man world, Gretel takes no longer than five minutes getting ready to look so pretty. But Gretel isn't real. I am just playing her part. I'm pretty enough. I've been told by a few men, without asking, that objectively I'm beautiful (I refer to these compliments as 'unforced errors'). But I'm not a model, and so it takes quite a lot of make-upping to achieve the desired Gretel look.

There's a banging at the door just as I'm wiggling a mascara brush through my eyelashes. 'Are you dead?' Mike calls. 'It would be a terrible shame if you were, especially as I really need the loo.'

I smirk. 'Sorry, I'll be right out.' I scoop up the contents of my make-up bag and stuff it all back in. I've 'only' got on primer, light-reflecting foundation, eyelid brightener, mascara, a tiny smudge of eyeliner, blusher, highlighter, and a red lip stain to achieve Gretel's natural beauty. I pull my jeans down, kicking off my Converse so I can yank them off over my feet. Then I shake off my blouse and bra, sniff my armpits to see how they're holding up, and step into a strappy maxi dress. I lean on the door, because you can only unlock it if you get the angle completely right, and stumble out into the raised eyebrows of Mike.

'You look nice,' he comments, but not in a pervy way. He's one of those extraordinary men who manage to exude absolutely no weird sex-vibes whatsoever. We were all surprised to learn he was, a) heterosexual, and b) married with children.

'Thanks. How late you working?'

He pinches the top of his nose, while letting out a small sigh of exhaustion. 'Hopefully not much longer. Though I've missed putting the children to bed. Again. Anyway, have a good night, I really do need to pee.'

I make my way back to my desk to collect my things. Still no nerves. I stuff what I can into my bag, and leave the bulk of my crap under my desk to take home tomorrow. I doubt Gretel's the sort of girl who drags along an overflowing bag. Every man I've ever dated seems to take it as a personal insult that I need to carry things around with me. 'Why is this so heavy? Do you really need all that stuff? It's OK to leave the house without the whole kitchen sink, you know?' And then, hilariously, it is mostly them who end up rummaging in my bag to retrieve all the useful items you've stored there. 'Can I have some of your water? Do you have any paracetamol? Are those mints? Can I have one? And, oh, can I put my wallet in your bag?'

The office is empty as I leave it, Mike still in the toilet doing whatever gross things men do in the toilet which is the same as women but somehow grosser.

The heat still lingers, the air lethargic with humidity.

Josh: Hi, I'm here a little early. I've got a table in the corner. See you soon.

Then another message just as I'm about to hop on the Tube.

Josh: Unless you've stood me up. In which case, I hope this makes you feel really guilty.

I smile as I read the second one. Josh seems a smidgen different in that he's not scared to turn up early. Simon made me wait twenty minutes on our first date, claiming he got held up at work. He was very apologetic but still late. Letting me know, from the off, that his time was more important than mine – that he was comfortable with the idea of me waiting for him. I've timed it so I'm exactly ten minutes late for Josh. Only ten minutes because men are less forgiving of late women than women are of late men. Enough to keep him on his toes, while also not enough for him to fuss over.

Gretel: We had a date tonight? . . . Kidding. On my way. Running a few mins behind.

The Tube has calmed down enough from rush hour that I'm not moist with sweat and the contagion of other people's bad moods by the time I reach London Bridge. I emerge up the stairs into the brightness, and use my phone to figure out where the cocktail bar is. Still not nervous. A bit worried I'm a total psychopath for lying about my name, but not nervous about meeting Josh. I just feel slightly sorry for him.

I find the entrance on this tucked-away little street where a sign hangs discreetly in front of a black door. I've walked past this a thousand times without knowing it was a bar. I'm not sure whether I'm supposed to knock the big brass knocker, or if I can push my way in. I'm not even that late, after all that. I'd planned to leave a little bit of extra time in my lateness strategy so that I wouldn't be too late, and that's worked out with me being only five minutes behind. I stand for a moment, feeling more anxious about this dilemma than I should. Gretel is temporarily lost, and me, April, and my general inability to human sometimes, forces herself to the forefront and stands paralysed with indecision. Luckily I'm saved when the door swings open and a group of giddy smokers emerge with cigarettes clutched in their hands. They smile and hold the door open for me. I take another deep breath, find my inner Gretel again, and stride in to meet Joshua.

There he is. Joshua. Strong name. Sitting in the corner. Strong choice of table. Not playing on his phone to compensate for sitting alone. Strong character. He sees me. Well,

Gretel. Must recognise me from the photo. He stands, and we both, within milliseconds, make ten gazillion micro-decisions about the other based on nothing but body language and scent and the filter of our past experiences. And hope. On his side, maybe, there's a filter of hope. He's on a first date after all, he must not have given up just yet.

'Hi, Gretel, nice to meet you.' He strides over and we awkwardly kiss on the cheek.

'Nice to meet you too.' It's insane that he's just called me *Gretel*. What am I doing? What the actual fuck am I doing? I have totally lost all my marbles. My voice is a bit too shrill and I try to drop an octave. 'Sorry I'm a little bit late. I couldn't find the place.'

He guides me to the table, bumping into another bloke on the walk over.

'Watch it mate.'

'Whoops, whoa, sorry,' Joshua says, before swearing under his breath once we pass. I catch a whiff of his nervousness. Normally I'm so consumed by my own nerves that my date could be bleeding from the eyeballs and I wouldn't notice, but, tonight, I can sense his anxiety bubbling. A jolt of power crackles through me. Again, a totally novel experience on a first date. 'Sit, sit.' He gestures to a chair. 'I didn't order you a drink because I had no idea what you'd like. But I can make eye contact with the waitress for you.'

'Umm, shouldn't it be me you're making eye contact with on a first date?' I settle myself in my chair, enjoying the way his gaze subtly registers my appearance. 'I don't want to be competing with the waitress.' We both laugh at the same time, though I can see the joke has thrown him off-kilter. So I lean in and look up at him through my eyelashes. 'A bottle of beer would be great to start with, thanks,' I say. 'And I'm rubbish at getting attention from waiting staff, so please do the honours.'

His ego soothed, Joshua's shoulders loosen. He takes pride in beckoning the lady over and ordering me a Corona and lime even though April doesn't really like beer.

My drink arrives, just as Joshua and I finish filling each other in on the thrilling details of our journeys here.

'Oh, yes, the Jubilee line really is weirdly exciting and grown up, isn't it?'

'Oh, so you can walk from Blackfriars? That's useful.'

'One Corona.' The waitress bends and places it on the table between us.

'Cheers.' I pick it up and take a swig, trying not to pull a face. 'Sorry, it's terribly undignified to order beer on a first date, isn't it?' I place the bottle back down. 'It's just so hot today. I promise I'll be sophisticated and order red wine later.'

Josh laughs again. 'Are you one of those people who understand wine?'

Always make them feel at ease, Gretel's voice whispers to me, so they associate feeling at ease with being around you.

I shake my head. 'No. Are you?'

He shakes his head too.

But don't hand yourself over on a plate; make him feel mildly uncomfortable so he knows he doesn't certainly have you.

'Good,' I say. 'Because if you are one of those people who actually knows what to do in a restaurant when they make you try the wine, then I don't think it's going to work between us.'

Another hearty laugh. I've never made a man laugh this much so quickly on a first date.

Ask them lots of open-ended questions about themselves.

I gulp down another mouthful of beer. 'So, Mount Kilimanjaro then?'

That's all I need to say. I don't even have to explain why I'm bringing it up, or remind him he put it as a picture on his app. His face lights up with the opportunity to talk about it. 'Yes, it was completely amazing. I'm still buzzing, I swear, even though it was over six months ago . . . so we camped in this beautiful place called . . . most challenging thing I've ever done, you learn so much about yourself . . . got the bug now, planning the next one . . . the important thing is that you have to train, you can't skimp on the training . . . altitude sickness is the worst of course.'

I prompt his monologue with the occasional 'wow' and 'why?' so we have a deep emotional connection, but mostly use the time to take in Joshua's appearance. He is neither good-looking nor bad-looking, I decide. He is neutral-looking, like Switzerland. He just looks like 'a bloke'. Definitely one of those faces that you need a slight emotional connection with before you want to rip his clothes off. Then, once all those problematic bonding hormones flood in, I can imagine the mole by his lip would be magical, and his eyes, green, well that's unusual enough to find riveting once your unmet childhood needs make him an attachment figure to glue yourself to.

'Yeah, so three peaks next . . . as an amuse bouche . . . hahahahaha . . .' He's made enough of an effort with his appearance. The grey of his shirt suits him and brings out his eyes. I imagine a past girlfriend told him that information and he's clung to it ever since. The shirt settles well around his normal body, toned enough by the mountain-hiking side of him, but he definitely isn't a gym-goer – he would've mentioned protein by now if that was the case. He maintains an acceptable level of hygiene. My guess is two serious relationships, the last one hurting enough to plough his grief into climbing Mount Kilimanjaro. Maybe the girl who told him he suits grey is the one who made him need to climb the mountain to get over her? All in all, if I wasn't using him as a social experiment, he seems a good bet. Especially at my age. Aren't I lucky to be on a date with someone like Joshua? Better not fuck it up by being myself . . .

'So, yeah, Everest is the dream, but it's like thirty fucking grand. Whoops, I just swore. Sorry, you don't mind swearing, do you?'

I shake my head and smile. Gretel doesn't mind anything, that's the point of her.

'Phew!' He mock-wipes his brow like he's a comedian from the eighties making a joke about his mother-in-law. I giggle. He remembers himself, recognises how much he's been speaking. He picks up his drink, and gestures out to me. The way he gulps it reveals he's still nervous. And, despite myself, I feel a pang of sorrow for him. God, the things we put ourselves through, on the quest to find someone. 'Anyway, how about you? You like the odd adventure?'

I nod because I know that you have to pretend you want adventures. God forbid if my idea of branching out is ordering a slightly different type of coffee one day and then regretting it instantly. 'Oh yeah,' I say, forcing myself to take another swig of beer. 'Of course I love an adventure. Who doesn't?' *Me me me me me me me.* 'I'm thinking of going to Africa, actually.'

The line has the desired effect. He looks impressed. 'Wow.'

'I just think it would be so amazing, you know?'

'Oh yeah, of course. I'd love to go back at some point. I didn't see enough of it, for sure, when I was there. Whereabouts in Africa?'

'Oh, all over. I want to see it all, you know? It's such a fascinating place.' I realise, much like saying you're writing a novel, or running a marathon, just saying you are planning to go to Africa instantly gives you so much social gravitas, you never have to really bother following through with it. 'So, what is it you do?' I ask, chasing it with more 'why?'.

And Joshua, whether it's nerves, or his personality, or just that men really do think the best thing that can be happening at any given moment is a woman listening to him talk, happily fills the silence until we've finished our drinks and decided on sharing a bottle of red. 'Oh, I work in computers. Why? I've just always loved them. I got into code before people even knew it was a thing. Why? Well there's a real beauty to it, it's its own language. Coding is so much more creative than anyone thinks. It's problem-solving, it's building worlds out of nothing . . . Oh, yes, the company I work for is great. It's a Start Up offering office perks. Really chilled atmosphere. We all get to finish at four thirty on a Friday. I know, great, right? Especially in the summer . . .'

I listen and listen and listen and listen. I nod and nod and agree and agree. I occasionally make small witticisms, to show that I'm not completely bland, just totally interested in what he's saying. It's so relaxing not being me. I sip my red wine and listen some more. 'That's great about the Friday finish,' I say. 'Wow, I don't know much about coding. How interesting.'

By the time the bottle of wine's been finished, and the bar's more crowded, I would estimate that it's been roughly eighty per cent Joshua talking compared to twenty per cent me talking. And, by the way he's blearily looking at me, with hope in his slightly-drunken eyes, it looks like, ladies and gentlemen, we've found the golden ratio.

'You're pretty,' he states. Throwing it out there with the confidence of alcohol. 'I like your eyes.'

I accept the compliment because that shows good levels of self-esteem. 'Thanks,' I say. 'I grew them myself.'

'BAHAHAHAHA.' He laughs so hard he almost spits out his wine. 'That's funny,' he states. 'HAHAHAHAHA. Wow, a girl has never made me laugh like that before.'

I raise my eyebrows and absorb the micro-aggression because Gretel is chill about things like that. It's almost ten and I'm starting to wane. It's exhausting constantly listening to somebody talk at you and arranging your face into a neutral listening pose. Also, Gretel has been a bit too easy up until now. It's time for the power switch. Sensing it, Joshua leans over and taps the empty wine bottle. 'Fancy another?' he asks. 'I won't tell if you won't.'

I smile with warmth and nothing threatening. 'I'd love to,' I say. 'But I probably shouldn't. I've got a crazy early meeting tomorrow morning.' Joshua's face dims, rejection rippling through him. So I lean over, put my hand on his hand, and start the never-ending routine of using up my energy soothing his ego. 'But I've had a really good time.'

He looks at our touching skin. He feels what I feel. Because, annoyingly, despite everything, the skin on skin contact is sending zings up my arm. Stirrings of electricity yawn through my body. 'Me too,' he says. 'What's the meeting about? It's so cool that you work for a charity. That, like, makes you a proper good person.'

'Yep. Worked off three years of purgatory already . . .' *Make sure you're clever, but not too clever, don't be intimidating.* 'It's just a meeting about funding, but it will be all mathsy, so I need to have my wits about me.' I remove my hand. 'So I should probably go.'

Joshua stands as I stand. 'OK, I'll walk you to the Tube.'

I pick up my bag. A group of aggy businessmen push past us to claim our table before I've even wiggled out. 'Sorry, sorry,' they say, hands up, but not meaning it, because they're doing it anyway. How many sorrys do I accept from men who are saying sorry but doing it anyway?

The sun's yet to set as we emerge onto the lively streets. A trillion cyclists whirr past us, the pavements clogged with people spilling out of pubs. Heat from the cemented roads rises and mingles with the hissing exhausts of buses. The air smells like it has no oxygen in it. Joshua's nerves have returned now we are out of the dimmed lights of the bar. We walk, side by side, but nowhere near touching. I act like the awkwardness isn't bothering me at all, swinging my arms and humming under my breath. Silence has always been something I stumble into, desperate to fill. It's where I give away so much of my power. But Gretel doesn't ever feel awkward. She's too busy planning out some tune to play on her ukulele when she gets home, or wondering if her new nose-piercing is accidental cultural appropriation.

'Big day tomorrow?' I ask, when enough time has passed for him to think I've been comfortable with the conversational lag. 'Are you going to code the shit out of some stuff?'

He giggles again. 'Oh yeah,' he riffs off the energy I created. 'Coding isn't going to know what's hit it. I'm going to code like there's no tomorrow.'

'You'll have to teach me sometime.'

Josh takes his cue. He stops us on the pavement and turns towards me.

'I'd like that,' he says. He reaches out and takes both of my hands and looks right into my eyes. I'm a bit thrown because I wasn't expecting this. I'm still not completely sure if Gretel kisses on a first date or not, but there is definitely the hint of a kiss on this muggy, polluted horizon. I look up at this strange man, who is holding both of my hands. I think about how I rarely touch the people I know, how, normally, skin on skin contact is something that comes with time. How friends build up to the ability to hug one another. And, yet, in a dating context, you allow random individuals the privilege and intimacy of touching you after, what, a few messages sent back and forth and a bottle of red? Men no longer have to earn the right to touch women. And, even if they do, they often lean over the counter and help themselves anyway. I feel prickles itch their way across my skin.

I look into Joshua's green eyes, and then down at our hands, and try not to let April's rage seep into Gretel. But it must've leaked out because Joshua gives me a cheeky smile and then lets go of my hands. 'Right, come on then. Let's get you home, Miss Important Meeting Tomorrow.'

'So important,' I counter, walking a tiny bit closer to him so he knows Gretel is still into this. 'I mean, sometimes, when I think about how important I am, it overwhelms me and I can't get out of my office chair.'

He laughs loudly again. I should be kinder about him to be fair. He may be a man, and I am pretty much certain that they're all awful and deserve to be punished for existing, but he didn't lean over the counter and help himself just now. He read my April vibes, and didn't kiss Gretel. Credit where credit is due. Though so many of them seem nice at first . . .

We reach the steps that will take me down to the Tube. It's still bustling with summer evening foot traffic, everyone ignoring the man with a mike and portable speaker who is yelling at us to accept God into our lives. Joshua manoeuvres us into an alcove next to Borough Market entrance so we can stop and awkwardly say goodbye to one another without the added awkwardness of people trying to walk past us and tutting.

'So,' he says, looking like he wants to kiss me again.

'Thanks for the wine,' I say. 'And for not being a scary psychopath. You never know with dating apps.'

Another big hearty laugh. 'You're welcome.'

I don't tell him I had a good time because I reckon Gretel is the sort of person who doesn't dole out compliments easily. You have to earn them from her; you have to draw her attention away from whatever incredible adventure she's on, or whimsical thought she is having. I can sense the cringey hug/back-pat goodbye of previous dates, so I lean in, kiss him gently on the cheek, and say, 'You get home safe now.' Then I turn and go. Down into the gullet of the London Underground, not once looking back.

I get out my card to let me through the barriers, and smile at the busker as I float down the escalators past posters for West End musicals I'm never able to afford because I live in London. I slump onto a germ-ridden seat with an *oomph* and the Tube snakes through the darkness and back home. I love riding the Tube at this time of night. When everyone is heady from alcohol and either going home happy after a few too many, or off out to make the evening into a bigger one. Giddy anticipation drips from the ceiling, and it's that sort of atmosphere where, if someone was to start singing 'Bohemian Rhapsody', everyone around would just join in. I change onto the District line, grinning as I skirt around a gang of tourists, blearily following someone holding up an umbrella as a guide. I plop onto my second train and get the pang I sometimes get. The I'm-so-lucky-to-live-in-London pang, when I think about how those tourists saved up to come here and goggle at what I mindlessly walk past every day. I open my planner and jot down some notes for tomorrow's meeting. I work out what time I need to set my alarm and set it on my phone. Then I plan what to have for breakfast, running through the ingredients I know to be in the fridge. If I get up ten minutes earlier, I can scramble eggs. I smile at the thought of this as I walk home. Already wanting it to be morning so I can eat breakfast.

It's only when I reach the end of my road, that I realise it.

I've gone the whole journey home without thinking about my date with Joshua.

He left my thought process the moment I walked away without looking back. I didn't even wonder if he watched me as I walked away, and I normally always wonder that.

I have not analysed my behaviour for anything I did or said wrong, and then tortured myself with all the nuggets of non-perfect-humaning I'm quickly able dredge up. I have not pored over every single thing he said, sifting it for evidence of commitment issues, personality disorders, a desire to have children, and/or ex-girlfriends he may still be in love with. I've not obsessed over the moment he took my hands, and how he almost kissed me, or berated myself for not letting him kiss me, because it may have put him off, even though I didn't particularly want to be kissed anyway. I've not checked my phone the instant I'm above ground to see if he's messaged, and let the outcome of that dictate how I feel about myself and my life. I've not rung Megan immediately to debrief her on all the above and to get her take on it because I do not trust my own instincts because, well, have you seen my track record?

This has never happened before.

I actually stop on the pavement and say 'huh' out loud.

Then, of course, my phone buzzes and comes up with his name.

Joshua: Hey Gretel, I had a really lovely time tonight. It would be great to do it again soon. X

The perfect post-date message. The message we all hope for. Straight away. 'I liked our time together.' *Bish bash bosh*. No game-playing. Saying they want to see you again. Oh, you've clearly hit it out of the ballpark. One kiss at the end. Already. Just the one. But one is good. Any other number of kisses at this point would be weird. All in all, as I said, the perfect message. It says, 'I like you, and I'm not going to be a dick about saying as much or play games, but I'm still a normal human who isn't going to pin all my hopes on you.'

Way to go, Josh, I think. I don't deliberate about how to reply. Or squeal with happiness. I just think, *I hope Megan hasn't eaten my bloody eggs,* and then speed-walk home to check.

• *Easy Breezy Lemon Squeezy – Gretel's Guide to Messaging Between Dates*

The most important thing to remember about messaging between dates is that none of them mean anything. They're just *fun*, ok? Their only real purpose is a) to sort out admin details, and b) to flirt and entertain.

Certainly no woman worth any worth is going to read anything into them, obsess over their content and their own replies, and jump into the air like a startled cat whenever they receive a new message. Like, who does that? Not Gretel, that's who.

Definitely do not reply straight away regularly. That's an instant way for him to lose his hard-on. The minimum reply time is an hour. Not because you've set an hour timer on your phone, but because you're literally just too busy being amazing and fabulous and Gretel to have time to reply sooner.

Make sure every message you send will make him smile in some way. Cheer up his day. Cheer up his life! Not too often though. Don't want to freak him out with all your availability. You need to strike the perfect balance of reassuring him you're thinking about him, while also reassuring him that you're not *constantly* thinking about him.

Keep in mind that he's probably messaging other girls too. That's cool. You're cool. That's so totally fine, ISN'T IT? I mean, you are totally messaging other guys too. And by 'messaging' you mean receiving unsolicited photographs of pubey, flaccid penises; constant requests for bra sizes; hate mail from that psychopath you dated three months ago calling you a 'slut' for not sleeping with him and considerately telling him you didn't want to see him anymore; countless messages from people who literally cannot spell; countless messages that just say 'hey' at you, over and over again, followed again by good ol' 'slut' when you don't reply. And you regularly look at your phone in complete despair and wonder how anyone meets anyone when it's so obvious all men are broken and you can't believe you've managed to find one, just one, you've vaguely clicked with so you're pouring all your remaining hope into him and cannot fucking believe it's been two hours now and he's not replied and you have no idea if he's going to ask you out again and you may cry if he doesn't . . . yeah, he doesn't need to know all this. All he needs to know is, like, you're totally playing the field too. This over-ploughed, scorched mess of a field scattered with the decaying corpses of all your past hopes . . . So, yeah, a really good message to send is a frothy cool one to let him know how busy and fun and spontaneous you are. One like: 'I'm out in so-and-so playing badger-themed, glow in the dark, minigolf – you should totally join!' or 'OMFG did you know you can currently buy mint choc chip Viennetta for a pound?'

Gretel: Did you know you can currently buy a mint choc chip Viennetta, a whole one, for only a pound?

Joshua: No way? I love those things! Where?! Other than in my dreams?

Gretel: Iceland. Yes, I'm a classy broad.

Joshua: Can't talk. On my way to Iceland.

Joshua: *Sends photo of a mint choc Viennetta*

Gretel: I can't believe you actually got one!

Joshua: Do you want me to send you a video of me cutting a slice?

Gretel: Too early to send porn to each other, right?

Gretel: Food porn, I mean.

Joshua: Glad I've got this Viennetta to eat now to cool me down.

Joshua: It would be nice to see you again.

Gretel: Oh would it now?

Joshua: You free tonight?

Gretel: Alas, I'm out with my housemate Megan. But maybe another time this weekend?

I'm slightly worried Megan is about to fall off the wagon the moment I've climbed onto it.

'I'm too stressed out,' she announced on Thursday, her head facedown on the table – where it's been so often this week that I'm surprised it's not started to make a little head-shaped mark. 'Can we go out tomorrow? I need a ride.'

My eyebrows drew up. 'A *ride*? Since when are you Irish?'

'Since I'm overworked and horny.'

'And that makes you . . . *Irish*?'

'Oh for God's sake! Will you come out with me or not? I promise I won't get emotionally attached to my ride.'

'Please stop saying *ride.*'

'It will just be sex.' She raises her head from the table. 'I'm so stressed with work, April. I have this stupid fucking launch to do, but they've not given me enough budget. And then my psychotic cuntbag of a manager is micromanaging me so hard I can't get anything done, and then she keeps complaining that we're behind and I'm like, HELLO, it's because I'm having to reply to all your psychotic cuntbag emails.'

'Why are so many managers so bad?' I ask, deciding it's probably a good idea to open a bottle of wine. For both of us. Megan's stress is highly contagious when she's like this.

'Shit floats to the top, doesn't it?' she wails, before returning her face to the wood.

'Megs, I love you, you know I love you, but are you sure this is a good idea?'

'What's a good idea?'

'Going ride hunting?'

'It's fine! We'll go somewhere super awful so I'll find someone super awful who I have no chance of falling for. It's just stress relief, April, honestly! I'm a modern woman.'

'Whatever you say.'

Twenty-four hours later, and I'm all dolled up for Megan's ride hunt, standing in a queue in a part of London I never go to, and feeling way too old for this.

'I've not been to Calculus since I was 25,' I whisper as we inch forward. 'And even then it was terrible.'

'You could totally pass for 25,' Megan says, reaching out and squeezing my arm.

'That is not my point.'

'You should take that as a compliment. You never know if and when you'll ever hear it again at our age.' She smiles and rakes her fingers through her hair to fluff it. 'And thank you for coming. It's the easiest place to pull someone. That is the point of Calculus.'

'Easy if they're looking for an older woman. The boys here are so young they look like the kids wearing suits in *Bugsy fucking Malone.*'

Megan laughs. They really do. We're sandwiched by a thick bread of fresh-faced and recently-graduated boys on banking graduate schemes, dressed in their first tailoring, hardly needing to shave yet, and playing at being grown up.

The queue moves forward and we step along, being pushed slightly by a rowdy group of equally fresh-faced girls giggling behind us.

Calculus on a Friday night is where humanity comes to puke up just before it dies. A club in Bank made for one purpose and one purpose only – for bankers to go to pull girls who are only there to pull bankers.

'Why bankers again?' I ask Megan, quietly marvelling at the girls' toned legs and wishing I was still at the age you could eat crap without your body noticing.

'Because I hate them.'

'That's a very healthy reason to be trying to have sex with one.'

'You don't get it. That's precisely why it's healthy! I have literally no chance of getting psychologically attached to one. And you know how much I like to get psychologically attached to men.'

'Who *you*? *Really*? *Oww* don't hit me.'

We inch along towards the hell mouth, while I try to calculate if it's possible that I could've mothered anyone here yet. Maybe I'm still a year or two away, but, regardless, this group of girls are doing nothing for my self-esteem. I twist around to grab a peek at them and their youth oozes out of them. A scent of naivety, optimism, and loads of still-viable eggs lurking in their ovaries. They're conducting some complicated verbal orchestra – each of them interrupting and hardly listening – as they psychoanalyse an ex-boyfriend's behaviour.

'And then I said, look, at our age, it's normal to want to label it. But he made me feel like I was crazy . . .'

'They'll do that. They'll do that. How long had you been seeing each other anyway?'

'Six months . . .'

'And he still wouldn't call you his girlfriend?'

'He said labelling it ruined it, and he thought I'd be cooler than that.'

'I'm so confused.'

'Me too.'

'Tim was like that, remember? I went to his grandma's fucking funeral but he still wouldn't make it official.'

'Fuck him.'

'Fuck all of them.'

'You can't message him tonight.'

'I won't.'

'You will. If you have more than five Jägers, I'm taking charge of your phone . . .'

'No, I'll be fine . . .'

Megan overhears too and rolls her eyes at me, before digging in her bag for a kirby grip. I twist back to the front, exhausted just from listening. I remember all those conversations. How my girlfriends and I would meet up and no matter how exciting the rest of our lives were, talk mainly about some guy: 'Why did he do that?' 'What does it mean?' 'No, I do think he loves me, he's just not making it clear at all with any of his behaviour.' I remember feeling exhausted even back then, as we collectively squeezed ourselves out of juice trying to convince ourselves men did really like us, despite all the evidence to the contrary. There were so many luxurious excuses we could lather on back then. Like we were young, and of *course* men don't want to settle down at this age. We could sort of give them the benefit of the doubt, even though it hurt us and made us worry they wouldn't get there by the time we needed them to. I remember wishing, just wishing, to be the age I am now, when I assumed all men's lights would turn on, like taxi cabs that are finally ready to take you home. I imagined that once you were older you'd fly over previous hurdles, because we'd be grown-ups now and now is not the time to piss about any more. But nothing has changed. No one has evolved. Not really. Even my female friends who have managed to catch a husband in their determined butterfly nets whinge about men. Their marriages are more like an elaborate charade to cover the fact they're essentially just babysitting a resentful, overgrown Man-Child:

'Brought back all his friends the other night. Insane drunk. They all thought it would be hilarious to take their trousers off. Woke me and Charlie. Found that even more hilarious. I honestly thought he'd grown out of this . . . It's his job. A bad influence. If he could just change companies, then I think it would all be fine.'

'Oh April, I probably shouldn't tell you this. I'm drunk. It's just . . . I guess I just assumed, since we were married, that we'd start a family, but he says he isn't ready, which is fine, but I'm 33 and I want a big family and I'm not sure how wise it is to wait but he said it's selfish to rush him.'

We step forward again. The bouncers are in sight now, standing in direct sunlight in their black uniforms and looking like melted icing on a cake. The sun is still high and honking in the sky. I don't think it's ever going to rain again, or that this new anger I feel will ever wane.

In a surge of efficiency, we're suddenly past the bouncers and entering the throbbing darkness of Calculus. The summer sun becomes a instant memory as the doors swing closed behind us. The place is covered in red carpet, so the rich men can feel like, yes, this is how things are supposed to be. And gold everywhere, because of the aforementioned rich men.

'This is going to be terrible,' Megan announces, with a wild smile on her face. 'God, you're a good friend for coming.'

'Can you please just pull quickly so I can go home and watch *Dawson's Creek*?'

Megan pouts. 'Honey, please, you are dealing with a profes-sional. Though God it's uncomfortable wearing a bra,' she adds. 'How do you do it every day?'

We clop along the red carpet towards the bag check at the top of the stairs, where cheesy music burps up from the mouth and lights scatter the wall. After a swift argument with the security about why I'm not allowed to bring in my emergency cheese and celery sandwich, we descend, sand-wichless, to the bar.

In the space of one staircase it's gone from being 7 p.m., still light outside and 27 degrees, into feeling like 3 a.m. and that the night could go on for weeks. The place is dark, crammed, and everyone seems incredibly drunk already. There's a five-person-deep queue at the bar. People are sunburnt and bleary-eyed and stumbling into one another, and then holding each other when they apologise and using that as a way to start kissing. Couples already grind on the horrendous light-up dance floor. Young women bend over and rub their pert arses into the groins of older men in expensive suits.

'Let's get some drinks,' I say, steering Megan away. 'Try to catch up with everyone here.' We push our way through the throngs of obliterated people to join the scrum waiting to order £8 Jägerbombs. Megan's already on the scout, standing with her shoulders back, breasts popped, hair flipped behind one ear. A green light from the club hits her face, and, for a second, I'm afraid to admit that she looks her age. There are wrinkles around her eyes that aren't around the eyes of many of the surrounding girls. Her foundation might be expensive but it still sinks into the wider pores of her skin. Her outfit, like mine, is just that tad too conservative compared to everyone else's. I suddenly feel desperately pathetic to be standing in this bar and can't believe my life has come to this, when I really, truly, thought that, by now, I would be spending my Friday nights putting the baby to bed. That me and my imaginary husband would be sharing a takeaway, laughing about how old we are now, and reminiscing about how shit it was to go out in London on a Friday night 'back in the day' . . . Then the light swings around again, and Megan looks just like Megan again. I blink away the pain of the life I thought I would have by now.

'Shall we get shots?' I call over.

'Let's start with three each.'

It's just as well I'm drunk, I think, as I look at the carnage around me. My phone tells me it's somehow still only eight-thirty. I keep checking it to try and look less like a lemon while Megan talks to Potential Ride Number One. A girl is already vomiting in the toilets, crying about the state of her life while her friends slur, 'He's not worth it, love. You can do so much better.' There's nowhere to sit down. Steam rises from the dance floor in giant clumps around me, and I'm getting hungry because I wasn't allowed to eat my emergency sandwich.

But I'm drunk, totally freaking drunk, so I don't mind much.

Megan's talking, her hands gesticulating wildly, as she leans into Mr Potential Ride. Snatches of their conversation float towards me over the general din of cheesy music. 'No way! You boarded at Glenalmond too? My sister went there before our family moved to London.'

Mr Potential Ride leans further in, puts a hand on the small of her back. 'Really? How old is she? Maybe we were there at the same time. Was she on the lacrosse team?'

Megan's already-posh voice has gone up a gear now she's found someone of her own kind. It may be the music distorting it, but I swear she just said 'yah' instead of 'yes'. It's hilarious, yet ultimately unsurprising that she's found the poshest banker here. Upper-classers have this extraordinary ability to find one another in any given social situation. Like they emit a sonar signal if their family goes hunting on Boxing Day.

'Yes, no. I don't normally come here. I'm just out with a friend, it's her favourite place.' Megan gestures towards me, and Mr Potential Ride smiles over. He's dressed how every other wealthy finance type is dressed in here – navy blue suit he probably dropped two grand on, red tie, statement pocket hanky, shiny pointy shoes, a self-satisfied smirk.

I smile back and return to my phone. God, it's dull, waiting for people to copulate. Hopefully she'll close soon and then I can go home and have the flat to myself, strip to my pants and point the fan at my body while watching Joshua Jackson. I've just been paid, so I may even be able to get an Uber. Then, I'll be sobered up by eleven, and won't be hungover tomorrow, and can do yoga or something in the morning – not that I ever do yoga, but I could always start.

At least 'Come On Eileen' is on. This is so exciting that I forget my purpose and catapult into Megan, yelling, 'THIS IS MY FAVOURITE SONG.' I don't think that's true, but it feels true in this moment. I drag both of them onto the consti-pated dance floor and start dancing like an actual madwoman.

I'm having the very profound realisation that when 'Come On Eileen' starts going slow and then speeds up again, it's impossible to feel anything but euphoria.

'Come on, EileentaloorahYAY,' I scream into Mr Potential Ride's ear. He looks mildly alarmed and it's ruining my vibe, so I turn away and fling myself into a circle of people as excited about the song bridge as I am. Suddenly I'm in the middle of them, lunging for some reason. Young people surround and clap me. I get a smidgen of sadness when I realise I've become that crazy older person in the club you call a 'legend' but secretly hope you never end up like. However, the drum beat's coming up and the chorus is about to drop in the most wonderful way, and I don't give a flying fuck about anything any more, so I jump and twirl and let this circle of youth worship me, and get lost in Eileen and how she must come on. The song merges into the 'Cha Cha Slide' and I'm shocked to find everyone knows the routine. 'But HOW?' I yell into a girl's chandelier earring. 'You must've been a fucking . . . fucking . . . FOETUS when this came out.'

I can't remember the moves though – maybe my memory is going with old age – and suddenly I don't know what to do with this group of children dressed in expensive suits who probably spent more money on shots tonight than I earn in a week. They are cha cha-ing and they are sliding, and this isn't fun and I'm lonely now.

I turn back to Megan and instantly feel lonelier. She's snogging Mr Potential Ride against the wall; their hands are all over one another. And, even though he doesn't look like the nicest of kissers – Mr Potential looks like he kisses how most posh men kiss, like he's trying to burp up Hugh Grant – she's still kissing someone and I'm not. I'm just alone in a nightclub. At 33. The pitiableness of it hits me like a cartoon tonne. I cannot stay here. I trudge up the stairs to reclaim the bag I checked in and emerge, blinking, into the fading light of the summer's evening.

Realising I need to tell Megan I've left, I dig about for my phone and find it has a message waiting for me.

Josh: Hi Gretts. How's your Friday night out going?

It's only 9.02 p.m. Too early for a bootie call, so what the hell is this? Is it a genuine message? Because he likes me and wants to know how my night is going?

I grin as I realise I can finally send one of those breezy flirty messages you're supposed to send men in the early phases. The message where you're out having an amazing time and invite them along all spontaneous and carefree. Normally on a Friday I'm in bed, reading *Little House in the Big Woods* and wondering if it's problematic that I fancy Pa, and feeling smug about no impending hangover. But tonight I've morphed into Gretel. And Gretel is totally out at 9 p.m. and can send that message. Josh won't be able to meet me anyway. London is too big, with everyone always at least fifty minutes away from everyone, so it's a win-win. I can get the Tube home and be the hermit I'm longing to be but without him realising I'm a hermit. This is perfect!

I fire back a message as I stumble, blinking, out onto the streets, struggling to adjust to the sun still in the sky; the weird twilight zone of Calculus's downstairs drunken universe fading.

Gretel: I'm out in Bank. It's terrible! You should totally come along.

I'm lost in a side street when he replies. I don't look at it immediately as I'm in the midst of deciphering the little map at a Boris Bike station. 'Where the hell is the Tube station?' I ask it, like it's a person, tracing a path with my finger before I check his reply. 'Oh bollocking fucking hellfire.'

Joshua: No way! I'm around Bank too! Are the stars aligning Gretel? Where you at? I'll come over and say hi.

'No!' I say, because I'm not Gretel and therefore I'm *not* OK with this totally spontaneous change of plans. 'No no no no no no *no*.' I'm stuck in a moment of complete indecision. Right now, I cannot compute that Joshua is nearby and I may have to meet him. I'm tired, I'm drunk, I've lied to him about who I am. The map blurs as my mind sifts through the options. The most obvious being: *stop this madness, April. Just don't reply to him. Let Gretel die. It's only been one date. You pretended to be someone else for one date. That is fucking weird and concerning, granted, but you're having a hard time right now. Laugh it off. Nobody will ever find out. But don't reply. Gretel can ghost him. There is no way this situation is anything other than nuts, so please for the love of God, April, stop it, go home and get a good night's sleep.*

Gretel: This is too weird! I just left a club and I'm on my way west soon, but I can drop in and meet you for one?
Josh: I'm in Forge. You know it? I'm a bit smelly in my work clothes, just warning you.
Gretel: See you in ten. And fret not, natural musk really does it for me. X

I lean against the bike map for a moment, revelling in how smooth that was. I would never have the confidence to send a message like that usually. I message Megan, to let her know I've left. Then give myself a moment to collect myself in this weird multiple-part evening. The sun's finally started to slink down the sky, offering the city a breeze and some respite from the heat. The tall buildings filled with self-important people doing questionably-important jobs cast long shadows through the sunset's gold. Tranquillity settles in me. There's the noise of fun being had and memories being made and, tonight, I am part of it. So often this is a city where you feel like an outsider looking in, hands pressed against a glass box, watching everyone else doing it better and having more friends and knowing the places to go and getting the hang of it. You're all breathing the same highly-polluted air and yet you've never felt lonelier. However, sometimes, like right now, you break down that wall and are able to crawl under London's skin and feel its heartbeat pulse through you . . .

These are all very grand thoughts to be having for someone who was, less than half an hour ago, dancing like an eejit to 'Come On Eileen'. I laugh at that. Out loud, into the setting sun. Loud and carefree and, oh my God, sometimes maybe I am capable of occasionally being like Gretel . . .

Gretel.

Shit!

What am I doing? I have to go and meet Joshua in, like, five minutes and I'm a drunken state! I can't be Gretel like this.

Shit shit shit.

I pull out my compact mirror to assess my face and it's not great if truth be told. I've sweated off most of my make-up. My eye make-up especially has drizzled halfway down my cheeks, and my mascara's clumped into the biggest black booger you've ever seen, like a mouse shat in the corner of my eye. My hair's moist and lank, yet has also managed to add 'frizzy' to its repertoire.

I do not look like a Manic Pixie Dream Girl Next Door Slut With No Problems.

I look like April, a thirty-something woman who has lost it, gone weird, and got hammered in a nightclub meant for people ten years younger than her.

How much highlighter do I need to apply to undo that?

I get to work quickly. Setting up a little workstation in the front basket of one of the bikes. I pluck out my eye booger with my fingernail and wipe it on the back of my dress. I retrieve a dirty cotton bud from the depths of my handbag, pick off the outer layer to reveal a vaguely white bit, then scrape it under my eyes to wipe up the melted make-up. When the worst of it has been erased, I quickly apply more (subtle) make-up to the blank canvas. I then miraculously find myself able to French-plait the front section of my hair to pull the sweaty bit away from my face. I can never usually French-plait but the alcohol's given me this weird ability, in the same way it can make you inexplicably good at pool sometimes.

I check myself again.

There. Done.

I use my phone to figure out where Forge is. I'll be ten minutes later than I said I would be but that's only because there were so many people to say goodbye to before I left. Sorry. You know how it is when you try to leave somewhere. God, isn't it hot today? I hope I look OK. It's been go go go since I woke up, I swear my face must look like a melted snowman's. Oh, I look perfect, you say? No way! You're lying. Bless you.

I get into character as I dodge the clusters of loud office-workers spilling out onto pavements, clutching pink pints of flavoured beers, and delaying going home to their lonely flat-shares. I smile at everyone I saunter past, and receive many smiles back. I arrive outside Forge, which is surrounded by a dense moat of drunken sunshine seekers. It's not rained for weeks now, but we're still all desperate to make the most of it. My confidence wavers as I realise I know no one here, and I'm about to meet not only Josh, who is basically a stranger, but all of his workmates too. It takes a moment to shake April off and find Gretel again, who isn't even thinking about what it means to meet a man's workmates on a second date, she's just enjoying this crazy little adventure we all share called Life with a capital L.

Gretel is such a fucking dick, I swear.

'Gretel!'

There's a delay between Josh calling my name and me registering he means me.

He tries again. 'Gretel!'

This time I kick in, twisting in the direction of his voice, a playful smile already on my face. I spot him amongst the ocean of loosened ties, and raise a hand to wave hi. He's standing with a group of all men cradling mostly finished pints. I feel their eyes on me as I make my way over, weaving gracefully through the throng, keeping my smile on the whole time. I reach Josh, and, without hesitating, lean in for a hello kiss on the cheek. 'This is so weird that you're here,' I say, faking excitement at the odds of it. 'It was a good thing you messaged when you did, I was about to get on the Tube.'

I can tell Josh is drunk from the sweetness on his breath and the way he clutches me a bit too intimately for only one date.

I wave at the clutch of IT men. 'Hi, I'm Gretel,' I say, picturing my floating Pocahontas trail. 'Who wants a drink?' I point to their mostly empty pints and, bewildered by my sudden arrival, they nod.

Shit. That's all my payday money gone within one evening.

'Great! Same again?' I turn to Josh who's still grinning at me with his slightly sunburnt, excitable, drunken face. 'And you?'

'Yes, that would be great. Cheers.'

That's another fiver.

'Brilliant!'

The bar inside is dark, cooler, and adorned with fake flowers hanging inexplicably from the ceiling. It's mostly empty apart from the scrabble of people at the bar. The staff wilt behind the counter, leaning over and letting people yell instructions, nodding, while also frantically scanning the rest of the queue to see if they'll ever get a breather. One lines up a queue of Magners, splashing each bottle into pint glasses filled with ice, a sheen of sweat glistening on his face like a glazed doughnut. I scan the queue for the best entry point, doing the maths of crowd flow to figure out where to stand to get served quicker. I pick a spot, push in, and, I'm just in the process of trying to make eye contact with a barmaid when I feel Josh's presence behind me. I arrange my face into a smile and twist around. His face is already in a giant grin.

'Well, fancy seeing you here,' I say, blinking more than I normally do.

His grin stretches wider. He's too drunk to hide how very glad he is to see me. 'I thought I'd come and pay for your round,' he explains. 'It's very polite of you to offer and every-thing, but I don't feel it's right for you to blow fifty quid on beer for my work friends.'

The thoughtfulness almost makes me stumble. That, and the relief that I don't have to financially cripple myself buying six London Pale Ales. 'Thank you,' I tell him, just as I manage to grab the bar lady's attention. I lean over and shout my order at her then I turn back to Josh as we wait. 'That's really kind, thank you.'

'Just the right thing to do,' he mumbles, blushing at my gratitude.

'Well now I don't have to remortgage my house in order to pay for this round.'

He laughs. 'No, now I'll have to remortgage mine.'

'And live in an empty pint glass.'

'Hey, at least the pint glass is branded with the logo of this super cool pale ale that's brewed on-site.'

'All the hipsters will be living in these pint glasses in a year's time. You're so ahead of the curve.'

He lets out another seal-bark of laughter, putting his hand on my back to reiterate how funny he finds me. The physical contact, again, ignites annoying chemicals that dance around the spot where we're touching.

'It's nice to see you again,' he layers the come-on.

'You too.'

We stare at each other, and his green eyes really are very pleasant. I think it's impossible for any woman in my age bracket not to find green eyes have some kind of kryptonite effect. The drawing scene in *Titanic* came out at a very influ-ential time in our sexual development.

'Six pints of pale ale and a rum and coke,' the bar lady announces, gesturing to the cornucopia of glasses in front of her. 'That's forty-two pounds ninety, please.'

Keeping his hand on my back, Joshua steps forward with his card. He's standing so close that most of his left side touches most of my right. I start collecting up the drinks to distract myself from my bodily stirrings. There's no way I can continue with this if I lose sight of myself and get chemically involved, even though I'm not really sure what 'this' is. Apart from maybe a very significant psychotic melt-down. That, or I'm living in someone's intense revenge fantasy fanfic.

We weave back to his workmates who are at the point of drunk where they cheer our arrival. I hand out their drinks and they thank me, not realising I'm not the one who paid for them. Then they return to their huddle and their boring conversation about office gossip.

'So, yes, if we don't launch till October, then Michael will definitely resign . . .'

'The problem with that operating system is it's so hackable, how they cannot see that . . .'

'When do you think they're going to announce if we get Christmas to New Year as extra annual leave? I don't know whether to book a holiday in September or not . . .'

I clutch my glass and try to nod in the right places but there is literally no way to join in office conversations regarding an office you don't work in. Not even Gretel has that superpower. Luckily, after ten minutes about the upcoming pension meeting, Josh saves me, twisting me away from the huddle.

'I'm sorry,' he smiles apologetically. 'I didn't mean to drag you away from your crazy night out for you to listen to dull talk about operating systems.'

'But it's my life goal fulfilled.'

'Where have you been tonight anyway?'

I flash back to only an hour ago. Flinging myself around a cheesy and morally questionable bar with a bunch of youths like a geriatric mess. 'All over,' I say. 'My housemate Megan met someone though, so I thought I'd move on.'

'So you have a housemate then?' he asks.

I nod. They're maybe not the most aspirational thing to still have at 33, but Gretel lives in London and doesn't have rich parents who can help her afford somewhere gentrified in Brixton. I can't fake that. 'Yes, Megan. It's her flat. We're university friends. How about you?'

He shakes his head. 'No. I live by myself. I'm scared of housemates. After I had to move out from my ex's, I ended up living with this terrifying guy called Donny from SpareRoom. He was so racist I think he should have been entered into some kind of Olympics. He managed to make literally every conversation racist. You'd say, "Morning Donny, it's a lovely morning, isn't it?" and his reply would be, I'm not even joking, "Yeah, it's supposed to be twenty-three today. The blacks will fucking love it, won't they?"'

I almost spit out my drink.

'I know! I was stuck in a fucking contract with that man till the break clause came up. And in that time he'd actually tried to make me go on a British Pride march.'

The mention of the ex has not gone unnoticed amongst the other shocking parts of his story. April brain rushes in: *Does he still love her? Wow, they lived together, that means it must've been serious. This means he's capable of a long-term relationship. Well, is he though? Because they broke up. I wonder why?* I shake my head to dislodge the thoughts.

'Sounds like you had quite the escape,' Gretel says.

'From my ex, or my crazy replacement housemate?'

'Only you know the answer to that,' Gretel says, because she is not threatened by the mention of exes. She understands that we all have a past, that's just life, isn't it.

'I'm still trying to figure out the answer to that,' Josh mumbles into his pint.

I raise my eyebrows. Uh oh. Emotional baggage. Here it comes. We made it to almost-date two before it surfaced. I find the exchanging of 'why-I'm-fucked-up' suitcases comes earlier in a relationship the later into your thirties you get.

'Sorry,' he says, smiling again. 'I take you away from your night out to chat about operating systems, and then take you away from them to tell you about all my problems.'

I smile like it doesn't bother me at all. 'It's great. You should turn it into a themed club night.'

'It will be the talk of London.' We both look at one another and laugh over the rims of our drinks. Mutual attraction obvious and unfurling. Joshua's workmates have re-clumped with their backs to us, like penguins, leaving us to flirt.

'So, no skeletons in your closet then, Gretel?'

I point out my finger. 'Hey, this is technically only date one point five. Surely it's too soon for the skeleton chat?'

Joshua takes another sip of his beer alongside another appreciative body scan of me. 'I just don't get how someone like you is single.'

Gretel smiles serenely. 'I'm just picky, that's all. If I'm going to jump, and change my life, it's going to have to be for someone pretty special.' I return his glance, to give him a hint that maybe, just maybe, he is the someone special. I want to vomit down myself as I do so.

'That's wise,' he replies. 'That's very wise.'

I let there be silence so he can talk more because men so very love talking. I expect him to go off on a monologue, like he did on our first date, but he surprises me by asking more questions about me and acting genuinely interested in my replies.

'So Gretel, that's an interesting name. Where did that come from?'

I'd already rehearsed this answer. 'My mum always loved fairy tales,' I reply. 'We used to read them all the time when I was little. It must've come from there.'

'Why Gretel though? Why not Cinderella or I dunno . . . what's another fairy-tale name?'

'Rumpelstiltskin?'

He barks his seal laugh. 'Yeah, why didn't she call you that?'

'Oh, you know, the usual. Cos it would've been child abuse.'

'Well, Gretel's a good name. Congratulations.'

Gretel curtsies, that's just how cute she is. 'So do you like your job?' I ask him, to make it less about me.

'Does *anyone* like their job?'

'I like mine.'

'You work for a charity, don't you?'

I nod. 'Yes, it's great. I genuinely love it.' It feels nice to have just one part of April match with Gretel. My job is that. 'Like, I rarely get sad on Sunday evenings because I really like going in most days. Not every day, of course, but most of them. I sound like I'm in a job interview, but honestly, working for a charity is so rewarding.'

'That's amazing,' he says. 'Really amazing.'

We launch into mutually drunken conversation, becoming one of those pissed couples you see, standing outside a pub on a summer's evening, leaning in a bit too much to hear what the other is saying. He asks me about my plans for the summer, and I say I'm saving up for Africa. He is going to Green Man festival with his friends from university, something they do every year. Apart from the ones who have kids now, of course. We stumble into politics, relieved to learn that we are both of the left-voting persuasion. This excitement dims a bit on my part as now, predictably, Josh is explaining politics to me. Regurgitating facts he has read on the *Guardian*'s website, claiming them as his own, subconsciously dismissing the fact that I have just admitted to him that I, too, read the *Guardian*, and therefore am likely to have read the same articles and know the same facts and know where he's got them from.

But Gretel is so grateful that he's teaching her more about politics. 'Oh, yes, you're right,' she says, putting her hand on his, just for a moment. 'I've not thought about it like that.' She's careful to chime in with a tiny titbit here and there, just to reassure Josh that she's well-informed *enough,* just not as much as he is. 'Oh, yes, I read about that. It's so sad for Jerusalem,' she chirps. He looks momentarily surprised, then a bit relieved, then a bit enchanted, and then a bit threatened. He tells me more facts he's read off the *Guardian* about Jerusalem. His workmates are forgotten. The sun is finally down. Some come over and say goodbye and we reluctantly break for Joshua to say 'I'll see you on Monday' and for me to say 'it was nice to meet you'. We lean back into one another before they've even left. We share stories of being young, of both growing up in boring suburban towns and the weird stuff you used to do in order to pass time as a teenager.

'Do you remember, when you were, like, 11, downing loads of own-brand cola from the supermarket to get "hyper"?' I ask.

'Oh my God, hyper! I forgot about getting hyper! We used to do the same, but we added sachets of sugar into the cola to make it extra strong.'

'Yikes. Speed balling. Aged 11. You sound like a right rebel.'

He takes my hand and squeezes it, and it's annoying how good it feels. 'Oh Gretel,' he says. 'I work in IT. You have no idea how long I've waited for someone to use the word "rebel" in reference to me.'

'Rebel.'

'Please keep saying that.'

'Oh my God, Joshua, you're such a rebel.'

'This is the best day of my life.'

I lean my head to the side. 'What can I say, rebel? I'm here to make all your dreams come true.'

Then he's kissing me, just like that. On the pavement, with the braying of pissed humans all around us. I didn't see the kiss coming but I go with it, my head bleary with too many different types of alcohol. Joshua's too pushy with his tongue and I have to concentrate on breathing through my nose. I wonder for a moment how he can get to his age and still think this is an appropriate amount of tongue.

Then I remember a fact I read in one of the self-help books about how men use tongue kissing to get you to taste their pheromones. He lets out a little groan and kisses me even deeper, pulling me closer and spilling a bit of beer down the back of my dress. I let Gretel ignore it, as she is supposed to be so into this kiss. And, again, what's annoying is, even though Joshua isn't a very good kisser, my body is still doing all sorts of things in response to this kiss. I can taste our compatibility. I can feel my heart thud harder under the thin fabric of my dress. I can feel feelings brewing, a desire unfurling, the urge to be with him and win him and keep him and grow mini hims in my stomach. Sex is such a trap. I forget every time how much it sucks you in, and sucks you dry, makes you lose sight of yourself and your actual needs – rather than the needs activated by biological tripwires and unmet childhood developmental stages. I refuse to be caught though. I am done done done. I can override this. I must. I let him kiss me a while longer, but then I break it off. I put my forehead to his.

'Well I wasn't expecting that to happen,' I whisper, which is the truth actually.

'I really fancy you,' he says, before pulling me back into a kiss despite my clear signal to stop. I try not to roll my eyes as I let his need to kiss me overrule my desire to not be kissed any more. I am well-rehearsed in this sort of thing. It's as easy as tying a shoelace, letting men push past my boundaries. Easier than sneezing. I pull away as quickly as I can get away with though.

'So, you fancy me, huh?'

'I think it's obvious that I do.'

'Makes dating so much easier, doesn't it? When you fancy them?' I am careful not to tell him I fancy him back. Now is not the time for that card. He needs to worry and stew that maybe I don't.

He laughs. 'Yes. Much easier. So, can I see you again?'

I pretend to think about it. 'I guess.'

'Will that make it date two or date three?'

'It's so cute that you're counting.'

'Why? Aren't you?'

I tap my nose and he seems to find that so attractive that we have to kiss some more and even more urgently. He's drunk and he's horny and I know I could easily have sex with him tonight if I wanted to. Not that I want to, but I allow myself a moment of feeling powerful that I could.

I pull away, again, as my phone buzzes. 'Hang on, I need to check this.'

Megan: I'm in a cab back to his. I'm fine. I'm fully consenting. This is a message to say I don't think I'll end up dead in a ditch tonight. Xxx

I'm just typing out a reply when my phone goes again.

Megan: WHAT IF I'VE FORGOTTEN HOW TO HAVE SEX? IT'S BEEN AGES! IS IT STILL THE SAME?

'What's so funny?' Joshua asks my neck as he kisses it.

'Oh, just a message from my housemate. I have to go and meet her now.' The lie falls effortlessly from my mouth. 'I really have to go. This has been great though.' I twist my neck out of his grasp, quickly peck him on the lips, and then pick up my handbag which I've let fall to the pavement.

'Are you really going?' His mouth is still half-open.

'Yes I am.'

'But date three, right?'

'Only if you bring a mint chocolate Viennetta.'

Megan: I'VE NOT FORGOTTEN HOW TO HAVE SEX! IT'S JUST THE SAME.

Joshua: Hey Gretel, it was great seeing you tonight x

April: It's like riding a bike, isn't it? Ha ha. RIDE. Congratulations on getting laid. Do you want to get brunch tomorrow and debrief?

Gretel: Had a great time too. Night!

April: Are you dead? Has he killed you?
Megan: Not dead. Just shagging. Won't be back till tomorrow.

Megan: Maybe Monday.
Megan: I'm FINE. He's really nice!
April: Megan . . .
April: Are you relapsing? You've been clean for two years.

*

Joshua: Hey Gretel, good weekend? When is it going to rain? I've forgotten what rain feels like. Anyway, how about a picnic in the

158

park this week? I'll cook* and bring you that ice cream you
wanted x

   *buy stuff from M&S

Gretel: Hey, weekend good thanks. I'm pretty packed this week,
but can maybe do Wed?

Gretel: PS: Assembling M&S pots of stuff defo counts as
cooking.

Joshua: Wednesday it is x

Joshua: I'm looking forward to seeing you Gretel x

*

April: Just checking you're still alive? It's now Monday morning.
MONDAY. Just in case you've forgotten.

Megan: Still alive! Back tomorrow I think.

April: You're not falling in love with him, are you?

Megan: Maybe . . .

April: Megan . . .

Megan: IT'S FINE!

*

Message received: 08:02

*Hey, I've never written into something like this before. Sorry if
I'm being stupid. Sorry. I'm just a bit confused about
something that happened with my boyfriend. We were having
sex and then he just sort of started having anal sex with me
without asking. It really hurt but I didn't tell him to stop
because I was quite confused and just sort of froze. He says
he loves me. I really love him. Do you think it was an
accident? Soz. I'm prob just being dramatic. Thx in advance
for your reply.*

From: Matthew@WeAreHere.com
To: April@WeAreHere.com
Subject: You OK?

Just saw there's a few tricky ones in there today.

From: April@WeAreHere.com
To: Matthew@WeAreHere.com
Subject: RE: You OK?

I'm fine buddy. Don't you worry about me. A x

*

Joshua: How's work? My colleagues all said how nice you were when I came in this morning.
Gretel: Work great! The joy of Mondays. Aww, that's nice of them. How's the crazy world of coding going?
Joshua: Yeah, good. Every day I can pretend I'm hacking into the Matrix.
Gretel: There is no spoon.

*

Joshua: Still on for tomorrow? What are your thoughts on chicken and avocado sandwiches?

Gretel: Hey, sorry for the delay in getting back to you. Crazy day. How did you know that chicken and avocado is my one true vice in life?

April: MEGAN COME HOME. I've not spoken to another human outside work for four days now.

Megan: Sorry April. I'll be home tonight.

Megan: April, I think I love him.

April: Get home now!

*

Joshua: I had such a good night tonight, Gretel. Though I do think we should apologise to the pelicans for our gross PDAs x

Gretel: The pelicans loved it. We should've charged them.

Joshua: You free next week?

Gretel: I should be. I just need to juggle some things around.

Joshua: Wanna find some different animals to disgust with our snogging?

Gretel: Did you just use the word snogging, Joshua?

Joshua: Yes. And I'm not ashamed.

Joshua: Is that a yes then?

Gretel: Hey, sorry, fell asleep. Yes. Let's do it next week x

*

April: Staying at Malcolm's again tonight? I thought Friday night were our nights.

Megan: I love it when you message me when we're both in the same flat. Yes. Sorry! I'll be back Sunday. Have you seen my pink lacy knickers? Argh! Staying at a boy's house is so stressful!

April: Sorry. On the loo. Why don't you have him come stay here then?

Megan: Bring him here? Are you kidding me? I can't bring him here.

April: Why not?

Megan: Because he'll see how I live!

April: What's wrong with how you live? PS: We need toilet roll.

Megan: It's a flat. I don't want him to know I live in a flat. He lives in a house. A proper one. With its own door, April. It's own door! In Dulwich. He has a garden. A front door and a garden.

April: We have a front door . . .

Megan: Yeah that we have to SHARE with people. I can't let him know that I share a front door. He might be the love of my life. It will all go out the window if he knows I share a door.

Megan: I've never felt this way about anyone before . . .

*

Message received: 13:17

hi my friend steve walked me home the other night because i was too drunk and he said he wanted to make sure i got home safe but then he came into my house and pushed me to have sex with him and then acted like nothing had happened the next morning had to take the morning after pill. v confused pls help

*

Message received: 12:04

My uber driver raped me last night. What do I do?

*

Joshua: Another great date, Gretel. You're quite good at this, aren't you?

Gretel: What can I say? You bring out the best in me.

Joshua: I could say the same about you.

Gretel: This is too cute, I may throw up.

Joshua: 😍

Gretel: Did you just heart eyes emoji me?

Joshua: 😍 😍 😍 😍

Gretel: Ever heard of playing it cool, Joshua?

Joshua: Ever heard of taking it easy on a guy, Gretel?

Gretel: 😍

Joshua: The modern equivalent of a sonnet.

*

Megan: Hey hon. OK, so this sounds crazy, but I looked up his ex-girlfriend and is she prettier than me?

Megan: There's this photo here. I like her dress, but she looks a bit old, right?

Megan: And then there's this one. She looks better in this one. I am prettier, right?

Megan: Right?

Megan: Sorry. I'll stop being mental now. I've deleted Facebook off my phone and I'm working really hard on this launch party. I'm fine! Sorry! Ignore me. Silly moment.

Megan: How about in this photo?

Megan: I put Facebook back on my phone.

Megan: Sorry. No more being crazy. Phew! I'm going to concentrate on my CAREER and this launch I'm in charge of and stop worrying about some stupid bitch called Regina who looks like she's got chew and spit disorder.

Megan: OK. But in that last photo? Botox, right?

*

Joshua: Morning Gretel! Happy Thursday! It's the weekend tomorrow. Whoop! I was just thinking, how about we remove animals from our dating agenda and add in a roof? Fancy coming around to mine tomorrow? I'll actually cook, rather than just arrange pots of things.

Gretel: Sounds great. Can I bring anything?

Joshua: Just your gorgeous self. 7?

Gretel: Can't wait x

On our third date, Joshua pulled out all the stops for the picnic. He brought a folded blanket, a cold bottle of prosecco, a giant assortment of chilled foodstuffs from M&S and a melted Viennetta in a seeping box which I laughed at. He kissed me the moment I rocked up to St James's Park station, with tongue, just to reaffirm that we'd already crossed this sexual boundary and were going to continue to do so. The conversation flowed as easily as the alcohol. He's a funny man. He's easy to talk to. Effortless and bubbly and also very happy to talk about himself, which Gretel let him do of course. We made out in front of the pelicans. I let him kiss me and stare at me with the hope and wonder you can only have in the very early days before you really know anything about someone.

'Maybe, this time; maybe she is different', I could imagine him thinking.

He was better at kissing when less drunk. Less tongue. It was not unpleasant. I fancy the guy. I'll admit that. I fancy the guy. But I also have no heart left to give him, and, even if I did, that is not why I'm doing this. We talked about his job some more and how he feels frustrated with the current management structure. We talked about his parents and how they wear matching cagoules to go on really long walks, and how they never leave Norwich. He briefly mentioned his ex again when I mentioned Chrissy's upcoming hen do – slipping it out like an accidental fart. 'Fiona was *obsessed* with getting married,' he mumbled, before apologising.

I wondered silently what he did to her in the relationship to make her insecure enough to be obsessed with getting married. Or what he didn't do. His poor ex.

'Weddings are ludicrous, aren't they?' Gretel said, stretching her arms up into the sun. 'They're so over the top and I think people get married for the wrong reason.'

He beamed at me. 'That's exactly what I think.'

I laughed inwardly when I thought of the amount of time I've spent planning my wedding since I was a child. The flowers, the dress – and how it adapts over time depending on the current fashions – the food, the playlist, the location, the readings. And then I considered all the time I've spent pretending I *don't* think any of this, to men, so they think I'm someone I'm not and can love me better and therefore I can have the wedding.

We kissed again. I started it, to change the subject. We kissed and hardly ate anything. We kissed and were shouted at to get a room. We kissed every twenty or so paces as we walked back to the Tube, and, once there, we kissed some more.

On the next date, we went to London Zoo for their Zoo Nights event. Joshua paid, which was just as well because it's bloody expensive to get in. We walked with our arms around one another as we skidded around groups of excitable drunk twenty-somethings to look at lions dozing in the heat that still won't go away.

'Look at that otter,' Joshua said, leaning his chin onto my

head as he pointed one out. 'He so thinks he's better than the other otters with that rock.'

'I think his name is Jarvis,' I replied.

'Jarvis the cocky otter. Sounds like a great children's TV show.'

Several minutes of our lives were lost to imagining Jarvis's day to day existence. Giving him a back story and a narrative thrust, and, ultimately, a redemption arch. Then Jarvis appeared to give another otter his little rock and we both squealed in delight that our story had come true. This required a celebratory kiss that was so intense someone threw an empty bottle at us and we moved on giggling, like teenagers.

'So, it's rather frustrating that you're not very stalkable online,' he said, as we walked holding hands and licking overpriced but lacklustre ice cream. 'Literally you were nowhere to be found on social media.'

I grinned as I imagined him typing in the word 'Gretel'. 'I'm not on any social media,' I said. 'Why? Are you on it? Doesn't it just make you unhappy?'

It occurred to me that, like him, I usually would've checked by now. If I'd had a quiet moment at work, or a low moment at home, I'd have typed his name into the search bar of various websites, feeling uneasiness and guilt in my stomach, like he could sense I was doing it. Feeling sicker if I found an album still open from the holiday he went on with his university girlfriend in 2009 because people didn't use privacy settings back then. Wondering if she was the best sex he'd ever had. Knowing he'd been to Croatia, but when he brought up the place in a real-life interaction later on, having to act surprised to learn he'd been to Croatia, rather than say, 'yes, I know, you went with your ex, didn't you? Tell me, are you still in love with her and only dating me because she dumped you, but you'd drop me the moment she returned? Did you do a sixty-nine together? And, can you remember what shampoo she uses because her hair is really nice?'

'Yes, for my sins.' Joshua took a lick of his vanilla cone, as I reflected on him being the sort of person who actually says 'for my sins' out loud. 'I just assumed it's something everyone is on, whether they like it or not. It didn't occur to me there's an option.'

'There's always an option. You don't have to do everything the world expects of you.'

It was such a Gretel thing to say, and it went down a treat. He stopped us next to a sign that explained how deforestation works and kissed me next to it, ice cream rolling down our hands. 'You're so right,' he half-whispered. 'Right, that's it. I'm deleting Facebook off my phone so I can be carefree like you.'

I almost choked on my cone. I'd never been called carefree in my entire existence no matter how hard I have tried to hide my anxiety. The adjective people most use about me, and when I say 'people', I mean men in the process of dumping me, is 'intense'.

No, the dates couldn't be going better. Joshua has surprised even me in his lack of aloofness – how happy he seems to be that this is quickly heading into relationship territory. Revealing vulnerable things like the fact he's tried to stalk me online, rather than playing it cool. I've had the occasional thought blip that maybe it's because he's actually nice, but mostly I marvel at the Gretel effect, and how easy a man finds it to give his heart to a unicorn. Either way, I have felt like I'm walking three inches off the pavement by having so much power, by seeing him fall for me, by knowing it's false and I'm not the one who is going to get hurt here.

But when I look at the latest message I feel scared for the first time.

Because . . .

Because . . .

I could only keep it up for so long. We're entering date five. He's been patient. He will worry something is wrong if we don't have it soon, and nothing's wrong with Gretel in that department thank you very much.

Gretel needs to have sex with Joshua, which means I need to have sex with Joshua.

• *Fucking Without Fucking It Up — Gretel's Guide to Hot Sex*

First-time sex with anyone new is nerve-wracking, so it's natural to be apprehensive which, sorry, is really unsexy. Confidence is what he desires. A woman who loves her body, and loves his body, and has no hang-ups and is totally up for anything. Make sure you get ready 'down there' and now's the time to dig out that super-hot lingerie. It's bound to make him go wild. The most important thing is to relaaaaaax and enjoy it and be up for anything and maybe hum when you go down on him and blah blah blah blah. . .

Sex after rape is a complicated beast. First of all, it's worth making it clear that rape isn't sex. It isn't sex at all. Yes, it involves the components of sex – a body entering another body – but rape is not sex, rape is violence and rape is power. Rape is the entitlement someone feels to someone else's body, regardless of the consequences on the soul inhabiting that body, who has to spend every moment of the rest of their life knowing their body is not as important as someone else's entitlement. And because sex is so very different from rape, what people don't understand is that you can have been raped and still really want to have a sex life. You can have been raped and still desire. You can have been raped and still desire angry, hot, thrusty, sex. You can have been raped and still want to initiate. You can have been raped and be sexually aggressive yourself. In fact, take every weird and wonderful thing that human beings desire on the giant spectrum of sexuality – the fetishes, the fantasies, the toys – a victim of rape can desire any of these things and it has nothing to do with their rape. You still want the things you want, crave the things you crave. Because sexuality and rape have nothing to do with each other.

What's strange about your sexuality after being raped is that it changes nothing and yet it also changes everything.

Sex is never the same, not quite. Because once that act of

violence is ripped into you, it's almost impossible to not let it bleed into sex. On an intellectual level you know this is different – loving, consensual, hell you're on top and you're the one who started this thing. But, emotionally, your body remembers, it wonders if it's happening again. And even though rape has nothing to do with sex, it still takes your sexuality away. It's snatched from you. In your head, much as you don't want to admit it, you are now a victim of rape. Well, you think you are. You're never quite sure if you're allowed to use that label. Not for you, not for your violation. Not when so many women are violated much worse. This messes with you on so many levels. How can you be a victim of rape when the rape itself was quiet and by someone you know and maybe you've just been over-reacting? How can you be a victim of rape when you weren't dragged into an alleyway? How can you be a victim of rape if you still want sex? Surely that diminishes it? Surely you're taking a label away from someone, someone more deserving of it?

But you *were* raped. You know you were. Your body and soul knows you were.

On your bad days you curl up into a ball and sob uncontrollably about the fact you were. Or you know you were but you can't handle it and don't want to open up that box thank you very much because you're terrified it will destroy you when you finally do, so you push it down and numb it out and continue getting on with this torturous business of living a life hoping eventually that the big ball of shame and confusion and pain will erode away, rather than blobbing after you quietly, tapping you on the shoulder every so often, saying, 'I'm here because you were raped, and I'm sorry but I don't think I can go away.' And you bat it off and numb it out and drink too much and fuck fuck fuck men to prove how well you can do it, even though the blob of emotions is hanging like a limp balloon in the corner.

Or you have learnt to wear the label, to talk about the label, to get up and say 'I am a victim and this happened to me' and other people say you are brave and other people are wondering if maybe you are making it up. And you tell people you want to have sex with and hope beyond hope it doesn't change how they see you, how they screw you, but, also, at the same time, you secretly want them to be more gentle, more caring, more understanding, but also really fancy you and not see that label ever, and not let it change how they have sex with you. And you know it's an impossible task and you wonder whether it's better not to tell anyone, because you are so much more than a victim of rape, but then, also you are still a victim of rape. You are both, and that is inescapable.

You wish every day that you'd just never been raped.

You feel sick with jealousy at women who have never been raped. You fantasise about how amazing their sex lives must be without all the 'rape clutter' that you're constantly rummaging through and trying to make love through, and you hate them for having it so easy. Then you start talking to other women and realise there are hardly any women you've met who *haven't* been raped. They say one in five and I call bullshit, probably more like four out of five.

But people get uncomfortable when you say things like that.

The thing about being a victim of rape is you are constantly a source of discomfort. To yourself, as well as others. So many men have sex with women who have been raped, and yet they do not know it. Because the women don't tell them, because, here's the thing: it's so hard to admit . . . Being raped is the least sexy thing ever.

It has nothing to do with sex and yet everything to do with sex.

It's too complicated and painful and there's nowhere for the shame to go, so you bury it and bury it and try to be like the other women. The other women who do not carry this ball of anger and shame and can fling their legs open and pant and scream. You pretend to be them. Sometimes you can con yourself, and him. Other times you can only con him. You tuck your sexual trauma away to make yourself sexier to the species who took your sexuality away from you.

There are so many of us, and yet maybe there aren't. And you don't want to be the broken one. Especially as it wasn't your fault this happened to you, although, of course, sometimes you worry it *was* your fault.

So you pretend, a lot, that you're fine. That you're like the other girls. But . . . maybe you are pretending to be a woman everyone else is pretending to be too?

I take the morning off work.

I shave my legs. I sit in the bath and do it properly, with shaving foam and everything. And a new razor blade, even though they cost a fortune. I lift my arms out from the bubbles and scythe off the regrowth in my armpit. It takes me a while to decide what to do about my pubes. In the end, I decide that perfect Gretel would have a perfect amount of them. Enough so she doesn't look like a child, because men can feel a bit guilty about that, even though porn has trained them to crave it. But not too much because she's a grown woman. It's so hot I hardly need a towel to dry off. But I still roll myself up in one, like a jam roly poly, and spend several minutes sitting in the sunlight that is chucking itself through my window, having lots of thoughts about what I'm planning to do, and how I know it's such an act of self-harm, but I'm going to do it anyway.

I stay in my towel and stare at the wall. Even with the morning off, I may still be late for work.

'Get ready,' I say out loud. 'Get up April and get ready.'

I don't get up.

'No,' I reply to myself. 'I don't want to.'

'But you've got to go to work.'

'Living life and being an adult is terrible. Why does nobody tell you how terrible it is?'

'April. Stop being weird and get ready.'

'FINE then, I WILL.'

I rub scented body lotion into my skin, and lie naked on my bed waiting for it to sink in properly while I look at the crack in the ceiling and wonder if anyone would do anything about it if I were to scream. I should probably use my trainers to 'prep the area'. In all the sex advice, 'prepping' usually refers to trimming your pubes with a pair of IKEA scissors or something like that, but, in my case, it involves stretching the muscles of my traumatised vagina. I roll off the bed and open the drawer under it, sifting through all the things I hide under there: my vibrator, lube, condoms that I rarely get the chance to use. Right at the back I find the ghastly pink bag of equipment the NHS gave me two years ago. My stomach tightens as I pick it up – just the gross hue of pink is enough to ignite several painful memories associated with this bag and the things inside it. I get out my hand mirror and a cotton bud from my dressing table, then reach into my bag and unscrew the small bottle of lidocaine numbing gel. I examine my genitals for a moment. It's always a shock, looking at your vulva in a mirror. Even with all the practise I've had through using these trainers over the years. I always find it vaguely grotesque and worry it's different and wrong. Which, considering I need to use vaginal trainers, it sort of is. I squeeze the lidocaine onto the Q-tip, then, using my mirror, I apply the gel around the entrance of my vagina like I was taught to at the hospital clinic. It burns like it always does. I get a flashback to my first appointment. My legs in stirrups. Screaming as they tested me because it hurt so much. 'I can't even use tampons any more,' I cried at them. 'What's happened to me?' They looked sympathetic. They told me how normal this is for survivors of rape. They reassured me the trainers would help, but they also said, 'You may not ever be able to have penetrative sex again.'

Now in my bedroom, one tear drizzles down my cheek but I pretend it hasn't, even though I flinch as the cotton bud hits each gland. I get out the dilators while I wait for the effects of the gel to take hold. They slide out of each other like white plastic Russian-doll dildos. I pluck out the smallest one, the size of a mini tampon, and hold it between my thumb and forefinger. I lay back on my pillows, open my legs, and, like I was taught to, take three deep breaths to relax my muscles. On the last breath, I push the plastic inside my body. It slides in fine with not even a wince. Relief gushes over me. The success of this relaxes me enough to go up one size and repeat the process. It slides in fine too. I go up a size and up a size, stretching myself bigger with each one. 'A bit like driving a car', they told me. 'Always go up through the gears, never start with the largest dilator.' After five minutes, I'm ready for it. 'Mr Big' as I've affectionately nicknamed him. I extract the giant, white, plastic penis-replicate from the pink bag, rub a little lube onto the end, take another deep breath and push it up slowly. It's slightly uncomfortable as it's made of hard plastic, but it's up it's up it's up. I lie back on my pillow, legs askew, and leave it in there for fifteen minutes like I was taught to do. Smiling.

I can still do this, I can still let things into my body. You didn't take it away from me after all, no matter how hard you tried, you rotten bastard. I won't let you win. I'll never let you win.

When the time's up, I slide the trainer out, collect them

all up and give them a big wash in the sink, drying them with a clean towel before replacing everything into the pink purse. I'm feeling triumphant when I open my top drawer and rummage for my good pair of matching underwear. I pluck out the black lacy bra and knickers and shove them into my bag. It's still too hot today and I want to put them on fresh after work. I know, of course, that what I'm planning to do later is potentially really stupid. Giving myself to someone who doesn't even know my name – for what? An end-game of revenge? But it's not just that, I think, as I shrug on my short-sleeved shirt dress. Every time I have sex with someone, part of me feels like it's payback against Ryan. Like I'm proving that he didn't win.

Eventually, I'm ready to leave the house. I step outside and it's like being slapped in the face by the heat. No breeze offers any respite. People walk slowly on the pavements, sweat pulping down their foreheads, suits ruined before lunchtime. The cold showers of the morning seeming like a million years ago.

They say it might rain later. Finally rain.

'Hi everyone,' I announce to the office when I get in just after 1 p.m.

A few people raise their heads from their keyboard in vague acknowledgement of my arrival, but most remain glued to their screens. The Friday vibe is yet to hit. I mouth 'hello' to Matt and Katy and sit down at my computer, getting right into my shift.

Message received: 08:43

I'm probably overreacting but I've been thinking a lot about something that happened a few years ago. My boyfriend was 18, and I was only 15, and one night, when I was staying at his, he just had sex with me without talking about it, without asking. His parents were out and I went over and I was expecting us to do some stuff, but not that because we'd not been going out very long. But he just did it, and I was so shocked I just went along with it. I didn't know how to say no. I figured it was obvious I wasn't ready, but it clearly wasn't because he did it anyway. We went out for a year after that and had consensual sex throughout our relationship. But now I can't get that first time out of my head. I've struggled to be in a relationship since. Am I weird?

Message received: 12:37

I was kissing some guy in a club the other night when he just shoved his hand up my skirt and into my vagina. I pushed him off and he laughed and I cried when I got home. Not sure why I'm typing this. Just feel a bit strange.

'I'm *fine*,' I snap at Matt, as he loiters behind my chair.

'Are you su—?'

'I SAID I'M *FINE*, OK?'

He and Katy glance at one another but neither of them say anything, and let me get back to my shift.

I'm helping. It's worth it because I'm helping.

The afternoon passes. The sky gathers itself into a tight grey knot, rumbling softly every so often, like a stomach awaiting lunch. The air's so humid you can stick your tongue out and drink from it. We have all the windows open, uselessly, and arguments have started about who has the best fan. At 3 p.m., in an attempt to be Friday and jovial, Mike goes down to the Tesco Express and comes back with a packet of already-half-melted Fabs.

'Ice-cream party in the kitchen,' he announces, more excitable than a children's breakfast-TV presenter.

Everyone lurches up like zombies and clugs themselves next to the kettle, reaching out and grabbing at the ice lollies. Matt sets up his speakers and a Spotify playlist and we're forced to hang around, making small talk and bonding as an office.

'What are your plans for the weekend?' I'm asked a dozen times by the IT guys, the fundraisers and the one HR lady we can afford to keep on.

Forcing myself to have potentially triggering sex for a weird vendetta against a man I've catfished, I think. I *say,* 'Oh, no real plans. It's hard to do anything in this heat. How about you?'

Between slurps of the red bits of their lollies, they tell me about their plans to BBQ or to swim at the Lady's Pond, their fingers sticky from the drips. Katy ends up next to me and gives me a wet wipe without asking.

'Thank you,' I say, taking it, and using it to wash the goo off my hands.

'Are you OK?' she asks again. 'Your shift this afternoon . . .'

'I told you I'm fine.'

'I know, I know, I was just double-checking.'

I want to snap at her, but, instead I force myself to smile. 'Thank you but I really am fine.'

'You sure it's not a Ross-from-*Friends* "I'm *fiiiine*"?' she does the impression perfectly and I snort out an unexpected laugh.

'I promise. Ta. Though I think I'm going to go back and do some work before Mike inevitably lets us go early.'

'He's such a soft touch.'

I pick up another lolly and return to my computer, trying to work through the happy chattering and loud music and not think too much about later.

Joshua wants me there at seven. So Gretel should turn up at around seven fifteen. I wonder if he wants us to have sex before, or after, dinner. I'd rather before, if I'm being honest with you. I still don't understand how anyone can be in the mood with a full, swollen stomach digesting a hunk of beef or whatever it is he's going to cook to impress me. I'm clenching my mouse so tightly that my entire hand is sweating, droplets of it pooling onto the mouse mat. I stare at my hand, like it isn't my own, then somehow it is four thirty and Mike's told us we can all go home early because it's so hot, and the storm is coming and HAPPY FRIDAY!

I'm one of those martyr arseholes who doesn't leave though. As Matt and Katy pack their stuff around me, I just hold my mouse and look at my computer. People must think I'm working. If you just hold your mouse and look at the screen you can pretend so easily that you are working.

'You staying here?' Matt asks.

I nod. 'Yeah. I took a half day. I shouldn't leave early.'

'And you're sure you're—'

'Please. Katy's already triple-checked. I'm fine.'

His eyebrows draw up. He doesn't believe me. 'If you're sure,' he says, doing up the buckle of his cycling helmet with a loud click.

'Surer than sure!'

Katy nods to confirm my mental health while packing up her bag. 'She's finer than Ross from *Friends*,' she says. 'Right, I'm off to enjoy having the flat to myself before Jimmy gets home. Have a good one guys.' She shoves her basket bag over her shoulder and leaves with most of the rest of the office. Mike stays only an extra half an hour before, he too, gets up and starts packing his bag.

'Don't stay too late.' He stands over my desk, where I have a volunteer spreadsheet open that I've not done anything with for two hours. 'It's Friday.'

'I won't.'

I can't anyway. I have to go and have sex with someone. I

wonder what it must be like, to be a girl who looks forward to having sex with someone new. Who anticipates it because she's so un-fucked-up about such things.

I hate that girl.

'Do you mind turning the fans off when you leave?'

'Yep no probs.'

I'm left. It's only five. I have exactly one hour and twenty-seven minutes before I need to leave. Of course, Gretel would not be watching the clock. She'd be too busy working hard at her job, going out for after-work drinks and laughing with her head thrown back, mouth wide and open, her teeth white and clean and straight.

'Hahahaha,' says Gretel. She probably hasn't even decided whether she'll have sex tonight or not. She is the sort of person who 'sees where the night takes her'. It's only coincidence that her body is hair-free and moisturised, and that her underwear is matching. 'How well did that work out?' she'll laugh gleefully afterwards, pointing to her perfectly groomed pubes, full of naked body confidence.

I, meanwhile, pass the time by laying my head on the desk, my neck twisted to one side, staring at the blades of the fan whirring around.

It's fine, I mutter to myself. *It's just sex, stop being weird, April. Stop being so goddamned weird. You fucking fucked-up mess. Stop it.*

I go to the tiny bathroom with not enough natural light and make my face look pre-sex-ready. I brush my teeth so hard that a little speckle of blood splatters out into the sink when I spit. I use toilet roll as a flannel and wash under my armpits, wiping off the odour of the day. I use Citymapper to work out how to get to Joshua's. My phone goes as I'm planning my route.

Joshua: Just got in and cooking up a storm. Hope you like Mexican! X

Joshua: PS: My door bell is a bit confusing. Press the button that says '7' and make sure you're already pushing the door when it buzzes. Any probs, I'll come down and let you in x

I wish he'd stop being so nice. It puts me on edge. Leaves slug trails of guilt glistening through my blood. I remind myself that he's only being nice because he is dating an illusion of a woman rather than an actual woman. If I was being me – tired and too hot and not ready to have sex yet and likely to burst into tears at any given moment – well . . . he wouldn't be so nice then, would he?

I pack my bag, checking I have everything. I turn the fans off, one by one, till the air in the office is so still and muggy you could cut it into slices. Then I make my way to his.

He greets me holding a giant mixing bowl filled with chopped vegetables. 'Gretel! You managed to work the buzzer. Congratulations! That makes you infinitely smarter than most of my friends.'

I am beaming with smiles, there is no insecurity inside this body of mine. Gretel is here and it's Friday and what a wonderful adventure life is. I hold up a bottle of tequila. 'You said we were having Mexican?'

He leans in to kiss me on the cheek. The bowl clashes between us. 'Tequila! You're a legend.' He kisses me again on the lips this time, slipping in a tiny bit of tongue. 'Thank you. Right, come on in. Welcome to my flat!'

He takes the bottle in one hand and returns to the kitchen with the bowl in the other. I take off my sandals and follow him, barefoot, trying to sneak glances around as I do. There isn't a hint of female touch anywhere. The sofa is black and made from cheapish leather. The art's nondescript – masculine lines hung in basic frames. The gadgets are all top-notch however, showing off his IT nerdery. The TV is massive, with all sorts of fancy wireless speaker set-ups. In the corner there's a desk with a giant computer with two monitors and all the gear, plus a laptop. In the kitchen, I see further gadgets littered around the place. Cooking thermometers, and a posh coffee-maker. Things with fiddly bits and instruction manuals that would need to be read properly in order to get them to work.

'Margarita?' Joshua asks, holding up a state-of-the-art blender.

'Oh yes please!'

'Coming right up.'

He leans over to kiss me once more, before blasting the ice into submission. He pulls out two proper margarita glasses and tips the pale green slush into them. He decorates the rims with salt and everything, and I can't help but be a little touched at the effort he's made, even though it's not for me but for Gretel. We 'cheers' and take a sip, keeping eye contact as we do. I raise an eyebrow, tell him that I know what he's planning and I'm totally OK with that, and, without a word spoken, the tension rises in this one-bed new-build in an up and coming area. Joshua swallows too hard. 'So, fajitas are OK with you?'

'Totally OK with me. Can I do anything to help?'

'Nope. Just sit down and delight me with your company, Gretel.'

I perch on a black faux-leather stool and watch Joshua cook. I chug my margarita and he pours me out another one, deliberately brushing my hand as he gives me back my glass.

'You make a mean margarita,' I tell him.

'What can I say? I'm a very talented man.'

'I'm sure you are.'

Another explosion of sexual tension. This one less daunting, what with the tequila whizzing through my bloodstream. In fact, I almost enjoy it. I sip and stare at Joshua over the rim of my glass, and he's the first to look away, blushing. He returns to stirring his pan of sizzling beef, making the entire flat stink of seasoning because his extractor fan doesn't work properly.

Second cocktail down and he's pulling a chair from under his circular glass dining-table. 'I've given you the non-wobbly one, lucky girl.'

'Wow. You really know how to treat a lady.'

He puts down bowls of homemade guacamole, salsa, and sour cream. He brings our third margaritas over and puts them on coasters. Then, with an excitable 'voila', he produces the grill pan of sizzling meat and veg, placing it between us on a wooden chopping board.

'This looks amazing.'

'Thank you. Tuck in.'

We pile things upon other things and wrap them into tortillas and then both find it difficult to bite into them delicately. The end of Joshua's fajita spurts open and drips onto his plate. 'Oh dear,' he says, fingers covered with a hybrid of Mexican sauces. 'I'm doing well, aren't I?'

Always make them feel safe and comfortable. Soothe their egos. Make them feel loved for exactly who they are.

I bite into mine vigorously and the same thing happens. 'Don't worry, I just equalised.' We laugh together and make more eye contact.

'How was your day anyway?' he asks.

I remember the hour I spent lying with my head twisted to one side. 'Yeah, it was *great!* Our CEO brought everyone ice cream this afternoon so we had a party in the office.'

'What a man. This heat's really something, isn't it? They're saying it's going to rain.'

I put down my fajita. '*Finally*. I love the rain. Sometimes

I like to go out and just stand in it, like I'm in the last bit of *Shawshank Redemption*.'

The second I say it, I feel weird. That was a slightly weird thing to say, I must be drunker than I thought. I wait to see Joshua's disapproval, yet he's somehow laughing.

'I *love* that film,' he says. 'And I love Freeman's voice. If I had all the money in the world, I'd use it to pay him to read me bedtime stories. Can you imagine?'

April's laughing too, picturing Joshua tucked up in his pjs with Morgan Freeman sitting at the edge of his bed, reading *Goodnight Moon*. 'I can actually do quite a good impression of him,' I say, 'If you want a cut-price dream come true?' I cough in announcement, lowering my chin. 'You can either get busy living,' I gravel. 'Or get busy dying.'

Joshua's face falls into shock before he bursts into laughter and breaks into applause. 'That is scarily accurate! Oh my God.'

'Thank you. It's a gift. I've always been weirdly good at doing accents. It's saved me through many a conversational dead patch at parties.'

His face is red and grinning. 'How did I not know this about you? Hang on . . .' Before I know it, he's up and gone into his bedroom. I sip at my drink, the further tequila joining rank with the rest already in there – feeling happy and squiffy that I've been a bit like April and he seems to like it. Joshua returns with a book. His eyes are as red as his face, slightly unfocused. 'Right, this is my current read,' he holds out a crime thriller. 'Come on Morgan, read to me.'

I take the book from his hands and I can't help but smile. 'Well, you need to lie down first if I'm going to tell you a bedtime story properly,' I instruct.

Joshua takes my hand and leads me to the living room section of the flat, before he flops back onto the sofa. He folds his arms behind his head as a pillow. 'I'm ready for Freeman.'

'Is this weird?' I ask. 'It feels like things are getting weird.'

'It's definitely weird, but let's go with it.'

'OK.' I sit by his feet and suppress a giggle. I open a page at random, cough again, and start reading it out loud in my best Morgan Freeman voice. It really is very good – it always used to be my party trick at university. Megan would some-times get me to read back our lecture notes in the voice while we were revising.

Joshua's vibrating with laughter. I get down the page best I can, but I'm starting to laugh too. I manage a few more sentences before I lose it and we both shake with silly hysterics for a good thirty seconds until Joshua reaches out and pulls me on top of him, and the book slides to the floor. We laugh into one another's mouths as we kiss. It's a strange moment of total and utter happiness. For two seconds, I'm laughing as I kiss a very nice man who seems to like me and get my weird. It's enough. For me, at least. One of life's slivers of brilliant moments – the sort you wish you could suspend and bathe in. I'm lost in the connection throbbing between two humans. But then Joshua groans into my mouth. His hands slide up the back of my dress. The mood shifts. I can sense he's been activated. A surge of panic gurgles in my throat. Suddenly all I can smell is the acrid scent of the fajitas we are supposed to have forgotten about. I feel like prey . . . like Joshua is gone. The bits of him that make him reasonable and trustworthy shut down with the power of his lust. A thousand small birds take flight in my stomach, flap through my limbs, and Joshua moans again.

But *Gretel* wouldn't feel like this. She'd be going with the flow. She'd be kissing back. *Fajitas? What fajitas?* She's just so totally lost in the moment. She's so like that with moments and getting lost in them. She enjoys the impact she has on men. It makes her feel strong, rather than vulnerable.

And I'm Gretel now so I push my panic down and I kiss back. I lace my hands around Joshua's head, threading his hair between the webs of my fingers, relaxing my body into his. If we could just stay kissing long enough, even April could probably get into this. If he could just stroke my face like he loves me, and take his time, and look at me adoringly, and kiss my neck for at least ten to fifteen minutes and ensure I feel totally comfortable and relaxed and ready then we could have incredible . . . oh, hang on, he's pulling me up off the sofa and into his room.

We stumble around, trying to find our way to his double bed – still attached by our groaning mouths. I open my eyes, keen to see what his room's like. There's a curious painting of Paris hanging over the bed.

'You're so sexy,' Joshua mutters.

'I know.' It seems the sort of confident thing Gretel would say. And it works because he groans again as we fall back onto his bed with freshly made sheets. He lands on top of me, pinning me down, tongue fat and heavy and plunging into my mouth. I twist my head so he's kissing my neck, and he takes the hint and stays there for a good while. I'm able to find peace in the moment again, in how good his lips feel on my skin. I close my eyes, to hone in on the blissful sensation. If I had the money, and if it wasn't strange, I would totally just hire someone to come and kiss my neck for ten minutes every day. That is really strange actually. But it feels so good. I let out a sigh, and I don't know if it was April or Gretel, but it reactivates Joshua, and, typically, rather than thinking 'she's sighing because this is really enjoyable, so it makes sense for me to carry on doing exactly what I'm doing,' he instead thinks 'hmm, that sigh has really turned me on, let me act on that and go back to what I want out of this foreplay.' So he stops kissing my neck and starts fumbling to take off my dress. I take a deep breath in the moment the fabric's pulled over my head, so I'm able to smile up at him when my head reappears. He grins back, his eyes lingering over my body, hungrily drinking me in. Then he kisses me with renewed vigour, taking my hand and guiding it to his erection in his jeans.

Clothes come off.

Mouths emit moans.

Skin finds skin.

I don't even know this man's favourite colour and yet he's unwrapping a condom. While he is faffing about with putting it on, the stench of plastic itching my nose, I lower my head and take some more deep breaths to relax my muscles down there. Gretel would probably be putting the condom on with her mouth or something, but I forgot to google how to do that before I got here.

He smiles.

He kisses me.

He leans me back.

He pushes in.

We're having sex.

Me and this man who doesn't know my name. And I'm doing OK.

It's OK. It's OK it's OK it's OK.

Gretel, of course, is loving it. She's letting out weird deep moans, even though he's not touched my clitoris for at least ten minutes now. I'm careful to get the exact pitch and depth of moan right – enough for him to know I'm enjoying it and that he's so good at sex and wow he can feel good about his ego right now, but not too much that he thinks I'm some loud, slutty porn person. I seem to have got the balance right. Josh's moaning too. We're in missionary, which is good actually. My favourite, although you're never supposed to admit that, are you, because it's boring. But the boredom of intimacy helps me feel safe. I put my face into his neck and smell him. A moment of being April, of needing this. I know my time allowed in this position is limited. Gretel will want to be on top probably and Joshua's a man who's grown up with porn, so it's only a matter of minutes before he'll try to get us to do doggy. But, right now, I bury my nose into just below his ear and wrap my legs around him, pulling him further into me. I try to freeze time and stay in this moment, this one moment where it feels intimate and connected and loving and how I wish sex could always feel. I pretend that he loves me, and will always love me. That it's the one thing I'll never have to worry about. That he respects me but also fancies me. That he cares for me while also knowing I'm able to take care of myself. That he's strong enough to accept and work through his personal weaknesses. That he'll hold me when I cry and never think the reason I'm crying is silly. That he will worship me but never in a co-dependent, suffocating way. And, strangely, lost in this weird trance of make-believe, fantasising about the love Joshua could have for me, I find I'm enjoying the sex. I'm gasping and clutching his back and can feel my body building towards it, which literally never happens to me during penetrative sex ever. Is this the secret they don't tell you? Hallucinate your way to orgasm? Replace the actual man who is penetrating you with some Colin Firth rom-com character fantasy? They never told me that in Cosmo growing up.

I'm enjoying it. I'm enjoying it. I'm not even having to fake it I'm enjoying it so much. So, of course, *of course*, Joshua pulls out.

He smiles down, like he hasn't just done the most annoying thing in the universe. Gretel smiles back. We wrangle about, mix it up. He half-heartedly tries to touch me when I'm on top but then gets lost in how good it feels for him so stops after twenty seconds – but probably still considers himself a good lay because he bothered to try. Gretel loves it. She can't believe her luck at how good this *not-as-good-as-a-moment-ago* sex is. Joshua's face below me looks like he's won the lottery though I'm not used to being this naked and confident and exposed.

'You're so hot,' Joshua leans up and whispers in my ear.

And, without warning, always without warning, the past regurgitates on me.

'You're a fat slut,' Ryan whispers in my ear. Pain and shame and being too confused to do anything other than freeze up.

Josh is below me, and he's looking ever so into it, but . . . but . . .

I'm not here any more.

I'm there. Staring at the white wall.

The white wall.

The

white

wall.

I can see every pattern of the embossed wallpaper. I'm too shocked to move. It's hurting. It's hurting so much. My body is screaming in pain though I stay silent and perfectly still, a primal part of me telling me this is the safest way – the quickest way – to end the hurting. Oww, it hurts so much, but I just look at the wall. Focus all the pain on the wall. A vague part of me, the tiny part of me that hasn't numbed out completely to keep me safe, is aware, so aware that this is damage. That what he's doing to me is damage.

Damage damage damage.

Damage.

I'm damaged.

I'm no good and I'm damaged and it hurts so much, but it's all I deserve. God it hurts. Why isn't he stopping? I can't find the words to make him stop. My throat is stitched up. Vocal chords ripped out, screaming silently into the empty hole of my throat. He keeps hurting me. It won't stop. I just need it to be over. Please be over.

Please

Be

Over.

But it's not. It seems to go on and on, time as slow as the pain is burning, hurting more and more. My whole body is on fire. Hands on my waist. Pulling me back and forth roughly while I'm as limp as I can go, whimpering. Why can't I open my mouth? Why can't I scream? Why can't I push him out and away and run run run? Why am I frozen?

Just staring.

At the white wall, the white wall, the white wall.

No no no no. Come back, come back, come back. It's over, it's over, it's in the past, the past, it can't hurt you. My lungs are small, so small. There are tears pricking. Breathing is hard. *But come back. Come back.* I can't, I can't . . . I'm back there. So scared. So hurt. So helpless. Staring at the wall. *No no no. April! Come back! Come. Back.*

I take the fingernail of my second finger and bury it into the side of my thumb as hard as I can. Pressing, pressing until I almost draw blood . . .

Here. In Joshua's room. The art print of Paris. Joshua is squeezing my hand, slowing it down. 'Hey?' he's saying. 'Is everything OK?'

His face is concerned. *Shit. I lost Gretel. I lost Gretel and I lost me, I'm fucking it up.* 'I'm fine. Why have you stopped?'

'I just thought. You seemed to zone out there. Is everything all right?'

No no no. He can't see this bit. The plan won't work and he won't fall for me if he sees this bit. Cover it up, make it good for him, power through. Power. Through.

Gretel pulls it together. Gretel reaches out and drags him closer. Gretel makes it clear he's misread this entirely. 'Don't stop,' she says. 'Please don't stop.'

And, it's not like he needs further convincing. He smiles, relieved, that I am not one of those damaged ones he has heard so much about. No no no, don't want one of them, do you? They're not sexy, those damaged ones. Can't spunk in their faces without feeling mildly guilty about it, and who wants to ruin an orgasm with guilt? Luckily, he doesn't try anything too risqué but I'm still fighting the trigger and losing. I need to hold it together. I'm not holding it together. I need to distract him to his finish. Gretel ramps it up. She cannot believe how amazing his thrusting his. She asks for him to go deeper, she says how big he is, how big and hard. Predictably, this sends him over the edge very quickly. He lets out a guttural squawk and judders into me. I just need to hold it together, hold it together. *Wait wait wait. You can unravel soon, I promise. Just not yet, not yet.*

Joshua stays still inside me, his head buried into my neck for some time. I twist my head to one side to let gravity roll the tear off my cheek. I can physically feel his penis deflating inside me, like a helium balloon days after the party. My trauma's surfacing; it's boiling in my skin.

Joshua finally lifts his head and looks down and Gretel's face is tear free and smiling as their eyes meet in a post-coital lock. His face bursts into a grin, and he has the good grace and manners to lean down and plant a kiss on my lips before holding the end of his penis to ensure the condom stays on while he tugs himself out of my body.

'Hi,' he whispers, collapsing to my side, giving me another kiss.

'Hi,' I reply.

I want to scream so loudly that it would scatter every pigeon living in London.

I watch him attempt to fight sleep for, oh, twenty whole seconds. He reaches out and heavily pats my naked back, all like 'there there son'. I reach out and rub his back, comforting him into unconsciousness so I can be alone. Quickly, his arm collapses as his body finds sleep, pinning me to the bed.

I focus on my breath, the rise and fall of my ribcage. I have to wait; I have to make sure he's fully gone before I get up. I do not want him to wake. I need to be alone so much right now that I'd kill him if I could, just for the peace, just to ensure he stays sleeping.

In and out, in and out.

Breathing really is quite painful sometimes, isn't it?

Gretel isn't here.

It's just me. April.

In this strange flat, with this strange man who doesn't know who I am. I check his sleeping face one more time. He is out. The slimy dead slug of the used condom dangling from his other hand. I delicately remove myself from under him, rolling until I'm standing, naked, looking down at him.

Still sleeping.

It's just me in this flat. My throat throbbing with screams that want to be screamed till my voice runs dry, but that would wake him up. I find my dress discarded on his wooden floor and hold it to my cheek with shaking hands. Then I pad out barefoot, gently closing the door behind me.

The living room is still how we left it. The scene of the wooing. The ice in our margaritas hasn't fully melted yet. Our meals lie half-eaten – the bowls of handmade dips still full and waiting to be scooped. A clock ticks on the wall. It's not even eight thirty. I clutch my dress to me tighter and I enter the tiling of Joshua's bathroom. The tang of Mr Muscle punctuates the air. I picture him scrubbing it moments before I arrived. The heat seeps through the small, open window above the sink. I can hear the laughs of Friday night bouncing through. I close it. I pull the string of the extractor fan, the hum giving me the white noise needed to cover the gasps escaping my mouth.

I lock the door.

I fall, naked, onto the bathmat.

Reasons why I've cried in bathrooms

- Because I don't want a man to know I'm crying
- Because I don't want a man to know I'm crying
- Because I don't want a man to know I'm crying
- Occasionally, work stress
- Because I don't want a man to know I'm crying
- Because I don't want a man to know I'm crying
- Occasionally, PMS
- Because I don't want a man to know I'm crying

When I'm finished, you would never know how hard I fell apart. My breathing is back to normal. My face is blotch-free. My shoulders unhunched. I've managed to get the nine-yard stare out of my eyes.

The white wall, the white wall, the white wall.

No.

Joshua's still dozing as I climb back into bed, fully naked, because that's what Gretel would do. I dream up the scenario of what she's been doing for the last forty-five minutes. She would've slept too, dozing happily in her post-orgasmic bliss that was real instead of faked. Then she would've done something fun! Oh, I know, she'll want more cocktails. I climb back out and retrieve the melted margaritas, placing them carefully on Joshua's side table before getting under the covers again.

My movements stir him. He half opens one eye.

'Oh hello.' He reaches out and pulls my head into his chest.

'I've brought in the margaritas.'

'You're a legend.' He kisses the top of my head. 'Sorry, I didn't mean to doze off.' He kisses my head again. 'You tired me out.'

I twist in his arms to look up at him. He has quite a lot of nostril hair for a man not yet 35. 'You tired me out too.' I lean over to get the drinks. He sighs exhaustedly and props himself up, saying 'thank you'. We sit, sipping, conversation temporarily not flowing. I know I should be bright and sparky, like Gretel would be, but I used up a lot of energy climbing my way out of hell on Joshua's bathmat.

'We didn't finish dinner,' Joshua opens.

'We bloody better. I'm starving.'

He pats my thigh. 'I'm glad my cooking didn't put you off.'

'What can I say? The man can cook . . .' I take a syrupy salty gulp. 'Among other things . . .'

My words visibly relax him, his body softens into his pillow. 'Oh,' he says, the corners of his mouth tugging upwards. 'So you . . . ?'

I nod hard. 'Oh yeah! Couldn't you tell?'

'Yeah, I mean, no. I wondered. So you did? Of course. Sorry. That's great. Great.'

I lean over and make myself kiss him. I wonder why men worry about women not coming when, during sex, they regularly do things that it's common scientific knowledge do not lead women to come. The kiss leads into a snog and I can feel the duvet cover twitching with the stirring signs of Joshua's second erection. I know I won't be able to avoid having sex with him again tonight but I don't think I can face it yet. Especially as it always takes much longer the second time around. I break off the kiss. 'Mmm, I'm starving,' Gretel breezes. 'And I've not tried your guacamole yet.' I'm up, stark naked, padding back to the dining table. 'You coming?' I call, sitting down. He practically runs after me.

'I think the food is cold,' he says.

'That's fine. I'm too hungry to care.' I pick up my fork and stab it into the remnants of my fajita. I get this urge to eat and eat and eat until I throw up. 'Mmm,' Gretel says. 'Top marks for the guacamole.'

'You know, I've never eaten fajitas naked before.'

'How have you coped your whole life without me?'

And he actually, momentarily, looks like he's considering the question. 'I honestly don't know, Gretel.'

We eat. We flirt. We wash up together. We chat about all the things we have yet to learn about one another. We're past the basics now – where he grew up (Norwich), where he went to uni (Leeds), and are getting into the slightly more detailed. We finally get to favourite colours. His is blue. Gretel's is orange. Mine's green.

It gets dark, but the promised rain doesn't fall. The storm never arrives. The sky outside gives off the vibe of someone who grossly overate, but not quite to the point of being sick. The sky is a long, uncomfortable, indigestion. I want it to rain so much.

We settle on his sofa, entwined, acting like the couple we are not yet. I can tell he's been single a while by how much he craves physical touch. He keeps putting a hand on my back and his hugs last a bit too long.

'So, apart from Morgan Freeman, can you do any other impressions?'

Apart from of a carefree woman who doesn't exist and can orgasm the first time she has sex with someone with hardly any clitoral stimulation? I think to myself.

'Give me an accent and I'll be able to do it.'

'OK, say something in American.'

'Something in American,' I parrot, but in a perfect US accent.

'All right, harder now. Scottish.'

'Oi, Joshua, you're a wee bit sexy, aren't ya?'

He laughs while also beaming at the compliment. 'I like this game,' he declares. 'Can you do anyone else famous apart from Morgan?'

'I do a great Ronan Keating actually.'

'Niche, but let's hear it.'

I sing a line and Joshua cracks up again.

We open the windows to let in the non-existent breeze. I ask him about the print of Paris in his bedroom. 'Oh, that? I bought it when I was travelling around Europe the summer I graduated.' The topic drifts to backpacking, an activity I've always considered exists solely for boring middle-class people to feel better about themselves and give them something to talk about at boring middle-class parties. No personality? No worries – just talk about *IndYA*! But Gretel's riveted – she just loves travelling – and so I have to sit through some of the same stories he's already told me about Mount Kilimanjaro.

We start kissing again. The kissing escalates and we end up having sex on his sofa. It's better than last time. When Joshua has finished removing the second used condom of the evening and collapses in a sweaty mess into me, I try to make sure I get my Madonna:Whore blend just right. 'That was amazing,' I say, even though it wasn't. It was only OK.

He grins and kisses my fingers. I can smell myself on his breath.

'I never usually sleep with someone this fast,' Gretel admits.

Joshua props himself up on his elbows. 'Seriously?'

She nods, shyly.

'I thought . . . I mean, you're so confident. I assumed . . .'

'What?'

He's clever enough to back away from the loaded question. 'Never mind.'

Gretel lets it go, like any normal girl would ever be able to let an 'I assumed' go ever in the history of life. 'Well I don't normally do this.'

Joshua's still for a moment, clearly thinking. Then he suddenly hugs me, really tightly, making me so suffocated it's a miracle I don't hit him.

After a moment, I tap his back. 'Can we sleep now?'

He tucks a stray lock of hair behind my ear and looks like he's falling in love with me. 'Let's sleep.'

I lie awake and stare at his ceiling, only catching an hour or so when dawn sneaks around the curtains and birds who wish they lived somewhere nicer than London chirp their morning announcements and wake me up. I want to scratch my skin off. I want to cry for a thousand years. I want to take a man, any man, and make him feel true, pure, fear. I want violence. I want to watch him bleed. I want the whites of his eyes to grow bigger with terror. I want him to freeze as a survival mechanism and then torture himself for the rest of his life for not fighting back. I want him to blame himself for it. I want him to scream and . . .

Joshua rolls over in the bed. His eyes are open. He's smiling.

'Good morning!' I chirp.

'It's a good morning indeed if I'm waking up next to you.'

'Oh, that is cheesy Joshua.'

He pulls me into him (all the better to let me poke my

morning erection into your thigh, my dear) and we roll into the inevitability of morning sex with morning breath and both of us pretending I'm not a bit too dry for it, what with it being the morning and all, and Joshua doing absolutely no foreplay beforehand. Even Gretel can't fake wetness. But Joshua doesn't seem to mind, or notice. When he is done, he falls off me head-first into the pillow, patting my back and muttering compliments.

'I need the bathroom.' I get up, pee, shower, and start tugging my clothes on. My skin's itchier. That last bout of sex was too much. I'm running out of time. The trauma's closing in. My ribs are tightening on my lungs.

The white wall.

The

white

wall.

He appears in the kitchen just as the kettle boils, shrugging into a casual white T-shirt.

'Tea? Coffee?' I ask, in an air hostess voice.

'Coffee, but let me make it. You're the guest.' He steps behind me, squeezing my sides to move me and it takes everything I have left not to flinch.

I sit at the table and watch him make proper coffee with his gadgets. He's finicky about it. Scientific. He uses the measuring spoon to make sure he's scooped up just the right amount. He takes the kettle off just before it hits boil so it doesn't burn the grains. He even squats down when he pours the water in to make sure he's measured it right. It's like watching an enthusiastic student in a secondary-school chemistry class, and it's bordering on adorable. When he passes the cup of coffee over, it tastes brilliant too.

'Thank you. Wow, you know how to make coffee.'

He pulls his chair over and uses his legs to clamp one of mine. 'It's both my greatest superpower and my greatest weakness,' he says. 'I'm such a dick about people making coffee for me. It causes me actual stress.' He leans over and tucks my hair behind my ear again. 'You look lovely without any make-up on,' he comments.

I'm wearing under-eye concealer, mascara, a touch of blusher and a lip stain.

'Thank you.' I keep sipping my coffee and can't bring myself to look at him. The urgent need to leave pulses through my body. And, before I can see the bottom of my mug, I'm done. I stand, using everything I have to keep smiling.

'Hey, where you off to?'

'I've got to go I'm afraid.'

The disappointment on his face is palpable. 'What?'

'Yeah, I've got this thing.'

'A thing?'

Smile smile smile. Breeze breeze breeze. Lie lie lie.

'Yeah, I'm working an extra shift this morning, and then I'm at a barbecue with some friends.'

'Oh, right.' He looks at his coffee.

I've never been with a man so openly needy before, and can't figure out if it's the Gretel effect or just Joshua. 'I had such a great time though.'

'Yeah, me too.'

'Sorry, I didn't realise you wanted us to spend the day together too.' It's *so weird* to be on this side of the next-day conversation. I'm usually the one assuming we'll be spending the weekend together, turning down other plans just in case, and then acting all meek and 'I don't mind' when the other person reveals they'd not considered a whole weekend together an option at all.

'No, I'm sorry. I shouldn't have assumed you didn't have other things to do.'

I reach over and squeeze his hand to let him know not to worry. 'I really did have a great time though.'

His eyes meet mine. 'You did?'

I nod. 'We should do it again.'

He waggles his eyebrows. 'Now? I'm quite sure you've exhausted me.'

I fake a laugh. 'Not that. Well, that. But also, you know, meeting up. Conversing. Sharing the same oxygen. We should do it again.'

'Monday?'

Wow. Right in there, Joshua. 'Monday works for me.'

Get my bag. Collect up my things. Resist the urge to flinch again when Joshua kisses my neck. Make dinner plans. Say thank you for such a great evening. Kiss goodbye at the door. Sigh with relief when door closes behind me. Act happily surprised when Joshua comes and stops the lift to kiss me again. Wave and keep smiling. Get outside. Wonder how I'm going to make it through a day so hot when feeling like this. Get on stuffy but mostly-empty Tube. Look down at hands. See they are shaking. Remember the white wall. Tell myself not now. Soon, but you have to get home first. Make it to Tube stop. Get off. Get through ticket barrier. Have message on phone from Joshua when I get signal. Don't read it. Can't. Not now. Slog through London streets, unable to cope with other humans who dare to be on the pavement with me. Steam rising from concrete. Can't get his face out of my head. His face afterwards. Not Joshua's face. Ryan's. How he slept soundly and I watched him sleep and couldn't understand how he could sleep after doing that to me. Could it have really happened if he slept that soundly afterwards? How much it hurt. Sore. Burning. He slept all night through. By morning I'd told myself I'd imagined it. But my body didn't forget. Couldn't. It closed up. Clamped shut. Get to the end of my road. I'm almost there. I want to peel my skin off it itches so bad. Breathing is hard. Lungs are smaller. I gasp more than I inhale. Keys won't go into the lock. Try again. No. Please go into the lock, why is this so hard? There. There we go. Push into the flat. Empty. Mine. Alone. Finally all alone. I can let it out now. The hiccup I've been holding in since I heard Ryan's voice in my head. I'm ready to cry. I lie on the sofa. I want to let it out. But now I'm here, now I can, the tears won't come. I feel nothing. Empty. Numb. I lie on my side with my knees up. I stare at the wall. This wall is pale pink. Megan's mum picked it. The other wall was white at the time. With embossed wallpaper.

Can't breathe.

He's here. It's hurting. I don't know how to say stop. Why is he doing this? The tears are here. Pouring. The numbness has gone but I want it back because now it hurts too much. Too many feelings. Too strong. How am I going to live my life with these feelings that won't ever dull, no matter how much time passes?

I hate you.

I hate you.

I HATE YOU.

I FUCKING HATE YOU RYAN SO FUCKING MUCH YOU FUCKING PRICK. YOU RUINED MY FUCKING LIFE AND NOTHING BAD HAPPENED TO YOU IN RETURN. MY LIFE IS RUINED AND I WILL NEVER BE ME AGAIN AND YET YOU GET TO CARRY ON LIVING THAT FUCKING LIFE OF YOURS YOU FUCKING FUCKING FUCKING FUCKING WANKING SHITTING FUCKING WANKER MADE OF SHIT I HATE YOU. GOD I HATE YOU. I HATE YOU SO MUCH IF I COULD KILL YOU I

WOULD KILL YOU. I'D MAKE IT HURT SO BAD. LIKE
YOU HURT ME. FUCK YOU.

FUCK

YOU

FUCK YOU

HOW AM I SUPPOSED TO DO ANYTHING WITH
ANY PART OF MY LIFE?

Crying so hard now. I can't see for the tears. This anger.
This anger is too much. It's always too much. I have a scatter
cushion in my hands. I'm pounding it against the sofa. I'm
screaming. I'm screaming 'I HATE YOU I HATE YOU I
HATE YOU I HATE YOU I HATE YOU I HATE YOU
I HATE YOU I HATE YOU I HATE YOU I HATE YOU.' I
can't stop screaming it. I hate you I hate you. *Smash smash
smash* goes the pillow. Why can't it be your face? Why can't
it be your fucking face? I don't think I can stop. 'I hate you I
hate you I hate you. I HATE YOUUUUUU.'

Smash against the sofa. *Crash*. I don't care if the neighbours
hear. Nobody will do anything anyway. Nobody ever fucking
does anything. *Thud thud thud.* I see your face thudding into
the sofa. I imagine it's concrete. Your nose breaking. Blood
everywhere. Why did you do this to me? Why did you take
what wasn't yours? You were supposed to love me. I let out
the largest scream of my life. It's not even a scream, more a
primal grunt of pain. My vocal chords tear in my throat at
the effort of it. I don't know how to stop making this noise.
Then the cushion has exploded. Feathers are everywhere.
Falling like snow. I keep hitting it until every last feather is
out. Still yelling 'I hate you'. Then there's just an empty skin
where there used to be a cushion. A bit like how I am just

an empty bit of skin where I used to be a person. A person who trusted in love and didn't think she would be one of those unlucky people whom bad things happen to and who thought the best in people and didn't ever think love could hurt as hard as it hurts now. Irrevocable hurt.

The skin of cushion drops to the floor.

Small hiccups of scared sobs.

I collapse onto my side.

I curl up my legs into a ball.

The tears fall so heavy and strong. I let out a small mew of pain.

I wish my life wasn't this.

I cry until my body runs out of water. That's the only way to make it stop when this happens.

Then I sleep.

I sleep like I have the flu.

• *Love Sick – Gretel's Guide to Dating Self-Care*

It's so easy to lose sight of yourself in the initial exciting hormone flurry of early dating.

Don't.

Remember you need to keep your independence and high-value worth and all the other things he's fallen for. Yes, your body basically feels like you're snorting twelve lines of cocaine every twelve minutes, but override all those natural human impulses. I do.

While it's easy to get carried away, make sure you spend some time looking out for yourself. Dating can be exhausting, even if it's going well, so get well-rehearsed in the empowering act of self-care. Run yourself a bubble bath; put on a facemask; light a candle; treat yourself to some cashmere-covered stationery and write lists of everything you feel grateful for. You deserve it. I mean, there's no significant trauma with resulting long-lasting mental-health issues that can't be fixed with a sheet mask and writing you're glad it was sunny today in calligraphy.

I sleep till eleven on Sunday morning, and even then I'm only woken up by the stifling heat. I need to pee, and to drink all the world's water, but the thought of getting up is unbearable. I lie on my side in yesterday's clothes and whisper 'get up get up get up' to myself for at least five minutes before I do. I force myself to take a shower. I smell Joshua all over my body and I exfoliate and loofah him off my skin, wondering if there is ever going to be a part of my life where I don't find existing so very hard.

Joshua: How was your shift this morning? I've been out jogging. In this heat! Are you impressed?
Joshua: Happy Sunday. What do you want to do tomorrow, O Gretel, Gretel, wherefore art thou Gretel?

I stare at my phone and the post-sex-reassurance messages I didn't even have to worry into existence. In fact, *I'm* the jerk who hasn't replied. I shove my toothbrush in my mouth and reply while I dozily shove it around my teeth.

Gretel: Battery died! How are you not dead after that run? I am impressed, but also scared you are doping. Are you doping, Joshua?

He replies before I've even spat out my toothpaste.

Joshua: Sometimes I ask for two shots in my coffee? Does that count?
Gretel: Most IT worker version of doping ever.
Gretel: Also, movie tomorrow instead of dinner? I need air con in my life right now.

We are to meet at seven in Leicester Square. We are to watch that summer blockbuster with all the special effects. We are to go back to Joshua's afterwards for yet more sex. Though that bit's assumed rather than verbally added to the agenda. With that all organised, Gretel leaves my body and I slump onto the sofa and stay there until Megan comes home.

'It stinks in here,' is how she announces her arrival. 'And why are there fucking feathers everywhere?' She stops and looks at me, lying sideways and staring glassily at *Dawson's Creek* with the sound off. She knows instantly. 'Oh my God, hon.'

'I'm fine,' I tell Dawson's big fat forehead. 'Sorry about the cushion. I'll clear it up. I'll buy you a new one.'

She dumps her giant bag of overnight gear onto the floor and sits by my head, reaching out to put her hand on me. The kindness of it makes me start weeping.

'Sorry,' I keep saying. 'I'm so sorry.'

'Don't be sorry! Don't worry about the cushion. What's going on? Oh hon.' She lifts me up from under my shoulders and kind of drapes me into hugging her. I cry onto her shoulder, tears flowing, my muscles too heavy to move myself. I'm like one of Taylor Swift's highly malleable cats. Megan strokes my hair. 'Oh honey,' she whispers into my hair. 'There, there, it's going to be OK. It's in the past, remember? It can't hurt you now.'

'I'm being stupid,' I manage to get out. 'It will pass. Sorry. I think Dawson pushed me over the edge.'

She laughs. 'He has that impact on most people. Right, come on. Sugar. You need sugar.' She strokes my hair one last time, then gets up and goes into our kitchen, returning with the Dairy Milk she's smart enough to keep in the fridge. She breaks off a block of eight fat squares. 'Eat,' she commands, pushing the chocolate into my mouth. It's hard to bite into without chipping a tooth, but I chew and obey. It starts to melt and turn to thick, creamy sludge, squelching in between my teeth. It tastes nice. I swallow and open my mouth like a baby bird. Megan laughs, cracks another line and feeds it to me, before having some herself. Within minutes, the sugar has done what it's supposed to do and I feel slightly lifted, slightly more able to hold up my own muscles again. I wiggle so I'm sitting upright.

'Sorry,' I say again.

'Stop saying sorry.'

'Sorry.'

'I will hit you.'

'Why is Dawson so annoying?'

'He is actually the worst. What episode you on?' She sits next to me and we press play and watch the rest of it. It's the one where Dawson and Joey finally kiss and Megan lets out a sigh when they do.

'I can't believe they've not noticed it's raining,' I say. It's what I always say when we watch this one.

'I know. Even Andie fucking MacDowell noticed the rain when she was kissing Hugh Grant. And Hugh Grant is way more distracting to kiss than Dawson.'

We watch the two teenagers swap saliva and return to our predictable arguments about why Pacey is so much better. When the credits kick in, and Dawson has gone on to patronise another day, Megan and I turn to one another.

'What set it off?' she asks.

'I love you, but I really don't want to talk about it. Please, can we talk about something else?'

'I love you too.' She switches off Dawson and the screen goes black. 'I'm a bit too worried to leave it though. I mean, you've gutted a Laura Ashley cushion.'

'I told you I'd clear it up!'

'OK, OK, that's not why I was saying it. I just hate seeing you like this.'

'Honestly, it was just a wobbly moment. I'm probably just hungover. Sorry.'

'I'm sorry too.'

'What's going on with *you*, anyway? I hardly seen you these days. Is everything all right?'

Megan nods, then shakes her head, then nods again. 'I think I'm really falling for Malcolm,' she admits, her hair covering her face.

I shift up on the sofa, glad for the distraction. The heat moves around my skin and I peel myself off the stick of the sofa. 'Seriously?'

'I know. It's a disaster, but I'm hoping a good one.'

'Good disasters. The ultimate catchphrase for love.'

She smiles. 'It's so nerve-wracking getting feelings for someone. I've been going a bit crazy. I'm not sure if you've noticed.'

'Not at all.'

'Liar.'

'I mean, all your thoughts about shared doors are so rational.'

She throws her head back into one of the puffy cushions I didn't destroy and they let out a gasp that matches her sigh. 'I didn't want this to happen. I honestly just wanted a one-night stand. But it's taken me totally by surprise how much we have in common, and he's such a gentleman. We get on so well, like I feel like I've known him forever, and the sex is really great, and it's like we're addicted to one another and I can't stop thinking about him . . .'

'So?'

'So?'

I kick her gently. 'So, what's the problem?'

'The problem is that I've gone from being a sorted, uncluttered career woman who is top of her game and happy and calm, without even having to do fucking mindfulness or whatever, to becoming a distracted, jumpy, insecure, jealous freak who can't go five minutes without checking her phone to see if he's messaged back.'

'Five minutes? More like five seconds.'

It's her turn to kick me. 'So, I'm a nightmare. We know this already.'

'What are you going to do about it?'

Megan shakes her head slowly. 'I'm not sure. There's this weird inevitability, isn't there, when it comes to falling in love with a man. It's never anything other than a huge trap and a massive act of self-harm. I know this. I'm self-actualized enough to know this, and know how it's played out in the past and how unhappy it's made me, and yet . . . I'm walking right into it anyway. I'm literally staring the mousetrap in the face and then shoving my big toe on it. And then I will scream and wonder why it snapped and why it hurt so much. But, April, what if it's different this time? What if Malcolm is different?'

He won't be different, I think. *They are never different.* 'He could be?' I say, obviously not meaning it, but she lifts her head and acts like I did.

'You really think so?' I don't have time to reply. 'Gah!' She stands up in one fluid motion, her arms in the air. 'I need to not go crazy. I need to just get my head together. I've not done any work all weekend and the launch is coming up and I have so many decisions to make and yet I can't think about anything other than whether or not our children will inherit his bone structure.'

'Well then, do some work.'

'I will.'

'Go on then.'

'I'm going.'

'Well do it.'

'I'm doing it right now.'

We laugh together. The first real laugh I've managed for

days. Megan reaches out and takes my hand. 'Are you really OK?' she asks one more time.

'I promise you that I am,' I lie. I glance at the puddles of feathers scattering our floor and wonder once more if I'll ever feel OK again.

The feathers are off the floor at least. Megan and I cleaned them up and I helped her brainstorm launch stuff until late last night.

She was at the kitchen table this morning, putting together a massive spreadsheet made of varying coloured Post-its. 'I'm channelling all my anxious nervous energy about Malcolm into my work.'

'How many times have you checked your phone this morning to see if he's messaged?'

'Two hundred and twelve.'

'So it's working then?'

'Shut it, you.'

I'm capable of smiling, and I'm capable of getting onto the Tube, even though it's crowded and still so hot, and when will it ever rain. I push through into the office and say a jolly good morning to everyone. I make a cup of coffee. I drink it. I catch up on my emails.

Matt arrives late because the Central line was being the Central line. 'I'm so hot I think I've sweated out my soul,' he says instead of hello.

'You have a soul?' See! A joke! I'm capable of making jokes.

We have a Monday morning catch-up meeting. Everyone's favourite thing. The fundraisers are trying to pretend everything is going to be fine, even though we lost out on a key bid last

219

week. The IT team have fixed the bug in our CMS system but, in fixing it, they have found a new one. The press release team have found someone from *Love Island* who may want to be our charity ambassador but they're asking for money to do it. I update them on volunteer uptake numbers for the next big training drive we have planned for the autumn. There're not as many as we'd hoped, but that's because we don't have the budget to advertise. We finish and I have another coffee.

'You all right for your shift?' Matt asks me. 'I've got another bloody meeting now, but I'm free at lunch if you need to debrief.'

'I'm fine,' I say. Maybe it's true.

It's not true.

At half eleven, I get my third cup of coffee which is probably a mistake because I already feel jittery as it is. I put on my cupped headphones so no one bothers me, and I open up the inbox. Twelve questions to get through. That's not so bad. I fly through the first three, all of them run-of-the-mill, everyday type questions.

Message received: 04:42

I'm in love with my best friend, do I tell her?

Message received: 08:57

Am I pregnant? I've taken a pregnancy test and it says I'm not but where the hell is my period?

Message received: 11:07

I watch gay porn sometimes but I don't think I'm gay. But maybe I am? I don't want to have sex with a man, but does my porn mean something? Help me pls.

I pull up template answers. I write back that you should weigh up the hurt of keeping your feelings a secret against the hurt of the possible rejection and ruining of the friendship. I write that periods can be late for any number of reasons but, if they're really worried, they should go to their GP. I reassure them that many straight men watch gay porn and your sexuality isn't something you should feel under any pressure to define. I'm in the groove. I'm doing OK. It's all going to be fine. Work is fine. It's a great distraction actually. I'm glad I . . .

Message received: 12:02

This is a weird one but my gf is being really offish because the other morning she woke up to find me having sex with her. I thought it was a sexy way to wake her up but she said it's made her feel a bit strange. I'm sorry cos i didn't mean to upset her but i also think shes overreacting a bit. I wouldnt mind if she woke me up with a blowjob would i? How can i make her see that its not a big deal?

My stomach is the first to go. Like someone's tied a tonne weight to it and then dropped it off a cliff. Then my hands start wobbling. I feel the rug being tugged out from under all my rationality. White rage pumps through my blood. With each beat of my fluttering heart, the anger pulses harder and harder and then I'm typing. Pure, putrid rage. Anger filling me from the tip of my toes up. I can't any more. I can't any more. Why won't they stop? Why do they never stop? It's not fair. How dare he? HOW DARE HE? I'm typing without thought or reason or time to get myself together. I'm done, so done. Aren't we all done? Aren't you? Because I am.

*You are a fucking disgrace. You have RAPED someone you
claim you love and now dare to be upset that she's upset about
it. Why are you all such dicks? What's wrong with you? WHAT
THE ACTUAL FUCK IS WRONG WITH YOU? I hope you die. I
hope you fucking die. Because if you did the world would be
better because at least then there'd be one less of you, fucking
women up and then making their pain all about you. Go die
now please, you pathetic cunt of a human being. I feel so sorry
for your mother.*

I stand. Matt is still in his meeting.

I hit send.

Oh well. Whoops. Butterfingers!

I start giggling to myself. 'I'm just getting some lunch.' I
smile at Katy like nothing untoward has happened. 'Do you
want me to get you anything?'

She looks up and catches my smile, beaming it back. 'Oooh,
where you going?'

'Probably just the corner shop.'

'If you bring me back a Twister I'll love you forever.' She
reaches to retrieve her wallet from her bag.

'Don't worry about it. One Twister coming up.'

'Thanks April, you're a legend.'

I give her a double thumbs-up.

I feel light when I step outside into the relentlessness of
the glaring sun. I laugh out loud, startling the line of tourists
waiting to get into the Sherlock Holmes museum.

I'm probably going to be fired, I think, as I look up at the
sky, but I don't even care. It's totally worth it.

I don't get lunch. Or a Twister from the corner shop. I just walk around the park, beaming at everyone. 'Isn't it a lovely day?' I say to a mother feeding the ducks with her children. She's not sure how to reply to this uncustomary London bout of friendliness and just ignores me. But I feel better for being nicer, they can go fucking fuck themselves if they can't be polite back. I walk off.

It's so goddamn hot. Not even the tears that I'm now crying are cooling me down. They keep coming. Falling down my face, splashing into my dress. It's quite an accomplishment to cry and walk at the same time – requires real determination – but I'm pulling it off. My feet hurt in my sandals, the heat making them swell and the straps rub, and I can't believe I've just done what I've just done . . .

What the hell have I just done?

I'm so fired.

So totally fired.

I sit on the empty bench dedicated to Gladys. I put my head between my knees. I'm not ashamed of what I did. I imagine that boy opening my reply and I feel good that he will read what I've written. Even though it's unethical blah blah blah. He needs to read it. He has to be told. They all need to be told. I think of that poor girl and what she woke up to and how confused she must be and how confused she'll always be because he did what he did. I just detonated my life like a landmine but it's worth it. Even though my job is the only thing in my life I ever feel good about. It's where I've carefully allocated all my worth and self-esteem and sense of self. It's what rebuilt me after Ryan, the way I felt I was in some control of it, able to make sense of it in some way. And I've ruined it but I'm glad I said it, but I don't want to have ruined it . . .

Matt finds me soon enough. He sits down. 'Oh April,' is all he says.

'I'm not sorry.'

'Your response didn't reach the user. I saw it and cancelled it before he was able to open it. I've sent the template perpetrator reply instead.'

My whole body stiffens. I dig my nails into the soft wood of Gladys's bench. 'You shouldn't have done that.'

'I think, in time, you'll be glad that I did.'

I wipe under my eyes. I can't think of anything to say. I can't think how or what to feel.

'What's happening April?'

I shrug.

'Talk to me.'

'There's nothing to say.'

'These questions come up a lot, and you've never done this before. What's going on? You can tell me. I'm your buddy – in both senses of the word.'

I wipe my eyes again. I guess it's worth pointing out that today's question isn't, indeed, anything that remarkable. During training, they dedicated half a day to perpetrators who use our services to alleviate their guilt. It's a tricky ethical one. Some of them just want to be told that what they did was OK, even though they know it isn't. Some of them get off on telling services about what they did. Some of them haven't even done anything but get off on pretending they have. And some of these questions may come from victims, using a story to 'test' a service before they feel brave enough to open up. I've been trained in how to spot these questions immediately. I've been trained to treat them as genuine users who want help, because there's no way of knowing that they aren't. I've been trained in handling the difficult emotions these questions evoke. They're never easy when they come up. I often push them straight over to Matt and need a long walk and some deep breathing. But not today, not any more.

'I just can't do it.'

'Do what? Your job?'

I shake my head and wipe a stray tear using my finger. 'Any of it. Just waking up and living my life when it's all too much and there's no point anyway.'

Matt hangs his head, quiet. I don't fill the silence either. We sit and look out at the scorched grass that looks like crushed Weetabix. I can't remember what it was like for grass to be green.

Eventually he says, 'I've had to tell Mike. You know that, right?'

'Whatever.'

'April, you know I had to.'

'Don't worry about it.'

He looks like he's about to reach out and take my hand, but he stops himself. Instead he raises his face to look right at me. 'Look, I know we're just colleagues but I also think this job makes us more than that. If you need to talk about anything, I'm here. I'm a friend.'

I look into his eyes behind his thick glasses and I'm glad there is at least one man in this universe that I can believe is good. Of course he's fucking gay, but it's a start. 'Thank you. I don't know what's going on with me.'

'Burn out?'

'Yeah, I guess that's a good way of putting it.' I look up, the sun making my eyes crinkle to slits. 'I don't think I can go back in there, Matt,' I say. 'Everyone's going to be talking about me.'

'They won't. I've only told Mike.'

'It will get out. Everyone will think I'm crazy.' I mean, I am crazy. I'm starting to realise just *how* crazy after years of blocking it out and pretending otherwise. Only since becoming Gretel and having to withhold so much have I realised the true extent of it all and how much I leak it out, like a malfunctioning madness sprinkler.

'Anyone who works for a charity is a bit crazy, that's the law.'

I manage a smile.

'I won't tell anyone, April. I promise.'

We lock eyes again. 'You're a pretty good buddy, you know that, yeah?'

'Right back at you.'

'Will you go and get my stuff? Tell everyone I'm not feeling well?'

'Yes, of course. Mike said to take the rest of the day off. He's organised for Carol to come in tomorrow though.'

My smiles fades. 'What?'

'April, you're amazing and I'm very fond of you, but you can't call a user a rapist and not get called in for an extra supervision.'

'But he is a rapist!'

'April—'

'Thanks for getting my stuff,' I interrupt him, needing to get rid of him before I cry yet more new tears. 'I'll wait here if that's OK?'

He wants to say more but he doesn't. 'That's fine. I'll be back in ten minutes.'

I'm left alone until Matt returns. I don't cry actually, just stare at the sky quite a lot, trying to remember what overcast feels like, what needing a cardigan feels like, what sanity feels like.

We hug when he gets back. I thank him again. Then I slouch my way to the Tube and back to the flat that I left not so very long ago and lie on my bed and stare at the ceiling again.

It's time to get ready for Joshua. I peeled off my work clothes the moment I got in, so I collect them off the floor and step back into them. I check my phone. There's an email from Chrissy, reminding me of the upcoming hen do.

'You can fuck right off you smug, fucking prat,' I find myself saying out loud, and then laughing hysterically.

I email back. 'Can't wait!!!'

I get back on the Tube. I practise smiling like I might mean it. I imagine a different day from this day, and wonder what Gretel would've done. 'Isn't this weather the best?' she would say. 'I had lunch out in the park. It was lush.' I get off at Leicester Square and fight my way through the sweaty throngs of tourists who don't know where to go or how to find out, weaving through them with the directional arrogance of a seasoned Londoner. I dodge past the M&M's shop and wonder why and how it is a) allowed, and b) so popular. I see Joshua waiting for me outside the cinema, and enjoy watching him for a moment in screensaver mode. An anonymous face in this city too full of anonymous faces. He looks up and spots my face. A grin splinters his in two. He is genuinely happy to see her. He cannot hide that at all. I walk forward, smiling back. We meet. We kiss. He slings an arm over my shoulder, and steers me towards the entrance.

'I've been dreaming about this all day . . .' he starts, leaning over to kiss my neck. 'The air con, I mean.'

'You're hilarious.'

'You know that's not the only reason.'

We kiss again and cause a little bit of a blockage on the packed pavements. I push him away like I don't want to push him away. 'Air con. Now.'

'Whatever you want, O Demanding One.'

'Not demanding. Just hot.'

He kisses my face. 'So, did you have a good day at work?' he asks, just as we push through the double doors and have our skin erupt into welcome goosebumps.

'Today?' I ask. 'Oh yeah, it was great. I had lunch in the park. It was lush.'

The Top 5 Most Common Lies I've Told Men

1) 'I'm fine.'
2) 'I don't mind.'
3) 'That's fine.'
4) 'Oh, I hadn't even thought about it.'
5) 'Yeah, of course I did.'

Carol has her special voice on. Her soft as a feather dipped in three-minute miracle voice. Her 'I'm here for you' voice. Her 'you can tell me' voice. It's quite hard to hear above all the fans whirring around us, fruitlessly combating the heat.

'What was that?'

'I said, how are you feeling today, April?'

I cross my arms. 'I think we both know I'm not feeling great. This wasn't a scheduled supervision, was it?' It's not like me to be so spiky. But I'm not really sure who me is any more. Not so very long ago, I used to be hopeful and optimistic, a tad dramatic but in a cute, jolly way. Now I'm apparently a psychopathic compulsive liar who can't stop crying.

'Do you want to talk to me about what happened yesterday?'

I shrug into the wind of the fans. 'I just couldn't take it any more.'

'Take what?'

Seriously, it's like she's put her vocal cords into the wash with extra-strength fabric conditioner. It makes me feel as fragile as thin glass. Like I need to be handled with special cotton gloves. 'I'm so bored of pretending,' I say. 'How are any of us making it through each day without screaming? Do you not think that's a miracle? Don't you just want to scream and scream until your voice is gone?'

She makes a note. 'It sounds like you are dealing with some very strong emotions right now.'

'Aren't you?' I stare right at her.

She doesn't take the bait. 'April,' she says, kindly. 'In our last session we talked about your mental capacity to handle this role, and I suggested the strain may be too much. After yesterday's indiscretion, what are your reflections?'

'I know you're going to take me off shift,' I reply. 'Let's not pretend I have any autonomy.'

She leans forward. 'April, I'm not here to decide what happens about your role. That's between you and your CEO. I'm here to see if you're all right, because, from the sound of things, you're not all right.'

I start laughing in a witchy cackle until my throat closes up. Then a rush of sadness crashes over me. It hurts to talk. 'I think I'm going crazy,' I get out. 'It's not just work,' I tell her. 'I'm dating a man and I'm pretending to be a totally different person. I'm pretending my name is Gretel. It's totally out of hand and fucking nuts and yet I'm still doing it. I don't know why.' And, under the breeze of half a dozen fans, all the things I've been doing spill out. From the messages with Joshua, to the first date, to the having sex and the giant flashback, to last night and pretending it's all fine going to the cinema, and even sleeping with him again, despite the fact my whole life has disintegrated. Carol's nodding and putting on her listening face, but you can tell she's excited by what I've just said.

'I don't feel like any of my life is mine right now, does that make sense?' I tell her. 'So it doesn't matter that I'm lying to some dude about who I am, or calling out rapists at work. It doesn't seem real.'

Carol puts her biro down and looks genuinely sorry for me. Which I wasn't expecting at all. More a telling-off lecture about why being a psychotic catfishing liar isn't appropriate. 'When you were assaulted,' she says, 'part of you was taken from you, totally without your permission.' I sniff and clumsily try to push a tear back with the back of my hand. 'Some disassociation is to be expected if you've not had much treatment. April, do you really think you've properly processed what happened to you?'

'It's in the past, I can't change it,' I say. 'There's nothing I can do. I just want to move on and be happy.'

How do you process what happens to you when *that* happens to you? Is it even possible? I changed the day Ryan did that to me, and I can't go back to before. I left him, and I wrote about it in my diary, and I got my body working again, and I wouldn't let him win, and yadda yadda yadda, heal heal heal, fight fight fight, survive survive survive, don't let it define you, embrace the scar, use it to make you stronger, wank wank fucking wank. I'd just rather not have been fucking raped by my abusive boyfriend in the first place, ta very much.

Carol passes me a tissue as I keep sniffing. 'I just feel all these emotions all the time,' I tell her, through a tight throat. 'I wake up and it's there, like a giant ball of energy spitting into my face, and I don't know what to do with it so I just keep pushing it away. It's not like I'm in denial about what happened. But I can't cry all day every day, even though I want to. It's not realistic. I don't know how to make all these emotions go away . . .'

There's a brief interlude because I'm gasping for breath. I panic as stale oxygen gets trapped in my chest. Carol squats down in front of me, repeating, 'Breathe, April, come on breathe. In for five, out for seven, in for five . . .'

This morning, Joshua and Gretel were so cute. They got up and danced around to The Boo Radleys, him twirling Gretel under his arm. What would he think if he saw her now? An irreparable mess. A pile of shattered glass. A ball of ugly emotions. He would not find it as cute as dancing to 'Wake Up Boo' let me tell you that for certain.

'Have you considered boxing?' Carol asks me, once my human functioning comes back. She sits back on the chair and crosses her legs.

'*Boxing?*'

She nods. 'There's this class. In East London, I think. It's women only and they have special classes for survivors.'

'There's a pop-up rape-victim aerobics class? Wow. East London literally thinks of everything.'

She ignores my joke which is annoying because I'm pretty pleased I've found the energy to be sarcastic at a time like this. 'Lots of survivors find it a really good outlet. It may be a way of letting out all these emotions you've been talking about.'

Despite my cynicism, I can't deny that the thought of violence immediately appeals to me. To hit. To destroy. To hurt. I log what she's suggested, making a mental note to look the class up. Then return to a more pressing concern.

'Is it . . . normal?' I ask her. 'To be pretending to someone that I'm someone called Gretel?'

'You know that "normal" isn't a useful word in these kinds of sessions.'

'Blink once for yes, twice for no.'

Her smile is tight now. 'I guess it's worth asking yourself what you think this behaviour is going to help you achieve?'

The answer tumbles out of my mouth. 'Power,' I say.

'*Power?*'

I nod. The fans lift my hair around my shoulders. 'Being Gretel is the first time since I started dating when I was 16 where I feel like I have any power at all.'

'What do you mean?'

I shrug, my eyes widening. 'Just that. I've never, ever, felt like I've had any power with men. I've constantly been on the backfoot, because I want the love too much, and they've made me feel like wanting love is a weird thing. A wrong thing. A needy thing. Even when I've gone for men who I actually, initially, think are a little below my league. Once we've got into it, they've still all ended up rejecting me. Do you know how powerless it makes you feel? To lower your standards to try and love someone and even then they don't want your love? But, when I'm Gretel . . .' I can hear her singing into the breeze of the fans, laughing like she's never worried about anything in her whole goddamn life, '. . . I feel powerful. Like I'm in control. Like I'm finally the one who is less into it. Like *I'm* the one who needs convincing. And, most importantly, *I'm* not the one who is going to get hurt this time. I even feel *guilty*!' I laugh Gretel's laugh. 'I've *never* felt guilty before. Never in my whole life. Guilt is the luxury of the powerful.'

Carol makes a quick note in her book before she finally looks up. 'Do try and get to that boxing class,' she advises. 'This feeling of disempowerment may be able to be channelled through . . . er . . . well, less destructive ways.'

'I will go.' And I will. When you are at rock bottom with only a pickaxe to dig further down with, you are willing to try just about anything. 'But this feeling of powerlessness pre-dates what Ryan did to me,' I tell her. I reach out and tickle the truth, burning my finger. 'I've always felt like I'm on the backfoot, that I'm chasing a rainbow I don't deserve, that I'm not worth anything.' My throat's smaller. Hands shakier. 'In fact, when he did it,' I say, hardly able to get the words out, 'it wasn't even a shock.' I pause again. 'More a confirmation of the inevitable.'

A huge hunk of silence follows that.

Then, 'Go to the class,' she echoes.

I'm signed off for a week, and taken off the rota indefinitely, even though they definitely can't spare me. I get sympathetic looks as I leave the office at 11 a.m.

'I hope you feel better soon,' Matt says.

'I'm sorry to be leaving you in it.'

'Don't worry about that.'

I cry the entire journey home.

Joshua: How's work going? I can't stop thinking about last night.

Gretel: Me neither. That air con really was very powerful.

Joshua: You're hilarious.

Gretel: Just wish we'd had air con in your flat for everything that happened afterwards.

Joshua: Messages like these are very hard to receive when I'm stuck in the world's most boring meeting.

Gretel: Bet that's not the only thing that's hard, huh?

Joshua: Stop. Killing. Me.

Joshua: What you up to tonight? I've purchased a fan. It would love to meet you.

Gretel: You know how to tempt a girl, Joshua.

Gretel: But alas, I have to work late tonight.

Joshua: Never mind. It was late notice anyway. What about Friday? You around? I'm meeting some friends for a curry.

Gretel: In this heat?

Joshua: Yeah. My friend Neil found this really good deal at Dishoom. Up for it? Me and my uni mates? They're a nice bunch. Very good at sharing poppadoms.

Two hours later . . .

Joshua: It's just a curry. No pressure. We can do it some other time. They just want to meet this girl I can't stop talking about :) :)

Joshua: Seriously, no dramas.

Gretel: Chill Joshua. I'd LOVE to go for a curry. I was just tied up at work. What time's the table booked for? xx

Joshua: Eight. That OK?

Gretel: Better than OK.

• *So No One Told You Love Was Going To Be This Way – Gretel's Guide to Meeting The Friends*

The meeting of The Friends is a much bigger deal than either of you admit. You casually ask the other to come along to a thing, and they casually reply that yeah that sounds great – neither of you pointing to the giant elephant in the room that's wearing a painted banner saying *'BIG DEAL, BIG TEST'*. Because if they introduce you to their friends, that means they have to explain to their friends who you are, and why you are in their life. And you don't tend to do that unless you're hopeful you won't have to explain at a later date why you'll never be seeing each other again.

It's a fucking minefield.

You need to look pretty, but, of course, you cannot look like you've tried. You need to resemble an accidentally-beautiful eunuch essentially. Because you can't let out any sexual vibes whatsoever. There is no room for sultry – we don't trust women like that. The best case scenario is to be a sexy children's TV presenter. Think Konnie fucking Huq. Everyone would love to introduce Konnie fucking Huq to their mates.

Conversationally, remember that you don't have to say anything and anything you do say could be held against you. This is a first impression. The approval of friends matters. You will sour before his very eyes if they do not think 'jolly good girlfriend choice, well done'. As always, bland is a good starting point. Remember, it's easier to add than to take away – a bit like doing a smoky eye. Start unremarkable and build from there. Slowly. Whatever you do, do not mention politics or religion or sex or mental illness or past relationships or comedians you like.

Only say nice things about your partner. Do not tease him, or laugh at him. They are not ready to be co-conspirators with you yet. And whatever the hell you do, do *not* ask them for advice about the relationship. Do not look to them to quash your neediness, to tell you how much nicer/prettier/thinner you are than the previous girl he introduced them to. In fact, part of the 'ignore the elephant in the room' game is you all pretending there *was* no one before you. That they didn't smile politely and shake hands and say 'hello nice to meet you' to girls before you. Maybe they even went on fun minibreaks with her. Maybe some of them are still in touch with her. Maybe some of them are hoping they'll get back together and you are just a phase.

Ignore it. Push it down. Let's all play nice and act like you're the one, the only one, and that they're not comparing you to the people before.

Do. Not. Flirt. Never flirt. Remember, in this context you're all asexual with no urges whatsoever. Yes, of course his male friends will wonder briefly what it might be like to have sex with you but no no no, let's all pretend that's not true.

Be bubbly.

Be light.

Be a radiator, not a drain.

Smile a lot.

Say please and thank you.

Be interested in their jobs.

Comment on the weather or something but don't be too boring.

And if his male friends scare you, don't worry, the female friends are much more terrifying – much harder to get right. They will not like the fact you are now on their territory. Even if they never wanted him, they'll want him to want them. Compliment them on what they're wearing. Ask them where they got it from. Reveal a minor insecurity about yourself. Offer it up to them like a sacrifice while remarking on their shoes or hair style.

Don't discuss the future in any way. If you fuck this up, there won't be a future, remember? So don't start suggesting group holidays, or even meeting up next weekend. It will only make everyone uncomfortable, you desperate pathetic bitch.

Before I'm thrown to the lions of Joshua's university clique, I have to wear jogging bottoms for their actual purpose for the first time in years. I've booked myself into Carol's trendy trauma boxing-club beforehand, hoping it will dislodge the guilt I'm harvesting about spreading my Gretel lie to a wider net of people.

I forgot that jogging bottoms are for exercise, rather than changing into the moment you get home. I'm going to boil to death, I'm sure, but I can't commit to buying shorts until I've seen if this class is as useful as Carol claims. I dig out my sports bra that still has the tag on. I've tied a novelty T-shirt into a knot. When I look in the mirror before I leave, I could definitely pass for someone who understands how exercise works.

The sky above me is a light grey, gurgling in pre-thunderstorms that none of us believe will actually come. The country's collectively given up on the idea of rain. On TV they tell us to only flush the toilet after pooing. That baths are the enemy. That hoses are a banned substance.

I've packed my overnight stuff as I have to meet his friends straight after the class. I've managed to successfully dodge him all week with lies about working late and cocktails with friends I didn't see. Gretel's been so busy while April's been so preoccupied with lying in bed, sweating into my sheets and staring at the old faithful crack in the ceiling.

It takes an age to get from the red brick and leafy squares of West London to the chaotic concrete and smell of bins of East London. It's a side of the city where I've never felt I belong. Where the air of hip is so intoxicating you feel the need to pull everyone you pass to one side to convince them you drink cold brew coffee and really dig it. I clutch my phone in one hand, using maps to steer me past Banksy-decorated walls and homeless people with no teeth begging outside flats that cost eight hundred thousand pounds. The pollution pouring off the clogged roads makes it feel even hotter. I cough and turn left, before realising I've turned too early and have to retrace my steps past a queue of people waiting to get into a café where you can drink bubble tea surrounded by cats.

I find the class five minutes before it's due to start. It's in a little dilapidated hall in a tiny piece of green you'd easily walk past if you were on your way to trendier things. The noticeboard outside advertises a cornucopia of different activities. There's a Legs, Bums and Mums class, a Bitch 'n' Stitch knitting circle, a self-help group for victims of narcissism, *and*, every Sunday, a religion-free church ceremony.

'This might help,' I say out loud, crossing my fingers like a child wishing for a pony. 'This might help, this might help, this might help.'

I push through the doors into an empty entrance hall that smells of cheesy feet and old sweat. School pegs adorn the wall, clogged with bags. I bung my stuff on one with a sticker of a smiling giraffe on it and listen to the chatter of the main hall through the glass door.

'This might help,' I whisper again before I make myself push through into the hall to the squeak of trainers.

'Hello, are you here for the class?' A woman clad all in canary-yellow Lycra beams at me. 'You look new.'

I nod nervously.

'Welcome! We're just stretching, then we'll start in a few minutes.'

There're about twenty or so women clotted into groups around me, all with ponytails and in an array of limbering-up poses. Two dozen pendulum boxing-bags hang from the low ceiling, and two giant fans whirr at full pace in each corner. When I researched this class beforehand, it advertised itself as a female-only martial arts class. Only in the small print at the bottom, it read 'this class is for survivors of trauma.' As I look around me, I feel like there must be some kind of mistake. All the women here look confident and functioning and . . . trauma free. They're laughing with their friends, or holding their calves back against their buttocks and remaining perfectly balanced as they do so. Most of them are smiling. I mean, the instructor is wearing all yellow. I find a space in the corner near the fan and pretend to stretch too. As I lunge forward I wonder if, from the outside, I also look as untraumatised as these women do.

Canary claps. 'Right guys, are you ready? Find a punching bag.'

The women who all look like nothing bad ever happened to them disperse. I weave myself into the most inconspicuous spot at the back.

'Right, we're just going to start with a warm-up. One punch with your left arm, then two short jabs with your right. Punch, punch-punch, punch, punch-punch.' She attacks her bag forcefully but gracefully in demonstration, her French plait swirling around her head. Then she walks to the front of the hall and presses her phone attached to some speakers. Little Mix blares across the polished wooden floor. 'Let's go!' she calls over the music. 'Punch, punch-punch.'

I feel silly as I throw my hands into the hefty mass of the swinging sack. It hardly moves. Everyone around me attacks theirs with much more vigour. Maybe I could try hitting it a bit harder? I pull my shoulder back, curl my fist tighter and heave my arm into it.

Oof. Oof-oof. The sack wobbles. *Oof. Oof-oof.* That feels quite good actually. I whack it harder, then harder still. No matter how much I hit it, the hanging sack can absorb it, like it's ingesting all my pain. I start thrusting the full force of my weight into each swing. The noise it makes as my fist connects is weirdly pleasurable, like the feeling you get when you hear snooker balls clonk off each another.

Thwump thwump-thwump.

I like this. Can I go harder?

Little Mix sing about how they've got the power and how they make it shower. I don't usually like pop music, but their voices ignite something in me, make me want to punch harder, fight harder.

'Now we're going to add some kicks in,' the instructor chirps over the chorus. 'Eight punches, followed by four kicks. Like this.' She attacks her bag with her foot, arching her body sideways to land her shin into it sharply. I clumsily try to copy her, and it takes me a good few goes to get my balance right but, by the time Christina Aguilera's 'Fighter' booms through the speakers, I've got the hang of it.

My leg sinks into it, *thwack thwack*. My arms are going for it too. It's like I can't attack the bag hard enough. I start to picture Ryan's face and imagine my punches and kicks landing squarely. *Fuck you*, I think as I punch him again and again. *Fuck you fuck you fuck you.* I feel amazing. Powerful. I picture his nose breaking. Blood spurting out of it, like in a Tarantino movie, soaking that stupid blue T-shirt he always used to wear. 'Stop,' I picture him pleading, his arms up to protect his stupid face. '*Please.*' But I don't stop. Why should I when he didn't? I punch eight times and kick four. His face becomes pulp and yet I still keep attacking.

This is how it feels when someone doesn't stop, I say to him. *You don't like it, do you? You don't like it at all, you pathetic piece of shit.*

He falls to the floor and I rain down more kicks, sweat flying off my body. The words from Christina Aguilera's 'Fighter' fill my head and spur me on. She sings about how she won't forget, and neither will I. I remember everything. That's what makes it so intolerable sometimes. The complete inability to forget it. How relentlessly the memory haunts you. I lose sight of everyone around me. I forget to be embarrassed by my sweat, or the potency of my rage. I'm just lost in feeling like I am finally in charge for once. That *I'm* the one to be scared of. *I* am one who decides whether or not I'm going to stop. So many defensive men put their hands up whenever women dare talk about it. 'Not all of us,' they say. 'Not all men,' they say. 'How dare you suggest,' they say. 'That's actually quite offensive,' they say.

I punch eight times, I kick four times.

Yes yes yes yes yes, I think. *Poor diddums. Getting all upset. Not wanting to feel like baddies when they're goodies. How unfair to all be lumped together. That must really hurt. I mean, it doesn't hurt even the millionth of a fraction compared to being sexually violated, and yet we make the poor men's feelings more important than the violated women's.*

My kicks get harder. I'm using every muscle in my body and it all already hurts but in the most brilliant way. Punch punch. Kick.

Imagine the blood.

God, I feel powerful.

Is this how men feel all the time?

If only they'd listen rather than call me hysterical, I would scream, YES, I KNOW NOT ALL OF YOU DO IT, BUT ALL OF YOU *CAN* DO IT. THAT'S THE POINT, THAT'S THE FUCKING POINT.

The fear is always there. The threat always there. Because, really, unless you are a fucking championship kick-boxer or something, if you are ever alone with a man, all he has to do is decide to do it and he'll be able to. They can hold both of your squirming arms down with only one of their own. They can pin you to your back with just the weight of them. You close the door and make it alone with just you and a man and they can always do that. You get into a cab with them and they can always do that. You get walked home by them and they can always do that. Not all men do, but almost all men *can*. If only they could have a day of feeling as scared as we do. Please just let them have one day. Of not having the power, of us having it instead. I feel like it would give me such release, but it won't ever happen, not in my lifetime, so I just need to keep punching this bag and pretending I have a little.

My feet are soaked in his blood. My clothes are soaked in my sweat. I have no worries in my head right now. I'm not feeling lesser than, or crazier than, or silly because, or sorry for. I'm just feeling good.

I annihilate my punch bag until the braided instructor tells us to stop. Released from my spell, I blink as I look around me, reality coming back into focus. The other women are all equally sweaty and beaming. I make eye contact with a short girl with a peroxide-blonde crop. We smile at one another.

'Great guys, just great. Well done for bringing it so hard in this heat.' Canary claps. 'Right, now, let's do some sparring. Kit is in the corner.'

My triumph wanes the moment I realise this next part of the session involves getting into pairs. Instantly I'm transported back to school PE lessons and never being picked for the team. But Peroxide Girl heads over. 'Want to partner up?' she asks. 'You're new, aren't you?'

'Is it that obvious?'

She laughs. 'No, don't worry. We just all really know each other here.' She gestures towards the box in the corner and we walk over with everyone. 'It's great, isn't it?'

'It's brilliant,' I say. 'I wasn't expecting to feel so instantly great. I feel like a superhero or something.'

She laughs widely again, revealing a tongue piercing. Holes line up like soldiers along her earlobes, the ghosts of multiple piercings removed. 'The first class is always such a rush.'

The instructor has climbed into the box and is tossing out boxing gloves and oversized pads to the sea of grasping hands. Peroxide Girl collects our stuff, before we step back to make room for the other women. 'Right, have you ever sparred before?' she asks.

'I have no idea what that means really.'

'It means we're just going to hit each other, but in a really, nice, empowering kind of way.'

I place my hand in a boxing glove which belches out an old-sweat smell. I yank on the other, marvelling at my giant cartoon-like hands. The instructor tells us to space out and practise our hits. 'Remember, not too hard. Check in with your partner, make sure they're OK with your force. No dick-measuring please.' We all titter. She explains how to punch the pads properly, how to hold them in a way that protects you. 'And remember the most important lesson of all: have fun with it. Let it all out.'

'Do you want to punch first?' Peroxide Girl asks.

'I feel like I need to know your name first.'

'Charlotte. And yours?'

I pause for a second before answering. 'Er, April.'

'That's a lovely name.'

'Thank you.'

She leads me to the corner, sensing my newbie embarrassment. The room's filled with the grunts of punches and the *thwack* of received hits. 'Right, so I'm going to hold the pads up here like this, OK? We'll do twelve reps in each position. Then we can swap over. Don't worry. I'll go easy on you since you're new.' I nod and she holds the pads up to her chest. 'Right, go on.'

I throw a feeble punch, followed by another not much better. It's hard to get over the initial discomfort of punching someone, anyone, even though they're encouraging you to.

'Come on, you can go much harder than that. These pads are totally absorbing.'

I attack her meekly for a few more reps before I gain enough confidence to go harder. Spurred on by her enthusiasm, I turn up the power until she's lungeing to absorb me, grinning like I'm her child who just won a school prize or something. Fist connects with padding. Flexed foot connects with a block. My smile connects with a stranger's. I swipe and attack until there's no oxygen left in my lungs, and then we switch over. I can tell she's not giving it her all as she lays into me, but it feels fine.

When we're both sweaty, giddy messes, the instructor calls it quits. We return the equipment to the corner, everyone smiling, everyone moist, everyone friendly.

'Right ladies,' she claps again. 'Game time.'

'You'll love this,' Charlotte whispers. 'It's the best bit.'

'Right, sit in a circle everyone. Newbies, this will be weird for two minutes, and then will be super fun. It's just some kid-like cardio games to release any excess nervous energy before you have to face the universe again.'

We all sit inwards, cross-legged, like pass the parcel is about to begin. 'So, this game is based on "Fishes in the Sea", a game that you may've played when you were little. But we've changed up the words a bit, so you ladies can reclaim any negative labels you may've been called in the past.' She walks around us and starts patting us, one by one, on the head. 'Needy, crazy, nagging, desperate.' She doles out the words like she's allocating school teams. 'Needy, crazy, nagging, desperate. Needy, crazy . . .' She gently pats my head at 'crazy' and it's the first time I've been called it that doesn't make me want to instantly cry. In fact, I hear a giggle and realise it's me. When we've each been allocated our word, she explains the rules. When our label is called, we have to get up and start running around the outside. Sometimes she'll call 'times are changing' and we'll have to run in the opposite direction. Sometimes she'll call 'when they go low' and we have to run on our tiptoes and yell back 'we go high'. Sometimes she'll call 'progress is one step forward' and we have to run backwards. Finally, whenever she calls 'the patriarchy's coming', we have to race back to our space, and the last one to sit down is out.

It's a whole new realm of bonkers. I crane my neck around, trying to make eye contact with Charlotte to make a 'this is crazy' face, but she's nodding and smiling like it's totally normal. Everyone is.

'Right, let's get going. NAGGING!'

A quarter of the room full of otherwise normal-looking women stand up and start running around the circle.

After five minutes, I totally and utterly get it.

'CRAZY!' I'm up and I'm jogging, my heart thumping, trying to keep pace with the rest of the crazies.

'WHEN THEY GO LOW!' I rise up onto my tiptoes and we all laugh at how hard it is to run like that.

'TIMES ARE A CHANGING!' I almost twist my ankle as I spin to change direction.

'NEEDY!' Another quarter of the room hop up and start running with us. Every single one of us is smiling, in that free way that hurts your face. My trainers thud on the wood. My arms swing by my sides.

'THE PATRIARCHY'S COMING!' We all squeal and peg

it back to our spots. I thrust my body forward, chuck my legs into a crossed position and land my arse heavily onto the ground. Charlotte, a needy, comes in last. She grins as she faces outwards, shrugging, unbothered, her face red from running. I smile at her as the word 'DESPERATE!' is called and feet thump around me once again.

'CRAZY!' Oh, me again. We all laugh, acknowledging the total lack of break we've had from the last run. Our breath comes out thick and heavy. It's hard to run fast when you're laughing so much. We run backwards, we scurry back to our places, we swap directions. NEEDY, DESPERATE, CRAZY, DESPERATE, NAGGING, NEEDY, NAGGING, CRAZY . . . I've never laughed at these words before. They are words that I'm usually incapable of having a sense of humour about. Because these words are always loaded. Even if the man holds his hands up and says, 'Oh come on, I was only joking', you cannot laugh, not properly, because these words are never a joke, they are only ever a method of control. But today, times are a changing. I run and run and I see these silly labels for the silly labels they are. I shoot back to a memory of Ryan standing over me as I cried in the corner because he told me I was too fat and he couldn't get an erection because of it. 'God, why are you crying, AGAIN? You're crazy.' And I see the craziness of that word being used, when my behaviour was the most normal response to what he'd just said. 'I wasn't crazy,' I whisper as I run, *thud thud thudding* on the floor. 'You made me crazy.'

I've never truly believed that before, no matter how many times Megan protested it. But with endorphins surging through my blood, and other women jogging around and laughing at that word with me, the message begins to bed in. It curls up in my soul, nestling in, and part of me releases a tiny squib of tension I've been holding in for years.

Nobody stays out for very long. The instructor keeps saying 'Oh, don't worry, just join back in' so we can all continue playing. The air is loaded with giddy. We land our feet in unison. Our hair swings madly from side to side. We apologise whenever one of us gets too excited and accidentally runs into the back of someone else.

'WHEN THEY GO LOW!'

'CRAZY, DESPERATE!'

'THE PATRIACHY'S COMING!'

In the last round, she calls 'WE'RE ALL IN THIS TOGETHER', the signal that everyone has to get up and run in a circle. It becomes more of a conga line than a circle – too many of us in the hall to really run properly. We hold each other's clammy shoulders, getting one another's sweat smeared into our palms, we push each other through the tiredness, draining ourselves of the very last droplets of energy. My face feels redder than it's ever felt in my life. I'm sweating out of every pore of my body. We all are. Ugly and breathless, but smiling and powerful.

'Right, game over! Let's dance it out to finish!' The speakers crank on. 'Just a Girl' by No Doubt blasts out. We all whoop like we're in a nightclub. I'm skanking like I used to as a teen, and everyone around me is doing the same. No one is dancing to look pretty. Half of us are screaming along with the lyrics. I jump, flick more sweat around. I've never felt happier than in this moment. Charlotte is next to me, yelling along even louder. Her sweaty arms are around me. We pogo up and down. I feel drunk with happiness. Lost in whatever is happening. We all are. We scream out the final words, punching our fists into the air, swinging some of the bags. Then the song dies, and it's quiet again. We become two dozen female strangers, soaked through in sweat, hugging one another in a tiny dilapidated hall.

'Well done ladies. That was a great one. Oh my God, it is *hot* in here. Luckily the shower is just about working.'

We let go of one another but the bond doesn't feel broken. Charlotte is eyeing me, her cheeks raised with her smile. 'So, how did you find it?'

'That is the weirdest but best thing I've done in a while.'

'Isn't it? It's like kick-boxing slash crazy children's-birthday-party slash trauma recovery slash dance party.' We walk towards our pegs and stop by Charlotte's otter sticker. 'Some of us go for a drink after, if you're up for it? There's one tiny shower we all have to take turns with, or you may want to go home and just shower there?'

I lift my bag away from its giraffe home. It's filled with Gretel gear for tonight. A nice outfit to meet Josh's friends in, but one that doesn't look like I've tried too hard. And overnight stuff to take to his house later. I reach into my bag and retrieve my phone.

Joshua: The countdown to poppadoms begins! See you at eight x

The time at the top of my phone says six thirty, and it's a thirty-minute journey at least to the restaurant.

'I'm supposed to be meeting someone, but I can be a bit late.'

'Great. The pub is only around the corner. Come on, let me show you the terrible shower.'

The shower's a tiny trickle in a gross, grey bathroom that must've once had white tiles. I let the water fill my cupped hands and splash it over myself. It's way too weak to wash my hair, so I just wet the front of it to dilute the sweat and figure it won't look too awful. Even if it does, I don't give the flyingest of fucks right now.

About five women wait for me when I emerge, including Charlotte. 'Hey everyone, this is April,' she says, giving me their names, which I instantly forget. They all wave hi. Ask how I found the class. They laugh when I rave about how good it is. We call goodbye to the instructor, asking if she wants help with the punching bags, but she doesn't. The fans have been turned off and the hall's eerily quiet. I can taste the salt of our sweat on my tongue, and the air isn't much better when we get outside. Heavy and unforgiving with a sallow, grey cloud-coverage.

I shuffle at the back of the group, feeling new and nervous as I'm steered towards the pub, listening to their conversations.

'How did your presentation go?'

'Did you see Jane at the weekend? Is she OK? Oh my God. A three-bedroom detached? This is why I need to leave London.'

The pub they pick is too busy with Friday. You can hardly get through the door with so many office workers standing outside, seal-laughing and gesticulating. It's empty inside though, apart from the throng at the bar.

'Shall we just sit in here, rather than stand around outside?' Charlotte asks. 'My legs are dying.'

'Yes, let's.' A woman with long black hair strides forward to claim a tucked-away table in the corner.

Charlotte points at the table. 'Wine? White? Two bottles?' Everyone choruses yes.

'Do you want some money?' I ask, digging for my purse.

'Don't be daft.'

'Need help carrying anything?'

'Nope. Just save me a seat.'

I'm left with the group and grin at them. The power from the class is fading out here in the real world, without Gwen Stefani and a giant punching bag for company. But the lady with black hair turns to me and saves me from my feelings of social inadequacy. 'April, was it?'

'Yes,' I nod. 'And you?'

'My name's Anya.' She holds out her hand and then introduces the others once more, giving me a chance to get their names this time: 'And this is Hazel, Steph, and Jenny.' They all wave hello and I wave back self-consciously.

'So, how did you guys all find out about this class?' I ask.

Anya replies first. 'My GP recommended it after the NHS couldn't continue my therapy any more,' she says. 'They keep refusing to acknowledge complex PTSD as a thing.'

Steph nods knowingly. 'Oh, yes, we've all been there . . .'

'Complex PTSD?'

'It's basically the same as PTSD,' Hazel answers, 'except it's caused by long-term exposure to trauma rather than a one-off one.' She rolls her eyes. 'In my case, my abusive prick of an ex-boyfriend.'

Charlotte arrives just in time to overhear, brandishing two bottles of wine and multiple glasses wedged on a tray.

'Snap!' she cheers, squatting to unload her spoils. She high-fives Hazel while the table laughs and they start handing out the glasses and tipping wine into them like a production line.

Charlotte sloshes a generous amount of wine into my glass, winking like we've known each other forever. 'You all right?' she asks.

'I guess I'm a bit surprised by what you just said,' I admit, taking a cool sip, already embracing the inevitable headache it will bring after sweating so much.

'God. Sorry! We're not very good at stiff upper lipping here,' she smiles. 'We all feel so safe with each other that it just kind of spills out.'

'No! Don't be sorry. I'm not upset, just . . . I dunno . . . I've never heard anyone come out and just say it like that.'

'That's what's so great about this group,' the girl called Jenny tells me. 'There's no hiding here, or pretending to be OK when you're not. The whole point of the class, and of chatting afterwards, is about letting it out.'

'Better out than in.' Charlotte holds her wine glass up and everyone repeats it and does a 'cheers'. The circle bleeds into groups of different chatter and I listen hard, trying to get the grasp of everyone. Charlotte works for a start-up in East London. Anya with the black hair works in finance. Jenny's a secondary-school science teacher. Hazel has two children and has had to move back home with her parents after leaving her ex. And Steph's only just graduated from Oxford a month ago, and doesn't know what the hell to do with her life. They update one another on the week's dramas, compare notes on their punching techniques. Hazel jokes about how she's finally losing the baby weight even though that's the last reason on earth she came. There's an easiness in the air. There's no whiff of any female competition – just camaraderie. I drink it in as I drink my wine, wondering how any of these women have any trauma at all when they seem so very fine. Until I hear Jenny mention to Hazel, 'God, I had the worst flashback on Wednesday. I literally couldn't get out of bed all the next day. I had to call in sick. Me. A teacher.'

'Shit love. I'm so sorry. What set it off?' Hazel pulls her in for a quick hug.

'A school fucking assembly. We had some guy come in to talk to the girls about personal safety, and it just set me off. Shaking. Crying. Reliving it. The worst! And it was only 9.30 in the morning. I had to hold it together the whole day. I just shoved the students in front of *Osmosis* fucking *Jones*, even the Year Elevens, and cried at the back of the classroom in the dark.'

'I'm really sorry,' I say, then worry I've just butted in.

But Jenny looks up, takes me in. 'Thank you,' she smiles.

'I had a really bad flashback the other day.' I'm not sure why I'm blurting this out but I keep going. 'They're the worst. I've been signed off from work this week.'

'That's awful. I'm sorry you had to go through that.' And, even though we don't know each other, Jenny reaches over to squeeze my hand. 'What brought you to the class? If you don't mind me asking, of course?'

'I don't mind at all,' I say. 'I was in an abusive relationship with this guy for two years. He . . . he raped me.' Saying it feels like pulling off a pair of pinching shoes at the end of a long day. I've hardly told anyone this. Only Megan, Carol, Matt, Katy and the odd badly-chosen romantic dalliance. I've not even told my mum. I twist my hands in my lap. 'He only did it twice though.'

Jenny shakes her head wryly. 'Oh yes, only been raped the two times. That's nothing.'

I giggle at the ridiculousness of what I've just said. 'You know what I mean.'

'Unfortunately I do. We're so good at diminishing it, aren't we? When we really shouldn't.'

'I'm so sorry that happened to you,' Hazel says, as I wipe under my eyes. 'You've done the right thing, coming to this class. I was raped too . . . if you haven't figured that out by now.'

'Essentially we all were, in some way, somehow,' Charlotte says, running a hand through her crop. 'It's what links us.'

'It's something that links many women,' Hazel adds, picking up her wine and taking a big slurp. 'Once I started coming here and talking about it, the more I realised it's a case of who's been lucky enough *not* to have this happen to them rather than the other way around.'

'Hear, hear!' Charlotte cheers the air.

I've never felt more understood and less alone than I do in this precise moment. The world's turned clear, like I've finally got the right prescription lenses with which to see it. There's a happy sharpness to this pub. The colours are brighter, the voices louder, my heart softer.

'Just nipping to the loo,' I say. 'Do you mind looking after my bag?' I squeeze around the table and push through into the toilet which doesn't have any paper left. It doesn't matter, I don't need to pee anyway. I lean over and grip the sink with both hands.

There's a table of women behind that door and they look normal and they sound normal but, like me, they spend every day applying the same veneer of normal over the huge struggle to get over what shouldn't have happened to them. The endorphins from the exercise still pump through me. They mingle with this newfound feeling of . . . belonging. I smile as I stand up and look at myself in the mirror. My face is still red from too much exercise but it glows.

I exude Gretel.

I wave and she waves back at me. 'We're going to be late to meet Joshua,' I tell her.

She shrugs through the reflective glass.

The sky belches an angry rumble of thunder as I drag myself away from the pub. 'I will *so* be at the class next week, thank you, thank you.'

I'm scrolling through my phone crammed with new numbers, grinning, when I'm interrupted by the noise. I look up to see the London skyline blanketed in a heavy dark-grey mass. The air has the iron tang of rain – I don't dare hope.

Gretel's late but she's told them she's on her way and she's sorry. Josh sends her a photo of the menu so they can get her order in.

Joshua: I've had half of your beer xxx

It's a slightly pass-agg message which is appropriate for my lateness. Luckily I'm glowing with so much post-class joy, I reckon I can charm my way out of it. I fling myself out of the clammy Tube, and up the stairs of Kings Cross, taking the secret shortcut only Londoners know about. I skip up to Granary Square. The sky's even darker now, practically black. Another attention-seeking clap of thunder shakes the sky and people stop and look up, like we're at the start of an apocalypse movie. There's a giant queue to get in to the restaurant and I slink past smugly, skipping the line of people all saying 'do you think it will rain?' and staring upwards.

'Table for Neil?' I ask at the front desk, checking I've got the booking name right on my phone.

'Up the stairs and to the left.' The concierge nods the direction and I turn and glide upwards, taking in the insta-gramness of the restaurant's interior. It's kitted out with sleek chequered floors and mahogany tables. Whirring overhead-fans push the flat air around fruitlessly but photogenically. I spot the back of Joshua's head and my stomach lurches in a swell of unhelpful affection. He's sitting at a table with three men and two women and hasn't noticed me yet. He's talking with his hands, as I've learnt he does a lot. I put on a friendly smile and hurry over.

'Yeah, she works for this sex and relationships charity called We Are Here, it's really great, though their CMS system sounds like a nightmare . . .' He cranes his neck backwards, a big grin right there. 'And here she is! Gretel, this is everyone. Everyone, this is Gretel.'

I wave at the table widely, trying to make eye contact with each one. 'It's so great to meet you,' I say. 'I'm so so sorry I'm late. I was at this boxing thing and it ran over.'

'Boxing thing?' The man sitting to Joshua's right is clearly the alpha of this group. I can tell by the way he's sitting – legs astride. He's tall, arms crossed, typically good-looking. He must be Neil.

'Yes and it was in East London so the Tube was a pain. Anyway, hi, I'm Gretel.'

They stand, one by one, to greet me, with an array of handshakes, cheek kisses, and an awkward hug from a slightly pudgy guy at the end of the table. If I'm guessing correctly, this must be Luke, their roommate from uni who's never had a girlfriend though none of them are sure why. He seems the friendliest. 'It's lovely to meet you,' he says mid-hug and slightly too loudly into my ear. 'I've heard so much about you.'

I raise both eyebrows at Joshua over his shoulder. 'Is that right?'

'All good things, all good things,' Josh reassures me as I sit next to him. He squeezes my hand under the table, and winks, giving me reassurance I don't need. 'You OK?' he whispers.

I can't pretend I'm not touched by the gesture. 'I'm fine.' I kiss the side of his forehead. 'Sorry again for being late. Hey, is that my beer?'

He hands it over, looking right into my eyes. I point to the half-empty glass. 'Still half-full,' I say.

'I knew you'd be a half-full person.'

I take a knowing sip and brace myself for turning up Gretel's megawatt charm. I lean over to Alpha Male, knowing he's the one to impress. The most unlikeable is always the most important to impress. 'So, tell me everything I need to know about Josh,' I say. 'You guys met on your course, right?'

Neil nods and leans over, all the better to show off his biceps with. 'Yes, we met in Freshers' Week and were in the same halls.'

'So, who here went to Leeds then?'

He points them out. 'Me and Lucy and Luke.' The table listens in now their names have been mentioned.

'And the rest of you know each other . . . ?' Gretel asks, so, *so* interested.

'I'm Lucy's husband,' says a tall man sitting next to her called George.

'And I'm Julia, Neil's wife,' the remaining woman says, who

is very done up for a curry. She's wearing false eyelashes and her hair is perfectly curled. She squeezes Neil's arm and he sort of shrugs her off while also smiling.

'So, what was Joshua like at uni?' I take a poppadom from the pile in the middle and ping it in two to fit onto my side plate.

'Just like I am now,' Joshua replies, taking half of my poppadom. 'Intimidatingly cool.'

'Umm, yeah mate,' Neil nods his head. 'Very cool . . . Apart from trying to start a Coding Society that no one turned up to, and let's not forget the cereal box business cards.'

The table collapses into laughter while Joshua blushes slightly.

'What business cards?' I ask.

Joshua shoots a 'thanks mate' glare at Neil before he explains. 'So, on my first night of Freshers' Week, I *may* have cut up a Kellogg's Cornflakes box into small squares, written my name and email address onto them with biro, and handed them out to all the people I met.'

Everyone chortles, sprays of poppadom crumbs falling from their mouths onto the tablecloth, while I play the part of surprised-but-delighted-at-the-cuteness-of-it girl. 'I don't know where to even begin with that one,' I say. 'I mean, why business cards? Why out of Kellogg's? Why your email address? Why did you not just make friends the regular way?'

Luke points to the air. 'These are all very valid questions Joshua.'

Joshua gets redder and nuzzles into my shoulder for support. I smell the sweet tang of too much beer on him. 'In my head, having business cards would make me seem really suave,' he says. 'But, no. Not made out of cornflakes boxes anyway. I promise you I'm really, really cool now,' he protests.

'I mean, cool people always tell you how cool they are,' Lucy quips while we laugh at Joshua again.

'Well I think that's adorable,' I declare, patting him on the head while they all laugh harder.

'Great. Adorable. Men just love being called adorable.' Joshua puts his head face-first onto the table.

'But it *is* adorable!' I pull him up and give him a quick peck on the cheek. He squeezes my knee again, his reddened face curled up into such a smile. Gretel is doing well. I'm fitting in perfectly. Of course I am.

'*You're* adorable,' he whispers, pulling me in for another quick kiss.

And I wonder if he'd still think that if he'd been sitting at the pub earlier and hearing me share what I shared.

The poppadoms are demolished. Loaded with chutneys, sprinkled with sliced onions, chomped down into, crumbs flailing onto the white tablecloth.

'Oh my God, do you remember that time in the third year, Josh? When you were so determined to make us go to Alton Towers before we graduated. But it came the night after the Otley Run?'

'Vomit. So much vomit.'

'It was Air that did it.'

'Hahahahahahaha,' says Gretel.

The mains arrive. Naans are torn apart and added to our tiny silver plates. We ask one another if they would like to try a bit of ours.

'So, what are your plans this summer?'

'Oh, George and I are going to stay in this villa in Crete with a bunch of his friends.'

'Ooo, nice.'

'Yes. I just can't wait to have the time off work. How about you two?'

'We're diving in Indonesia. Trying to get our PADIs, aren't we love?'

'How about you, Josh?'

'Working, I'm afraid. Used up all my annual leave climbing the mountain.'

'I can't believe you climbed a mountain, you've never mentioned that before.'

'Shut up.'

'Hahahahahahaha,' says Gretel.

'Don't let him fool you, Gretel. He might act like an Iron Man but he has literally only climbed one mountain, and he hasn't even walked up the left side of the Tube escalator since.'

'Hahahahahahaha,' says Gretel.

'And you Gretel? What are you up to this summer?'

'I want to go to Africa,' Gretel says.

They all nod. They all say, 'Amazing. Isn't Africa just amazing?'

Another round of drinks. The men point to their beer glasses and nod. The girls pluck out the cocktail menu, pour over it as a means of bonding, discussing which one they are going to go for.

'Mother's Ruin sounds great,' Gretel tells Lucy 'I'll get one too.'

'Why is gin so delicious?'

'Oh, I know. And, can I just say? I've been obsessing over your shoes all night.'

'Oh, thank you! I was just thinking how nice your bag is.'

'Oh, thank you!'

Nobody orders pudding because nobody ever orders pudding at an Indian restaurant. We have another round instead. Josh is slippery with drink, his hand constantly reaching for mine under the table, sweaty, squeezing my fingers too tight. His craving for physical affection overwhelmingly constant. I listen a lot more than I talk. Neil speaks the most, the loudest, interrupting, but no one seems to mind. Reminiscing about university is clearly the group's conversational safety blanket. They remember old lecturers, and pubs they used to love going to that aren't there any more, and compare living in the north with living in the south.

'A taxi home was only four quid, can you imagine now?'

'Snakebite. A pound.'

'We could sell our one-bed and buy a castle up there. Well, not quite a castle, but you know. Four-bed detached. A garden.'

'Yeah, but you wouldn't be in London.'

'True, true.'

Gretel's doing well. I can feel she's doing well. Julia has already nodded at Joshua when she didn't realise I was looking.

I tune out whenever they drift into nostalgia I can't join in with and busy my brain with reliving the boxing. *Punch punch, kick kick kick.* I want time to hurry up so I can go back and do it all over again. I don't think I've stopped grinning since

I left, and it's contagious. The table smile with me, reflect it back, catch my happiness like a summer cold.

Eventually a waiter approaches the table with a bill. He's sorry but they need the table now for the next booking. The air ripples with mild annoyance, no one wanting to leave the sanctuary of the table. Neil's eyes flick to the queue below us, as if he's trying to make out the group who dares expel us. He then picks up the bill and takes charge, calculating the amount we all owe.

'Don't worry, I'll get it,' Joshua says to me as I'm rifling through my purse for my card and praying I've got enough to cover it. I can't afford to be as independent a Gretel as I want to be right now. 'Thank you.'

'I'm the one who asked you to come.' He pulls me in to kiss me on the cheek. 'They like you, I can tell,' he murmurs, the smell of beer on his warm breath.

'I like them too.' It's true enough. I certainly don't dislike them. They're just like any other group of uni people who have all ended up in London, glad to have ties and roots in this relentlessly lonely city. Neil's a bit of a dick but every friendship group has a bit of a dick that only an outsider can pick up on. We wait impatiently as the waiter hurries through all our respective card payments, wiping his forehead with the back of his hand. 'It's started to rain,' he announces to no one in particular and nobody really takes it in. We're all too busy collecting our bags and figuring out where to go next.

Neil decides it's best to stay here. 'There's a nice bar on the lower ground floor.' His word is decision. We nod and clatter downstairs, walking through clouds of various aromas from different dishes carried past. My phone has a notification on it, telling me I've been added to a group chat called 'Better Out Than In' and my smile settles into my stomach.

'You staying at mine later?' Joshua asks, lips brushing my neck.

'If you want me to?' Gretel says, looking right at him innocently as we reach the ground floor. A grab of my arse indicates he does.

The bar's crowded but dying down enough that we're able to cram ourselves onto a circular table.

'Right. Shots! Shots?' Neil says and everyone groans but accepts the challenge. He returns shortly with a tray of tequila and limes, and good old Gretel downs hers effortlessly, licking the salt and munching the citrus, the very definition of fun fun fun – aren't I such fucking fun?

We order more cocktails. I'm able to afford a round as Joshua paid for my meal. It costs seventy pounds. I check my phone while I wait for the cocktails to be made.

Better Out Than In

Charlotte: Welcome to the group, April! How are those endorphins treating you?

April: WHY DOESN'T LIFE ALWAYS FEEL THIS WAY?

Hazel: We have a convert.

Hazel: Oh my God, my butt.

Hazel: Why did I kick so very hard? Must. Stop. Imagining. His. Face.

Charlotte: The whole point is to imagine his face.

Hazel: Shouldn't I be over it by now?

Charlotte: Yes, set a time limit on your trauma recovery. Very helpful.

I wish I didn't have to return to the table. I'd rather go home, shower properly, get into my pyjamas and spend all night sending messages to these women. I contemplate just leaving – vanishing – once again thinking I should just end whatever the hell this mess is that I've started. The need for revenge has quietened since just one boxing class. Carol must really be onto something. Yet I find myself staying put and carrying the tray of drinks back from the bar. 'Ta-daaa!' I say, plonking the tray down. Everyone thanks me, plucking their drinks off it, before returning their attention to Neil who's waxing lyrical about something or other. I settle next to Josh, who pats my knee, and take a sip of my drink.

I'm a little bit more than tipsy actually and finding it hard to sit up straight on my stool. I try to tune back into the group's frequency – leaning forward to hear what Neil's saying.

'Did you see it in the news? It's getting ridiculous. You can't say anything if you're a man these days. It's a complete witch hunt.'

My ears prickle. I sit up a bit straighter. I turn to Joshua who's holding his head up with bunched fists under his chin. He's blinking blearily, but nodding.

'I *loved* him in *Under the Apple Tree*,' Julia adds. 'And he's such a nice man. He's clearly so in love with his wife.'

A very determined chill settles across my skin as I realise who and what they're talking about. I've been trying to avoid it in the news but it's almost impossible. It's everywhere. A famous actor's been saying that the sexism backlash in Hollywood has gone too far. That some women have over-reacted to minor incidents and the climate of fear is affecting how films are made. The phrase he's coined that's caused all the upset is 'rape spectrum'.

'I mean, I totally agree with what he's saying. Why is there such a backlash?' Neil continues. He leans forward, his strong arms bulging out as he re-postures. He speaks with the confidence of someone who's never feared for his safety before.

The table nod their heads heavily, giving him further confidence to continue as my stomach curdles with newly-arrived bile. 'Having your arse pinched is not the same as being, like, violently raped.' He throws his hands up. 'Where's the controversy?'

My feet are on the ground because I'm standing up. I didn't mean to stand up, but it appears to be happening. My mouth is open, with words tumbling out of it.

'Pray tell me,' I'm saying, loudly, sourly, 'what a *non-violent* rape is please, Neil? I'd love to hear.'

The energy switches within a millisecond. The table falls quiet. Mouths drop open. A tightness encompasses the group. Portcullises shut down. Neil and I size each other up and I put on a smile, like I'm asking the question innocently. A child who doesn't know the answer: 'What does Santa Claus do in the summertime? Why can't I go to bed as late as I want? Why do I have to eat my main course before I'm allowed my pudding? What's a non-violent rape? Can I have a cookie?'

Joshua stiffens next to me. He and Neil share the smallest of looks. My malfunction is loud and aggressive and inappropriate and ruining everything. I should be panicking now. Trying to stuff myself back into my box, folding in my limbs like a rag doll at the end of her children's TV show. Quietening myself, making it easy, smiling and nodding because it will make for an easier hour now, even though I won't be able to sleep for the rage I'll feel later. Gretel would laugh it off. Gretel would know maybe it's not the time or place. And Gretel could handle this conversation anyway, without it setting off a thousand tiny landmines in her perfect trauma-free body. But April is too full from her class to back down. I can't let this slide, not when I feel totally able to take him on.

Neil turns so he's fully facing me while the rest watch our stand-off. 'I didn't mean it like that.' He may as well be holding his hands up and stepping away from his weapon. 'I'm just saying, there *is* a spectrum to these things. You can't lump in something like pinching an arse with something more damaging. That's all he was trying to say, and I don't think that's an unfair argument.' He sits back, puffing his chest, spraying his alpha scent over me like a skunk that's been stamped on.

'And *you* get to decide what's damaging and what isn't?' I ask. 'You don't see a problem with a man who probably hasn't ever been violated getting to decide what counts as a violation? You don't see the problem with even measuring a violation in the first place?' I shake my head, like he's being stupid, because he is. 'It's the violation that's the violence, don't you see? It's knowing your boundaries mean bugger-all that's the trauma – that anyone can touch you, that how you feel about it doesn't count. *That's* the trauma. That's the violence. Anything else that happens on top of that is additional.' I'm darting my finger at him. The table looks utterly horrified. Neil's doing his best not to snarl. 'It's not a spectrum,' I continue. 'It's a line that shouldn't be crossed. Ever. In any way. It's all violence and it's all traumatic. And, for someone who clearly has no experience of it, why do you feel like you're the one who gets to decide?'

Neil's wife has got the alert. *Husband under attack! Husband under attack! Must protect, must do my duty.* Julia jumps in while I'm pausing for angry breath. She must defend her husband. 'I don't think that's what he was saying . . .'

'What *are* you saying then?' I ask Neil, but now Joshua's bumbling in.

'Let's change the subject,' he says brightly, lifting his beer to his mouth. 'No politics on a Friday night, eh?'

I twist to him and shake my head, stupefied. 'This isn't politics, Joshua, it's women's fucking lives.'

There's a collective flinch at the table. A Mexican wave of friction to my inappropriate swearing.

'Hey, hey, hey,' Lucy's saying, trying to keep the peace.

'If we could all take a minute maybe, to calm down,' Luke suggests.

Nobody's having fun all of a sudden and it's all April's fault. I'm breaking the rules. I don't even care. I'm so *bored* of this sort of bullshit and I've finally got the confidence to say as much.

Joshua is po-faced. His voice soft. 'Gretel, I didn't mean it like that. I just—'

'I'm really sorry, but I have to go.' I don't care that I've made it awkward, and I don't care that they're all going to bitch about me, and right now I don't even care that I've messed up my weird social experiment with Joshua. This is the time to end it, like this. With April's energy soaring through my veins, finally having her say, revealing that even Gretel has some fucking limits. All I care about is leaving this table. Leaving this debate about something that is too painful to be debated.

'Gretel!'

'Sorry, it's just, I've got this thing, early tomorrow.'

I'm still making a polite escape considering everything. I'm letting the side down by not just storming out. My urge to be likeable, even when storming out of a curry house, still wins. 'It was lovely to meet you all,' I pretend.

We even all kiss each other on the cheek before leaving. They tell me it was nice to meet me too. Joshua's eyes are wide with drunken confusion. I kiss him on the cheek the same way I'd kiss my grandma. 'Bye babes,' I say, then I walk out of his life.

I practically run up the stairs. If I don't get out of this stuffy air, I will suffocate. I push past waiters and around tables of people eating. The concierge wishes me a good evening but I hardly hear him. I'm through the doors and outside, and yes yes yes, it's raining! It's finally raining! Sheets of it plummet from the sky, drenching me within seconds. I stop and stand in it for a moment, not quite believing it. I'm not the only one in wonder. Soon there are several of us standing there on the grey slippery pavement of Granary Square, staring upwards, our arms outstretched, like we're in rapture. I throw my head back, open my mouth, and let the polluted raindrops fall onto my tongue. I will never see that table of humans again and they all hate me, but I could not care less. Gretel is gone, it's over. It wasn't quite the grand finale I wanted it to be, but I've still ended it. In fact, it's even better this way. Because I ended it while standing up for myself. In this moment I'm everything I want to be. Strong, alive, not taking any more shit. In this moment I'm invincible. I never want it to stop raining.

I duck into the Tube, shaking myself dry like a dog. My dress clings to my body, my feet slip in my sandals, my lungs feel clean from all the extra oxygen in the air. I don't let myself think about it as the train rumbles through the darkness, its damp passengers dripping onto the filthy floors. I'm not ready to unpack the emotions, the fall-out. I just want to feel good that it's finally raining, that I made some new friends earlier, that I stood up for something I believed in even though it was the harder thing to do.

It's still pissing it down when I get out at South Kensington. I have no umbrella. I've forgotten what it feels like to even consider taking one out. So I walk home with the fat rain splashing my eyelashes, taking it slowly as people dart past me, *Evening Standard*s held uselessly above their heads. I savour each step. I know things will get complicated once I'm inside and fully alone. So slowly I go, skin soaked and puckering, jaw chattering from the damp, unable to hear the noise of the city over the din of so much water falling from above and the low rumbling of thunder.

The flat is empty, once again. Megan merely a passing ghost these days. I stand dripping onto the wooden floorboards, laughing at how drenched I am. I peel my clothes off and carry the dripping bundle to the bathroom sink. I get my towel and rub myself vigorously, squeezing my hair until it doesn't drip any more. Then I wrap myself up like a burrito and walk back out into the sitting room.

I thought I would cry when I got in, but instead I just feel the vague sting of self-righteousness, burning gently like the first day of cystitis. I'm not embarrassed or ashamed that I stood up to that man, that I made the conversation difficult for him, although I do feel a tiny pang for Josh, and his embarrassment at my behaviour. I expect he'll call tomorrow, probably, after he's cooled down. He'll ask to meet for coffee and then make an excuse about why he doesn't think we should see one another any more. His friends are probably going through his escape plan right now, reassuring him he's making the right decision. Maybe he isn't ready to date again after that last one, the girl he lived with. I pull up my phone to see the group chat's been busy.

Better Out Than In

Hazel: How am I drunk after two glasses of wine? Why does this always happen to me? Especially when I see you lot?

Steph: Because we're amazing.

Hazel: I mean, apart from that . . .

I wish I'd stayed with them. I should've. Why did I even go and meet Josh's friends? Considering I have no interest in him whatsoever, why did I put that above my healing and recovery?

My phone rings in my hand, and my eyebrows furrow in utter shock when I see it's Josh's number. It takes three tries to accept the call as my fingers are still wet from the shower.

'Hi Gretel.' I can hardly hear him over the roar of the storm. 'Whereabouts in South Ken do you live? I'm at the Tube station.'

'You're *where?*'

'Are you OK?'

'You're at the *Tube* station?'

'Yes, but I don't know where to go next. Is it OK to come round?'

'It's pissing it down! Aren't you soaked?'

'Yes. Look, I'm sorry about what happened. Can you just give me your address and we can chat about it?'

I'm too shocked to do anything other than give it to him.

Unsure how to proceed next, I perch on the sofa, staring at the wall until the urgent trill of my buzzer makes me jump. I open the door, still wrapped in my towel.

Joshua looks like he's just clambered out of a swimming pool. His mouth is set in a thin line. 'Hi,' he says nervously, running a hand through his hair and dislodging a hidden tidal wave of water. 'Can I come in?'

I step to one side and close the door after him. 'You're drenched, I'll get you a towel.'

'Thank you. That would be great.'

He's balancing on one leg to take off his shoe, dripping more rain onto the floorboards, when I come back with a dry towel.

He takes it wordlessly and rubs his face into it. 'Do you mind if I take my clothes off? Not like that . . . it's just, I really am soaked.'

'No, that's fine. The bathroom is through there.'

I sit on the arm of the sofa again and it occurs to me that I should probably get dressed while he's in there, but I don't seem able to move. The noise of the storm pushes out most of my thoughts. The floor creaks and I look up. Joshua is back, also wrapped in a towel, like we're on a couples spa holiday.

'I've never been to your flat before.' He's looking around, digesting it. I've not had any time to Gretel it up in any way. It's just my home. April's. With the giant framed picture of Dawson crying that I got Megan for her thirtieth hanging over the sofa. The unwashed plates from this morning's break-fast festering in the sink. The general mess caused by being signed off work for a week for stress.

'Here it is.'

'Your flatmate not in?'

'No.'

Silence approaches and stays put. I'm not particularly in the mood to be the one to break it. I'm still angry. Joshua shuffles over in his towel and lays a hand on my shoulder. I look up.

'I'm sorry,' he says, like he might mean it, adding to my surprise. 'I'm not sure what happened back there.'

'Your friend was implying there's a rape spectrum . . .'

'Well that's not exactly what he was . . .' he sees my face. 'He's a really nice guy. There's no way he meant it the way you took it.'

'If you came over to defend him then you may as well leave. I know he's your friend, but this is my job, Joshua,' I say. 'I deal with girls who have been victims of that all day every day. If you had any idea, *any*, of the damage it causes, the pain, the confusion, the ripples of shit . . .'

What I *don't* say is, 'and I was raped. Me. Me! And it is something I can never take away. It's something that will never not hurt whenever I think about it. It's something I didn't deserve or ask for and ouch it hurts, so much. Do you have any idea what it's like to have someone fucking DEBATE your entitlement to pain? I WAS RAPED, OK?' I don't know why I don't say it, but I don't.

'Things are so much worse than people think,' I continue, staring right at him. 'When you do the job I do, you see how widespread it is and it's hard, and therefore it makes it *impossible* to listen when someone tries to diminish it in any way.'

'He wasn't trying to diminish it, he was just saying some things are worse than other things—'

'You can't quantify damage!' I throw my hands up, almost losing my towel. 'Do you have any idea of the privilege you must have to be able to debate sexual violence from a place of emotional detachment?'

Joshua goes quiet because I've said the word 'privilege'. They always go quiet when you bring that one out of its box. Not in a respectful way, but in a quiet, fists-slowly-curled, face-getting-red, feeling-like-it's-not-fair way. I let him bathe in feeling silenced. I think, *that's how we feel every day Mister.*

'I've never seen you like this,' he says eventually, gaze determinedly on his hands.

'Like what?'

'This. All . . . angry.'

'And let me guess? You don't like it?'

'I'm not saying that . . .'

I'm not Gretel right now, that's for sure. I'm too fired up to be her. I think of the years of my life where I've doubted what happened to me and doubted the pain it has caused. That night, with the white wall, if I was asked to mark it on this 'rape spectrum', well, it would've been a two out of ten, I reckon. An SPF 15 kind of rape. A 12A kind of rape. A Nando's lemon and fucking herb sauce rape. I wouldn't be able to win rape top trumps with it, that's for bloody sure. I wasn't held down. I didn't try to run and get caught and dragged backwards on my stomach while I dug my fingernails into the ground. There wasn't more than one of them. I wasn't too drugged to move. I wasn't in a dark alleyway, crying for home, wishing I'd not taken that shortcut. I didn't even bleed afterwards. I didn't even cry. In fact, I lay next to him and stroked his hair after he fell asleep. I didn't even think it was rape until a year or so later, after he left me for that other girl, when my body clamped shut and I couldn't get tampons in, and the specialist at the hospital asked in the kindest voice if I'd ever experienced any sexual violence. Then the memories of that time with the white wall, and the other time, came screaming out of me, hitting me full-force, delighted and dancing in the wind that they had finally been allowed out of their container. Months of dabbing lidocaine on my vagina and sitting with my legs apart with a trainer shoved up it, mourning the loss of everything I was before. Thousands of tears. Hundreds of mini-breakdowns. Sex ruined, potentially forever. The fear, every single time, that my body wouldn't let me have this part of my life again. All of it so awful, and yet the worst bit being the doubt that you deserve this trauma. Have I over-exaggerated what happened? Was it really that bad? Isn't it much worse for other women? Why am I so fucked up about something so minor? Am I just weak? Am I one of 'those' women who over-dramatise for attention? The doubt is sometimes worse than what actually happened. I've sometimes wished for a fucking rape certificate. I wish I could've invited some independent rape adjudicator to join me on a jolly jaunt back in time to watch what happened and verify that it was what my trauma is telling me it is. So much pain and doubt and fear and confusion and shame . . . and then men, around a table, happy and glowing from alcohol, never worrying that this could happen to them, saying your worst thoughts out loud, debating the validity of your pain, then wondering why you cry or get angry. How unreasonable you are.

'What are you saying?' I put both hands on my hips. He

looks up at me, mouth wide, ready for all kinds of comebacks and defences and arguments, but his mouth closes again. It's like he's seeing me for the very first time.

'I don't know,' he says. 'I'm really sorry.'

'Sorry why?'

'Because you're right. What Neil said wasn't OK. I'm just trying to defend him because . . . OK, I'll admit it, I'm embarrassed all right?' Joshua runs his hands through his wet hair. 'I mean, it's the first time you've met my friends and Neil bloody starts talking about that? He *knows* about your job. I've told him. He's always arguing about that kind of thing. He gets off on playing Devil's Advocate. I worried he'd bring it up and then he did . . .' He rests his face in cupped hands, shakes his head with them still there. 'I'm really sorry, Gretel, it wasn't cool.'

There's a crack of thunder. The rain drums even harder on the pavement outside. I don't know what to do with this. This honesty, pure and white, spilling from his mouth. This genuine apology. It undoes everything I think I know.

'Why would he deliberately bring it up?' I sit next to Joshua on the sofa and the sinking cushion makes our knees fold in together.

'Like I said, he's antagonistic like that, always has been. You know what it's like, with uni friends. You're in these weird pre-set social dynamics that are hard to change. I'm really sorry he upset you.' He takes my hand, laces my fingers. For the first time since I started this, my body craves him back, enjoys his touch.

'I didn't mean to make it awkward, I just couldn't stay.' I'm so proud of myself for not apologising back to Joshua. For not automatically replying to an 'I'm sorry' with an 'I'm sorry too'. Though it takes considerable effort to override the urge.

'I get that.' He groans. 'God, that could've gone better, couldn't it? You don't think I'm one of those old-fashioned men's rights mentalists, do you?'

'I don't think that,' I say. In fact, I'm thinking, *maybe you are different*.

'You never talk about your job,' he says. 'I think it's really cool what you do yet you don't talk about it much.'

I shrug. 'It bums people out. Makes them uncomfortable. I've learnt not to.'

He begins to stroke my thumb. 'But I want to know.'

'Know what? How many rape victims I deal with every day? How awful it is? How relentless? How we never have enough money to help properly? How sometimes I feel like we're just shoving novelty plasters onto a giant seeping wound?'

'I'm interested. I want to know.'

'You *think* you want to know,' I tell him, 'but then you'll get all defensive and want to pick holes in the things I tell you. Like Neil.'

'That's not fair. I'm not like him. I really am sorry.' He leans his head towards mine until our foreheads are kissing, needing to make it OK. He cups my face, and grazes his lips against mine. They instinctively kiss back before I turn my head.

'Do you really want to know all the awful parts of my job?'

'Yes.'

'I mean, I literally deal with terrible sexual violence every day.'

'And that makes me sad but it's something I need to know more about. For Christ's sake, I work in coding, Gretel. I just don't know about this stuff. I'm woefully ill-informed.'

'I don't feel like talking about it right now,' I say. I just want him to kiss me again. I want it so badly that it throws me.

'Well then, we don't have to. But some other time. Talk to me. Tell me more about what it's like to be you . . .' He kisses me again and I kiss him back in surprised relief. The way he's looking at me, the way he sounds like he means it. Gretel sheds her skin to the floor. April is left, kissing him, running her hand through his hair. I can feel his goodness; it radiates like central heating. I want to get closer to it, closer to him.

'My towel's falling off,' I say, because it is. We both look down to see one exposed breast hanging out, my nipple grazing the towelling. We both laugh quietly.

'What a shame. Mine too.'

We fall backwards onto the sofa, dislodging the remnants of our towels and kiss slowly, heavily, like we mean each and every part of it. Joshua's hands run down my back. I find myself clutching him tightly. It all falls away. The night. The anger. The embarrassment. Even the angry thrashing of the storm fades to white noise. We kiss and kiss. He doesn't try to turn it into anything more than kissing. He doesn't assume it will lead anywhere. It feels so good just to kiss, to feel like the man is just enjoying the kiss rather than wondering how long he can use it to segue into something else. My muscles relax. I lose sense of time, logic, the lies I've told. I find myself whispering into his ear. 'You've not seen my bedroom yet.'

'I've not.'

'I didn't know you were coming round. I haven't tidied up.'

'I couldn't give a flying fuck.' He picks me up like he's rescuing me from a plane wreck, both of us completely naked, and carries me towards it.

'Not that door, the other door.'

'OK, right.'

'Hang on, you have to turn the handle. I'll try to do it with my foot. Hang on. No. Put me down a second.'

And we fall, giggling, onto my unmade bed.

Maybe he is different
Maybe he is different
Maybe he is different
Maybe he is different
Maybe, he is . . . different?

The first tickles of morning light hit the crack in my ceiling as I wonder how to arrange my jumbled thoughts into coherency.

Something peculiar happened last night you see.

Joshua made me orgasm. Not just a regular one, but an earth-shattering, lost-all-sense-of-myself, made-noises-without-embarrassment, one.

That's not happened to me since It happened.

I still can't stop smiling when I think about it. How the sex was long, and slow. I didn't orgasm *through* sex, because I never have, even before Ryan. But he stopped halfway and went down on me until I did and . . . and . . . God I want to have sex again just thinking about it.

I watch his sleeping face crumpled into the pillow. Fondness stirs in my guts. I want to reach over and stroke his cheek. I cannot help but smile when I look at him.

After we finished, and were lying there and listening to the storm outside, he asked me more about my job. How I got into it. What the day is like. How I cope with all those hard questions. I told him about starting as a volunteer manager, about being asked to take on some shifts, about how much joy I get when I hear that I've helped someone, about Matt and how close we are, about clinical supervision and identifying triggers and how terribly hard it is some days.

He listened while stroking my hair. 'I wish my job was important like yours.'

'Coding is important.'

He laughed.

'You could code for a charity. They have websites. They need coders.'

'You know what? I could actually, couldn't I? Sorry again, about Neil.'

'Oh God. Your friends are going to hate me now.' A pinch of anxiety rippled through our post-coital bubble. I suddenly cared about it, the awkwardness I'd caused, how I would face them in the future.

'Don't be daft, they won't hate you. They all said how much they liked you.'

'Yeah right.' I buried my face into his armpit. It smelt of sour sweat mingled with new sweat, and yet I could not get enough of his scent. Would bury my face further in if I could. Snort a line of him.

His voice was heavy with sleep, but he still made an effort to be reassuring. 'It could've gone better, for sure. But you'll meet them again. And it was Neil who kicked it all off anyway. It's about time he was told, to be honest.'

'Are you sure?'

He tilted his chin down and planted a kiss on the top of my head. 'I'm sure.'

The next peculiar thing is that I slept after that. Wrapped up in Joshua's arms. A deep, heavy, dreamless sleep. The sort of great sleep you get when you accidentally nap in the afternoon. I only regained consciousness fifteen minutes ago, when the heat between our bodies got too much. The fresh air cleared by the storm is already forgotten – the heatwave well and truly back in action. But, when I woke, I was still in his arms, wrapped up in him, totally naked and comfortable, like we were a pack of wolves but without the rest of the pack. I've not been able to sleep next to a man since It happened either. I force myself to look away from Joshua and back at the ceiling crack.

I don't know what any of this means.

I'm very confused right now, it has to be said.

He's not behaving how I know men to behave. Intellectually, I'm certain this is only because I've been Gretel. That his lack of game-playing and mind-fuckery and not-really-knowing-what-he-wants and emotional-whiplashing is only a non-event because Gretel is a non-event. A safe, make-believe woman for him to be infatuated with. I mean, I've never met someone that it's got so serious with so quickly, so it must be the Gretel effect, right?

But a tiny part of me is starting to believe. In him. In men. Maybe he really is a good guy. Maybe they do exist. Maybe I've been lucky enough to stumble across one because, for once, I wasn't looking. They always tell you it happens when you're not looking. The mattress shifts. Joshua stirs. I turn towards him and watch him wake up to this morning and my face.

'Hello.' His voice is gruff, sexy.

'Hello.'

He pulls me into his naked body. I can feel what he wants pressing into my thigh. But he's also staring at me in wonder. He leans in to kiss me on the lips. 'Come here,' he whispers. 'I want a cuddle.'

Though inevitably we do more than cuddle.

★

'You don't have a coffee machine.' Joshua's wearing only yesterday's boxers and looking around, offended, at our tiny kitchen. 'You don't even have a cafetière. I can't cope under such conditions.'

'I've got Nescafé.'

'That's it. I'm out. I'm leaving.' He smiles to check I know it's a joke. I smile back. We've been doing this all morning. Talking. Kissing. Grinning. Kissing. Grinning. Every sentence the other utters is worthy of a joyful smile and a congratulatory peck on the lips.

'I have tea? Lots and lots of tea?'

'I suppose it will have to do.'

I get out two mugs and the special Teapigs bags that I always get from my mother for my birthday – alongside the obligatory Richard and Judy Book Club novel, a small vial of Jo Malone Pear and Freesia, and the yearly lecture about how men are all shits and she can't believe Dad just left her to bring me up alone. I boil the kettle, splash water onto the teabags, tip on some milk, and hand a mug to Joshua who says thank you. We return with them to my mangled sheets and sit up against the wall, legs twirled around one another, sipping even though the drinks are still too hot.

'I like your bedroom,' he comments.

It's very much April's bedroom, not Gretel's. I'm not sure what Gretel's bedroom would look like. I guess she'd have framed photos of all her travels. Or maybe not. Maybe she's someone who 'doesn't need to take photos because the memory is enough.' She'd probably have a vinyl record player, not because she's a hipster, but because she genuinely understands music and genuinely knows it sounds better on vinyl. There'd be a glass filled with wildflowers that she'd somehow managed to pick herself in inner-city London. Her bookcase would contain *The Catcher In the Rye* and *Catch 22* and all the other books men love women to read because they're all about men and written by men.

But Joshua only gets April's bedroom.

I try to see it through his eyes afresh. There are quite a lot of clothes on the floor, and a big pile on my chair, which never gets sat in, what with the constant pile of clothes. The top of my wardrobe has a nice framed photo of Megan and me on it, from that one good holiday we managed to take together in Greece. But it's somewhat obscured by the scattered bottles of all the things I apply to my face and body each day in order to pass as a functional woman. Deodorant. Moisturiser. Night cream. Day cream that I'm still not sure is different from moisturiser. Make-up remover. Cotton pads. Eye make-up remover. Vitamin C that stings my face and I don't understand why I need it, just that I do. E45 anti-itch cream for whenever I shave my legs or bikini line. Tweezers to pluck out my nipple hairs. There are piles of make-up-blackened cotton pads I haven't been arsed to transfer the whole metre to the bin yet.

'I really like that poster,' Joshua comments, pointing to the one by the door. It's a framed *Harry Potter* print I got as a leaving present from my last job. A quote about finding light in the darkness.

'*You* like *Harry Potter*?'

'Yeah, of course. Doesn't everyone? I even dressed up as Dumbledore once at a uni party.'

'And, there I was, thinking people in IT are all geeks.'

'Oi!' He tickles me in protest and I shriek and spill tea down my chest and then shriek louder. He takes my mug from me, puts it on the side, and pulls me into him. I nestle in, take another inhale of his scent, ignore all the nagging in my brain.

'I had a really amazing night last night.' He kisses the top of my head again.

'Even though I stormed out on your friends?'

'Especially because of that. In fact, I'm glad that happened. I mean, I'm sorry it made you sad. It was nice to talk to you about . . .' He picks up my palm, and starts to stroke the inside of it with his thumb. He's about to say something deep and meaningful.

'About . . . ?' I prompt, hungry for it, even though I know how deliciously dangerous such moments are.

'Just about . . .'

There's the crash of our front door. A wail like a dying animal has been trodden on. We jump comedically. I pull up my sheet to cover myself.

'Are you here?' Megan howls.

'It's my flatmate,' I whisper. 'Shit.'

'ARE YOU INNNNNN?'

It sounds bad. Really really bad. I get out of bed and shrug into a T-shirt and knickers. 'I'm here,' I call out. 'Hang on. I'm coming.'

Joshua is still, watching me, eyebrows drawn up in confusion. *What was he about to say?*

'I think she's upset,' I tell him needlessly. 'I'm just going to check she's all right.' I skid out of the door, closing it behind me, but it doesn't quite catch. No time to worry about it though, as Megan is right outside my room. She's fallen to the ground, bag exploding at her feet, and she's gone into full-on child's pose, her back heaving as she cries.

'Megan? What's happened?'

Worst case scenarios ricochet through my head. She's been raped. She's been mugged. She's just been fired even though it's Saturday. She's just been diagnosed with incurable brain cancer.

She raises her blubbering face, shot through with red-raw emotion. I brace myself for the impact. 'It's . . . it's . . . him.'

I close my eyes for a second. Malcolm. I allow myself a moment's relief. This is a problem we have overcome many times before. I should've known, really, the moment she got into the foetal position. 'Oh hon, I'm sorry, I'm so so sorry,' I say, even though I'm not sure what he's done yet. I drop to the floor. Pat her back. Tug her armpits. Encourage her to come and sit on the sofa to tell me what happened.

'He . . . he . . .' she leans forward onto her knees and starts crying again. All I can do is keep rubbing her back, waiting for her to get the words out. I glance at my door. I can feel Joshua's getting-ready movements. Is he going to stay in there? Or come out? How do I explain any of this? But Megan howls again and snaps my attention back.

'Tell me,' I urge. 'Tell me what happened.'

'It's stupid. I'm so so stupid.'

'You're not stupid.'

'Yes I am. So fucking stupid. I'm pathetic. I'm JUST SO PATHETIC.' She lurches up and she looks like a possessed demon. Snot smeared over her, hair matted from tears, last night's make-up streaming down her face. It's at this exact moment that Joshua decides to make his sheepish entrance. Megan jumps. 'Who the fuck are you?'

I leap up, step between them and grab Joshua's wrist. 'This is Joshua.' I don't know what else to say. Megan's mouth is open. She shakes her head.

'*Joshua?*'

'Hi,' he says. 'I'm sorry. I'll leave you guys to it.'

The shock's at least snapped Megan out of her hysterics. She watches as I lead him to the door. We step into the corridor, just as I hear her sobs start up again.

'Sorry,' I say. 'Umm. Boy trouble.'

'I could hear.'

'I think it's going to be a while.'

'And there I was, looking forward to making you eggs.'

'I don't have any eggs.'

He does the smile again. 'And there I was looking forward to going out and buying eggs and then making them for you.' There's a twinge in his voice. The smile is covering something. But Megan's pain echoes through the ajar door and I have no time to contemplate it.

'I'll see you soon,' I promise. 'Have a good Saturday.'

'Call me.'

We kiss goodbye. He wraps both arms around the small of my back and mashes his lips against mine more angrily than I'm expecting him to. I look up to see that he's kissing me with his eyes open, staring vacantly over the top of my head.

'Um, bye then,' I say.

'Bye.'

There's no time for psychoanalysis. Not with the sounds

coming from inside. I go back in and find Megan sprawled across the sofa, face down in a cushion, convulsing with grief.

'Hey, hey, it's OK.' I bend down, balancing on the balls of my toes as I comfort her. 'Please tell me what happened.'

'I'm so embarrassed.'

'Don't be. What happened?'

'I'm so stupid. I'm so crazy and fucking stupid!'

'You're not. What's going on?'

She flips over and pushes herself up, her knees bent. She hiccups and can't look at me she's still crying so hard.

I try humour. 'You look like Dawson in that meme.'

It lands. She snorts and wipes her face in a useless attempt to get rid of all the snot, but instead just turns it into a paste. 'Don't.'

'Sorry Dawson.'

Another burp of giggles. 'Stop it.'

'Tell me what happened.'

She whimpers and clutches her knees further into herself. 'It's all my fault anyway,' she starts. 'I shouldn't have said anything, but I really honestly thought we were on the same page. Argh.' She shakes her head. 'We were having such a good night. I was feeling proper loved up. Malcolm took me out for cocktails, he got us such a good table. He kept staring into my eyes, putting his hand on my back, telling me I was gorgeous every five minutes. We got back to his and things were still great. We ordered in Deliveroo and ate it in our pants. We felt like a proper couple, you know? I wouldn't have said anything if I hadn't . . . ARGH!' She clutches her head in her hands.

'What did you say?' I'm rubbing a figure of eight into her back with one hand, and patting her foot with another.

'We were lying there, and he was staring at me, and playing with my hair. You know how you can just *tell* when a man is really into you? Well that was the vibe I was reading, and I said . . . I said . . . I said, "So, are we exclusive?"' Her bottom lip trembles, cheeks flushing at the memory. She looks up at me with her wide tear-glazed eyes. 'The mood changed right away. Oh my God, April. He honestly flinched like I'd just revealed I had fucking herpes or something. The first thing he did was take his arm away and didn't look at me. And I started fucking backpedalling, saying shit I didn't mean, like "don't worry, I don't mind if we label it or not". Even though of course I fucking want to label it. That's why I asked.'

'What did he say?'

Her head sways like a pacing elephant in a zoo. 'He said . . . he said . . .' her voice is on the cusp of breaking again, 'he said what he liked about me was that I wasn't that type of woman. Well, that he *thought* I wasn't. And that now he's thrown that I was.'

'What does he mean? What type?'

'He said the insecure type. The type that needs to label it like that.'

I let out a sigh of exasperation. Honest to God, if we were able to put together all the air exhaled by the sighs of exasperated straight woman dealing with useless straight men then we could send an air balloon into fucking outer space. 'What?'

'I know, I know. So, of course, instantly I'm all like "oh

yeah, I'm not like that at *all*." Even though I am, THAT'S WHY I WAS HAVING THE CONVERSATION. And I fucking apologise. And he says "good", and then goes back to acting all couply like it's all sorted. I lasted two whole episodes of *Breaking Bad* before I broke. For two hours, April, I managed to contain it.'

'That's real progress.'

'I know. I just sat there, trying to squash down all the questions and protests. Like, "does this mean you're still sleeping with other people? And, what the hell am I supposed to do now? And who are these types of women who don't want to know where things are going? Are they real? Because if they are I want to hunt them down and fucking slap them for ruining it for the rest of us". And it was that really boring fly episode that so many *Breaking Bad* twats are obsessed with, which didn't help. Anyway . . . I lost it. I burst into tears and started attacking him with the questions.'

I can picture the scene. Even though I've not met Malcolm since Calculus, I can see the bulge of his freaking-out eyes, his eyebrows furrowing in distaste, the calm snarl of his voice as he rationally explains why all of Megan's emotional responses are, in fact, incorrect.

'He just kept shaking his head, like I'd let the side down. He said I'd read too much into everything. When I pointed out that we'd spent almost all our time together, that I was practically living there, that we message every day, he had his mouth wide open like that was all nothing. He came back with all this stuff like, "yeah, but you've not met my friends" and "I thought this was just fun" and "I never said I was signing up for anything serious". Oh, April, what's wrong with me?'

'Nothing!'

'I just hallucinated a relationship.'

'You didn't! Anyone would've thought the same.'

Her crying starts up again. 'Why did I do this to myself? I knew it was trouble when I started getting anxious. My instinct was spot on, and yet I hoped so much this time was different, that maybe because I wasn't looking . . . because I didn't think I cared . . . But I was just tricking myself. Because I do care, I DO.'

She cries and talks, cries and talks. Tea is made multiple times, and left unsipped, what with all the crying. Sometimes she'll say, 'Sorry, I've not even drunk any of that tea,' and I make more, but then she's crying too much when I get back with the fresh cup that it goes cold once more. The heat permeates the flat. We stay in our pants and T-shirts. I feel Joshua all over my body, inside my body. I want a shower but I can't leave her when she's like this. We psychoanalyse every minute interaction between her and Malcolm, looking for red flags she ignored, signals she could've picked up on. We pore over every detail she managed to glean about him in their time together. His parental blueprint, past girlfriend history, the ethos of the boarding school he went to.

'He's right. I never did meet his friends,' Megan ponders, finally managing to take a sip of tea. 'And he never called me. It was always me calling him. I thought I was being all modern and pro-active. But actually I was just shoving my heart and vagina on a plate for him to rub into his ego and ejaculate inside.'

'That's quite a descriptive metaphor, Megs.'

'Sorry. It's true though. That's all I was, wasn't it? God knows what lies he's telling himself about what just happened to make him "the good guy" in this situation, but it's clear enough, isn't it? I was obviously developing feelings for him, and he was eking out how long he could get away with fucking me and having me cook him dinner before I mentioned it, so he could argue we'd never even talked about it.' She looks up at me. 'I feel so worthless, April.' The fact that she is no longer crying almost makes me sadder. 'What's wrong with me, that I get myself into these situations time and time again?'

I shake my head. It's not like I know the answers. 'There's nothing wrong with you.'

'Maybe I am just crazy.'

'You're not! Who is this cool girl who just totally goes with the flow and doesn't want to label it, and is really easy-going, and doesn't worry about having children before her eggs run out, or where a relationship is going, and wants to feel safe she's not wasting her time with an arse? Show me to her. Because she doesn't exist.'

Even though I'm pretending to be her, so maybe she does exist. Is every woman who is doing well romantically just pretending to be Gretel?

'I miss him.' The tears start up again.

'You will for a while.'

'Why did I do this? I was so happy a month ago.'

I squeeze her into a hug. 'It's a normal and natural thing to want a relationship,' I tell her. 'There's nothing wrong with you for hoping this was it. He's just an overgrown man-child.'

'He is. Why did I pretend he wasn't?'

'Because you wanted to believe.'

It's getting dark by the time she's fully calmed down again. Late. We open the windows to try to let in some cooler air. I made her delete his number because we know what she's like. We've agreed she needs to focus on making her jewellery launch the best thing that's ever happened. I tell her about the boxing class and she perks up. 'That's great, April. Oh my God, I'm so glad you've finally found something that helps.'

'Well, it's only been one session, but still.'

She hugs me, then starts setting up *Dawson's Creek*. It's only when we're sitting back down, her head resting on a cushion in my lap, that she remembers. 'Hang the fuck on.' She twists up to look at me. 'I was in blackout mode so almost forgot. Who the hell was that actual man in your bedroom?'

My fingers pause in her hair. 'Oh,' I say. 'Him.'

'Him? Him? How the hell did I not know there was a him?'

I don't know what to tell her about Joshua. I've not had time to think through Joshua and last night yet.

'I just . . . er . . . brought him home last night. I don't want to talk about it.'

'But you *always* want to talk about it.'

'Please, not tonight.'

And she must be really upset because she doesn't push me on it. 'OK then.'

The night turns inky outside, and we watch a teenager with a prominent forehead cry so that we can better forget our own problems.

April: Do you think Joshua is like all the others?

Gretel: Yes.

April: But what if he's different?

Gretel: None of them are different.

April: But he might actually be different. He's kind, he talks about his feelings, he calls when he says he's going to call . . .

Gretel: Because you're pretending to be me! The fact that he's falling for it is proof that he's like the others.

April: But I stormed out of that dinner. I was difficult and not easy-going, and he came over and didn't seem to mind.

Gretel: Yeah, about that. Don't fuck up like that again, OK? You really showed me up, bitch. Don't let your pathetic trauma rub off on me like that again, OK? You really could've messed things up.

April: So Joshua *is* just like Malcolm and Simon and all the others?

Gretel: Yes!

April: It's just, with him, it feels . . .

Gretel: Feels what? Different?

April: Yeah.

Gretel: April, sweetie, how many times have you given your heart away to some pathetic useless man-child because you convinced yourself it felt different?

April: Err . . .

Gretel: That's what I thought. And, let me guess, the more you got to know them, the more evident it became that they weren't

301

different at all? You came away feeling lesser and scared and like you were crazy for wanting normal things? And yet, because you'd decided they were different, you hung on and got more and more hurt.

April: Stop it!

Gretel: What? Telling the truth?

April: Yes.

Gretel: Nope, babes. Sorry. You need to hear this. Stop thinking a man will be different for you when you are so messed up. Your damage is unlovable. *You* are unlovable.

April: Please, stop . . . This isn't fair.

Gretel: I know hon, but this is why you have to carry on being me. This is the only way you'll feel you have any power at all.

April: I don't want power, I want to be loved.

Gretel: People love people with power. Anyway, I thought you let go of love? I thought you'd freed yourself of that?

April: I thought so too, but then . . . He's so nice.

Gretel: Because you're not being yourself.

April: I am a *little* bit.

Gretel: Go on then! Tell him about Ryan. Tell him about the rape. Get out your dilators. Cry on him and tell him all the horrible things you've been through. Sob and weep and cling to him, like you secretly want to. Vomit up all your pain and trauma. Beg him to make you feel safe. Beg him to write down a schedule of all the big promises of commitment he's going to make to you and when he's going to make them, to the minute, and get him to sign it with his blood. Show every inch of your needy, gross self. Do it all and then demand he love you forever. See how that works for you.

April: Surely maybe—

Gretel: And have you forgotten the *hugely* important fact that YOU HAVE LIED TO THIS MAN ABOUT EVERYTHING?! How can you explain that to him? Men don't want anything real. Joshua only likes you because you're not real. Megan was real with Malcolm, and look what's happened to her. And she's a million times less broken than you.

April: But . . .

Gretel: Haven't you been enjoying the power of being me? Hasn't it felt nice?

April: It felt nice the other night, when I was me and he seemed to like it.

Gretel: You're actually kidding yourself, you know that, right?

April: Maybe I'm not.

Gretel: Think of everything you've hidden from him. Think about all you've not told him. Think about how you've pretended to be compared to what you're really like. Do you honestly believe he'll stay if you reveal who you really are?

April: But it's not my fault I'm like this.

Gretel: Yeah, so? Doesn't make it any more sexy though, does it?

April: . . .

Gretel: Break his heart. Make him love you then break his heart. Stop being a sap and enjoy having some power for the first time in your life. Why on earth would you want to let that go?

April: You sound crazy.

Gretel: Honey, with all due respect, I'm not the one talking to myself in the mirror right now.

Joshua: Hey. Is your roommate OK? Free any point tomorrow? We could go for a roast?

Gretel: Aww how sweet of you to ask after her. She's not, but she will be. Think I need to be on duty the rest of the weekend though.

Joshua: OK. She's lucky to have a good friend like you.

Gretel: Thank you.

Joshua: How about Monday?

After several hours . . .

Gretel: Monday I can do I think.

I hate men.

I hate how you fall for them. I hate how weak that makes you. I hate having feelings that you can't stop and how hard they are to put back in their box. I hate how they make you feel like you're always slightly wrong somehow, and how that makes you change who you are so they can love you. Then I hate how disempowering it feels to know you're only loved because you've locked parts of yourself away to be acceptable. I hate how, once you've fallen for one, it feels so physically insurmountable to sever yourself from them, even if you're fading away by being with them. I hate the fear you carry that they'll find out what you're really like and not want you any more.

I hate the women whom men find easy to love.

I hate myself for not being like them.

I hate how I have no idea what to do.

Predictably, everyone is weird when I return to work. They all talk slower, like I've had a week off for hearing problems or something.

'How *are* you?' they over-enunciate.

'Fine, I'm fine.'

'Did you have a nice break?' Katy asks, like I've just come back from a week in Cephalonia.

'Yes, lovely thanks.'

Mike, at least, is brisk and business-like. 'Nice to have you back, April,' is all he has to say on the matter, before summoning me into the meeting room to ask how recruitment for volunteers is going. It's good to feel professional again.

'Numbers aren't brilliant, but they're also normal for this time of year,' I say. 'Once we get ourselves in front of eager Freshers in September, I'm sure we'll hit our targets.' I show him the postcards I designed, encouraging people to become advisors.

'This is great, really great. Good work.' He doesn't mention the other part of my role, or my absence, or anything else. And I almost feel like hugging him for it.

When we walk out of the meeting room, I feel people's necks craning in my direction, examining me for signs of madness. At least six people offer to make me coffee. 'I've already got one, thanks.'

All the fans are whirring, making no dent in everyone's

bombarded basal core temperature. Matt is the only other one who treats me normally. He sends an email, which I don't see until just before lunch as it takes me all morning to catch up on the deluge of mail I received when I was away – mostly informing people that ice lollies were in the kitchen.

From: Matthew@WeAreHere.com
To: April@WeAreHere.com
Subject: You OK?

I missed you buddy. You feeling any better?

I look up from my screen, just as he happens to look up from his. I smile.

From: April@WeAreHere.com
To: Matthew@WeAreHere.com
Subject: RE: You OK?

I missed you too! Sorry I can't be your buddy for a while. Feeling a bit better actually. Though guilty that it's put more work on you and the volunteers we are yet to recruit.

From: Matthew@WeAreHere.com

Don't be stupid! I'm just happy you're feeling better. Lunch?

From: April@WeAreHere.com

I'd love to actually! Shall we see if Katy wants in too?

Katy looks thrilled to be invited, and we plan a park picnic for 1 p.m. I'm proud of myself for saying yes, though I know it's going to take a lot of self-control to not ask him about the inbox and what's come in. One piece of advice Carol gave me before signing me off was to imagine I carry a container around with me. I can make it any type of container I like – basket, Tupperware – but it has to have a lid. And, whenever I have thoughts about all the abuse that happens and how overwhelming it is, I have to visualise myself putting my thoughts into the container and pushing the lid down.

'That's not to say you're never going to think about these things again,' she said. 'It's not about repression. But it's a way of not having to think about it all, all of the time. Really work on that mental image of storing it away.'

It seems to be working. At eleven, my calendar tells me that my shift is coming up because I forgot to cancel the reminder. *Go to the inbox. Even though you're not supposed to. See what's in there. I bet it's bad. I bet so much bad stuff has happened, and you're not even going to help are you? Because you're so selfish and weak?* I picture a giant Tupperware box and I shove these thoughts into it. I hold the top down with my palm so I can snap the clips into place. There. Thoughts fully contained.

I drink a cup of coffee at my desk and work out the volunteers' rotas. I have to re-jig a lot as they're taking on an extra shift each because of me. *Because you're too weak and pathetic and useless and . . .*

Into the container. Push down the top. Snap down those clips again.

It works as a coping strategy until after our lovely team

lunch, where we stuff ourselves with strawberries and yogurt and do very well at not bringing up difficult subjects.

Megan calls me as we're walking back to the office from the park, providing further distraction. 'I miss him.'

'No you don't. You miss the idea of him.'

'Since when did you become Yoda?'

'Throw yourself into your work.'

'I can't ring celebrity publicists when I am crying in the loos.'

'Give yourself five more minutes of crying, and then promise yourself you're allowed to cry as much as you want tonight. It hurts now, but it will pass. It always does.'

'I know. I'm just so mad at myself.'

'Don't be stupid. Right, five more minutes and then back to work. Do you want me to stay on the phone?'

'No, it's all right. I'll cry alone and leave you in peace.'

The last five minutes of my lunch hour is stuffed with other electronic communication. Chrissy checks I know the details of the upcoming hen weekend and prompts me again to send over my deposit. My mum sends a trail of pictures of bridge club.

Mum: Came 3rd!

Mum: Would've been second but Margaret was cheating.

Mum: She can't see this message can she?

I go and stand in front of the biggest fan to cool down from being outside. I tell more people who ask that I'm fine. I have a cup of tea. The bad thoughts stay in the Tupperware during my meeting about volunteer retention. Though I look out through the glass wall at Matt, knowing he's covering my shift and wondering what's come up and if he's OK and back it comes – feeling guilty and worried and wondering what's in the inbox and and . . .

Oops.

Better Out Than In

April: Any of you ever been told to use the container method? It work for you?

Anya: Ahh, that old chestnut.

Anya: It only works for me in the first two weeks of my period cycle.

Anya: But then again, that's the case with every positive thing in my life.

Charlotte: OMG! The same! I feel like such a kick-ass trauma-annihilating warrior, then I get PMS and suddenly it's like I've never had any therapy at all.

Hazel: Yep. Me too! All my emotional spirals come in the days leading up to my period. Why do they never tell you this in therapy?

Charlotte: Recovery tip no.1: Never judge your recovery on days 26-28.

Hazel: I'm so jealous your cycle is only 28 days long.

Hazel: Since having Jack, I've literally never had a regular period. It's so hard to tell if I'm legitimately going mad or not.

Anya: In short, April, the container method is OK. But nothing works as well as coming to class and kicking the shit out of a punch bag.

Charlotte: Seconded.

Anya: You coming this week?

April: Hell yes.

When five thirty eventually comes around, I'm feeling much better. After a day of standard behaviour, no one's acting like I could spontaneously combust any more. I've dragged myself out of email backlog hell. I've organised the rest of my work-load for this week, and I have messages pinging in from my new boxing friends. Even Megan seems improved. She emails to let me know she's managed to send two whole emails.

Gretel: I've got a hankering for some ramen. Fancy changing plan to suit my urges?
Joshua: You want soup?! It's 30 degrees!

I'm applying my not-there make-up in the bathroom when I get his reply. 'Yes, in this heat,' I say to my reflection, before blotting my just-bitten lip stain. 'Gretel is just random like that. She'll be eating ice cream in winter next, crazy cat. Doesn't shit like that just make you feel aliiiiiiive?'

Gretel: Eating hot food cools you down. Science.
Gretel: Carpe diem, Joshy. YOLO. #BeARebel
Joshua: OK OK, O Captain, my Captain! Let's go for spicy soup.

He's there before me when I bluster my way into the empty noodle house, sweat pouring down my body from the long bus journey. He's sitting nursing a beer under the ceiling of fans, and he stands when I get in, looking slightly unimpressed.

'Gretel, hi.' He kisses my cheek formally. 'They wouldn't seat me until you arrived.' Pass-agg laces the sentence and I raise an eyebrow, looking around the deserted restaurant.

'Well, it's totally empty so I wouldn't panic,' I say.

'Hmm.' He turns his back to me, alerts the waiter. 'She's here now,' he says conspiratorially and I raise my eyebrows again as we're led past long tables with high stools to a little set up in the corner.

'Right under a fan, perfect.' I smile over, but Josh just picks up the menu. 'What are you drinking?' he asks it.

'Um, a white wine maybe?' I eyebrow him once more but he's too engrossed micro-reading the descriptions of extras. Something is up and I panic for a moment that he's found out somehow – my stomach turning itself into cinnamon rolls laced with anxiety.

'Your housemate any better?' he asks the menu.

'A little better. It will take a while.'

'Yeah.'

The waiter reappears with a notepad. She hasn't left us very long but it's not like there are any other customers to wait upon. 'You guys know what you want to drink?' she asks, pen poised.

I smile with all of Gretel's charm. 'A white wine please.' I gesture towards Joshua, who is forced to look up.

'Another of these please.' He points to his pint.

'Great. Coming up.'

Before I have a chance to make eye contact, Joshua's vanished behind the menu again. I scratch my neck, wondering what Gretel's done wrong. If he did know, I reckon he'd be less passive aggressive than this and more aggressive aggressive. My stomach loosens slightly.

'You know what you're going to get?' I offer one last olive branch for whatever crime I've committed.

'Well, ramen, clearly.'

That's enough now. Time to take the power back. I shake my head then jump off my stool, and, without saying a word, I walk out of the restaurant. I'm enveloped by the steam of heatwave Soho as I walk away slowly, waiting for him to inevitably follow. It feels deliciously overdramatic, but also fitting considering his behaviour. I wish I'd thought to do this all the moments in the past when I've been cold-shouldered. I've just reached the corner when I hear him.

'Gretel? Wait! What the hell?'

I keep walking a few more steps. One . . . two . . . three.

'Gretel!' There's urgency to his voice. The squeak of surrender as the power floats through the city's mugginess and lands back into my hands. I turn around, looking bored.

'Where are you going?' he asks.

'I don't do passive aggression,' I say. 'Don't meet me for dinner and then not speak to me. I won't stand for that sort of crap, Joshua.' I put my hand on my hip. 'We're not 12. If I've pissed you off, tell me.'

He glows red with guilt. 'I'm sorry.' He offers up the apology instantly. 'I'm, well, can we just go back inside?'

'I don't know. Are you going to make eye contact?'

'Yes.'

'Are you going to explain to me what's going on, like the grown adult man that you are?'

He stares at his feet, looking nothing like a grown adult man. 'Yes.'

'All right then. Let's go back in.'

The waiter's holding our drinks patiently when we return – nonplussed, unbothered – this city rendering her unshockable. I take my wine, thank her, and drink a giant glug as I clamber back up onto my stool. Joshua's still blushing as he sits. He takes a sip of his pint and places it down, before squeezing his hands together like he's trying to juice them.

The waiter holds up her pen again. 'You guys ready to order?'

I shake my head. 'Not quite yet. Maybe give us a few minutes?'

She nods and exits stage left. We're left alone and I lift my face to the ceiling fan, letting it whip my fringe off my forehead.

'I didn't mean to be weird,' Joshua starts. I don't say it's OK because it isn't.

'I just, well, I'm a little bit upset to be honest.' He looks up earnestly, still attacking his hands.

'Upset about what?'

'It's just . . . I know we've not talked about it, but, well, I

314

mean, you met my friends the other day. And I don't just, like, let them meet anyone. I thought that went without saying. I thought we were on the same page.'

I catch an inkling of where this is going, and, when I realise I'm right, a mist of surreal descends down on me. I'm in the middle of a 'what are we?' conversation and it's the first time in my life I've not started it. I am never, *ever*, on the *receiving* end of these kinds of desperate-but-pretending-they're-not chats. I take another sip of wine while my stomach tries to figure out what emotion it's feeling. Excitement that I'm winning? Or guilt? Or, maybe even excitement that he likes me this much?

Not me, I remind myself. *Gretel.*

Joshua stumbles in to fill the silence. 'Anyway, when your housemate turned up on Saturday, I know she was upset and everything but, well . . . Gretel, it was clear she'd never even heard of me.' He makes eye contact and it hurts to look back at him, confirming the emotion I'm feeling as 'guilt'. Guilt mixed with admiration that he's brave enough to say all this. 'She hasn't, has she? You live with her. You're clearly very close friends. Have you ever mentioned me at all?'

I shake my head and tell him the truth. 'No, I guess I haven't.'

His face collapses. 'Right.' He says it again. 'Right.' Another sip of beer as he faces the bittersweet relief of knowing you're not being paranoid after all.

'I mean, I've mentioned you *now*.'

'Because you had to.'

'It's not like that. Why are you being weird about it?'

Joshua flinches and the guilt intensifies, the surreal mist

getting thicker. I've had that hurtful collection of words chucked at me so many times and now I'm the one saying them. I panic. I do not like to hurt people. I start back-pedalling. 'Sorry,' I reach over my hand and take his. 'I didn't mean that.'

'No, its fine,' he says, when it isn't.

'I don't know why I didn't tell her. I didn't mean to hurt your feelings.'

His chest inflates as he tries to puff it out. 'You didn't.'

'Right.'

The waiter reappears and jolts us back to societal appro-priateness. 'Ready to order?'

We both want ramen – Josh orders the beef, me the chicken. 'Want a side of edamame beans?' I ask as we hand over the menus.

'Yeah, sure.'

With no laminated A4 to use as conversational shields, we both start plucking ramen accessories out of the tray as a distraction while I wait for Joshua to explain. I snap chop-sticks in two, rubbing them together to get rid of any splinters. Joshua grates peanut dust into his hand. The childlikeness of it throbs something in my gut.

I am hurting this man.

This is the first time I can see the hurt from my lies first-hand. He swipes the peanut dust into a napkin and smiles as he looks up at me, and the guilt sinks into my bones. This power doesn't feel liberating like I thought it would. It feels confusing, like a dull ache, like I've let myself down. *End this,* I think to myself, smiling back. *Now is the time to end this.*

All I need to do is say it's not working. Say it's not me it's you. Say we've just met at the wrong time. Say I'm not over my ex. Say I need to focus on work. Say there just isn't a spark. *Say it say it say it.* His heart will be mildly bruised. He may not want to frequent this particular ramen place for a while. It will hurt for a day or two but his heart will receive minimal damage. Say it can't go on. Say you've met someone else. Say you're emotionally unavailable. *Say it say it say it.*

But I don't say anything.

And, once more, Joshua flings himself into the silence. 'Gretel, I'm not seeing anyone else,' he says plainly. The man returned. Sitting up in his stool. 'I know we've not had this conversation. I thought it was kind of implied, but now I'm not sure. So we need to talk about it, I think. Are you seeing anyone else?'

I have a split second to grasp Gretel's answer. 'No.'

He takes a breath of relief which he tries not to show. 'Cool. OK. I mean, it would be cool if you were. As I said, we've never spoken about it.'

'I don't sleep around.'

'I know, I wasn't suggesting you do. Sorry, I mean, even if you do, that's fine. Gah. OK, look . . .' Josh picks up my hand and inhales courage from the air around him. 'What are we, Gretel?' he asks.

'What do you mean?' Though I know what he means, of course I know.

'I mean, are we together? Not together? Seeing each other?' He laughs. 'I've been out of the game a long time. I'm not really sure how any of this works.'

End it end it end it my conscious screams, as I watch his

hope and his heart being offered out, flecked in peanut dust. This is the line I can't cross. This is where staying makes me a bad person. Makes this social experiment something with serious collateral damage. Joshua and Gretel can't be together because she doesn't exist. The poor guy just asked a phantom to be his girlfriend. He doesn't know this, however. He's just thinks Gretel is Gretel. Why wouldn't he? I must stop this, stop hurting him. But I can't. And not because I just want revenge. I hate to admit it, but part of me can't stand the thought of not seeing him again.

'Joshua, are you asking me to be your girlfriend?'

'Well, I mean, I'm not sure what the term is when you're our age. And I know we've not known each other a huge amount of time. But I really like you Gretel.'

I clamp down on his fingers, feeling the pulse from his wrist beat through my hands. 'I really like you too.'

'So?'

'So, I guess that means we're "going steady".'

He digests what I've said and then his face splits into a smile, carving through the stubble on his cheeks. 'Really?'

'Of course.' My smile matches his. I laugh. He laughs. Happiness spews out of us. Our hands mesh. I feel like a confetti cannon should fire out over us. Joshua leans over to kiss me. He leans over to do it again. He's a different man – changed, loosened. We're interrupted by the food arriving, forcing us to release one another's grip.

'Coming out for ramen was a brilliant idea,' he says, picking up his chopsticks. 'The things you make me do, Gretel.'

I pick up my own chopsticks, smiling back. He's different

because he's relaxed. Because I've reassured him. He has pinned Gretel down. We are on the same page after all.

He, quite cutely, checks a few times. 'It's not too soon? I keep counting how many dates we've had and thinking maybe it's too soon.'

'It's not too soon.'

We kiss again. We slurp our ramen and giggle about how unattractive we both look. We order more drinks. We kiss more over the table, knocking over the nut grinder. We kiss out in the heavy air of Soho, pressed against a wall. We hold hands on the Tube. We stumble into his flat laughing and kissing.

The way he looks at Gretel . . . If only I could be looked at like that by a man. I pretend I am her, because it's easier, because it's nice to pretend for myself sometimes. Pretend I am fun, carefree, that I'm not dragging myself through life with tonnes of trauma and baggage trailing behind me like chains, pinning me to my sadness. I need a cold shower, I say. He needs one too. We shower together, shrieking at how cold we can make the water go. Kissing with our bodies slick, him looking like a child with his hair wet, teeth clashing with teeth, laughter turning into shivers, wrapping ourselves up in his towels and rubbing one another dry. We inevitably make love, and I not-so-inevitably find myself climaxing again. Clutching onto his hair and turning my head into the pillow.

'Are you OK?' he whispers, between my legs.

'Yes.' It's the truth.

We lie together afterwards like pretzels that weren't separated properly in the factory. A tangle of limbs. He keeps stroking my face. I can feel so much love coming off him, but it's not for me. It's not for the person I am. I want to hide in this moment. Curl up in it. Pretend it's the truth. Pretend a man is capable of loving me the way Joshua seems to love Gretel. Does any woman get to feel like this? Better women? Ones with less raggedy edges? It seems so unfair that the people who deserve love like this the most, the ones who have gone through the most torture, are the ones who are the least likely to get it. How the legitimate need for it repels it, and increases the odds that you'll never get it. We reward simple people with love. People without trauma. And we punish those who dare to get scathed by life, even when it's not their fault, like their pain is a contaminant.

I lie in Joshua's arms and focus on his touch as he traces my stomach with his thumb. 'I'm going to miss you this weekend when you're away on this hen do,' he says.

'I'll miss you too,' Gretel says.

I will miss him.

And what that means scares me.

• Gretel's Guide to Becoming The Girlfriend and Staying The Girlfriend

You're a girlfriend now. That changes things. Girlfriends have different requirements from girls who are merely dating. You've made it past the first round of tests, but the stakes are higher now, and therefore the prizes better.

Girlfriends need to be that bit more nurturing than dating girls. You need to cook him meals and rub his head and ask how his day was and actually give a shit about his response. Don't nurture too much though, it annoys them. If you overdo it, they will flinch and act like you're trying to break them. 'It's not a big deal, don't make it into a big deal,' is a sign of over-scrambling the nurturing eggs. Best not to talk too much when you're nurturing. Stick to the cooking and the head rubs, the silent nodding, and the occasional bland words of encouragement. Less of the hardcore talking, you annoying bitch.

You can be dirtier in bed now. In fact, it's good to save the filthier side of you for the Girlfriend Zone. He'll be worrying slightly that, if you do indeed pass all the invisible tests, he'll be stuck having sex with just you for the rest of his life. This will concern him, poor thing. I mean, he deserves a life of good, filthy sex. Can't give that up for just anyone, especially not you. Amp up the whore to counteract all this new commitment. You need to reward him for declining his natural impulses for the compromise of you, and reassure him that, if you do end up getting married, he can still slap your arse or jizz across your chest or do it hanging upside down, or whatever the hell it is he needs to do to feel like he's not sacrificing any of his sexual self by agreeing to put up with you.

By the way, now that you're his girlfriend, you have to be totally OK with every single thing he's doing with his life. Do not expect too much quality time, certainly don't need it. You're his girlfriend now, God, isn't that e-fucking-*nough*?

The elephant in the room at this point in proceedings is pretending you don't know that he's looking at you and thinking 'are you Wife Material?' That's the test. If he can't see you as Wife Material, you're out on your ear, sista. Table for one at Spinstersville. By the way, Wife Material is slightly different for every man so have fun figuring that one out. But being a girlfriend = imagining a future, so make sure you're fitting his version of what his future can be. Paint a masterpiece every day of the life he could share with you.

When it comes to kids, he's thinking about you and them now. Wondering how you'll mother up. How much you will fuck up his precious children – without considering whether he'll bring any fucking-upness into the equation. But he'll be looking for signs in you. So don't have any mental health problems, or hereditary diseases if you can possibly help it. Remember though, he may not be ready for children. He certainly doesn't want *you* to be ready for them until the exact moment *he's* ready for them. So, maternal-wise, walk the tightrope. Sure, yes, you want kids 'some day'. I mean, the man has to spawn his replicates and you are the vessel to provide that. Don't *not* provide that, you selfish twat. Don't be one of those weird women who hate children. I mean, there's just something *wrong* with women who don't want children, isn't there? But don't be *too* maternal either, jeez, that will freak him out. He doesn't just want to be a sperm donor, how hurtful is that to his feelings? 'I want children when I've lived my life enough,' is a good thing to say. Nice and vague. Say that a lot. When and if he brings it up.

Never, ever, bring it up first.

That goes for lots of things by the way. Do not say 'I love you' first. Do not want to move in. Do not want to know 'where things are going'. Why are you so needy like that? Don't put pressure on him. He's your boyfriend! That's what you wanted, isn't it? Why is it never enough for you? GOD! So ensure that every single step forward in the relationship is totally his idea. Pretend you've never thought about it. Be casual. You can be casual, can't you? I'll tell you who can be casual – people made out of fucking Wife Material, that's who. Wait for him. Just enjoy it. I mean, it's a huge massive test cluttered with landmines where the rules always change and, if you fuck it up, then you'll probably die alone or have to freeze your eggs, and you don't have the money to freeze them, and even if you did, it only has a twenty-six per cent success rate, but *definitely* don't let him know that you know that, but anyway, yes, it's really really important that you don't fuck up this giant test, but ENJOY IT OK? I DON'T UNDERSTAND WHY YOU'RE NOT ENJOYING IT.

Also, don't nag*. Nobody wants a nagging whiny controlling bitch for a girlfriend. How dare you reward his generosity of committing to you with *nagging*? Back off and show some fucking gratitude.

---

* 'To nag' = Express distaste at any legitimately bad behaviour and ask politely if this behaviour can be changed because it's making you hugely unhappy.

Punch the bag, punch the bag. Let it out, let it out, let it all out.

I picture Ryan's face.

I kick and grunt. I sweat. I jab.

Why why why why why? Me me me me me?

Punch punch punch.

Why why why.

Kick kick kick.

Me me me.

My forehead has its own tap of sweat. I look uglier than I've ever looked in my whole life but I don't care. I thrust my body into the sack. It never gives. Ever. It can take every punch I throw at it.

Why me why me why me?

It isn't fair it isn't fair it isn't fair.

I'm a good person and I don't deserve any of what happened, but happened it did and it's NOT FAIR.

Punch punch punch.

'Whoa, April, it's OK,' Charlotte takes the bag. Stopping it swinging. Stopping me. She hugs me. 'I know,' she says, this woman I've only met twice. 'I know, I know.'

'It's not fair,' I whisper into the moisture of her sweaty shoulder.

'It isn't. It really isn't. It's OK,' she says rubbing my back, my hair. 'It's going to be OK.'

Joshua: Hello girlfriend of mine. How was boxing? x
Gretel: Yeah, it was great! Such a laugh x

From: ChrissyHartley123@gmail.com

To: AprilS1987@gmail.com

Subject: This weekend

OH MY GOD APRIL I CAN'T BELIEVE IT'S TOMORROW.
What is HAPPENING to my life? Anyway, thanks for sending
the money. Can't wait to see you babe. Xxx

*

Megan: I can't believe you're leaving me here in my bed of pain
to go on a hen do of all things.

Megan: Who am I going to judge Dawson with?

Megan: HE IS SO EASY TO JUDGE.

Megan: Do you think Malcolm has a new girlfriend?

Megan: WHY AREN'T YOU HERE TAKING MY PHONE AWAY SO
I STOP STALKING HIM?

April: Sorry, train was in a tunnel. Don't. Stalk. Him. You are NOT
that person.

Megan: Well I just stalked him so I totally am that person.

Megan: No signs of a new gf tho so it's all good.

Megan: Though he did go to Sushi Samba without me when I
thought that was OUR place.

Megan: I meant nothing to him at all, did I?

April: Oh hon xxx

Brighton's a teeming cesspit of holiday makers, day trippers, sunseekers, and hen-and-stag-do goers. In fact, I feel like I'm stepping onto a bachelor party conveyor belt when I emerge in the stinking heat onto the platform. Clumps of women clutching almost-finished bottles of prosecco spill out of the crammed train carriages, the different groups only identifiable by their choice of sash. Some pink, some black, some decorated with cartoon penises. The brides-to-be hold court in their cheap veils, clopping along in inappropriate shoes, feeling the most special, marked out to ensure surrounding voyeurs know they are the most special too. *Look at this cheap veil I'm wearing off Hendoswag.com. It means someone deemed me acceptable enough to marry. Someone in this world approves of me that much. Take it in, bitches. Take it all in. It's all been leading up to this.*

I dodge past them and their 'Team Bride' temporary-tattoo-adorned bodies, feeling vaguely nostalgic for four years ago, and the many, many, nights I had the same tattoo emblazoned across my cheek. Those summers of back-to-back weddings are long behind me now, and funnily enough, I didn't actually find them that hard back then. There was still so much time to assume 'it would happen for me'. Which is exactly what was whispered at me during those hen dos, by swaying brides grabbing me by the shoulders, telling me how amazing and kind and beautiful and smart I was: 'It definitely will, I have no doubt.'

I use my phone to navigate my way to the restaurant where Chrissy's sophisticated hen do is located, bumping my way past the sunburnt and flip-flopped people clogging the pavements. I've deliberately arrived late to make tonight as short and painless as possible. Chrissy's an 'anomaly' friend, in that we've always been close but have literally no other friends in common. We met temping one summer as students and we just clicked and have stayed close since then. We convened several times a year throughout the rest of our uni years, the confuzzled mess of our early twenties, the quarter life crises of our mid-twenties, and the panic-stricken years of our late twenties. Chrissy's always been super smart and is now a tip-top lawyer specialising in copyright. Yet she's also always been a perpetual singleton – that is, until, she met Mark two years ago at a wedding. Anyway, suffice to say, I know nobody as I climb the steps to the top floor of the Greek restaurant and step into a room full of thirty-something hens.

'April! Hello! You're here!' Chrissy clatters over in shoes she most definitely can't walk in and envelops me in a tight hug. 'Everyone, this is my friend, April,' she announces, holding me out on her arm.

I wave at everyone, and get passed around the room; names are exchanged that we won't remember, but will be too embarrassed to ask for again. The tables have been arranged into a giant circle for maximum group-coherency with funny photos of Chrissy littered here and there to act as conversational prompts. But there's no penis confetti, or novelty sashes. Chrissy's bedecked in a tasteful veil, but Team Bride transfers are nowhere to be found. There's a projector screen set up at the far end, and a sound system plays a carefully curated playlist of Chrissy's favourite songs – mostly Jack Johnson.

'Hi, I'm April,' I repeat over and over. I shake hands, ask people how they know Chrissy. There's the other-lawyers-from-work-clump, the uni-circle clump, the home-friends clump, and the awkward-friends-and-family-of-her-and-Mark clump.

'Oh, so you're Mark's little sister? Mark's great, isn't he? Just great.'

'You're a lawyer too? Oh right, OK. In London? Of course. Yes, the train down wasn't too bad actually, was it? Whereabouts in London do you live?'

'So you grew up with Chrissy? Oh that's funny, that you all call her Tina. No, she's always been Chrissy to me. So what do you do? Oh, two kids you say? Yes, I'd love to see a picture. Oh, they are so cute. Congratulations.'

'Oh me? No. Not married. No, no kids. Just me.'

'Is that bottle of prosecco finished? No? Great. Yes, if you could pass it down.'

'Shall we order another bottle?'

I've never really liked prosecco, it's always tasted like piss put through a soda stream, but it's included in the deposit we put down for the meal so down the hatch it goes. I knock back a glass, then another. My teeth start to hurt from the sugar and I go for a wee I don't need, just to collect myself.

Megan: Is it bad?
April: Sitting on the loo, weeing a wee I don't need
Megan: So it is bad

April: Everyone is friendly. They're just all . . . so grown up

Megan: Fuck them

Megan: Fuck them all

Megan: Burn the fucking place down

April: Are you OK?

Megan: Quite clearly no

Megan: But I'm also fine. Go have fun now Xx

April: Doubtful

Just as I'm wiping, I get a message from Josh.

Joshua: Has the butler in the buff turned up yet? Hope you're having a nice time x

Gretel: A great time, thanks! No nudity yet, but it's only seven thirty. Have a good night with Neil x

The useful thing about sitting around mothers is that you only have to ask them a few choice questions and then you don't have to talk or think any more for a good hour or so. I'm settled by the home-friends lot, all of whom have at least two kids that I'm shown on their phones.

'So, do they sleep through the night?' I ask, and low and behold, we have conversation filler right up until the starter arrives, and even a little after that too. We are all handed out three stuffed vine leaves arranged on a limp plate of lettuce scattered with shaved red onion. We pick up our knives and forks and pretend this is an adequate starter for the forty-quid-a-head price, while I hear all about the power of white-noise machines.

'Wow, I've never heard of them before. Amazing. I'll keep

that in mind.' I bite into the sour, soggy mush of my vine leaf, and listen to Chrissy's friends talk about nursery places and how hard it's been to have small children in this heat.

'How's it going over here?' Chrissy's doing the rounds between starter and main. Eyes frantic, talking in caps lock, checking to make sure we're all having fun so determinedly that she doesn't seem to be having much fun herself. She slots in beside me and I pour her a glass of prosecco.

'Don't! I'm already way too drunk.'

'Yes. It's your hen do.' I top up my own glass. I must be on my fourth by now. I feel warm and like all my weird problems aren't so bad and weird after all.

'How *are* you?' she asks, arm around my shoulder, fizzy wine on her breath. 'April, it's been *forever.*'

'I know. I'm OK. Oh my God, Chrissy, you're getting *married.*'

She covers her face with her veil. 'I *know*. It's so fucking *weird*. Me, April. ME? Did you ever think you would see the day?'

'Of course.'

'Even after Sven?'

'Definitely after Sven. He was the rock bottom you needed to hit in order to find the portal to evolution.'

It's all hugs and squeezing and prosecco getting knocked over. 'Oh, I love you. I've missed you! I'm so glad you came. How are you— Oh my God, ROCHELLE! How ARE you? How are the kids? I'm so happy you're here.' I'm shunted aside. Chrissy now has Rochelle-with-the-white-noise-machine in a squid-like vice and I'm left holding my glass, which is somehow empty again already.

I sit staring at nothing for a moment, before taking a breath and swivelling to my other side to a woman whose name I've already forgotten. 'So,' I ask, smiling. 'Have they started talking yet? Ball? They can say ball? Oh, yes, that's so cute.'

By eight thirty everyone is a little bit too drunk to fully appreciate the nouvelle cuisine of halloumi skewers on a tiny mound of gigantes plaki.

'Halloumi!' a sozzled lawyer yelps. 'I just love halloumi.'

'Me too. Isn't it the best? I love how it squeaks.'

The table's united in our shared love of the cheese. We stuff it into our faces with our fingers, talking with our mouths full. Someone's turned up the music so we shout to be heard. Nobody eats their beans. A waiter brings out a tray of prosecco bottles and we all applaud him. We're all best friends by the time the sundaes are arranged in front of us; the clumps all united in how good cheese can be and do you want to try a bit of my ice cream. We swap seats and share stories about just how amazing Chrissy is. 'So amazing, isn't she?' 'Oh yeah, really amazing. Just the amazingest.' The ice cream melts to soup in its glass bowls, until we're snapped out of our tiddly haze by three assertive claps.

'Right ladies.' One of the lawyers-clump – I think her name is Janet – is standing by the projector screen on which is now a giant freeze-frame of Mark's head. 'Now that we've eaten, it's time for the games. Mr and Mrs!' Everyone starts cheering and whooping. 'Chrissy, get your cute butt over here.'

Chrissy saunters over in a flurry of netting and collapses into a chair, giggling. Her face is red with alcohol and happiness and I have a flashback to the Sven year and feel deep joy that she's got here. Well, seems to have got here. Every time we meet up she does complain a bit about Mark and his lack of verbal affection, but still, he must feel vaguely affectionate if he's agreed to marry her.

'We asked the lovely Mark here some questions about our girl, Chrissy, and she has to guess what she thinks he's going to say. If she gets it wrong, well then . . .' Janet holds up a bottle of Sambuca with the top already off. 'SHOT!'

Chrissy laughs behind her hand while we stamp our feet. 'I'm scared now.'

'Come on, let's play.' Janet clicks the laptop attached to the screen and un-freezes Mark who waves at us all.

'Hello girlies. I hope you're all nice and drunk.'

Raaahhh, waaa-heeyy! We are so excited with that. Mark's set the camera at a weird angle so his chin looks massive. *He's not the most attractive of men,* I find myself thinking. Not compared to Chrissy, who's an auburn-haired goddess. Whereas Mark looks like he hasn't had hair since Papa Roach were a thing, and his eyes look permanently sad.

The first question floats up on screen in giant novelty balloon-font.

'What were you both wearing on your first date?'

Janet repeats it out loud and we crane to look at Chrissy who's laughing hysterically from all the attention.

'Well?' Janet demands.

Chrissy sips from her prosecco glass. 'I'll be surprised if he gets this right,' she says. 'Umm, he was wearing jeans and a *Rick and Morty* T-shirt, because I distinctly remember being put off by that.' We find that way too funny what with all the alcohol. 'And I was wearing my denim dress, with yellow shoes. My summer date outfit.'

'Do you think *he'll* remember that?'

She shakes her head. 'No chance. He'll remember his own T-shirt though. He still loves that fucking T-shirt.'

'Well, let's see what he says.'

Mark's unpaused again. 'She won't think I'll remember,' he asserts. 'I mean, of course we both remember my failsafe *Rick and Morty* T-shirt.' *Raaaaaaah Wheeeyyy woooooooh,* we all yell. 'But Chris was wearing this really nice blue dress. And some yellow shoes; I remember really liking those yellow shoes.'

We howl. We point. We find ourselves chanting 'CHUG CHUG CHUG' as Chrissy screeches, 'I can't believe he remembered!' before downing her shot compliantly.

I watch her as she looks at the screen. It's frozen again – Mark's mouth slack and odd in the paused moment. 'Oh, Marky,' she whispers at the screen, and my eyes are not as dry as they were ten minutes ago when I hear her say that.

They both remembered their first kiss at the number eight bus stop when Mark lunged first. Mark's most disgusting habit is clipping his toenails into the loo and then not flushing it. Chrissy's is picking her feet in bed. Mark does not know Chrissy's bra size. 'Umm, E?' he stabs. We all *hee-haw-hee-haw* because Chrissy has never been more than a B her whole life. 'I fucking WISH mate,' she yells, getting up and slapping the projector screen. 'CHUG CHUG CHUG.' But he does know exactly how she likes her tea: white with two sugars. And how she will order her eggs when she goes to brunch: poached and on sourdough. And that her favourite movie is unashamedly *Titanic*. And that her favourite sexual position is on top. And they both correctly guess that her most annoying habit is using caps lock in messages. They both tell the proposal story in exactly the same way, including the bit where they had to smuggle the ring back through customs as Mark didn't realise you had to declare it. As question bleeds into question, my throat tightens, my eyes prickle, emotion inflates my stomach. Mark's chin doesn't look so chubby now, his eyes not so sad. I picture him scheduling the filming of this into his diary, secretly liaising with Janet to pick a time when Chrissy was out of their flat. Chrissy's equally bewitched. She reaches out at least twice to stroke the projection of her fiancé. She's doing hardly any shots as they keep syncing answers.

I cannot take any more of this.

I impatiently wait for Chrissy to get one wrong and use the 'CHUG CHUG CHUG' excitement to make my exit, my stomach swirling, hands shaking. The restaurant corridor whirls as my drunkenness catches up with me, and I stumble, half holding the wall, into the toilets and lock myself in a cubicle.

Here I try to digest the pure shameful envy it's sparked in me. The longing in my gut that won't leave, no matter how much I try to push it away. I sit with my knickers gathered around my ankles, peeing with my body bent forward so my head rests on my knees.

It's not that I'm not delighted for Chrissy – I am.

It's not that I want to marry Mark – I don't.

It's not because she has a diamond ring on her finger, or a white dress to wear in two weeks' time, or the honeymoon of a lifetime around the corner.

It's the *knowingness* that hurts.

Because no one romantically has ever known me the way

Mark knows Chrissy and Chrissy knows Mark. I want to be known, all of me known. All of me loved. All of me accepted. I want to have someone in my life who completely and utterly knows me, and has earned the knowing of me by their unwavering willingness to stick around while I slowly reveal it all. It only grows with time and commitment and dedication, and that only comes with someone deciding you are worth the investment to become knowable. Someone who believes the bits they will learn about you will only make them love you more, not less. I don't have that. I've never had that. I don't think I ever will . . .

Megan's quick to answer the phone. I didn't even realise I was calling her until she picks up. 'Hello? April?'

'He . . . he doesn't know me,' I slur out. 'He doesn't know anything about me.'

'What are you talking about? Are you OK? Where are you? Are you still at the hen do?'

'Joshua!' I shout, my voice bouncing off the metal encasement of my cubicle. 'He doesn't know me at all.'

'Who the hell is Joshua? Hang on, is he that guy who was in our flat the other day?'

I nod.

'April?'

'He doesn't know me, Megan.' My voice keeps catching. 'He thinks I'm Gretel. He only likes me because he thinks I'm Gretel.' Snot pours from my nose, tasting bitter as it seeps between my lips though I'm not quite crying. 'I thought being her would make me feel good about myself, but it's just made me feel worse because he only likes me because he, he . . . thinks I'm *her*.'

'I'm so lost right now, honey. I don't really understand what you're saying but I'm sorry you're hurting.'

'No one knows me,' I wail, my voice a squeaky wail.

'*I* know you.'

'You don't count.'

'Well, thanks April.'

'I'm not April, I'm GRETEL, that's the whole thing.'

'Hon, I'm worried about you. Are you alone? Are you safe? You sound really drunk. I'm here in the flat if you want to come home. I love you. I love you. It's going to be OK. Hen parties are triggering nightmares and it's totally OK to just come home. Say you're sick or something. I love you.'

Megan's kind words may as well be made with Teflon. 'I have to go Megan.'

'April!'

'Sorry, I'm fine. Just fine. I'm safe. Sorry. I love you.'

'April, wait—'

I ring off.

Stare at my phone.

I don't want to feel like this – lost and pathetic – the very cliché of being left on a shelf I don't want to be left on. A tiny part of me wonders if this is a good idea but the other part of my brain has already dialled his number. I sit up as it rings, pants still adorning my feet. I sniff and wipe my face.

'Gretel?'

'Guess whose drunnnnnnnnnnk?' I'm full of fun and joy and I'm having such a brilliant time in this wonderful life of mine.

I feel Joshua's smile break over the line. 'Well hello you,' he says. 'Hang on, I'm just in the pub with Neil. I'll duck outside.'

I find I'm smiling too. I wipe myself as I listen to him telling Twatface Neil that it's me. Cradling my phone under my neck, I pull up my pants, flush and then take myself out of the cubicle. I'm just done washing my hands when he's back.

'I'm here. Hello. I wasn't expecting to hear from you.'

'I missed you,' I say. So cute, so goddamned cute.

'Someone's been drinking.'

'There's that too.'

'Anyone shoved a penis straw up their vagina yet, or whatever it is that happens at hen dos?'

'Joshua, that has never, ever, happened at a hen do. Well, actually, it probably has.'

He laughs because I'm witty and fun and cool and brilliant to spend time with. 'And there I was, thinking I was missing out.'

I look at myself in the mirror. Make-up smeared off, hair sweaty from the heat, dress sticking to my clammy body. Face blotchy. My whole look reduced to the words 'train wreck'. I blink twice and picture how he thinks *Gretel* looks right now: grinning, red lipstick perfectly applied, sipping on an ethical straw, hair over one tanned shoulder, mischief in her eyes. Hell, her eyes might even be sparkling, though that doesn't even exist in real life. At no point in the history of hen dos has one ever prompted Gretel to consider her own life choices and romantic prospects. I blink again and see Gretel form in the mirrored glass. She waves hello. She winks at me, and I find myself winking back.

'I'm not calling for any reason other than to say filthy things,' I watch Gretel say seductively down the phone.

More laughter. 'Can I send you on more hen dos if this is what happens?'

'Why aren't you here right now? There's so much I want to do to you.'

I hear him gulp. 'Yes? Like what?'

'Anything you want, I'll do.' It's best to keep it vague, let them fill in the blanks with whichever porn they watch and feel shame about afterwards.

'OK, and now I have an inappropriate erection in the middle of Soho.'

'No such thing as an inappropriate erection in Soho.'

'How can you be crazy hot and crazy funny at exactly the same time, Gretel? That's not very fair on a man.'

I smile again and my reflection smiles back. That red lipstick really does suit her. I've never had the confidence to wear red lipstick before. 'What are you thinking about?' Gretel asks.

'Things that aren't helping this erection go away. Honestly, I've had to turn to face the wall.'

'I wish I was there. I could do things with that situation.'

'Please get on a train back to London now. I've said "please" and everything.'

'Sorry, no can do. But wait till I next see you—'

I hang up, mid-sentence, cutting him and his erection off. I laugh at how easy it is for them to believe your pretence. I sort out my real reflection. I wipe off the ruined bits of my face, sort out my smudged make-up, and tip my hair upside down under the hand dryer to reinvigorate it.

A better April stares back at me now. Not as good as Gretel, but much improved. One that's able to get through the rest of the evening. My phone buzzes.

Joshua: I'm going to be thinking about you all night xxxx

I do feel better.

Though, I worry part of me will be thinking about him all night too.

We end up in a club after all.

We shed the breast-feeders and the ones who could only get babysitters until midnight, and head to some awful place on the beach where all the other hen dos have congregated in some kind of rally. They're all much younger than us. Some of them clearly on their first, exciting, one – decorated with glitter and penises and wilting sashes and the bits of fancy dress that have made it to the end of the night. We're too drunk to mind though – dancing in a little circle, around the pile of our handbags, leaning in to shout 'I don't know any of these songs!'

Now I'm on the beach, smoking a Marlborough menthol even though I've never smoked a cigarette in my life. Chrissy's sitting next to me, also smoking. Our heels are off, toes buried into the cold pebbles.

'I can't believe I'm getting married,' she tells the quiet slosh of the sea, before nuzzling her head into my shoulder.

'I can't believe you're getting married either.' I pat the top of her head with my non-fag hand.

'I literally thought that was it. After Sven. When I left him, I left him knowing he was probably my only chance.'

'And now look at you.'

She throws her arms into the air and her cigarette lights a path through the darkness. 'FUCK YOU SVEN, I'M NOT

A SPINSTER AFTER ALL!' she yells into the black sea. Whoops and cheers from other inebriated people echo back at us and we both fall into one another, laughing.

'Sven was such a dick,' I say.

'*Such* a dick.'

'Remember when he forgot your birthday?'

'And somehow blamed it on me for "stressing him out"?'

We shake our heads and I take an inexperienced drag on my cigarette, sucking on its minty filter, trying to remember how it even came to being in my hand. I cough.

Chrissy cracks up then starts coughing too. 'God, we're a sorry state of affairs,' she says, grinding hers out.

'But we look so cool!'

She takes mine and stubs it out too, and there's a moment's calm, where the delicate crash of waves against shingle mixes with the thud of the bass spilling from the club.

'I can't believe I'm having a wedding,' she murmurs. 'I have a dress and everything. It's so surreal.'

'Are you excited?'

'Yes, I think so. I mean, it's also really stressful. Like just a giant project to manage, and you know about Mum and her MS and all the worry about how she'll cope with the day, but it will be lovely I hope.'

'It *will* be lovely! What are you looking forward to the most?'

I used to ask myself this same question about my own hypothetical wedding. During those moments when I used to plan it in my head, like I've been groomed to do since being born a girl. Of course, the most obvious answer is that thing from *27 Dresses* – the look on his face at the end of the aisle when he first sees you. That's the low bar heterosexual women set themselves as a romantic accomplishment: find a man who looks pleased to be marrying you on your actual fucking wedding day. *Dream big, April . . .*

'His speech actually,' Chrissy says after consideration, interrupting my thoughts. 'I'm really looking forward to his speech.' She picks up a pebble and squeezes it in her palm. 'The thing is, I know Mark loves me. I mean, he must do, right? We're getting married! But he's never been very verbally affectionate. I told you we've argued about it a lot. How he never really gushes over me. Never really says "I love you" or "you look gorgeous". Stuff like that. He says words don't mean anything and I get that so it's fine. It's totally fine. I mean, I'd rather he *did* say nice things, but that's not him, and he treats me like he loves me and that's what's important but, well, the speech is going to be special. Cos he'll get a chance to say it all. And it will be nice to hear it, just once, you know? I feel like he's saving it all up for then, and it makes me feel all warm and gushy. Does that sound stupid?'

I stroke her hair. 'It doesn't sound stupid at all.'

'I'm really looking forward to it.'

I turn to her and cup her face, like I'm the romantic lead in a film. 'You're beautiful, Chrissy,' I say, in a macho voice. 'And you're so smart, and kind, and I'm so so lucky to have you in my life.'

She giggles, and I do too. 'The funny thing is that, even though you're a girl, and you're joking, it does still feel really nice to hear it,' she laughs, before launching herself at me for a hug, her hair getting up my nose. 'I really want it to happen to you,' she says, mid-hug, pulling me tighter. 'It will honey, I promise. You're too amazing to end up alone.'

The hug feels suffocating. I have a deep urge to push her away, push her into the sea. I clamp my eyes shut and feel the bottom of my stomach drop out. I don't like being the charity case. I can't stand that I've become this one.

'I've met someone actually.'

Chrissy pulls away. 'What?' Her eyes light up from the moon.

'It's still really new. He's called Joshua.'

'Oh my *God*, why haven't you told me?'

'It's your hen do. It's not about me, it's all about you.'

'But I want to know. Wow! Joshua! What a great name.'

'Isn't it?'

'So, tell me everything!' She's grasping both of my hands. She's so happy for me, that I've got there. Well, that I've got a chance to get there.

'There's not much to tell yet. As I said, it's really new. He works as a coder. Umm, he has his own flat . . .'

'Great, great. Pictures?'

I retrieve my phone, pulling up a selfie he sent me the other day of him on a 'training walk' up Hampstead Heath. 'He's a bit sweaty in this one.'

She snatches the phone off me. 'Oooo, cute! I like the look of his face. He looks kind. Do you have any more?' She starts swiping through my pictures, finding additional shots, zooming in, telling me all the things that she can tell are good about him from the photos. I look over her shoulder, seeing him again through her new eyes and I feel . . . pride bubble in me, a smile sneaking up my cheeks, warmth in my stomach. Oh God, this is not a good sign. Not a good sign at all. And yet it feels *wonderful*.

My phone's returned with another hug. 'I'm so happy for you,' she says. 'You so deserve this.'

What a strange thing to say, I think, but the thought is then lost in a Sambuca fog. Lost in the feeling of this moment. How nice it is to be the girl who has found the boy and it looks like it's really going somewhere. The relief from others, from yourself. I find myself floating out of my body for a moment, and watching us, two friends, drunk, on the beach, hugging one another and sharing gossip about 'our guys'. The belongingness of it.

Though this moment doesn't belong to me. It belongs to Gretel.

Chrissy's hug judders to a halt and I'm held at arm's length again. 'You have to bring him to the wedding!' she says, so excited by the thought it's like she's discovered gravity.

'What?'

'As your plus one! You must bring him.'

I'm looking at my hands, twisting them in my lap, imagining how to get through that day without anyone calling me April. 'Oh, I'm not sure. I don't know. I mean, he might be busy.'

'At least ask him. Yay! I can't wait to meet him. I *knew* it would happen for you, April. I never gave up hope. Even if you did.'

'Shall we go in and find the others?' I'm already standing up, turning my heels upside down to dislodge the pebbles that have taken refuge in there.

'But it's so hot.'

'Come on Hen,' I hold out my hand to yank her up. 'You only get one hen do.' We both make a noise of exertion as I pull her to her feet.

'Let's hope so.'

We link arms, two old friends, and pick our way across the stones to get back to the club, leaving the black ocean behind us.

I stumble through our flat door, eyes red, the stench of last night all over me, random drunken bruises coming up on my legs. I drop my bags to the floor and groan.

Megan turns around from her spot on the sofa. 'You look like someone has vomited you up.'

'Everything hurts. I'm too old for this. I was too old for this even when I was the age it was considered the appropriate thing to do. Why is it so fucking hot? When will this fucking heatwave ever end?'

'In a good mood, are we?'

'No. Is it that obvious?' I kick my shoes off and flop down alongside her. I must smell bad because she inches away slightly. I look at the television. 'Oh, it's the episode where Joey loosens up and becomes Other Joey.'

'Yep, she's about to sing "Cheap Tricks" and act slutty.'

'God she's annoying.'

'The actual worst,' Megan confirms. 'I mean, they call her "Other Joey", like you can compartmentalise the fun, cool parts of a girl away from the tricky bits . . . Hang on . . . come to think about it,' she points at the screen with the energy of someone who doesn't have a hangover. 'How many times have we seen this scene in other incarnations?' I twist my broken head to where Joey's singing on stage and taking her clothes off, while Pacey looks on adoringly. 'There's always the woman who is too tightly wound or whatever, because she wants to do well in school or her career or whatever the hell else it is that's actually probably a pretty good aspiration to have. And then some slightly-fucked-up dickwad turns up and starts getting her to realise her "true self". But her "true self" is always some drunken, slutty, fun-loving twat who takes her clothes off and dances on stage while everyone cheers.'

'True,' I say, and then I can't say anything else. All other words seem impossible. I cuddle up to Megan's legs. 'Megs?' I start.

'Yes?'

'There's something I need to tell you.'

Sensing something in my voice, she picks up the remote and *Dawson's Creek* comes to a standstill. 'What is it?'

'If I tell you, you have to promise not to say anything.'

'You haven't killed a man, have you?'

I scramble so I'm upright, fold my legs into a crossed position, sitting across from her. 'No, I've not killed a man.'

'Then what is it? You can tell me.'

'I've . . . I've . . .' I savour this last moment where my weird little secret is still just that. Safe within the realms of only my knowledge. I close my eyes, open them. 'I've met a man . . . That Joshua guy.' Her eyes widen. 'But it's complicated. Because, well . . . he's my boyfriend now, except he isn't because I've been pretending to be this fictional woman called Gretel.' It sounds even worse out loud than I thought it would.

Megan's eyebrows lift, crinkling her forehead. 'Right,' she says slowly, picking up a cushion and hugging it. 'Right.'

'It's bad, isn't it?'

'I think I need a bit more explanation. Though last night, I got an inkling. You called me, do you remember?'

The moment she brings it up, I do. The fog from last night lifts and I'm smacked with the memory of my knickers down, wailing to Megan about not being known.

'Shit. Yes. Sorry. I didn't mean to make you worry.'

She waves the apology away. 'So, who's Joshua? And, who is Gretel? Isn't she that girl you used to work with?'

I take the cushion from her, clutch it to myself, and it all spills out. She listens, stopping me only once to say, 'I'm so sorry. I had no idea you were going through all of this.'

'. . . and, yeah, so now he's my boyfriend. I'm crazy, Megan. I'm actually fucking certifiably insane.'

I don't realise I've fully hidden behind the cushion until she pulls it away, forcing me to look up at her. She doesn't say 'no you're not insane'. She asks, 'So you're doing all this for what?'

'Well, initially for revenge?'

'Right, on who?'

'All men.'

'And that's all?'

I yearn for the cushion to be back over my face, muffling my shame. Talking about it has made it real and the reality of my behaviour is terrifying. It's like I've slapped myself across the face with myself. 'I thought that was all it was,' I admit. 'I was so fed up and just wanted to feel like I had some power. Any power . . . But now. I'm not sure. I kind of like him. He doesn't seem so bad. I keep wanting to spend time with him; I think about him a lot. Ironically, it's the closest I've felt to any guy before. And . . . I *like myself* when

I'm Gretel. Does that make sense? But then I also hate myself for not being her. I feel . . . I feel Gretel is the woman I could've been if all the bad stuff didn't happen to me. Whenever I'm her, I can pretend none of it was real. But it did, and it was, and I'll never be her. I can never be like her. Joshua would hate me if he knew me, and would think I was crazy anyway, even without the fact I've been pretending to be someone else because I'm a complete fuck-up.' Hangover and exhaustion and psychological break-throughs join together and a tear falls down my face. Megan launches over the sofa and lets me cry into her hair. 'I'm so crazy,' I keep saying. 'I hate that I'm so crazy.'

She pulls me back. 'You're not crazy,' she keeps whispering. 'You're not.'

'I'm pretending to be someone else.'

'So does *everyone* when they start dating someone. You've just taken it to the extreme, that's all. OK, so you've lied about your name and wanting to go to Africa, but that's about it, isn't it? The rest has just been hiding parts of yourself. Do you really think this Joshua guy is the person he's making himself out to be? No! He's showing you his best bits. He's hiding all his crap. But I don't care about him right now, I care about you. April. Honey.' She rubs her finger along my arm. 'I think you need some help,' she suggests, quieter than even a whisper now and her words fall like snowflakes, melting into my hair.

I.

Need.

Some.

Help.

Need.

Help.

'I know I do,' I say. The first time I've ever said it. Admitting it hurts more than I'd imagined, like I'm taking off my top layer of skin with an emery board. 'I've started to think that since going to the boxing classes. They're all in therapy . . . But I can't afford it.'

'I'll pay!'

I shake my head. 'That's nuts. You can't do that.'

'Why not? I have money. It's stupid how much money I have. You may as well have some. That lady, the one you see at work? She does private appointments, yes?'

'I think so . . . Yeah, I guess.' It's all got far too real far too quickly. I've hunched my legs up now, practically cowering into the cushion.

'Well maybe think about setting something up. She knows your back story, which will save time.'

'She does. I'm not sure though, Megs. I can't take your money. You already give me such cheap rent.'

'Don't be stupid.'

'I'd pay you back in instalments, maybe? But, well, I'm not sure I'm ready to let go of Gretel yet.'

'Are you going to keep seeing him in the meantime?'

'I dunno.' The thought of not seeing Joshua again feels too painful. This isn't good. None of this is good. 'Probably,' I admit. 'Is that a bad idea?'

She shrugs. 'Probably. But I can't tell you how to live your life. Besides, it's not like I have a clue.'

I yawn. 'God, I'm so tired. Can we just leave it for today, please?'

'OK. Sorry. I love you. It's going to be all right.'

'I hope so.' I curl up on my side. I've told someone and the reality is knackering. I don't have anything else to give today. We un-pause *Dawson's Creek*, and watch three episodes in a row. Megan is kind enough not to pry any further and grumbles instead about the launch. I grumble about my hangover. Sunday is back in perfect working order. Except it isn't.

My phone died early this morning and it takes me until night time to summon the energy needed to shower, unpack my stinking overnight bag, find my charger and plug it in. It vibrates straight away, with a message from my boyfriend.

Joshua: How's the hangover? When can I see you next? Xx

And sometimes in life, when there are too many emotions, and they are too strong and too conflicting to make any sense, the only feeling you can feel is nothingness. And the only way you can get through the nothingness is to carry on doing whatever the hell it is you are doing, even though you know it's wrong.

Gretel: Sorry. Phone died. Hangover brutal. I need cuddles and attention and distraction from my pain. Any ideas?
Joshua: Umm come over right away?
Gretel: Uber already ordered x

April: GOOD LUCK FOR THE LAUNCH TONIGHT. YOU ARE GOING TO TOTALLY SMASH IT! I BELIEVE IN YOU, MY DAD, PETER PAN xxx

Megan: OMG, I totally forgot that *Hook* exists as a movie.

Megan: That movie was so fucking weird.

Megan: Still can't believe hot Rufio died.

Megan: Or that in those days you were allowed to roll up a fat child and push him down a ramp as a weapon . . .

Megan: Anyway THANK YOU. I'm fucking bricking it and nothing is ready and I HATE that I let a stupid man distract me but hopefully it will be OK.

April: It will be more than OK. You're amazing xxx

Gretel: Hello you. So, my housemate is out all evening doing this launch thing. Wanna come over? I'll cook. xx

Joshua: Depends what you're going to cook.

Gretel: Something quick so we have loads of time for sex afterwards.

Joshua: Do we have to even eat first?

Gretel: You can eat something . . .

Joshua: What's the earliest I'm allowed to arrive?

Gretel: Six x

Joshua: I like you. A lot. Just so you're aware . . . x

I'm back to faking my orgasms again.

Joshua's doing exactly what he did last time, and the time before that, but it's just not happening. I throw my hair back and make my body judder because I know there is literally no way it's going to happen this evening. Not now I'm giving it so much thought. A female orgasm is like the opposite of a tree falling over in the woods – it only exists when you *don't* think about it.

My faking sets him over the edge and we cross the finish line together, collapsing into a tumble of limbs, panting and sort of half tapping each other on the back. 'It's too hot for such things,' he says.

'You started it.'

I guess I've ticked off the slut box; I need to check off the nurturing box now too. 'Give me a moment and then I'll cook,' I say.

'You're amazing.'

'Let's see how the stir-fry comes out first.' I get up to pee so I don't get cystitis, shrugging on my knickers and bra and wondering why I feel so terribly awful.

'Can I use your shower?'

'Sure.'

★

Joshua emerges ten minutes later, clean and damp, wearing just an open shirt and pants, his stomach bulging slightly over the elastic. 'Wow, it smells great.' He comes up behind me and kisses the top of my head while I'm stirring the pan.

'It's just stir-fry. But I chopped the vegetables myself.'

'Such a multi-talented woman.'

'You can lay the table if you want.'

'Of course Your Highness.'

I grimace as he walks away. I'm mad at him and I'm finding it difficult to override. April's pissed off for some reason and she keeps taking the steering wheel of my life. He whistles as he lays the table, and I tip the sizzling pan of gingered meat and veg onto noodles and then two matching plates. 'Ta-da!'

'This looks great, thank you.' He reaches out his leg while we eat, and massages my foot with his. I try to smile back as I tuck some hair behind my ear.

'This is really nice, Gretel.'

'It's just stir-fry.'

'Yeah, but still, it's nice.'

I bite into a miniature corn on the cob.

'That was really nice too.' He nods his head towards the bedroom, where you can still see the chaos of the sheets.

'Yeah, it was great.'

'Yeah?' he nudges my foot again.

I arrange the smile on my face before engaging eye contact. 'Yeah!'

'OK.'

We talk and chew and swallow. I ask him about his day. His manager isn't being very nice. 'I'm sorry to hear that.

What a douche. You could do such a better job.' He asks me about mine. 'Yeah, it was OK, same old, same old.' I do not say, 'It feels like I can finally breathe again after I stopped doing my shifts but I feel so guilty I then lose the ability to breathe again.'

'So where's your housemate tonight?'

'She's got this huge work-launch thing. She works in jewellery PR.'

'Cool, sounds cool. When do I get to meet her?'

Megan, coincidently, asked the same question this morning while I was checking it was OK to have Joshua around. 'Does this mean I'll get to meet him?'

'Well, maybe you'll see him in the morning.'

'And does this mean I'll get to meet Gretel?'

'Shut up.'

'Just saying! Oh shit! Is that the time? I'm late. Oh God, I'm so stressed I may vomit.'

I bite a pepper and chew delicately. 'Megan? Oh, soon. Maybe even tonight depending on what time she gets back.'

I'm flailing. I can't find Gretel. She isn't here. I can't find her buzz or energy, passion or enthusiasm. Maybe her period is due? Does she even have them? I'm not sure. But the atmosphere is flat and it feels like my fault. Joshua's eating but he's not smiling and it's my responsibility as a girlfriend to entertain him, to uplift him, to put him in a good mood. He can't associate his girlfriend with any negativity.

'Speaking of friends,' I start, not sure where I'm going. 'Umm, my friend Chrissy. The one whose hen do I went to. It's her wedding next weekend, and she gave me a plus one.'

He puts down his fork. 'Really?'

'Yeah, I mean, I know weddings are pretty boring, especially if you don't know anyone. But you're more than welcome to come. If you're not busy.'

The smile he smiles. 'I'm not busy. I'd love to come, Gretel. Where is it?'

'Just in Surrey. So we can get there and back on the train.'

'And you know Chrissy from?'

I wonder if I need to invent a lie for her too, to give our friendship a more dazzling edge, but it's too hot and I'm just . . . not today . . . so I say, 'We temped together years ago, and just clicked. I won't know many people at the wedding either, so you'll be stuck talking to me most of the day.' That wasn't a very confident thing to say. Argh. April's just seeping out of me, all into the stir-fry. But Joshua's still smiling and spearing a piece of pepper.

'Sounds great.'

'You sure you want to come?' *Why do I keep checking?*

'Yes!'

'But, weddings can be really dull and boring and long.' *Stop it stop it stop it stop it!*

'Not with you there.'

'OK, if you're sure?'

'I'm sure.'

'Great.'

We talk and finish the wine, and time passes as Joshua tells me all about his manager in a lot of detail, and all the different ways in which he isn't as appreciated in work as he thinks he should be, and all the ways he could do a better job if he was manager. At about nine, he crashes to a halt, and just looks at me.

'What?' I ask.

Then he's out of his chair, scooping me up in his arms, carrying me to the bedroom.

'What about the washing-up?' I squawk. Again, so totally un-Gretel.

'I'll do it later.'

But I'm still too busy digesting dinner to want to have sex right now, I think. *But the soy sauce will stick to the plates and take forever to scrub off*, I think. *But it can't still be there when Megan gets home because that won't be fair*, I think. *But I don't trust you to actually do the washing-up later*, I think.

But I've not been Gretel enough this evening. She doesn't care about something like the washing-up needing doing. Not when there's sex with her glorious boyfriend on offer, the boyfriend she wasn't expecting to get, especially as she wasn't really looking for one. So I let myself get carried to my bedroom and try to get myself into a sexy place, which is really hard with a stomach full of food. My head's so not in this. It's all over the place, cluttered with lies and guilt, and chicken that the enzymes in my stomach haven't broken down yet. I feel almost panicked as we start kissing, the taste of my cooking on his tongue. I don't feel aroused as he strips off his shirt, revealing his bloated belly. I almost want to push him away when he starts kissing down my own full tummy with a suggestive look in his eye. I don't think I have the energy to fake another orgasm, let alone think about even attempting a real one. I want to be alone. I want to never touch a man again. I never want one near me again. I hate them. I hate Joshua for touching me. I hate him for loving me, for caring, when it can never be trusted. Feelings. They always wane and then you end up fucked up and bitter and wishing you'd never got going in the first place. And I don't deserve these kisses, and I don't deserve what he's doing right now, with my knickers pulled to one side. I don't deserve a man like Joshua, even though he's still a man and they're all awful. I don't deserve anything good, and I want to cry but . . .

I let out a moan, because I don't want to hurt his feelings, because he's trying really hard down there.

He doesn't do the dishes. He falls asleep clasping me in his arms, and it's a really delicate procedure, getting out of there without waking him. I wiggle like Houdini until I've dislodged him and his affection and spend a good amount of time looking at Old Faithful, my crack in the ceiling. I watch him sleep, changing my mind about him every five minutes:

Look at his sleeping face. He really is quite handsome. I can't believe this man has chosen me. I want to touch his face, I want to kiss him, I want to be next to this face forever.

Then:

I can't believe you've just fallen a-fucking-sleep when you didn't wash up. I knew this would happen. I hope you don't snore because I have work tomorrow and I don't want to be tired. I just want to be alone. I wish I could vanish you away so I can be alone in my bed, without your body here confusing me.

I can't take it any more. I heave myself out of bed, holding my head as if that will stop it whirring so hard, shake on a dressing gown and pad out into the darkness of the flat. I can still hear Joshua's heavy breathing whistling through my door, so I gently push it shut. And it's just me again, April. I look at the dirty table, sigh, and get to work collecting the plates up and taking them to the sink.

I'm elbow deep in Fairy Liquid bubbles when I hear the scrape of Megan's key in the lock.

'I'm still up,' I stage whisper. 'Hey. How did it go?'

I twist to see her putting her bag down on the sofa, a tired wilt to her body. As she steps towards the kitchen, moonlight from the front window highlights her perfectly made-up face and hair – though there's a touch of 'end-of-the-night' to the look.

'Really well,' she says, sinking into the sofa. 'Thank God.'

'Amazing! I knew you'd smash it! You want a glass of wine? I've got some leftover.'

'Please.'

I shake off my soap-suddy hands and pour out the rest of the merlot that Joshua brought round. I hand her a glass before plonking myself next to her. 'So, tell me all about it.'

She takes a deep slurp before replying. 'It all went seamlessly. Right up to the last minute, of course. There was a terrible moment when we thought the flowers weren't going to arrive. Or Cara Delevingne. But then it all came together. Cara turned up with all her friends, which is a bonus, means we'll definitely get press coverage tomorrow. Everyone loved the line. They've sold out of the heart necklace ALREADY online.'

I reach over and grab her foot. 'Megs! This is amazing! I'm so proud.'

'I know, thank you. Our CEO was so chuffed. She said "well done Megan" as I was leaving, and, from her, that's like the biggest thumbs-up ever. Hopefully this will really help my promotion next year . . .' But she's not looking at me, and she's not glowing with pride like she should be. She's staring into her merlot instead.

'What? What is it?'

Megan shakes her head with her eyes closed. 'Sorry. I'm being stupid.'

'No. What is it? What happened?'

She puts her glass down on our messy coffee table and wipes under her eyes.

'Megan?'

'Sorry . . .' she's crying. 'I'm an idiot. I just . . . it went so well, and I worked so hard, and I should've been buzzing, you know?'

'I know, I know. You're amazing. What is it?'

She shakes her head again. 'But I couldn't enjoy the evening, April. I know it's pathetic, but I kept thinking about him. Even though I meant nothing to him, I kept . . . it sounds stupid . . . but I kept thinking maybe he'd turn up to support me, as a surprise? Make a grand declaration or something? And I kept imagining him seeing me in the press photos in tomorrow's *Metro* and realising his true feelings . . . Then I realised I'm insane and pathetic, and I just got really sad. It was one of the best nights of my career, and I couldn't enjoy it, couldn't get lost in the moment, because I liked a man and he didn't like me back.' She snuffles and wipes her eyes again. 'I'm such a loser.'

'You're not!'

'I am.' She puts her face into her palms, and wipes them back over her hair. When she looks up, her make-up is smeared in two lines from her eyes to her ears. She smiles meekly. 'I'm going to get help,' she says. 'First thing tomorrow. I'm booking an appointment. I know I told you *you* need help but I'm starting to think I need it too.'

'You don't need help, you just—'

'What? Need to never try with men ever again? Shut them out of my life?'

I shrug.

'It can't hurt, can it? I don't want to feel like this any more, and I don't want to be in this pattern any more, and those are precisely the two things they say therapy is for. Even if I use the sessions just to figure out it's better to be by myself, I still want to know I've made that decision from a healthy place.'

I reach out for her glass and take a sip of her wine. 'Well, if that's what you want to do, I support you,' I say. 'And I'm so pleased the launch went well. I never doubted for a second that it would.'

We stare at the blank television screen, passing her drink back and forth, taking it in turns to have some.

'What about you, *Gretel*?' she asks.

'Please. Don't.'

'Is he here?'

'He's here. He's asleep.'

'Can I go and look at him?'

'No!' I laugh. 'That would be weird.'

'Oh, because nothing else about this situation is weird at all, Gretel.'

'Don't. *Please*.' It's my turn to put my head in my hands. 'I've invited him to Chrissy's wedding.'

'What? What the hell are you doing, April?'

'I don't know,' I say, with total honesty. 'I don't know.'

Reasons not to trust men

- Every single man I've ever opened my heart to has damaged me
- Even the good ones are still dysfunctional man-children who never check their privilege and want a medal for being 'a good guy' every hour of the day
- Everything men have done

Reasons to trust men

- They are not all the same
- You must believe the best in people
- You will die alone if you don't get over this
- Barack Obama
- ~~Joshua???~~

Our trainers squeak on the floor, our bodies pant with exertion. Sweat drips from the ceiling. *Splosh splosh splosh.*

'Do you trust men?' I ask Charlotte, through short gasps for air. It's hard to be heard over Destiny's Child. She runs sideways and throws me the squashy ball. I crab-run in front of her, and manage to catch it.

'Now that's a question and a half.'

'Well? Do you?' I throw the ball back. 'And is it a good thing or a bad thing to do so?'

We're playing a game called 'Emotional Labour' where we have to run from one side of the hall to the other, chucking the ball of 'fragile masculinity' between us.

'Be careful ladies,' Gillian, our instructor calls. 'Don't drop it. Remember how fragile it is, it will definitely smash.' We all giggle which is hard with my heart pumping so hard from the crazy cardio. Will this ever stop feeling amazing? This hour of class, followed by the hour in the pub afterwards is the only time in my life right now where I feel good.

Charlotte holds on to our ball while she thinks of her reply. 'I didn't trust them for a really long time,' she says. 'I remember where you are so well. I didn't trust any of them. Thought they were all the same.'

'Aren't they?' I gasp.

She throws the ball. I catch it. We run. I throw it. She catches it.

She shakes her head. 'No. I don't think so.' She throws it back. 'Not all men do terrible things to women,' she says. 'I think there are some good ones. They're not all abusive. At all. But . . .'

'But?' I say.

'But they're all still men, I guess. They may not be violent or controlling, but they are all a bit . . . rubbish. They can't help it even.'

'And take a breather,' Gillian calls out, over the whirrs of multiple fans. I've since learnt that Gillian trained in kick-boxing after her husband kicked her down the stairs, broke five of her ribs, told her she was crazy to accuse him of such a thing, and then, when she eventually left him with two black eyes, told the custody court that she was an unfit mother.

Charlotte drops the fragile masculinity, and I bend over, hands on my knees, oxygen not getting into my lungs quick enough, my heart beserking its way through my chest. We heave in air together for a moment, like everyone else.

'So, they're rubbish,' I try and clarify, 'but you can trust them?'

'Oh no.' She lurches up. 'You can't *trust* them. I trust women, but I could never trust a man. But . . .' she picks up the ball from the ground, 'I do trust that they're not all abusive wankers. That some of them are just nice and hopeless. Does that help?'

'I'm not sure.'

She stops, wipes the sweat off her forehead, and pats me. 'I really feel for you,' she says. 'You're only just starting to see a counsellor for this. I'm a few years ahead of you in recovery, and I remember your stage so well. It's all still so raw, and you're still questioning everything, and you don't trust any of your instincts. It's exhausting!'

I well up a little.

It is. So. Very. Exhausting.

She pulls me in for a sweaty hug. 'It does get better,' she promises. 'In time, you'll learn to trust *yourself* again. And that's the only person it's important to trust. But it gets worse before it gets better. At least you're getting it out.'

I nod. I do feel some poison leaking out. I do feel like there's a little bit less than there was. But I also feel totally overwhelmed by how much there still is, and how long it will take to drain, and whether it ever will, and how much of my life I'm going to mess up in the meantime.

'It will get better,' she repeats, before releasing me.

Gillian turns the music off and claps her hands. She gleams with sweat. The air in here must be at least thirty degrees. My own sweat keeps dripping into my eyes. 'Good work, ladies,' she says. 'Now, before we cool down, I think it's time for an "It's Not Your Fault" circle.'

I send a questioning look to Charlotte who grins reassuringly. 'Just wait. It's actually exactly what you need.'

'If you could put your balls back in the basket, and sit in a circle. Oldies, show the newbies.'

There's only one other new girl, Hannah, a short brunette who turned up last week and hasn't spoken to anyone yet. Our eyes find one another as we're singled out as the new kids. I manage a smile, plop my ball back, and join the circle forming on the ground. A mist of contentment seems to rise off it. All of us filled with exercise endorphins and the

relaxed energy of being around people you don't have to try
with. I cross my legs beneath me and sit next to Hazel who
smiles too.

'What's this about?'

'Just wait.'

Gillian sits down in a perfect lotus, completing the circle.
'Everyone comfy?' she asks. 'And can everyone hear over the
fans?' We all nod. 'Great. Now, most of you know the deal
here, but for those of you who don't, here's all there is to it.
We are going to close our eyes and take some deep breaths
as a group. Then we're going to sit in silence. If you feel
moved to speak, speak. Say the things you need to say. I want
you to get in touch with your pain, and really sit with it. I
know it's hard, but you're safe here, and we're all here with
you.' She pauses. 'And, if someone else is speaking, know that
what they say applies to you, too. We're all in this together.
Feel every word, know that it's true, and know that you
deserve to hear it.' Nobody's acting like this is strange, even
though I have to say it sounds a bit strange.

Gillian jumps up and turns some quiet meditative music
on, the sort you shavasana to at the end of a yoga class, then
she sits back down again. 'Right everyone, close your eyes.' I
watch everyone close theirs without complaint before I do
so myself. My eyelids lower, the universe goes dark. 'OK, now
I want you all to take three deep breaths. Breathe in . . .'
There's a whistling noise as we all suck in oxygen. 'And out
. . . And in . . . and out. And in . . . and out.' My ribcage
inflates and softens. My shoulders drop slightly. 'Now, this
may feel hard, but I want you just to quickly think about what
brought you to this class . . .'

The white wall. White wall. Hurt. Pain. Shame. Too numb to move. Blame. No. Please. Don't. I can't believe this has happened to me. My eyes begin to prickle, even with them closed.

'Now, locate where it hurts. Do a scan, find the part of your body that holds this pain.' I don't even have to scan. I locate it right in my guts. It's like my small intestine is made of cast iron. Wow. I've never noticed it before.

'What shape is the pain? Can you find the edges of it? Sit with it. Don't push it away.' There is a big lump of pain in my gut that I didn't know I'd been carrying. I feel it now. It's about the size of an oversized banana, and spiky, pointing into me, hurting whenever I turn. I don't resist it. I try and soften its edges. I breathe into it, and notice how it moves as my ribs move. It really hurts. Tears leak down my face from behind my closed lids. There is pain. So much pain. In me every day and nowhere for it to go, and I'm not sure I'll ever feel right again. The only way to get through is to pretend it's not there and hope things get better and hope I don't make the same mistakes again, but then this pain catches up with me and knocks me down and, no, I don't think I'll trust myself ever again, let alone a man and . . . I begin to weep quietly, feeling ever so desperate, like I always do when . . .

'It's not your fault.' Gillian's voice. Calm. Loud. Authoritative. 'What happened to you. It wasn't your fault,' she says.

My stomach twists, resisting the words. No. The pain can't live under conditions such as this. It starts to argue with her, I start to argue with her. *Maybe it was my fault, just a bit. Maybe if I'd fought back. Maybe I'm overreacting . . .*

'Don't diminish your pain,' another voice in the circle says. 'Your pain is a totally appropriate response to what happened to you.'

'I'm so sorry this happened to you,' another voice says.

'It shouldn't have happened to you,' says one more.

I jolt. I clutch my stomach. I can't figure out whose voice is whose any more. I hear a whimper. Someone else is crying. Maybe it's me who made the sound. The iron in me hardens, rejects. *But it did happen to you, it did. It can't be undone. You will always be fucked up by this. So fucked up.*

'What happened to you doesn't define who you are.' It's Gillian's voice again, like she knows. I guess she must know. Because she's been here too. I gulp, and I gulp again, because if I don't, I will full-on sob. The tears keep on pouring. I keep my eyes shut, ears open, heart open.

There was a white wall and I looked at it because it was all I could do. I got hurt and I buried the pain of it because, at that moment in time, it was all I could do. I just tried to survive. I'm trying to heal but it's taking ages and it's hard and feels impossible but I'm trying, and that's all I can do.

My mouth cracks open. Words spill out. 'You *will* heal,' my voice is saying. 'I know it feels like you never will, but you will.' It's too much. All the emotion. Too much. I lose track of who is saying what, who is sobbing and who isn't, what time of day it is.

'It's not your fault.'

'You did the best you could.'

'It won't always hurt this much.'

'You are so much stronger than you give yourself credit for.'

'It could've happened to anyone.'

'He is the broken one, not you.'

'You will get through this.'

'You will get through this.'

'You will get through this,' I whisper.

And I know they're the sort of clichéd sayings you see posted on inspirational backgrounds in swirly font. I know they're just words, and words can't take the pain away, can't undo what was done, can't make me the woman I was before, can't make me forget, or forgive, or ever be the same again. But there's something about these words being chanted by women who get it, who have been there and not deserved it either. Some much further ahead than me on this journey of putting yourself back together again, able to add a layer of authenticity to what they're saying, because they're on the same road, but they're further along, and they can see the sun over the horizon, and they're calling back to me, promising me that, if I can hold on a little longer, I'll be able to see the sun rise too.

'And that's it,' Gillian says. 'Open your eyes when you feel able to.'

It takes me half a minute or so. My chest is sore from releasing grief, not one part of my face is dry. The room full of fans comes into focus. We are all crying, all of us. Some harder than others. But we're all smiling. My stomach feels the tiniest bit lighter. Like maybe I've soldered off the top layer of iron. I really am crying. Charlotte catches my eyes and sees how hard I'm sobbing, and she stands, pulls me up, and hugs me so tight. I hug her back, bawling into her shoulder. Howling and shedding tears all over her. She just hugs and hugs. Then there are more bodies and more hugs, and we all blend together. Arms mingling, breasts pushed together, ribs hurting as the entire class melts into a fused circle.

From: Carol@FreshStart.com
To: AprilS1987@gmail.com
Subject: Your first appointment

Dear April,

I'm just confirming your appointment for an initial consultation for this Wednesday evening at 7 p.m. Obviously things are slightly different as we've already worked together at WeAreHere, but I still think it's important to have a talk about what you're hoping to achieve out of this process.

Attached are the directions on how to find my office.

Kindest regards

Carol Knight

Clinical psychologist

*

From: April@WeAreHere.com
To: Mike@WeAreHere.com
Subject: Official notice

Dear Mike,

As discussed in yesterday's meeting, here is my formal

notice of resignation for the role of Advisor. Thank you for being so understanding.

April

★

From: Mike@WeAreHere.com
To: April@WeAreHere.com
Subject: RE: Official notice

April,

Thanks for this. Annoying legal formality, especially as it's not like you're leaving us!

Anyway, I accept your notice and we've started advertising for someone to take over your shifts permanently. I know we spoke about it a lot on Thursday, but I do want to reiterate just how grateful we are that you took on this role and everything you gave to it. These front-line jobs do take a toll; they take a toll on anyone who does them. Please don't chastise yourself for reaching your limit. You've given so much and helped so many people. I'm looking forward to continuing to work with you as a volunteer manager. Thanks for everything you gave us.

Mike

★

Gretel: Crazy week! Sorry I've not seen you. Shall we meet at Vic at 11 tomorrow for the wedding?

• And Happily Ever After . . . Gretel's Guide on How to Keep Him

Oh, look how far you've come. Look at all you've achieved now you've learnt how to play the game. Aren't you glad you've mastered the art of holding in all your totally appropriate responses? Remember how lonely you were back in those dark days of authenticity? But you made it. Well done. Let's all be honest, I really didn't think someone as pathetic as you would manage it, but you did. That's how desperate you must've been. Enjoy your prize of a man. Enjoy society finally accepting you now that you're not a lonely, pathetic singleton anymore. Enjoy the beautiful comfort of being in a loving, caring relationship with someone who truly adores you for who you are . . .

Hang on, what do you fucking mean you've not been being yourself?

Are you *crazy*?

You mean, you've not been being you? This *whole time*? Are you dim? Do you not know the most basic rule of dating – IT ONLY WORKS IF YOU ARE YOURSELF!! I thought everyone knew that. Jeez. I can't believe you've been lying to this poor guy from the start. How let down he's going to feel when he realises that you're actually a flawed human being, with needs and desires that may infringe on his own, and that you want to be loved despite all those repulsive flaws, which is totally unreasonable if you ask me. Yes yes yes, you need to be yourself. Duh. But, like, I thought you realised all of this wasn't about hiding yourself, but *changing* yourself. Making yourself perfect. Like he deserves.

Too late now. Can't open up now. Otherwise he'll claim false advertising and want his goddamned money back. Nope. If you don't want to lose him, you're just going to have to commit to keeping up this facade for the rest of your life. Just keep pretending. Every day. Fake it till you make it and all that. I mean, TRY to be yourself, but not too much. You don't want to go back to square one again, do you? I mean, if he doesn't love you for who you are then nobody else will. Life's not *that* long to act like a complete fake. Men tend to die before women too, so you'll get a few years when you're eighty-six of being able to let yourself loose for a while. You can hang on until then, can't you?

April: Gretel?

Gretel: Yes, babes?

April: I need to let you go.

Gretel: Me? But I'm not the one with all the problems.

April: Exactly.

Gretel: Explain your rationale please.

April: Gretel, you're not real . . .

Gretel: Well that's true.

April: And you're not different from me . . . you *are* me.

Gretel: Huh?

April: You're the me I never got the chance to be. You're the me I could've been if none of it happened. But it did happen, Gretel. It did. I can't take it away. It can't be undone. I am the woman I am because of what happened. I will never be you, and it hurts too much to keep you around. Because you're not real. You never were. You're just a stick to beat myself with.

Gretel: I thought I was a stick to beat Joshua with?

April: I thought so too, at first. But no.

Gretel: I thought you wanted to feel power. Haven't you felt more powerful being me?

April: No. I've felt worse.

Gretel: Surprise surprise.

April: I've felt worse because there's no power in denying who you are. No power in wishing things could've been different. No power in envying the other you that you could've been. No power in hiding away those bits in order to be loved.

Gretel: Bloody hell. Somebody's been to therapy . . .

April: I have. It's helping.

Gretel: I've never seen the need for it myself. All seems a bit self-indulgent.

April: You would think that. Because you've not had the life I've had. I've got to say goodbye now. To you, and to Joshua.

Gretel: April?

April: Yes?

Gretel: I'm sorry.

April: For what?

Gretel: I'm sorry you didn't get the chance to be me. I'm sorry it all happened to you. Truly, I am.

April: Thank you. Goodbye, Gretel. It was nice never quite knowing you.

Gretel: Goodbye.

Gretel: April?

April: Yes.

Gretel: He still might love you, you know?

April: Please, don't.

Gretel: He might.

It starts raining on the day of Chrissy's wedding, and the day I'm going to end things with Joshua.

'Poor Chrissy.' Megan pushes the living-room curtains to one side, her face dimly lit by the gloomy sky. 'Months of heatwave and then it decides to properly break on the day of your wedding. If it were me, I'd consider it an omen.'

I join her, taking the material of the curtain between my fingers. It's pissing it down in a determined, relentless, way. Already this summer of scorched grass, sunburn by 10 a.m., and it being too hot to sleep feels like a collective dream. Like it never really happened. 'Bless her,' I say. 'Such bad luck. Also, will my yellow dress look stupid now?'

'Nah, it will be fine. It will be warm in the church. Those giant, stone rooms are well known for their cosiness.'

'You're hilarious.'

We both stare out at the rain like we've never seen it before. I run through all the ways in which I now have to adapt my plans to fit with this new precipitation. I need to find a bag that fits an umbrella. I need to find a pair of skin-coloured tights that haven't laddered or make my legs look like I have jaundice. I need to get cash out for a cab from the station to the church, as a fifteen-minute walk will ruin my hair and make-up. I need to admit to Joshua that I've catfished him and listen to him tell me what a fucking psycho I am . . .

'So, this is your last engagement with Joshua?' Megan says to the misted windows.

I grasp the curtain a little tighter. 'Yes. I'll tell him after today.'

'And not before the wedding today because . . . ?'

'Because then he won't come.'

'And you want him to come because?'

'Because Chrissy says each guest costs sixty-five pound a head. You can't lose your plus-one wedding guest last minute when it's sixty-five pound a head.'

'That is true.'

'Unforgivable.'

'And you're sure there's no other reason? Like, you want to spend more time with him?'

'Stop it, Megan.'

Gretel isn't coming to the wedding – only April. I don't want to pretend any more and it's all going to end anyway. So April curls her hair, because she cares about looking nice on her friend's big day, and she checks the train times over and over because she gets stressed about being on time. She sends a message to Joshua, checking he's going to be on time too, even though he's never been late before.

Joshua: Bang on time. Look at me, the best-dressed dude on the tube.

He's sent a selfie, decked out in an uncomfortable suit, and I sit down on the edge of my bed and stare at the photo. All dressed up for me, getting up early on a Saturday for me, spending the day making boring small talk with strangers and eating dry chicken for me. *But it isn't for me, it was never for me*, I remind myself, and I put my phone in my bag.

The London streets are empty as I hurry under my umbrella to the station, like the rain is poisonous. I shake my umbrella off into a floor puddle, get a seat on the Tube, and as we career through the tunnel I stare at nothing, wondering how I'm going to make it through this. I remember my initial fantasy – breaking a random man's heart over an artichoke before dropping the mic and vanishing. I wish I'd had the guts to follow through with it. Maybe if the guy hadn't been Josh . . . or maybe I never had it in me anyway.

'You say that this Gretel is every man's dream,' Carol said in our first session the other day. 'But you're basing that on your own interpretations of what men want. Do you think maybe Gretel is nothing to do with men, but rather a fantasy for you? The woman you think you could've been if you hadn't met Ryan?'

Joshua's waiting for me outside WHSmith, cradling a news-paper he's bought. His hair is wet, childlike and juxtaposed with his suit, and he looks so adorable that I almost can't walk over and kiss him hello.

'You look lovely,' he says, drinking in my effort. 'Your poor friend though. Raining today.'

'I know. And they've paid a fortune for this big stately place too, so that they can get good photos in the grounds.'

'It will still be the happiest day of her life though.'

'Let's hope.'

'I bought our tickets while I was waiting.' He hands me an orange card and I want to hold it to my heart like it's a precious love-note.

'Thank you,' I say. 'Do you mind if we pick some food up at M&S? I live in fear of being hungry at weddings.'

I over-shop, buying two sandwiches, one pasta salad, crisps, and an overpriced collection of chopped fruit in a plastic cup. Joshua gets a bacon sandwich and a bottle of Coke. The train's on time, which is noteworthy enough for us both to comment on, and we settle at a table-seat and spread out our picnic. He keeps putting his hand on my knee, leaning over to kiss my neck. We've not seen one another all week as I've been ripping the plaster off slowly. His physical affection stings like my arm-hair getting caught in the glue.

'So, what's been going on at work?' he asks. 'Crazy week?'

I nod, stretch my arms, watch the rain splatter the window as we pull out the station. 'Yeah. I resigned from part of my role,' I tell him, getting the truth about myself out in little nuggets.

He puts down his sandwich. 'Wow, what? Are you OK? Which part?' He rubs my arm to comfort me and it stings again.

'Just the advisor role. I'm fine. I feel guilty, but also know it's the right thing to have done.'

'Oh OK. Woah, though. I thought you really liked that bit of your job?'

'Yeah, I did. But it was getting too much. I was struggling with how sad it was.' I raise both eyebrows and shrug, all 'well, what can you do?'.

Josh's hand drops off my arm. 'I had no idea,' he says slowly.

'It's fine. It's not a big deal.' And it isn't. I beat myself up about it for one sleepless night, then I only felt relief. I'm proud of what I did and who I helped, but I don't want to be angry all the time, afraid all the time, I don't want to believe that every dog in the world bites, even though they all have teeth.

Joshua stares over my head and at the splattered decoration of rain against the glass. 'OK, well, I'm glad you're happy. Sounds like it's been a bit mad.'

I can sense his pain about being left out of this life development and I put a hand on his arm. To comfort him, to try and make this last day a nice one. 'Sorry I didn't tell you,' I say. 'It was just a lot for me to digest, and it was all a bit heavy and I didn't want to burden you with it.'

His eyes are sad when he smiles. 'But I'm your boyfriend. I'm here for the burdening.'

You won't be my boyfriend for much longer, I think, *and you never were to begin with.*

'That's so cute.' I kiss him, to pretend that it's better. I should tell him now. Before we get off the train. I don't want to be screamed at in front of Chrissy's wedding guests. But his lips are so warm, and the way he hugs me . . .

We pull into the suburban station and I feel sorry for everyone who has to live here. Maybe it's just the rain and greyness, but the town lacks anything that makes anywhere something. There's just a paved shopping precinct showcasing the most basic selection of high-street stores. Chrissy always told me this part of Surrey was the most sterile place in the universe to grow up, and I'm now inclined to believe her. Joshua and I run to the taxi queue to make sure we're at the front, both of us ducking under my umbrella, and ask to be taken to St Luke's.

'I really don't know anyone,' I tell him as we're pulling into the sodden car park. 'I hope you don't get bored.'

'It's fine. I love singing hymns. They better have "Jerusalem". I used to go to church all the time as a kid. That was always my favourite.'

I glance at him as we pay the cab and dash to the door. I didn't know he grew up going to church. A further part of him is coloured in.

An usher hides under the heavy eaves of the church door, shivering slightly with a stack of papers. 'Hi, welcome,' he says, stepping out to greet us. 'Here's the order of service.'

'Thank you.' I take the tasteful, thick programme emblazoned with Chrissy and Mark's names in calligraphy. 'I still can't believe this weather,' I say to him.

'I know.' He peers out at the heavy sheet of rain from under the brim of his hat. 'But we've organised a coach from the church car park to the reception, so we should all stay dry. And there's a really lovely conservatory at the venue, too, so we'll be nice and cosy.'

Joshua and I nod our thank yous and enter the flower-adorned church. Adults wearing fascinators and their best suits congregate at the back, shaking umbrellas, twisting to inspect how wet they are, women getting out compact mirrors to see what ghastly impact the moisture has had on their styled hair. Even with all the flowers strewn everywhere, you can't quite shake off the smell of wet dog.

'I didn't know you were religious.' I find a space near the back to shake out my own umbrella.

Joshua takes it from me to give it a more vigorous going over. 'Only Easter and Christmas now,' he says. 'It keeps Mum happy. She's half-Irish, a Catholic.'

'You're a Catholic!' More parts of him are coloured in.

'Yes, sort of. Not a very serious one though. As I said, Easter and Christmas. I don't go to confession or anything.'

'And you've definitely had sex before marriage.'

He drops his mouth. 'I can't believe you just said the word "sex" in church! I'm telling God.'

'He already knows, mate. Omnipotent and all that.' We both giggle.

'Shall we find a pew near the back?' I turn to move, but Joshua pulls me into a tight hug. He smells so good – aftershave mingling with dampness. I let myself close my eyes and enjoy the moment.

'What was that for?'

'Just because.'

Maybe I can tell him another day . . .

I mean, nobody really knows me here, and the hens were probably too drunk to remember my name. I certainly don't remember most of theirs. And Chrissy will be too busy having the happiest day of her life to blow my cover. Maybe we can just have a nice day, a nice memory, a proper farewell to this weird situation I've created. Maybe, maybe . . .

We hold hands in our pew, waiting for everyone to dry off and settle down, ready for Chrissy's big moment. I recognise a few of the hens and we nod to one another, but thankfully they don't come over to say hi. People don't tend to be friendly at weddings until after the ceremony. Mark's at the front, chatting animatedly to all the people who approach him to pat him on the back and say good luck. He's relaxed, smiling.

'Do you know the groom?' Joshua asks, his hand hot in mine.

'Not really.'

'Do you like him?'

I laugh.

'That's a no.'

'No, he's fine. Mark's fine. I don't really know him. He's better than her ex.'

How many men win the love of women, simply by being better than her ex?

'He looks happy.'

'Well, he damn well should be. It's his wedding day.'

'Yes, I know. Sorry.' Joshua drops my hand, sulky at my snap.

'No, *I'm* sorry.' I am all over the place. I am not the in-control Gretel I used to be. My nerves are vibrating, thoughts flurrying around my skull, all of them contradicting the other. I pick up Josh's hand. 'I just hope he makes her happy. I'm very protective of Chrissy, she's a good friend.'

He kisses my cheek, happy to make up. 'She's lucky to have you.'

The church fills up. You can almost picture steam rising from the congregation as we collectively dry off. Chrissy's mother is wheeled to the front by her brother – neither of whom I've ever met, just know from social media pictures. She's got a lovely green hat on. She sits tall and proudly, daring people to stare at the chair.

'Is that her mum?'

I nod.

'Why is she in a wheelchair?' Joshua asks discreetly.

'MS.'

'Oh, that's sad.'

'Chrissy's just glad she's well enough to come today.'

Joshua kisses my bare shoulder. We open the order of service and spot 'Jerusalem', and he looks so genuinely happy at the prospect of singing it that I'm overcome with affection and kiss him all over his face. Raining them down like the cascade of water falling outside, while he blushes and grins.

Maybe you could trust him? Maybe you could trust it? I mean, he'll never be able to trust you but . . . never mind, let it go. Let him go.

The organ stops. We all know what this means. Everyone quietens. Expectation swells in the gaps between us. A signal's given. The organ starts up again. We all stand, twisting towards the aisle, ready for Chrissy to make her grand entrance. My eyes fill when I see her walk past. She really does look lovely in her ivory gown, though maybe a little overdone and not truly like her – essentially how every bride looks these days with professional hair and make-up. Mark looks glad enough to see her too as she arrives at his side. They share a smirk, all, like, 'well this is weird' and my heart's next beat is painful, and stays painful for half a minute or so. The vicar jollies up. 'We are gathered here today . . .'

We stay standing to sing 'Jerusalem'. Joshua surprises me by singing loudly, without embarrassment, face to the front, chest open. I grin to myself and colour in another piece of the Joshua jigsaw. More affection gurgles up and I can't concentrate for the rest of the song. I keep looking over and feeling warm yet inappropriate feelings.

We're told to sit. We do. The sermon starts. Vows exchanged. Tears spring up. I forgot how awkward it is to sit next to a boyfriend at a wedding. How it makes you confront the question of whether or not you two will one day be the couple at the front everyone else is watching.

Chrissy looks at Mark from beneath her veil and promises to love, honour, but not obey because she's a smart, educated, feminist, lawyer type. I can't help but revisit the anxiety spiral of wondering if this moment will ever happen to me. If I'll ever stand in front of a room full of people I love, and promise to love someone else the most? I remember a quote from a movie I saw years ago, about how weddings are supposed to be about the couple, but they actually make you spend the whole day thinking about yourself. I glance over at Joshua. His head's down, his hair falling over his forehead. *Is he imagining our wedding? Is he picturing me at the end of the aisle and realising how happy that thought makes him?*

I follow his gaze to his hands, where he's checking the football scores under the pew on his phone. So, that's a no.

He senses me catching him. 'Sorry,' he whispers, putting the phone back into the pocket of his suit. Winking at me and winking away the romantic fantasy I'd stupidly projected onto him.

There's a long sermon before the couple say 'I do'. They kiss. We clap. As always, it takes forever for them to sign the register. Joshua checks the football again. 'Sorry,' he says again. 'First game of the season, you see . . .' He's not even finished explaining to me before he's gone mute again, clicking away from the football tab onto the rugby one. I feel irritation pinch the top of my nose. I twist to an older couple sitting next to me.

'Wasn't that a lovely service?' I say to the lady.

'Oh, yes, lovely.'

'Shame about the rain.'

'Oh yes, what a shame.'

'So, how do you know the couple?'

They are family friends of Mark's. They drove here from Dorset. The traffic was really bad on the M25. Isn't that motorway just the worst? I can sense Joshua still on his phone beside me. Lost to his surroundings – scroll scroll scrolling. I'm not sure why it annoys me so much but it does. Yet, when I look around, I see Joshua isn't the only man on his phone. In my direct eye line, I can see the blue glow of at least four men's crotches as their wives and girlfriends pretend it's not happening and talk amongst themselves.

'Sorry,' Joshua says, hiding his phone again in his suit pocket.

Perhaps try not doing the thing, rather than doing the thing you know is annoying and then saying sorry?

Chrissy and Mark emerge, legally wed, level unlocked, new profile pic waiting to be uploaded. They walk slowly down the aisle to the triumphant organ, smiling into the sea of phones taking their photographs. Chrissy catches my eye as she passes, clocks Josh and raises an approving eyebrow. And I love her for that. In this moment, a moment that is truly only hers, she's still interested in my life. My complete mess of a life, but today is the end point of the mess.

The front rows start streaming out after the happy couple.

I check the time on my phone. It's two thirty. We have just under ten hours to get through without incident. It's about as likely as getting the popular boy to kiss you at the disco. I have no idea what to do. Gretel would know what to do, but she's not here.

'You ready?' Joshua holds out his arm for me to link. 'There's a bus to the reception right?'

I thread my arm through his. 'Super ready. Let's go.'

Here are some of the truly ludicrous thoughts I am having: you can get through an entire wedding without anyone calling you by name. You might be forgiven for lying to someone about what you're called. You might be falling in love with the person you've been lying to. You can get through an entire wedding without anyone calling you by name . . .

Have I already said that one? As I said, *ludicrous*.

The usher was right – the reception really is in quite a nice conservatory. Light pours in even though the sky is a sallow grey. After a ten-minute lurching bus-journey, everyone spilled into it, clutch-bags held over their heads, and we are now congregating in groups, drinking flutes of champagne.

'Sorry, I hope you're not bored,' I tell Joshua, as we stand in a clump of just us two, sharing a plate of pastry-wrapped-around-stuff. 'I'm not very good at mingling.'

'Me neither.'

'How's the football?'

'Oh it's great. We're playing well, which is a nice start to the year.'

'I thought it was really fucking rude that you kept checking the score during the service.'

I don't actually say that. But I want to. 'That's good,' I say instead. A waiter in a penguin suit passes and I grab two more flutes and hand one over to Joshua. 'Cheers.' I chink us and try to smile.

'Cheers.'

I chug down my drink, bubbles fizzing to my head. My brain feels like it's burning. I miss Gretel. I miss feeling like I'm in charge.

To pass the time before we're tipsy enough to mingle,

Joshua and I start grading the canapés in order of our favourites, hunting down the waiting staff that cradle our winners.

'So the salmon thingamajig is definitely worth a second round.'

'Good because I need something to take away the taste of the quail's egg.'

'I still can't believe you spat that out into your napkin like an actual child.'

Josh beams at me. 'You mean, it didn't impress you?'

We both laugh and affection gurgles loudly in my pastry-laden stomach – my anger about the football forgotten. I reach over and squeeze his hand tenderly and he squeezes it back. The moment feels really warm and lovely until claps start to echo around us in a Mexican wave. Joshua nods behind me. 'Oh look, it's the happy couple.'

I twist to see Chrissy and Mark arrive through the main doors. They're holding hands, eyes wide from the shock of their own day, too many experiences to drink in all at one time. My stomach flip-flops for a second but I push it away – they'll be swallowed by well-wishers and won't really speak to *me* all day, especially as I'm an anomaly friend . . .

But, for some reason, out of all the wedding guests in all the conservatories in all the world, Chrissy locks eye contact with me and decides to march Mark straight towards us. The crowd parts for them like they're Moses, and I have no idea what to think or feel about any of this, only that it's too late too late too late because now Chrissy is throwing open her arms and saying, '*April!* Oh my God, I'm married.'

She gives me a giant hug as she ruins it all, pulling me into her silk gown, while I'm thinking *fuck fuck fuck shit shit shit shit* as everything disintegrates. My life is in tatters on the floor. With all the netting in my face, I can't see him, can't see his response. I hug her back limply, my heart pounding, wondering if I can pivot her . . . then she lets go so I can shake Mark's hand and say congratulations. 'And you must be Joshua,' she says, dragging him into a hug too. 'It's so great to meet you.'

I scan Joshua for signs of freaking out, my body completely soaked through with adrenaline. But he might've missed the 'April' because it's not showing on his face. 'Thanks for inviting me,' he says, giving me hope as he's released from the netting. 'Congratulations. It was a beautiful service.'

'Thank you, thank you. I still can't believe it's fucking raining though!' She reaches up to readjust her veil, then shrugs. 'Never mind. *C'est la vie.* At least this conservatory is really nice.'

Mark and Joshua shake hands and Joshua congratulates him too. Mark's not quite with us, his eyes darting behind our heads, looking at all the other people he needs to meet and greet. But Chrissy's settling in. She summons a waiter and plucks herself a champagne flute.

'So, Joshua, I was very excited to hear about you,' she says, eyeing him over her glass, while my hand trembles on mine. I keep sipping and sipping and begging her not to say April again. 'April is amazing.' I flinch. 'I hope you realise how lucky you are.'

I close my eyes. That's it. Game totally over. 'Chrissy!' I protest, though she doesn't know the true meaning of my anguished yelp.

'What? You are. Meeting you was totally worth that terrible summer scanning-in ASDA reward vouchers for £5.50 an hour. So, Joshua, what do you do?'

Joshua certainly noticed the second one. His cheeks are red with confusion, his focus darting between Chrissy and me. The true horror of what I've done hits me in the stomach. I want to cry, scream, yell, run away – all the things it's totally impossible to do at one of your best friend's weddings. So I gulp the rest of my drink, tipping my neck back to ensure I get every last drop, and watch in awe as Josh acts as normal too.

'I'm a coder. Which is much more exciting than it sounds.' His social skills are impeccable considering the bombshell exploding in his face. His eyes flit between the two of us, like we're a maths problem he needs to solve. 'This is a lovely venue. Did you grow up around here?'

Chrissy doesn't notice his shock. Why would she? 'Yes, I spent my teen years living here. Did you see the train station? It's such a skank-hole. But my mum has MS so we didn't want a wedding far away, did we Mark?'

Mark jolts to attention. Looks at his new wife, and kisses her cheek. 'No. It's a nice find. Though I can't take credit for any of it. Chrissy planned the whole day.'

'Well, it's gorgeous,' I say. My voice is very shrill indeed. 'You don't notice the rain at all. Just perfect.'

'Thanks love. Right, I better go and speak to everyone before dinner. Joshua, it was great to meet you. Take care of April here, won't you?'

Three times. Three times she has said my goddamned name. I close my eyes. Breathe. Open them.

'Congratulations again,' Joshua calls after her, as the newly-weds turn to a group of lawyers, congratulations raining down on them as hard as the rain outside.

Joshua finally turns to me, his face unreadable.

I turn to Joshua, bracing myself for impact.

We look at one another honestly for the first time since we met. When he talks, his voice is polite, quiet. 'Umm, Gretel?' he asks, reaching up to scratch his neck. 'Why did she keep calling you April?'

There is no mic drop. There is no forgotten artichoke. There is no power. There is no winning. There is no time left pretending to be what I'm not. There is no explanation that can make sense to a reasonable person.

There is no going back now.

Josh looks me in the eye as he waits for my reply. Hopeful. Waiting to feel relieved by a simple explanation that I can't give him. A strange calm descends on me like a lazy fog drifting across the sea. I return his gaze. 'You're basically the only person who calls me Gretel.'

Josh's entire face drains. '*What*?'

'My name's not Gretel,' I say. 'It's April. As you've probably guessed.'

Josh's eyebrows furrow at the same time his mouth falls open. '*What the hell*? How come? What? I mean, why? What? I don't understand.'

I take a breath, preparing myself for the talk I've been planning in my head. My stomach sucks in under the netting of my dress. I've been rehearsing this all week since I decided to tell him, but now the words sit like sludge on my tongue, pleading with me to tell a lie instead, one that will make things easier. I blink slowly and Josh's concerned face flickers in my vision. 'Well,' I start, 'it's sort of strange because—'

But I do not get to say my prepared speech because

there's the dinging of a spoon on glass and the conservatory grinds to a silence.

The usher is standing on a chair. 'Ladies and gentlemen,' he claps, calling us to further attention, 'please come through to the wedding breakfast.' He points the way out of the conservatory down a short hallway filled with oil paintings.

'Err,' I say, as everyone starts moving towards the door. 'Well you see . . .' But there's no time to explain as Joshua and I are pushed gently forward by the crowd, past the oil paintings, and through to the dining hall. I shrug as I don't know what else to do, and try to take Josh's hand to reassure him. He pulls it away though and my stomach plummets further.

Our drama cannot stop the tidal wave of wedding convention, however, and we walk stiffly to the handmade sign explaining where we're sitting. All the tables are named after trips Chrissy and Mark have taken together. We've been allocated 'Aussie' – decorated with photos of the couple's trip there last year. As we approach in tense silence, I see Chrissy's put us with her lawyer lot and I overestimated how drunk they all were at the hen because—

'*April!* How *are* you?' Janet asks, standing up to say hello like we're the best of friends.

April April April April. I watch as the word hits Joshua like a bullet. I want to reach out and shield him, but he takes the hit, sitting down like nothing has happened, though he's gone paler than fresh snow, and pouring himself a giant glass of wine.

'This is my husband, Jonathan.'

'Hi, this is my, er, boyfriend, Joshua.'

We all shake hands over the table decorated with the

standard two bottles of white and two bottles of red. Joshua and I lie trapped in the strict social conditioning of appropriate wedding behaviour. I reach for a bottle of wine and he doesn't help pass it to me, just pours his own glass down his gullet with shaking hands. I pour myself a generous glug.

'Hi, nice to meet you. How do you know the couple? Where have you come from?'

I tell everyone my name is April as we all reintroduce ourselves, and I watch as each time makes Josh flinch. I wonder how long he'll make it through the meal. It's insane he's even sitting down and eaten his bread roll. Every time I introduce Joshua as my boyfriend, my heart stings, knowing this will be the last time I get to say that – which seems all the more painful considering this is really the *first* time I've ever been able to introduce him as my boyfriend. Joshua has already drained his glass and, not looking at me, he picks up the bottle of red and pours himself more.

I try to catch his eye again but he's determined to devour a second bread roll and we get lost in pointless small talk until the starters arrive, comparing who lives where in London.

'Oh, Greenwich? Lovely.'

'Herne Hill. Oh that's just lovely.'

'Hampstead? How lovely.'

A line of teenage waiters appear, presenting each of us with a tiny plate of food that is more artfully-splattered 'jus' than food. The table quietens as the hungry lawyers and their partners tuck into their starters, giving us the chance to implode.

'I still really don't get the Gretel thing,' Joshua whispers over his plate of mozzarella and tomato salad. 'Look, I have to admit, I'm freaking out a bit.'

'The thing is,' I tell him, spearing a baby tomato onto my fork and speaking pretty rationally considering everything. 'As I said, my name has never been Gretel.'

'I don't understand. I thought maybe April might just be a nickname or something . . . ?'

I shake my head. 'No,' I say. 'It's not that. I straight-up lied about my name.'

'But . . .'

'I didn't want you to know my real name, so I said I was called Gretel.'

There isn't one single part of Joshua's face that isn't utterly horrified. I can't stand that I've made someone hurt this much. The guilt arrives like a wrecking ball. I caused this. I made this person feel this awful. Me. April.

'Why?' he asks, shaking his head.

'I told you it was Gretel and then, once I'd done it, I didn't know how to undo it. And I got to know you and we kept seeing each other, and then it all got out of hand.'

'But why the hell would you lie about something like that to begin with? I mean . . .' He shakes his head faster, unable to complete the sentence. 'You know what. No. I don't care.' His chair is scraped back. His body is leaving it. 'Excuse me,' Joshua says to the table. 'I need a moment.' He rushes off so quickly that the decorative basil leaf wafts off his plate and onto the floor.

He crashes into a waiter collecting empty plates. I watch the back of his head weave through the tables and feel white-hot pain pulsate throughout my body at the sight of him leaving. Can I follow? Do I follow? How do I make this better? Will he come back? But the entire table is watching so, despite my inner unravelling, I smile at everyone around me like he's just popped out.

Janet gives me a thumbs-up. 'He seems nice,' she says, the ball of cherry tomato in her cheek like a hamster. 'How long have you been going out?'

'Only officially for a few weeks,' I reply, thinking it's funny how capable you can be of behaving normally when your life is so not in a normal place.

Jonathan leans over, teeth already stained with red wine. He waggles his finger at me drunkenly. 'Ooo, very new. Don't freak him out by trying to catch the bouquet later.' He laughs and winks, like he's just given me the best piece of life advice in the universe.

Don't do this. Don't do that. Don't be too much. Don't be too little. Don't scare him off. Don't make him feel like you don't care. Don't be too slutty. Don't be too prudish. Don't be too insecure. Don't be too self-contained. Don't be too fat. Don't be too thin. Don't be you. Never be you. You don't want to die alone so don't be fucking you.

I look around at the sea of circular tables, dotted with couples. All holding membership cards to the club I long to inhabit. The Belonging Club. The antidote to loneliness. The safety net of someone essentially nodding at me and saying, 'Yeah, you'll do.' That's all I've ever wanted. To be sitting alongside someone at a table covered with white linen, feeling slightly bored by the story they're telling the person on their right because I've heard it a thousand times before. All my life, I've wanted to be loved. I wanted to have someone pick me as their specialist. I wanted to feel safe in my being-lovedness. For someone to not be put off by the parts of me that were hard but that I couldn't help. But I never got the chance.

And so I wanted to be powerful, instead; to finally have the ball in my court. I wanted others to hurt the way I've been hurt. I wanted to have just one moment of feeling like I've won.

But it turns out I don't have it in me. I could've destroyed Joshua today. I could've laughed at him and his hope and his misguided faith. I could've revelled in the crackle of power that comes with holding someone's heart in your palm. I could've hurt him and humiliated him like so many have hurt and humiliated me. But, even with everything I've been through, I don't have it in me.

I've hurt too much to hurt others.

I like that I'm not Gretel.

I like that I'm me.

And I like that, despite everything, no matter how hard I've tried these last few months, I've found it impossible to run away from myself.

In fact, I love that.

'Excuse me,' I say, to the table full of couples who think I belong now. I get up from my tastefully-decorated chair. 'I need the bathroom.'

I dash in the direction Josh went, grinning like nothing is wrong when everything is. I don't know what I'm going to say when I find him, but I need to find him. I dart around waiting staff who are refilling glasses and scooping up empty plates ready for the pork or chicken or goats-cheese tartlet main course. Chrissy's laughing at the top table, her meal untouched, sharing a joke with her mum. I know I should stay and eat and pretend life is great for her, but the urge to find Joshua is too much. I feel ill at what I've done, the look on his face, at what I need to explain.

He's not in the hallway. He's not in the conservatory. He's not in the entrance hall where we left our wet umbrellas. My heart feels like it's rehearsing for a full-on attack and I'm shivering even though it's not that cold as I pace the stately home, dodging the glances of stressed staff. I wait outside the toilets for a while, listening to more well-mannered laughter from the dining room, but he doesn't come out.

He's left, I realise. He has gone. And I can't even blame him.

The loss is more intolerable than I imagined. I head back into the empty conservatory and wilt into a chair, feeling tears itch my eyes, as the echoes of wedding thud down the hallway. I sniff and wipe my nose with the back of my hand. I sniff again. The rain beats against the glass in pitter-patters.

I remember Josh coming to my house in the rain. I remember him saying sorry. I remember feeling in my guts that he meant it. I don't remember ever feeling like that when a man has apologised to me before. I close my eyes. They're wet when I open them. I look up at the glass ceiling, the dollops of grey rain hitting it. I wonder whether or not I should try to call him; if there's any point. Another shriek of laughter ripples from the wedding and I turn my face out towards the rain-smudged view. The stately grounds are hiding in the deep-grey mist of the storm. I can just about make out a patio, a gravel walkway lined with topiary hedges and sodden benches. And, on one of them, I see the huddled figure of Joshua.

Without forethought, I'm outside, soaked instantly. It's so much quieter out here, just the steady pounding of raindrops in puddles. I run over the gravel, arms crossed, and come to a stop at the bench he's sitting on, head in his hands. My heartbeat cranks up the amp. He looks broken, his body physically bent over on himself, hands shaking. I feel a twist of pain in my ribs as I examine what I've caused. The privilege of guilt . . .

'Joshua?' I say. His wet and sad body doesn't answer me. 'I thought you'd gone . . .'

He straightens, and pulls the sopping lapels of his jacket across his chest. He doesn't reply.

'What are you doing out here?' I ask. Every part of me wants to touch him but I know I'll be swatted off. I've lost the right to brush his skin. It's been left on the table, alongside the packets of sugared almonds. 'You're soaking.'

More silence. I think he may stand and stalk off. He didn't

ask to be followed. I don't dare sit. I don't dare break the silence again. And, finally, through gritted teeth, he talks. 'I've been sitting here,' Joshua tells me, his voice hardly a murmur, 'in the fucking rain, trying to work out why I keep getting myself into these situations.'

'What situations?' I ask delicately.

He sinks his head back into his shaking palms and I see his eyes are watering before they're hidden again. 'Throwing myself headfirst into relationships with women who lie.'

I freeze. I was not expecting that reply.

'What's wrong with me?' Josh asks himself, rain spilling into his collar. 'Why am I always here? Who the hell even are you? My friends warned me, they told me I was going too fast again, they said I needed to take it slower this time. But, did I listen? No, I never listen.' He massages his face with his balled hands. I reach out a hand to comfort him but I pause it in mid-air, tuck it back into the pocket of my dress. I don't know which words to use. There's no script to follow, no advice from Google or self-help books. 'There must be something seriously wrong with me,' he says, again, more to himself than to me. 'What the actual hell is the matter with me? Why do I always get it so wrong?'

'I'm sorry,' I say to the top of his head, my voice cracking. 'It was one lie, and it got out of hand.'

'I just don't understand why you'd lie about your name. I mean, what the hell?' He keeps shaking his head. 'Why would you do that? And you met all my friends and lied to them too? Why would anyone do that?'

I blink up to the sky, and let the rain merge with my tears. 'Because I'm bloody terrified,' I admit. 'I have had some really bad experiences and I lied about my name to protect myself and it was a total and complete fuck-up.'

The honesty causes him to look up. We lock eyes, and my heart surges with pain again. I shake my head sadly. 'I'm really fucked up, Joshua.' My voice chokes out the words in barks. 'I don't want to go to Africa either. I only said that because it was a first date and I was trying to impress you.'

He barks out a harsh laugh. 'Anything else?'

'I don't trust men not to hurt me, so, when I met you, I hid loads of stuff to try and protect myself.'

His mouth falls open. 'I've never done *anything* to hurt you!'

'No. Not yet. But you will. Anyway, you're about to break up with me, aren't you? That's going to hurt.' It will, more than I care to admit. Somehow I've fallen, once again, into the default setting of me getting my heart broken. I was stupid to think this would ever end on my terms. Nothing to do with hearts are ever defined by my terms. But at least I still have one, at least it's still functioning, still feels. It hasn't gone cold like it could have. I'm proud of that, even though I'm ashamed of the lies I've been telling him and myself. Even though losing him is going to hurt so much.

'Break up with *who?* Do you have any idea how much I'm freaking out right now?' He throws his hands up in the air. 'I'm at a wedding, with someone who I thought was my girlfriend, and now I realise I don't even know her real name!'

'I told you, it's April,' I say as another tear falls.

I look out at the grey bleakness of the wedding venue – something that I'm not sure I'll ever have in my life. Then I look down at the man refusing to look at me, and I realise

I'm in one of those rare moments in life where you can say whatever the hell you like, and it doesn't matter, because your life has already burned down. I literally have nothing to lose.

'Joshua,' I start. I perch next to him on the bench, the water seeping up my skirt and through it. He stills, to let me know he's listening. 'Look, I said I was called Gretel on our first date to protect myself. And, yes, I was pretending to be the very best person in the world, and then you liked me and I got worried that you only liked me because I'd been hiding parts of myself. Yes, lying about my name is weird and that enough is a good reason for you to end this. You must think I'm crazy. *I* think I'm crazy . . .' I almost laugh, and then shake my head, my wet hair sticking to my face. 'But, while I've been figuring out what the hell to tell you and how to come back from this, I've realised that, actually, my name's the only real lie I've told you. The rest of it has just been me hiding things from you. And, the thing is, you were always going to end it anyway when you found out how much I have going on. Because, you think I'm easy-going and carefree and laissez-faire, but I'm not like that. I can be those things some-times, but a lot of the time I'm not. I'm neurotic and skittish and exhausting and hard work and so many other unsexy things . . . I've not been lying but I have been hiding the bits you won't like.'

Joshua keeps shaking his head. He's not running away but he's definitely shaking his head a lot.

'Gretel . . . I mean April. Shit! Literally none of what you've said makes any sense.'

'What do you mean?'

He lets out an angry sigh and throws his hands up. 'The bits I won't like? *Like?* How do you know what I like and don't like?'

'Because you're a man! And you all want women to follow the rules. Like how you didn't like your ex-girlfriend because she wanted to get married . . .'

'What?' He's looking at me in stunned disbelief. 'I didn't want to marry my ex because she fucking cheated on me! And when I took her back, she kept pestering me to marry her as a way of proving I trusted her again. But then I found out she'd started sleeping with him again.'

'What?'

'Yeah! What? You thought I dumped her because she wanted to get married?' My silence answers that. 'Well, it's nice to know what you think of me.'

'Come on!' I hold my arms out. 'What was I supposed to think when you said that? Men always . . .'

'Always what? You don't know. You can't assume.'

'Are you really going to say "not all men" at me?'

'Yes! Because it's fucking true.'

I'm crying furiously now. Wipe wipe wipe my face. Out it all comes. He won't come near me now he's seen all this. 'You wouldn't think they were so great and harmless if you had to do my shifts.'

'I thought you'd stopped that role? Why?'

'Stop it!'

'Stop what? Upsetting you? I'm upset too! I only just found out your actual name.' Joshua twists towards me, looks at my tears. He doesn't seem repulsed by them, which is new. He still looks angry though. He lowers his voice again and I can hardly hear him over the rain. I shiver as I listen, digesting the story he just told me. About his ex. Realigning it with the assumptions I've made, wondering how many more I might've made about who hurt who . . . 'Look,' he says. 'As this is the surrealest thing that's ever happened to me and I have no idea what's going on, I may as well be honest too. I know I've been pushing things forward, but, I've . . . There have been moments with you when I have felt really . . . not good.'

Huh? I jolt in shock. *But what about Gretel? Surely he's head over heels for her?*

He holds up his hands. 'I mean, I obviously like you. I've not been leading you on. I don't do that. I like you, that's why I've carried on seeing you, but Gre— I mean, April. Fucking hell. You are hard to get to know. There are times when it's great! Like when you sang that song in the Irish accent, or the night of the curry and how you spoke and told me about your job and everything. There are moments where I feel like "Wow, this girl is cool and interesting and clearly really thinks about things", but then there's been a lot of . . . aloofness? Falseness? Like I never know where I stand. Like you're cagey about meeting me. Holding me at a distance like it's a test. It's weird that you brought up Africa, cos that's not one of the things I like about you. In fact, I've never really thought about that. I like the bits that feel genuine. And now your name isn't even Gretel and I don't know what the hell to think any more. That I need to go to therapy or something, as I seem to only be attracted to girls who lie.'

His words are almost too painful to hear because they're confirming what I was too scared to believe: the feeling that it was actually me he liked, not Gretel. That the real bits were pulling us together, rather than my lies. Those moments our barriers were lowered. But it hurts because, after what I've done, he should leave. If he has any sense he should leave. For his own sake, I want him to leave. I have revealed myself to be the crazy one they are all so frightened of. Yet, when I reach out and put my hand on his knee, Joshua, the idiot he may well be, doesn't flinch. Instead he reaches out and puts his hand on my wet knee.

I make myself look at him, and dare myself to hope. 'I know it sounds mental considering everything, but I really don't lie,' I tell him. 'I didn't before this name thing, and I certainly won't any more. You are the first person I've ever not been honest with, ironically, considering you hate it so much.'

'Lying really scares me,' he says. 'Like, after last time, I can't handle it. After my ex, I need to know someone. Really know them.'

We look down at one another's hands on one another's knees and I colour in the bits of him I just learnt, about his ex, about how he's been hurt, and he colours in the bits of me. Both of us hiding the broken bits and making up stories in our heads of how the other will respond to them, assuming the worst. And our heads push together, until they're almost touching, and I can't stop weeping, and he looks pretty close to crying too.

I open my mouth and words spill, unfiltered, from it, into the side of his face. 'I'm sorry I've put up so many walls but, as I said, something . . . really bad happened to me,' I tell him, terrified of how he'll take it but forcing myself to tell it anyway. 'It wasn't my fault, but it's left me a mess. And men haven't been very good at dealing with it in the past.' He opens his mouth, but I won't let him interrupt me. 'I . . . don't trust men,' I tell him. 'That may feel terribly unfair if you believe you're a good man who has never done anything bad. But please don't judge me for that. It makes sense if you know what I've been through. I'm . . . complicated, you see. I've had some things happen to me that shouldn't have happened.' Tears run more freely now, and I wipe my face with the back of my hand. He sits up, watches me cry. He doesn't comfort me, just lets me continue. 'I don't want to tell you all the horrible things that have happened to me, not right now. But, if this had continued, I'd have had to let it out eventually and you'd have ended it then. And that's why I'm cagey and tried to be someone different, because I don't trust you to still be here when I'm myself.'

There it is. All out there. I wait for him to drop his hand. I wait for the judgement to cave in on his face. I wait for him to look uncomfortable. I wait for him to be Simon. And the countless others before him, who see my trauma like a contaminant. As a shame they have to decide whether or not they can be arsed to deal with. I'm almost too scared to look at him, because I will not be able to stand it to see one more face fall at the revelation of the complicated reality that is April. But I decide to take one last leap of faith and force eye contact.

We look at one another. We hold one another's knees.

And Joshua's face . . . it doesn't fall. In fact, it looks like things are clicking into place for him.

'I'm really sorry you've been through something like that,'

he says eventually. 'Thank you for telling me.' He lets out a long breath and really looks at me. 'But you can't lie, not any more. I need to be with someone who is themself.' Then, his hand, it squeezes me in reassurance. A reassuring squeeze. My very first. A squeeze to say it's OK. It takes everything I have not to burst into tears or run away because I simply cannot trust it. 'It makes me sad that you don't trust people enough to be yourself,' Joshua says.

'It sounds like you don't trust people much either.' I think of what he's been through and how it must've hurt. How hard it must be for him to take any of this in right now, after I've so hugely pushed his buttons. I give him a reassuring squeeze back.

'I'm trying to. I've got good reasons not to.'

'I'm trying to too. And I've got good reasons too.'

'Is it a stupid thing to try to do?' Joshua asks.

'Trust people?' I ask. 'Well, my therapist claims it's worth striving for.' I let go of him and point both fingers to my tear-stained, mascara-smeared face. 'Yes, I have a therapist,' I announce. 'Welcome to April.'

His hand on my knee squeezes tighter. 'I want to trust you April.'

'Right back at you.'

We sit in the rain. We don't kiss. All that's gone on can't magically melt away just because we've had one honest conversation. I'm still at war with myself, unsure if I'm on the cusp of yet another bout of hurt, rejection, and reducing of myself. Yet I'm struggling to let go of his knee.

'We should probably go in,' I say, sensing that this is as far as we can get right now. That we've reached our limit on the emotional window being open and need to digest and think and come to imperfect decisions based on our imperfect actions. 'The speeches are before pudding, and I want to hear Mark's speech. Chrissy's really looking forward to it.'

'Yeah . . . um . . . sure.'

I take Joshua's hand and lead him over the gravel and back into the dryness of the very lovely conservatory. I can't believe he's letting me take his hand and it's awkward between us the moment we're inside – shivering and dripping onto the parquet. I wince a smile at him, and he winces one back. Both of us chilled in the cringe aftermath that follows deep heart-to-hearts. I can hear the echoing applause of a speech ending. I wonder if we've missed it.

'We'll distract everyone if we come in now all wet,' I whisper to Josh. 'Should we just peer around the door?'

He nods and we make sodden footsteps towards the threshold of the dining hall. Waiters are lined up in the corridor, brandishing martini glasses filled with Eton mess, waiting for the speeches to finish. They eye us curiously, but don't say anything. I peer in, watching everyone twisted in the direction of the top table. Chrissy's dad is sitting down, looking flushed and relieved. Mark is fiddling with the mic, checking it's still turned on. It feels a bit voyeuristic, watching through a gap in the door, but I don't think anyone would appreciate us rocking in right now, with half my make-up cried off. Mark stands, puts his hands in his suit pocket. I watch Chrissy's face. She's beaming up at him, so much love gooing out of her. He's so lucky that she loves him, I hope he knows it. I hope he tells her and makes this speech worth it.

'Hi, everyone, and thanks for coming,' Mark says, not

removing any cards from his pocket. Not a good sign. 'As you know, I'm not a man of many words but I just want to say . . .' I look at Chrissy's poised face, smiling, joyful, patient, waiting. Mark coughs. '. . . It's great that you all came here today. It means the world to Chrissy and me to have you here.'

Then Mark is sitting down.

Sitting down.

Back on his chair. Like the speech is over. Which it must be. Chrissy's face is on pause, as she computes whether that's it or not. I see the exact moment she realises that's all she's getting. There's a millisecond where her features collapse, where the hope he may be different, just for once, on their wedding day, because it's important to her, falls out of her stomach. She blinks. Smiles. Recovers. And stands herself as everyone claps half-heartedly, trying not to shrug at one another. Chrissy stands to repeat her thanks to everyone. My heart is breaking for her. It's her wedding day. The one thing she wanted on the one day she needed it the most and he didn't do it.

My anger and bitterness rush in, despite the damp, forgiving, hand holding mine. I want to drop it. I want to go and scream in Mark's face. I want Chrissy to get what she deserves. *Why do any of us bother?* I find myself thinking. *Really? What is the payoff for the disappointment?*

Yet Joshua's hand is still in mine in this doorway. I've cried on him, and told him my name isn't Gretel, and revealed all my chaotic mess, and he is still here. He's not run out of the door, or called me crazy, or assumed the worst. He's just asked for an explanation and listened to what I had to say. We still need to talk, oh boy, do we need to talk, but the fact he's still here is new. This is not what I'm used to.

And then . . . I feel his breath on my cheek.

'*That* was his speech?' Joshua whispers in my ear. 'Seriously? Just that? On his wedding day? I thought you said she was looking forward to this bit?' He shakes his head, clearly as disgusted for her as I am. 'Bloody hell. Your poor friend.'

I look down at our held hands, then up to his face.

Maybe you are different, I think.

I wait for Gretel's reply. Her warning. Her snark.

I get nothing.

Maybe you are different, I think again, as I lean over to kiss Joshua's cheek – which could be the making or the undoing of me. I will not know for some time. I may never know at all.

Maybe you are different.

And it begins.

Whatever it is. It begins.

One year later

I hate *some* men.

And you know what? I don't think that's over the top, considering what some men do. The ones who hurt and push, the ones who see you as decorations, the ones who are so sad and so messed up that they take and take and take and still feel empty. I hate that they refuse to admit that they hate women. I hate that they still blame it on us. I hate that so many of them seem so far beyond help, and all the damage they're going to cause as a result of that. I hate the ones who laugh at our anger, who diminish our pain. Who want to keep their slimy hands tightly clutched on the reins of this world, riding the rest of us and whipping us like horses.

I hate the men that did the things to me that made me hate men. I think that's appropriate. I believe only I am allowed to decide if forgiveness is something I'm willing to give them, and I choose not to. I will not turn the other cheek to the men who damaged me. I don't owe them anything.

But I love some men. I love the men who try to be different. I love the men who listen more than they talk. I love the men brave enough to hear what we have to say. I love the men who then talk to other men about it, even though it goes against everything they have been taught not to do. I love the men who want to break the cycle. Who want to be different from their fathers, or their brothers, their friends or their colleagues. I love the men who can confront the uncomfortable truth that it is their fathers and brothers, friends and colleagues who are doing this to women. Who have to admit maybe women see a different side to them, one we are not lying about. I love the men who don't need sisters and daughters and wives to make us human and not want us hurt. I love the men who cry.

I love a man.

I have managed to find a man who, for now, is worth loving. I love a man who has stopped and listened and tried to understand, even though he is a man so he can never truly understand. But he tries. The important thing is that he tries. I love a man who holds me when I cry and is there, but who is making me build myself back strong rather than letting me use him as my strength. I love a man who annoys me so much sometimes that I honestly, seriously, sometimes think I hate him too. I love a man who finds me equally annoying at times but who still chooses to love me anyway.

I love a man, and it has not solved all my problems. It has not made my entire life slot into place like I thought it would. It has not saved me from the huge amount of work I need to do to save myself from things that never should've happened to me. There is no 'the end' we can hide behind after we found out that we loved each other. There are still two complicated human lives to lead and no guarantee that we'll make it.

Some days are pure magic, some days are pure hell. Some days I feel like we're soulmates who perfectly fit, other days

I wonder what the fuck we are doing together when we're so incompatible. Sometimes he gets it, sometimes I can't even handle how badly he doesn't.

Some days I believe the hard work is worth it, and other days I don't.

I'm starting to realise this is what love is. I do not know if it's worth it. If it makes me any happier. If the pain and frustration of blending a life with another life is worth the gooey moments. I don't know if the good days will outweigh the bad days.

I don't know anything.

Yet I keep loving him anyway.

And he keeps loving me.

I'm starting to realise that's what love is.

Acknowledgements

I'd just like to start by quickly thanking all women, everywhere. Whenever I think about this book, and everything I read, everyone I spoke to, every painful secret that was whispered to me, I tear up when I realise the sheer strength of us. If your story is anything like April's story then I wish you peace, I wish you recovery, I wish you love. I hope I did her story justice. This story was partly inspired by the years I spent, like April, helping victims of sexual violence, and, like April, there came a time when it became too much and I had to stop. So thank you to everyone out there who continues to work for these services. It's such vital, important, brutally-hard work and you are all my superheroes.

There are so many women in particular I'd like to thank too. To Maddy, as always, my own official dream-maker and powerhouse – and to her amazing team. To Kimberley, my editor, for pushing me to make this book everything that it is. And to everyone at Hodder in general for not batting an eyelid when I sent over the opening line 'I hate men'. For getting it and believing in it, and championing it, and me, and the work I do. It means the world that I have a publisher who lets me tell these stories – thank you. Also a special shout-out to Becca, your passion and work ethic is as impeccable as your hair.

To my female friends – Rachel, Lisa, Emily, Ruth, Lucy, Ellie, Harriet, Jess, Christi, Non, Lisa, Lexi, Sara, Emma, Louie, Lizzie, Becky, Tanya, Katie, and so many more. Thank you for pulling me through this book, for always picking up the phone, for the insight and wisdom you give me, for the turn-taking we share in reassuring one another that we're not crazy. To my incredible women in my family – Mum, Eryn, Willow.

And, unlike April, I am proud to say that I don't hate men, and this is because of the wonderful collection of men in my life who challenge toxic concepts every day. Thanks to my father, to Josh, to all the great men I worked with at Youthnet. And to W, in particular – goodest of all the good eggs.

Finally, to anyone who needs further advice and support after reading this book, please do contact Women's Aid or Rape Crisis. And to anyone inspired to donate to these causes by this story – please do. They are chronically underfunded considering the huge scale of the issue of violence against women.

For more information and advice for those affected by rape or sexual abuse, contact Rape Crisis or Women's Aid – both of which are national organisations offering free and confidential support to those in need.

Rape Crisis
Helpline: 0808 802 9999
More information: rapecrisis.org.uk

Women's Aid
More information: womensaid.org.uk

Reading Group Questions

1. April has a complicated relationship with online dating and messaging apps. Can you relate to the pressure she feels to appear perfect when navigating the world of modern dating?

2. April creates the character of Gretel to cater to what she believes all men want. How does this persona differ from April's own personality? Do they have anything in common? To what extent do you agree with her assessment of 'what men want'?

3. Joshua challenges April's views on men's behaviour and motives. Can you think of any other characters in *Pretending* who challenge gender stereotypes? How?

4. April's pursuit of revenge initially makes her feel powerful and in control for the first time in her dating history. Can you sympathise with her actions? How does the book handle the subject of power dynamics within romantic and sexual relationships?

5. April's best friend Megan also embarks on a new relationship in *Pretending*. How does her experience mirror April's? How do their experiences differ, and why?

6. The boxing classes help April connect with other survivors of abuse. What else is shown to help this character begin to process her trauma? Consider April's job at the sexual health charity, her friendships, her meetings with a therapist, and her relationship with Joshua.

7. At the beginning of the novel, April is pretending to be someone she is not. Can you think of any other characters who are pretending? Why do you think people feel so much pressure to disguise themselves?

8. The book begins with the line 'I hate men.' Can you identify how April's views on men shift throughout the book? Why do you think her feelings change? What are the differences between the book's opening passage and the narrator's closing words?

Did you love *Pretending*?

Turn over for an extract from *How Do You Like Me Now?*

Month One

Olivia Jessen

Six month bump alert. The belly has popped people, the belly has popped. #BumpSelfie #Blessed

81 likes

*

Harry Spears

I liked it so . . . I put a ring on it.

Harry Spears and Claire Rodgers are engaged.

332 likes

*

Andrea Simmons

Poo explosion! But look at that cheeky face . . .

52 likes

> *Comments:*
> **Olivia Jessen:** Oh no, Andrea. I've got all that to look forward to.
> **Andrea Simmons:** I'll give you a nose peg at your baby shower!

*

Event invite: Olivia Jessen's super-secret baby shower.

16 attending

*

Tori's WhoTheF*ckAmI? Official Fan Page

Alright my f*ckers! Who's coming to the London show tonight? I
can't believe it's sold out! I love and adore you
all. See you at seven. I'll be the one on stage with the
microphone, wondering how the hell I got so lucky in life.

2434 likes. 234 comments.

★

I look out at a sea of earnestness.

There are too many faces to make anyone out individually,
but there is a collective look. A collective glow. Their eyes are
dewy; their hands are clasped.

They hang on my every syllable.

I'm getting to the good bit. The bit I know they've been
waiting for. The bit I've been building up to. I walk across
the stage in my designer heels and smooth down my designer
dress. I look exactly how a successful woman should look.
Groomed, plucked, highlighted, contoured . . . but not in an
obvious way. I look right out at them. At their anxious, eager
faces. And I say:

'That's when I realised it.' I raise one threaded eyebrow.
'Sitting there, cross-legged in that fucking tent in Sedona.
Chanting bollocks with a load of wankers, wearing a rosary
necklace for God's sake. That's when it hit me . . .'

I pause.

The audience stills. You could float a boat on the expectation
filling the air.

'I was trying to *find myself* how everyone else finds themselves,'

I say. 'I was having a nervous breakdown exactly how everyone else has a nervous breakdown and I was healing myself how everyone else tries to heal themselves. And I said to myself *NO MORE.*' I hold out my hand like I'm signalling stop. I pause again, waiting for the beat. '"Just who the fuck *am* I?" I asked myself. "What do *I* want?" Because life isn't a paint-by-numbers. You cannot find yourself along an identikit path. And, actually, even after my quarter-life crisis, even after this whole year of self-discovery, I was still twenty-five and doing exactly what had got me into this mess in the first place. I was doing what I thought I *should* be doing rather than what I fucking *needed* to be doing.'

A stray whoop. The audience softens into gentle laughter. I laugh, too, and it echoes around the walls, bounces out of the various speakers.

I nod. 'Exactly.' I pause to let them settle. I clop back to the other side of the stage. There is a hush. I blink slowly, trying to remember that moment. Trying to invoke the triumph I felt. Six years ago. On that day, that incredible day. The day where everything started going right for me.

'So,' I tell them. 'I opened my eyes, I uncrossed my legs, and I walked out of that stupid meditation yurt and never looked back.'

The applause is overwhelming, like it always is. It takes about five minutes for them to calm down, like they always do. I make my own eyes go dewy to show my appreciation, like I always do. Then I get around to telling them the rest of my story. The story they all know already. Because all of them have my book clasped in their hands, waiting for me to sign it afterwards. Waiting to have their moment with me. To tell me about their own messy twenties, their own terrible boyfriends, their own shitty jobs, their own smacking disappointments. And to tell me how my book, my words, my story helped them through. *Still* helps them through.

It's crazy really. I sometimes forget how crazy it is.

We don't sell many books despite the queue that snakes around multiple corridors. They all already have their copies. Battered copies with crippled spines and Post-its to highlight their favourite parts. I sign for over three hours – my grin stapled on, trying to keep my energy up for all the women who've waited so long for this moment.

This moment with me.

Like I'm special or something.

So I smile and smile and I high-five them when they tell me of their own adventures. I hug them when they cry. I lean in and listen carefully as they whisper their secrets. My publicist hovers, twitchy, and asks if I'm OK. If I need a break. If I want some water. I smile at her and say no. I'm OK. I'm fine. I'm managing. But thank you.

Every single person asks the same questions:

'So, when is your new book coming out?'

'What are you working on now?'

'Do you have a new project coming out soon?'

'I'm so impatient. How long do I have to wait?'

My smile goes tight and I tap my nose and say, 'Wait and see' and 'Watch this space.'

Then, of course, they also want to know:

'So, are you still together?'

'The guy you met at the end of the book? Are you still with him?'

'Are you still in love?'

They ask the way a child asks their parents if Santa Claus is real – their eyes big, wide with a mixture of excitement and fear. I know why they're excited and I know why they're scared. They're excited because if I can find him, they can find him. If I can make it work, they can make it work. If magic is real for me, it is real for them. I am the reflection of everything they want in their own lives. I'm essentially the Mirror of Erised.

They're scared because I could also be their albatross. If I can't make it work, who can? If magic doesn't work for me, it most certainly won't work for them.

I nod and simper and coo and look all bashful. I repeat the phrase over and over. 'Yes, we're still together. We live together now.'

Oh, how that makes them happy. They gasp. They demand photographs. They swoon, they sigh. Their eyes grow bigger and wetter and they are so relieved. It makes my own eyes water and I blink like crazy to stop it. Because they make me remember Us. The Us we were. The Us that we were when the story they clutch finishes. I can remember it so clearly – maybe because I've been forced to talk about it non-stop for six years . . .

'Are you OK?'

'Huh?'

I blink and look up at the face of a woman standing over me. Her entire body jolts with nerves; her fingers tremble on her copy of my book, which has over one hundred Post-its glued in.

'Sorry.' I smile and take the book off her. 'Now, what's your name?'

'Rosie.'

'Oh, that's a lovely name,' I say. It's what I always say.

'Thank you.'

I sign her book with the message I always write:

Dear Rosie,
Live the life you fucking need to live.
Love,
Tori xx

She's crying.

'Oh wow, thank you,' she stutters through her sobs. 'Can I . . . can I take a photo?'

I hand her book back. 'Of course, of course. Are you OK?'

She laughs a little and says, 'I'm fine, it's just so amazing to meet you.'

I hold out both arms warmly. 'Come here for a hug and a photo.'

Rosie hands her phone over to my publicist and is so overcome with emotion she forgets to even ask if it's OK for her to take the picture. Then she clatters around to my side of the table and quivers next to me. I pull her in, putting my arm around her. She's hot and sweaty. Her dampness sinks into the crisp fabric of my dress, but this moment is worth more than my dress.

'Smile!' my publicist says, holding up the phone.

I smile with my good side facing towards the camera – chin down to give me better jaw definition, eyebrows relaxed so my forehead wrinkles don't show. There's a flash and Rosie giggles and steps back to her side of the table, retrieving her phone and checking the photo.

'Thanks so much for coming.' I hand her book over.

'No, thank *you*. Thank you so much for writing it. You don't understand. When I was twenty-three, I was such a mess . . . then I found your book and . . . it changed my life . . . it really did.'

I am tired of smiling, but I need to smile at this because it's important to her. 'Wow, I'm so touched to hear that. How old are you now?'

'Twenty-five.'

She's only twenty-freaking-five. They just keep getting . . . younger.

'Well I'm so glad you enjoyed it.'

I'm looking past her now, to the next person. Because it's gone ten and I've got the wedding tomorrow. But, just as I reach out to take the book off the next shaking fan, Rosie discovers the courage to say one more thing.

'Hey, sorry. But, can I just ask? Rock man? The man from the book? You are still together, aren't you?'

Rock man.

The man who found me on the rock. Who found me on top of a vortex in Sedona screaming *'fuuuuuuuuuck'* and throwing my rosary beads off into the skyline, and somehow found that endearing.

Tom . . .

The man who could've been anywhere else in the world that day, but whom a thousand gusts of fate somehow blew to Arizona too. *Sedona* too. Climbing up to the vortex too.

My happily-ever-after.

The one you're always rewarded with in stories where a character decides to be brave.

'Yes,' I confirm, feeling like my smile might snap. 'We're still together.'

She lets out a little squeal and a yelp, arms flailing in the air. Then she blushes. 'Sorry. I'm fangirling.'

'That's fine.'

I'm looking past her again because, in the nicest possible way, she is taking too much time now. There are still at least fifty women waiting not-so patiently any more. Rosie doesn't read my vibe. My response has only given her more confidence. She is conducting the conversation that she needs. In her head, we are friends now. Already great friends.

'And you're still blissfully happy?'

I close my eyes for a second longer than I should. When I open them, my smile is still there. It has to stay on. For the next fifty people it has to stay on. I give Rosie my dimples and my charm and my glowing, golden happiness. My wisdom. My serenity. Everything she expects. Everything she has paid for in her ticket price.

'Of course,' I tell her. 'We're still blissfully happy.'

★

The adrenaline starts to ooze out of me in the taxi home. I feel each muscle clenching and releasing. The cocktail of performance hormones steadily filtering out of my tight stomach, unravelling my intestines inch by inch. I lean my head against the blackened glass and watch London twinkle outside. This city just keeps getting taller, refusing to let anything stunt its growth – much like the people who live in its turrets.

My phone lights up and buzzes angrily in my hand.

Dee: HELP ME HE IS A CRAZY PERSON

I smile as the taxi passes the looming ostentatiousness of Big Ben and we drive over the black currents of the Thames. There will never be a time when I don't want a mid-date message from Dee.

Tori: He can't be as bad as last week's surely?
Dee: He's married, Tor. HE'S MARRIED!!
Tori: Then why is he on a date with you?!
Dee: He said he WOULD get a divorce but he CAN'T FIND HIS WIFE BECAUSE SHE VANISHED.

I tap out a few replies as the cab plunges through the murky depths of South London – where glittering lights are replaced by concrete slabs of sort-of-affordable housing as long as your parents can help you with the deposit to dodge inheritance tax. I try to find the right mix of sympathetic, concerned, and taking the piss.

Tori: Seriously, are you OK though? It would only happen to YOU. X
Dee: I'm safe! I'm home. I really want to drink Merlot with my spritely young housemates but we've got the wedding of doom tomorrow.
Tori: Don't remind me. I'm still picking you up at 9, right? X
Dee: 9 it is.

Then five minutes later:

Dee: And, it's not me. This is just what dating is, Tor. Everyone apart from me is either boring or totally insane.

I put my phone away as we slow down around the park. The pavements are clogged with smokers and drunk people spilling out of bars, ripping into boxes of fried chicken, laughing loud and shrill and leaning into each other, and putting their hands on each other's chests. We pull up at a red light and the taxi throbs softly from the music blasting out of a flat above. London never rests. It doesn't do bedtime or catnaps or even dozing. It's so exhausting living somewhere this constantly awake.

The thought of coming home to Tom makes me feel safe. The thought that he will be there, and that he says he loves me; the thought that I don't have to go back out there into a world of ghosting and dick pics and messages with two ticks but no replies. But the thought of no Tom . . . I shiver. The thought of the alternative. The thought of starting again. Thirty-one and alone. Thirty-one and putting that number on an online-dating profile. Knowing the assumptions people make about that number. The wilting pair of ovaries they see. The desperation they smell. The sand you leave behind on the chair as the hourglass pours from top to bottom . . .

*

How Do You Like Me Now? is available to buy now

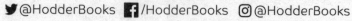